ALMOST A GENTLEMAN

"How dare you do such things to me?"

Grayson looked at Billie. She was on her knees a few feet away with her hair tousled, her hands clutching the shirt closed, and her chest heaving in indignation. She was the picture of outraged innocence. Another role or the truth?

"How dare I not? And you can rant all you want. You're not going to convince me you didn't enjoy what I did."

She wiped her sleeve across her mouth with careful dignity, but the action pulled the shirt up and revealed most of her legs. Following his gaze, she smothered a most unladylike oath and tugged her shirt down.

"If you don't mind, I would like to get dressed now."

He settled himself cross-legged on the floor and began loosening the bonds that wrapped his feet. "Good idea."

"A gentleman would turn his back."

"And have you knock me out? We've been over that plan already."

<u>BOOK YOUR PLACE ON OUR WEBSITE</u> <u>AND MAKE THE</u> <u>READING CONNECTION!</u>

We've created a customized website just for our very special readers, where you can get the inside scoop on everything that's going on with Zebra, Pinnacle and Kensington books.

When you come online, you'll have the exciting opportunity to:

- View covers of upcoming books
- Read sample chapters
- Learn about our future publishing schedule (listed by publication month *and author*)
- Find out when your favorite authors will be visiting a city near you
- Search for and order backlist books from our online catalog
- Check out author bios and background information
- Send e-mail to your favorite authors
- Meet the Kensington staff online
- Join us in weekly chats with authors, readers and other guests
- Get writing guidelines
- AND MUCH MORE!

Visit our website at
http://www.kensingtonbooks.com

TENNESSEE WALTZ

Ginger Hanson

ZEBRA BOOKS
KENSINGTON PUBLISHING CORP.
http://www.kensingtonbooks.com

*To Bob and JoAnne,
the best husband-daughter support
team a writer ever had.*

PROLOGUE

Tennessee, 1863

A gunshot cracked the summer morning air. Startled, Destiny shied backward with a frightened whinny. Billie hugged
the horse's neck, her body tensed for the searing pain of a
bullet. In a shower of leaves, a Yankee swaddled in an oak
branch dropped out of the sky to land in front of her and
Destiny.

He staggered upon hitting the ground but kept to his feet.
In quick, fluid motions, he shoved the broken oak branch out
of the way and pulled a gun free.

"Halt or I'll shoot."

Too late, Billie realized it had been the breaking of the
tree limb, not a gunshot, that split the quiet morning.

Beneath her, Destiny danced sideways.

"Easy, big boy." Even as she used her voice and hands to
calm the horse, Billie tightened her legs around his girth.
Sliding her feet back, she eased them outward to kick the
muscled sides.

"You do it and you're dead."

Fear raced down her spine at the callous challenge.

"Don't worry, I won't shoot the horse," the clipped voice said. "I need him. I don't need you." The barrel of the pistol pointing at her moved slightly. "Dismount, boy."

The gun didn't convince her of the futility of disobeying; it was more an air about the soldier that dictated obedience. An air that told her none of the many tricks she'd taught Destiny would help. The Yankee had caught her with her guard down and had seen a healthy horse. He wouldn't believe a sudden attack of lameness.

She sat in the saddle and contemplated the Yankee's gun for several long moments before she dismounted. Once on the ground, she couldn't walk away from the horse, who turned his head to whicker at her.

"Get away from the horse, boy."

She wanted to kill the man. Oh, yes. There were many Yankees she wanted to see dead, but this dusty Yankee now topped her list.

The fact she carried no weapon kept her from trying to kill the Yankee, and he would kill her if she didn't move, but her feet wouldn't comply. Instead, she rubbed the soft nose one last time, savoring the feel of damp breath blown across her palm.

"I'm sorry," she murmured to the horse.

"I'm not telling you again. Get away from the horse."

The outrage. The impotence. The tears. They clawed at her throat, but she couldn't give them voice. She had to move. With a playful butt of his head, Destiny shoved her. She stumbled a few steps away.

"Your horse shows better sense than you." The Yankee didn't bother to adjust the stirrups. He grabbed the saddle and swung a leg over it. Destiny circled, shaking his head at the strange weight.

She steeled herself for a harsh command or a spur dug into the horse's satiny flanks.

"I'll kill you if you hurt him." The thump of hooves obliterated her threat. She watched the Yankee settle in the saddle. To her surprise, he handled Destiny with patience and gave the horse time to accept his new rider.

And gave her time to memorize the man who took her horse, because when the war was over she would find Destiny.

She recognized the signs of an officer beneath the dust of the road. It was there in the double-breasted frock coat, the sword, the gilt spurs, and the hat made of the finest black felt. A well-dressed officer whose uniform contrasted sharply with the ragtag attire of the renegade troops from either army that raced back and forth across this portion of Tennessee.

The fact he was a Union officer placed him among thousands. Her gaze swung upward, searching for something to hold in her memory. To her dismay, his face was shadowed by his hat as well as the dark stubble of a young beard. Several days' growth framed a pair of lips curving into a grin.

"Aren't I the lucky one?" He slid his hand along Destiny's neck. "To find such a specimen of Tennessee horse breeding in the middle of nowhere."

As he bent to check a stirrup, the tardy morning sun broke free of the tree line to catch the dull gleam of a belt buckle adorned with two women leaning against a shield with the word *Excelsior* scripted across the bottom. She knew the insignia. He was a New York soldier.

The Yankee holstered the Colt revolver. "What's his name?"

The rich baritone crackled with an educated Northern crispness. Her gaze swung from his belt buckle to his face. She couldn't find one distinguishing flaw to lock the man in her memory. With his hat low on his brow and the stubble on his jaw, she was left with little to file away for future reference.

"I guess I could call him Brownie."

Billie stiffened at the insult to a horse whose bloodlines dated back to the founding sire, but her brain ordered caution. Destiny's future lay in her obtaining all the information she could before the Yankee left. She closed her mind to the carnage of the battlefields, which wrought as much havoc on animals as it did on men.

"Angel." She roughened her voice and slid back into the role of belligerent youth. "He be known as Angel." She anglicized Destiny's name with the hope the Yankee wouldn't realize what a prize he had taken.

"Angel? I'm not too sure I can ride a horse called Angel."

"Then don't ride 'im at all; just leave 'im here." She thrust her fists into her pockets. It took all the self-control she had learned in the past months not to rush the Yankee. In the deepest recesses of her heart, she wished she had perfected Destiny's latest trick, but she was afraid to signal the horse to rear. If Destiny hesitated, the Yankee would have time to control him.

"Impertinent young boy, aren't you?"

She swallowed her anger. Appealing to a Yankee made her want to vomit, but she only had these few seconds to plead Destiny's case. And for him she would grovel before a thousand Yankees.

Her anguish stripped away the bumpkin role.

"I don't mean to be impertinent, sir." A growing constriction in her throat made speech difficult. "Please, don't give my horse away when you reach your lines. Take care of him. He is a . . ." Tears vied with a tight throat to prevent her from talking. ". . . a wonderful friend."

The Yankee guided Destiny close, and the familiar mixture of sweat, leather, and horse filled her nose. Destiny's head dipped toward her, and his velvety lips grazed her cheek. She stifled the reflexive urge to run her hand along the white blaze that ran a crooked path from ear to nose. Playing a boy kept gestures like that out of her life. But it was hard not to cry out her despair. Destiny was all she had left. She contented herself with a whispered vow.

"Survive the war and I will find you." She could feel the

Yankee's impatience to be gone. As did Destiny, who restlessly shook his head.

"You have my word. I will keep your horse as safe as I can through this damnable war."

She glanced up, surprised at the bitterness lacing the man's voice. She had not thought a man could be anything except pleased by the war. The idea of whipping Yankees delighted all the local boys she knew. A pair of dark gray eyes met her startled gaze.

Stepping back, she nodded. For some unfathomable reason, she believed him. He would take care of Destiny.

Horse and rider turned and started down the rutted farm lane. They had not gone more than twenty yards when he wheeled Destiny around.

"If I should want to write the owner after the war to tell him of the horse's welfare, where would I direct the letter?"

She hesitated, then realized she had to anglicize all the names or admit she had lied. He probably wouldn't send a letter, but if he did make it easy for her, the postmaster would know where it belonged. Many of the local people called the farm by its English name.

"Angel belongs to my pa, Philip Angel of Angel's Valley, Sumner County, Tennessee." She stepped toward the horse and rider. "And who'd be writing my pa?"

White teeth flashed through travel grime and beard stubble. "Grayson Vanderlyn, Colonel, United States Army."

Grayson Vanderlyn. Grayson Vanderlyn! She stared after the disappearing horse and rider in astonishment. It couldn't be *the* Grayson Vanderlyn, could it? But all his Captain Dinsmere books were set in New York. It had to be. Fate had smiled on her at last. She had been given the way to find Destiny after the war. Billie almost clapped her hands with glee. Her horse had been stolen by a well-known Yankee author. If she couldn't find Destiny, then her name wasn't Wilhelmina Constanza D'Angelo.

CHAPTER ONE

New York, 1866

"Easy, old fellow. What ails you tonight?"

Holy Mary, Mother of God, he's in the barn! Billie D'Angelo froze midstep, five bare toes digging into the soft loam of the floor while her other foot hung in the air. Fear sang along taut nerve endings, prickling her skin with gooseflesh. Her heartbeat, already rapid, exploded into such a loud knocking, she was sure the sound echoed off the barn rafters above her.

She couldn't believe the one man who could stop her stood less than fifteen feet away.

Body stiff, she listened as a set of large teeth demolished something, probably a carrot, in several quick chomps. The sound relaxed her. She eased her foot back to the floor, willing her heart to slow its frantic beat.

"I thought you'd like that."

Time had not dulled her dislike of the crisp Yankee voice. Damn the man! His step was quieter than a bobcat stalking a hare. She'd had no idea he was in the barn, which had gotten as dark as the inside of a closed casket when a cloud hid the moon, but here he was. If he hadn't spoken, she would have walked right into him.

And that would have ruined her plans for Destiny.

She backed her way into an open, empty stall. Bracing herself against the wood, she eased to the floor. The musty odor of straw wafted upward as she settled on the floor, a rope halter in one hand.

How she hated sneaking around. It tied her stomach into knots and squeezed her throat shut. She may have spied for the South during the war, but she hadn't had to sneak around to do it. Few people, especially Union soldiers, heeded what they said in front of a boy they believed to be a crippled half-wit.

Something bit her ankle, and Billie almost forgot herself enough to slap it. In fact, her hand was poised for the kill when a horse's familiar nicker raised the hairs on the back of her neck. Her hand dropped to her lap.

The Yankee's voice crooned into her ears. "What's bothering you, old fellow? You've been restless these past few days. Too bad you can't tell me why."

Yeah, thought Billie as she massaged her left hip, *it'd take a talking horse for this houseful of Yankees to know someone was hiding on their farm. But if horses talked, you'd know I was here, and I've spent too long planning how to get Destiny to have everything ruined now.*

"What's the matter? Are you upset because Ackerly's mare spurned your attentions last week? There'll be other females, you know. There always are. And between you and me, one female is as good as another."

Billie was always surprised at how easily the careless words or actions of a Yankee ignited her rage. She couldn't be shut of these people fast enough. How dare this Yankee use her horse for stud! Fat lot of good it did him. She had the papers. None of these damn Yankees knew whose bloodlines they were getting. They didn't even know the horse's real name.

Tonight would change all that.

"Don't worry, there's another mare over at Three Acres Farm who will need your services any day now. I'd better let you rest up for her." The farewell pat sounded firm and final.

Billie held her breath as the man latched the nearby stall and walked past her hiding place. She made herself wait, counting to one hundred. Then she limped across the aisle to the stall that held her Destiny. A gentle whicker greeted her. It had been two and a half years, but the horse had known she was nearby from the first day. She'd watched his restless behavior from afar, pleased he had not forgotten her.

"Did you miss me as much as I missed you, big boy?"

The dark nose butted into her hand, then snuffled up her arm as if the horse had to touch her as much as she had to touch him. She stroked the large jaw, caressing upward to his forelock, where she buried her fingers beneath the stiff hair and scratched the velvet skin.

"I doubt anyone has done that in a long time," she whispered, needing to talk to her horse as much as she needed to touch him.

The horse nodded his head in agreement. She grinned and pulled a carrot from her pocket.

"You, sir, are a shameless beggar, and I ought not give this to you. Have you no pride? Taking carrots from a Yankee! I thought I taught you better than that."

Nibbling lips tickled her palm as the horse took the carrot she'd stolen hours earlier from the nearby greenhouse. Two tracks of tears slid down her cheek, but there was no time to cry. Instead, she wound her arms around the horse's neck and rubbed her cheek on his.

"Thank God that damn Yankee didn't get you killed during the war." Her words were thick with moisture. "I told you I'd find you, didn't I? And we're going to have a wonderful new life, but first we have to get out of here."

She slid the worn halter over his head, her fingers adjusting it more from touch than sight, although glimmers of moonlight now snuck through the cracks and crevices of the old barn. Within a few moments, they stood at the rear entrance.

"Stay here while I check the yard." Billie wasn't sure if she whispered the words to command the horse or to encourage herself. She did know the next few moments would either see them on their way to Fletcher and safety or . . . not.

She pushed open the door and slipped through. Melting into the shadows of a broken wagon, she scanned the quiet farmyard. She'd been fortunate. For some reason, these ignorant Yankees had no dogs to warn them something was amiss.

The faint odor of tobacco lingered in the cool night air, and she wrinkled her nose, trying to tell if it was fresh. Staring intently at the house, she searched for the telltale glow of a cigarette. Stephen had once told her the glow from a lighted cigarette could be seen from half a mile away at night. The dark, silent shape of the large farmhouse met her intent gaze. Later she would chide herself for becoming impatient, but she'd been patient for the past week, and all she wanted to do was shake the dust of New York from her feet.

Destiny shoved his head against the door, pushing it ajar. One hurried visual sweep of the yard and then she slipped back to the horse.

"Don't be impatient," she murmured into a silken ear as she grabbed Destiny's halter. The horse followed her to the wagon, where she used a heavy wheel to swing onto his broad back. As her legs gripped his barrel, the warmth of his body penetrated the thin cotton of her tattered pants.

It was sheer bliss to be on Destiny again. The intervening years disappeared. The bad memories of the war evaporated. She and Destiny were together. With her knees molded to his sides, and his four strong legs gliding over the grass beneath them, she was gracefully complete once again. A nudge here, a shift in weight, and his pace quickened into a canter.

Destiny's mane whipped into her eyes as she rested her cheek against the satiny neck.

"Ready, big boy?" Her voice and heels urged him to a faster pace. "We're going to take the fence. It's a smooth jump—simple for you. Trust me."

Beneath her knees she felt Destiny's remarkable muscles gather as they neared the fence. Intoxicated with the joy of riding Destiny again, she failed to understand the significance of a shrill whistle that cut through the night air.

Her concentration centered on guiding Destiny over the fence, but at the last moment he balked. Unprepared for the sudden stop, she flew off his back.

"Nooooooooooo!" Her denial split the quiet night while the moment hung in time, bookended by a shriek and a thud. The fall jarred her from head to toe, unleashing memories of that long-ago crippling accident. Suddenly, it didn't matter that time was of the essence, that she had to get back on Destiny and jump the fence. Nothing mattered except the dizziness, the nausea, and the welcoming blanket of black.

But she couldn't let the blackness win, and she fought it. "Destiny. I have to get Destiny. I promised Poppa."

The Yankees were coming! She had to hide Destiny. She'd promised her father she would protect the horse, but she hadn't protected him. One beautiful summer morning a Yankee had dropped out of the sky and stolen the future of the D'Angelo family.

But Destiny was here. She could feel his soft nose snuffling through her hair. Nausea badgered her throat, but she ignored it. She had to get up. She had to get back on Destiny. They had to run.

"Back up, Angel. I can't see if your long-lost friend is hurt with your head in the way."

Billie frowned. She recognized that voice. The sound of it set off warning bells, but her body refused to get up and run. The ground shifted beneath her as she was rolled onto her back. She gagged as the motion brought the two carrots she'd stolen for dinner to the back of her throat.

Darkness beckoned, overriding the bout of nausea. She

willed her eyes open, although they felt as if someone had tied two anvils to her eyelids. When strong fingers probed her scalp, all thoughts of swooning evaporated.

"Stop that!" She slapped at the hands. She wasn't sure which appalled her most, the feebleness of her defense or the weakness of her voice. Blinking, she tried to focus on the face above her.

"Take it easy, boy." The man rocked back on his heels. "There's no reason to get excited. I was trying to help."

She'd never seen the Yankee hatless, shaved, and at close range. A bright gibbous moon crept from behind a thin ribbon of cloud and glazed his features with light and shadow. Billie stared at him, wondering why her breath hitched in her throat. She wasn't sure if the difficulty was caused by the fall or the chiseled perfection of the Yankee's face.

"Can you get up?"

Billie welcomed the question. It cut off her appalling appraisal of the man who had stolen Destiny. His kind had ruined her family's horse farm. Self-disgust surged through her. If a handsome face could make her forget the past four years, then she didn't deserve Destiny.

"Of course I kin git up," she snapped, as much at the Yankee as at herself. "I jest got the wind knocked outa me. I been throwed by a horse before." Which was true—she'd been thrown before, but never by Destiny. What had that damn Yankee done, teaching her horse to respond to his whistle! What other bad habits would she have to undo?

She pushed herself into a sitting position. The movement jarred her hip into another level of pain. She sucked in a quick gasp, unwilling to let the Yankee see how much she hurt. She needed a minute to recuperate, and she knew getting to her feet wouldn't be easy.

"Grayson! I heard a cry. What happened? Has there been an accident?"

Billie squinted her eyes against the light of the lantern the woman carried. Although a dark cloak covered the woman's body, loose tendrils of brown hair floated around a plump face, signaling a full figure beneath the billowing cloak. From the braid hanging over one shoulder and the white material showing at the hem of the cloak, Billie figured her banshee shriek had driven the woman from bed.

"There was no accident, Lina." The Yankee rose to his feet, brushing dried grass from his trouser legs as he went. "I caught this boy stealing Angel. I whistled as they were about to jump the fence. Angel stopped midair. Physics being what it is, the boy kept going."

"You caught this young man stealing our horse?"

"It ain't stealin' to take what's rightfully mine." Billie jumped into the discussion as well as her role. She couldn't let the fall from Destiny rattle her.

"Is that why you came sneaking around here in the dark? If you're so positive the horse belongs to you, why not come to the front door in the daylight and make your claim?"

Billie shrugged away the sarcasm. "I ain't met a Yankee yet who'd freely give back what he done stole from a Reb."

"Young man, this horse is mine by virtue . . ."

"Of stealin' him!"

"I didn't steal your horse, damn it! I commandeered him for the Union Army!"

"Grayson! Your language, in front of a young person and a lady."

Billie watched the Yankee's chiseled jaw clench. She was surprised to see the ornery Yank heeded the woman's reproving tone. Strange, but the thought of this Yankee having a wife bothered her, as did the image of a passel of little Yankee young'uns. She shook off the flicker of depression. So the Yank had a wife. Perhaps appealing to a higher authority would win her case.

"The horse yer husband brought home from the war, ma'am, belongs to me. And I got the papers to prove it."

"This is my sister, not my wife, rapscallion. Sweet-talking her won't gain you what you want. And no one can make me return this horse to you. I commandeered it under authority of the United States government."

Pleasure rippled through Billie at the idea the Yankee wasn't married. She disregarded her reaction and concentrated on the firmness of his tone. He did not seem inclined to give up Destiny.

"Perhaps you should listen to the young man, Grayson."

Not a wife, but still sympathetic.

"I reckon it weren't enough you Yanks killed my pa, tore up our house, and set all our slaves free." The lie popped into Billie's mouth faster than she could say "pass the grits." When had lying to Yankees become second nature? She dismissed the flicker of conscience. If she had to lie to get Destiny back, she would lie.

"No, you gotta steal our horses, too. What'd ya think I'm gonna plow with? Iffn I don't get some seeds planted soon, my baby brothers and sisters'll all starve. Which they almost done last winter, no thanks to the likes of you."

"Grayson?"

Billie wanted to smile. She heard the hard question buried in the melodic feminine tones.

"No, Lina. You can't believe what a horse thief says. Any court of law will uphold my claim on the horse."

"Only a damn Yankee court. Iffn you was man enough to come to Tennessee, you'd see what a court of law thought of yer claim. Stealin' a horse is a hangin' offense in Tennessee."

No longer content to nuzzle Billie's head, Destiny decided to butt his head against her back. It seemed as good a time as any to try and gain her feet. She could use the horse for support and avoid any help from the damn Yankee.

Girding herself for whatever pain her hip might give her, Billie pulled herself to her feet. The ache had intensified, but she could handle it.

"I did not steal the boy's damn horse!"

"Grayson!"

This time Billie thought she heard the Yankee's teeth grind

when he clamped his mouth shut. Either he seldom cursed or he wasn't accustomed to being censured by his sister. Whatever the reason, his body radiated anger.

"It's not as if you need the horse to survive. And it's most important to this young man. Why won't you give him the horse?"

Billie figured the Yankee counted to twenty or thirty before he answered his sister.

"I realize the nuances between commandeering and theft might elude the civilian mind, but they are not the same thing. I commandeered the horse under the authority of the United States government because he was necessary for the completion of my mission. I then purchased the horse from the government. Therefore, the horse belongs to me. This boy trespassed and tried to take the horse in the dark of night. If he'd come to my door in daylight and requested the horse, I would have considered it. But I do not reward horse thieves."

The announcement was as firm as the ground beneath Billie's bare feet. The Yankee's sister was made of sterner stuff and ignored her brother's tone.

"But, Grayson, this young man's family needs the horse."

Grayson knew he was digging his heels in about the horse, but the boy had sneaked onto the farm and tried to steal it. As a matter of principle, he refused to reward underhanded behavior, no matter what the motivation. And he suspected the urchin had spun a tale to sway Lina's soft heart.

"As I recall, there were churches in Tennessee. Do you attend one?"

The boy met his question with silence, then nodded his head.

"You would consider yourself a good Christian?"

"A good Catholic, and that's a sight better Christian than most I know."

Grayson almost smiled at the indignation coloring the boy's answer. Looking down at him, he made his offer.

"In that case, why don't we march you into the house?"

He paused and wrinkled his nose. "Or perhaps we had better bring the Bible outside. Either way, you may swear on the holy book you have hungry brothers and sisters."

The lantern light flickered across the boy's face, bathing his thin cheeks with a warm glow but no telltale blush of embarrassment. Ah, yes, this boy was used to lying, but he possessed an underlying streak of honesty. Grayson knew the moment the boy decided to recant his tale.

"I mayn't have any starvin' brothers and sisters, but I'll put my hand on a holy Bible any day and swear the damn Yankees tore up my home and stole all our horses!"

His words blistered the air, causing Lina to step back half a pace. Not so Grayson. He had seen it all, the honorable and the dishonorable, on both sides. He had no reason to flinch before the boy's accusations. Nor did he regret preventing Angel's theft, although he hadn't intended to harm the thief.

Thank God he kept his gun in a drawer in his bedroom rather than strapped to his side as he did during the war. Had he been armed, he would have shot the thief rather than whistled.

"Well, what are you going to do with this young man?"

Lina's voice sliced through his thoughts. He looked down at the boy, whose bodily stance screamed defiance.

"The law jails horse thieves."

"Then why wasn't you jailed three years ago?"

"Now, now, Grayson." Lina stepped into the tense breach. "You're being much too hard on . . ." His sister's gaze swung from him to the boy. "What is your name, dear?"

"Billie."

"Billie?" Lina smiled. "Short for William, no doubt. Such a strong name, makes one think of kings, doesn't it?"

"Yes ma'am, I reckon it does."

"Well, William," continued Lina, "do you have a last name?"

Grayson folded his arms across his chest and settled himself for an interesting few moments. Lina might seem a gentle person, but he knew how determined she could be when seeking to save someone. He was curious how the little Reb would handle her.

More than a few moments elapsed before Billie said, "Yes'um."

Lina possessed patience with young people, Grayson had to grant her that. She waited much longer than he would have before she finally surrendered to her curiosity.

"And your last name is?"

"D . . . uh, Angel, ma'am . . ." He stuttered to a stop, then said more confidently, "Billie Dwight Angel."

"Interesting." Grayson jumped back into the conversation. "A Reb who isn't sure of his name. Are you perhaps not an Angel? Is this a false name?"

Billie scowled at him.

"William Angel needs our help, not your barrage of questions. He has been orphaned by a war which he was too young to have caused or even fought in."

"Oh, no, ma'am, I fought. I coulda gone with my pa, been a drummer boy. But he needed someone to stay on the farm to tend the horses. That was afore the Yanks stole 'em all. But I got to shoot me a few Yanks there at the end."

Grayson snorted at the boy's performance. The boy knew a softhearted woman when he saw one.

"I ain't lying!"

"I'm sure you're not, William."

"Honest, I wouldn'a shot them Yanks iffen I'd known any was as nice as you. I thought they was all like him."

To Grayson's surprise, the little Reb jerked a thumb in his direction. "Your compliment overwhelms me, rapscallion."

"We could put William in the attic."

Grayson could feel his heels digging deeper into the ground. If Lina was thinking what he thought she was thinking, he would nip her idea in the bud.

"We could also put him in the nearest jail."

"Grayson!"

He winced at the mingled shock and disbelief that drenched his sister's tone.

"Surely, you jest. Anyway, you bear some responsibility for this situation."

"And how, sister mine, might I be responsible for a ragamuffin thief who got himself caught while trying to steal my horse?"

"Didn't you commandeer the horse from a young boy in Tennessee? When you described the incident to Darrell, I got the impression you felt bad about taking the horse. You thought the boy and horse quite attached to each other. Since I'm sure William had no way to discover your identity, I guess you contacted William's family. How else would he know where the horse lived?"

To Grayson's dismay, Billie pulled an envelope from a tattered pocket and waved it in the air.

"He wrote me. See here, Miss Lina. He wrote me a letter."

"I wrote your father," corrected Grayson. He snatched the envelope from Billie. "I wrote Mr. Philip Angel, as I promised you I would when I commandeered the horse." He stuck the envelope under Lina's nose. "In this letter, I explained I had purchased the horse and he had a good home. I did not invite Mr. Billie Dwight Angel to New York to steal my horse."

Lina looked from the letter to Grayson. "Be that as it may, your letter brought the boy here."

Grayson knew the futility of arguing with Lina once she had her righteous tone in full steam, but he also knew he wasn't about to cave in easily, not with such a satisfied grin lurking on the young Reb's face.

"I didn't expect anyone to respond to my letter."

"Well, William has, and now he's your responsibility. By the looks of him, he's penniless. And I doubt he has eaten a good meal lately. Heaven alone knows what hardships this young man endured in his trek from Tennessee to New York."

His sister could be as tenacious as a lobster once she got her claws into an idea. He was not going to feel either guilt or responsibility for the presence of one Billie Dwight Angel in New York. One of them needed to inject a bit of reason into the situation.

"Your young hero tried to steal my horse."

"William came to take back what he believes is rightfully his. The war's over. You no longer need the horse."

Grayson felt the argument slipping into some female realm of logic where he couldn't follow. The Reb wasn't helping any; his face wore a pitiful expression guaranteed to sway the cruelest heart, and Lina possessed a generous one.

". . . and he can stay in the attic."

Lina's last words snapped Grayson's attention back to his own position. "This young man is not coming into my house to steal me blind while I sleep."

"Don't be silly. You know William is not going to steal us blind. He's going to sleep in the attic tonight. In the room father made for you when you swore you couldn't sleep in the same room with Darrell another night. Tomorrow we shall decide how we can best help our new friend."

Friend? Billie had never thought to call a Yankee "friend," or to have one pin that label on her. She hadn't met many nice Yankees in her experiences with the Union army and Union sympathizers in Tennessee. Therefore, she wasn't prepared for a woman like Lina. Up until this moment, it had been easy to hate all Yankees. Faced with such generosity of heart, she found it difficult to view Lina Vanderlyn with the burning hatred she reserved for her former enemies.

Billie watched the exchange between the two Yankees with bated breath. She liked the way Lina stood up to her brother, but part of her hoped the Yankee would stand firm. If she could stay in the barn, where a ragamuffin such as herself belonged, she had a better chance of claiming Destiny. She could almost feel the frustration stiffening the Yankee's body as his sister wore down his resistance. She also knew the moment the

Yankee agreed to his sister's harebrained plan, because he turned his frustration on the one causing the situation.

"If it stays on my farm," he said as he took a step toward her, "it has to have a bath first. I won't have anything that vile-smelling under my roof."

Billie shrank back against Destiny. From the look in the Yank's eyes, he planned to throw her in the nearest horse trough. She wanted to die of mortification at the thought of smelling as bad as he claimed she did. No gentleman of her acquaintance had ever said such rude things to her.

But then, she wasn't dressed as a lady, was she? Her clothes, permeated with the scents of horse, manure, sweat, and leather, had seen her safely through the war. It seemed reasonable to believe the smelly outfit would see her safely through this postwar escapade.

When he reached for her, Billie clamped her teeth together. If he was going to throw her in a horse trough, she wasn't going to give him the satisfaction of one howl. To her surprise, his hand continued past her, brushing lightly across her shoulder as he grabbed Destiny's reins. She would go to her grave denying the Yankee's touch had sent a spiral of pleasure down her spine.

"And if I let you stay, you will promise not to steal my horse."

It wasn't a request; it was a command, stated in a voice accustomed to taking control while others jumped. Tonight she would jump, because it would keep her near Destiny. Anyway, she would never steal one of the Yank's horses. She wasn't a horse thief. When she left with Destiny, she would be taking something that belonged to her. Always had, always would. She had the papers to prove it.

She didn't want to appear too eager to agree to his condition, so she looked at him, watching the lantern flicker shadows over his face.

The Yankee met her gaze, his voice slicing through the night. "Your promise, rapscallion."

She could tell from the Yankee's tone that his patience, nearly nonexistent to begin with, had almost vanished.

"Oh, aw right." She edged her tone with reluctance. "I promise I won't steal any of yer horses, but I don't want no bath."

"Good," Lina said. "It's settled. William will stay with us."

"Shall I put the horse back in his stall, Master Grayson?" A wizened old man appeared out of the shadows, his nightcap askew on his head.

Billie recognized the newcomer from her surveillance of the farm. If the Yankee had been as old as his groom, Billie knew she would have gotten away with Destiny. Earlier in the night she had tiptoed past this man's room, her footfalls masked by his loud snores.

"Thank you, Jacob." The Yankee handed him the horse's reins. "I appreciate your help."

Jacob clucked to the horse and started to lead him away.

"Wait! I hafta check his legs first." In all the excitement, she'd forgotten to check Destiny's legs after the aborted jump. The horse stopped at the sound of her voice, and without thinking, she stepped toward him. Pain shot up her leg, and she staggered slightly.

"Why, William, you've hurt your leg. And where on earth are your shoes? Your feet must be freezing!"

When she bent to check Destiny's leg, Billie gritted her teeth against the stab of pain. When it eased somewhat, she said, "My leg ain't hurt, Miss Lina. Bruised a little from the fall is all. One leg's shorter than the other. That's why I walk funny. And I don't got no shoes."

While she talked, she ran her hands up and down each of Destiny's legs. Then she stepped back.

"I don't feel nothin', but I better sleep in the barn tonight and keep an eye on him."

"Over my dead body," the Yankee said. "Jacob, take Angel back to his stall. We'll check him carefully in the morning light."

Billie watched the old man lead her horse to the barn. Unable to stop the scowl settling on her face, she turned toward the Yankee.

"I don't wanna bath." She might as well play her role to the hilt. "But I shore do need a privy."

The Yankee picked up the lantern and handed it to his sister. "Show our 'guest' to the privy, Lina. I'll go stoke the fire in the kitchen to heat water for his bath."

His tone told her she was having a bath. Billie bit back a blissful sigh of anticipation. How she had longed for a bath these past few days. When he stopped and turned around, she thanked the night shadows for hiding her expression.

"Oh, and toss his clothes out the back door," he commanded. "I'll have Jacob burn them in the morning."

Billie didn't protest his high-handed order. Instead, she watched the Yankee's ground-eating stride carry him out of the ring of light thrown by the lantern and into the paler moonlight. The alabaster rays caressed dark brown hair, slid over wide shoulders, and stroked a narrow waist. His back was straight, and he walked with the assertive grace she had come to associate with professional soldiers.

"This way, William."

Lina's voice jerked Billie's gaze from the Yankee. Limping after the other woman, she welcomed the sharp pebbles and twigs that jabbed into her bare feet. They were a form of penance, painful reminders that she was not in New York to stare at hateful Yankee men; she was here to get Destiny.

CHAPTER TWO

Grayson stared at the journals scattered across his desk-top. Ruthlessly killing off characters in the half-dozen Captain Dinsmere books he'd penned before the war had not prepared him for death. Four years of warfare had altered him, quenching his desire to kill anyone, even in a novel.

Or on his farm. While he was glad Billie hadn't been injured by his fall from Angel, he wasn't pleased to have the boy in his home. Nor did he like his own sister casting him in the role of despicable cad while Billie emerged from the fiasco with a chance to steal the horse again—probably with Lina's blessings.

Grayson sighed. Lina's reaction didn't surprise him—compassionate explanations for why people acted the way they did littered his sister's world. She thrived on rescuing the less fortunate, and he supported her projects although they disrupted the household. No, Lina could not accuse him of being unfeeling. She might not understand the line he drew between comandeering and stealing, but she would respect his decision—if he remained firm.

All he had to do was wait until Billie tried to steal the horse again. Then Lina would have to agree that a night in jail to ponder his misdeeds and a train ticket to Tennessee would be the best solution for the problem of Billie.

A soft tap at the study door roused him from his frowning contemplation of the open journals on his desk. "Come in."

"I'm sorry to bother you, but if you're going to burn William's clothes he'll need replacements." Lina entered the library, her dressing gown rustling as she moved. "Do you have anything in your wardrobe he might wear until Mary and I find him a suitable wardrobe?"

Grayson closed his war journal. "I apologize for the inconvenience my letter is causing you."

"It's never an inconvenience to help those less fortunate." He heard a minute note of reproof in Lina's tone. "The war didn't touch me as heavily as it did you, nor as heavily as it touched William. It's difficult to think he numbered among our enemy only eleven months ago."

"From the malevolent way he looked at me, I would say the boy still numbers me among his enemies." Grayson rose from his comfortable leather chair, deciding it would be best not to give Lina a chance to chide him again about the horse. "I suspect his bathwater grows cold. I'll get some clothes for him."

Once in his bedchamber, he selected a worn pair of trousers and frayed shirt because his plans for Billie called for old clothes. He sifted through the contents of his bureau, but his thoughts were on an oppressive summer morning in Tennessee.

Had the letter been an attempt to assuage his guilt over taking Angel? An attempt to erase from his memory the anger, frustration, and resignation that had chased each other across Billie's face as the boy realized the enemy had taken his best friend?

And perhaps condemned the best friend to death.

Had he been seeking atonement when he bought Angel and sent him to New York? Had he wished someone would come for the horse when he wrote Billie's family? Grayson looked down at the flannel nightshirt in his hands.

No, he shook his head. He had felt guilty about taking the horse and bought Angel in order to save a beautiful animal from an untimely death on the battlefield, but he never expected anyone to respond to the letter.

Now someone had. He would have to deal with it. And giving the horse to Billie after the boy's attempt to steal it wasn't the answer. Grayson refused to reward a thief.

He added a pair of drawers to the clothes in his arms, a decision reached. If Billie behaved himself and atoned for his attempted theft, Angel would be his. But something warned him Billie would rather try to steal the horse again than pay any price a Yankee requested.

Billie lathered more rose-scented soap onto the washcloth. With typical Yankee ingenuity, the Vanderlyns had converted a former buttery off the kitchen into a bathing chamber. But even its proximity to the cavernous kitchen fireplace wouldn't keep the little room warm forever.

Poking her left foot out of the water, she scrubbed at the grime-encrusted sole. A delicate shudder shook her frame. She never complained to Fletcher, who had invented her disguise, but she'd always disliked some parts of her masquerade.

Such as bare feet and greasy hair.

A tentative knock sounded on the door separating the bathing chamber from the kitchen. She tensed, sinking slightly into the water.

"William? Is everything all right?"

"Yes, ma'am." Billie put a whine in her voice. "I near 'bout scrubbed my ears off."

"Good for you."

Slipping down into the water, Billie pulled the washcloth

over her breasts even though the small patch of cloth didn't cover her well. She hoped Lina would stay on the other side of the oak panel that shielded the tub from the rest of the room. Something scraped across the wooden floor in the kitchen; then the door separating the bathing chamber from the kitchen opened. Billie's stomach churned as Lina bustled a few feet into the room, dragging something behind her.

"I've set a chair next to the door to hold your clean clothes. And I found a pair of Darrell's shoes. You might need to stuff some newspaper in the toes if they're too large." The sound of rustling newspaper accompanied her last sentence. "As soon as I make up the bed in the attic room, I'll come back and show you the way."

"Thank you, ma'am."

The slippered feet moved toward the door, and Billie relaxed. When they stopped, she tensed up again.

"And, William, I apologize for Grayson insisting your clothes be burned."

As if Billie would argue. Burning those clothes had been her fondest wish for the past four years, but she was a boy and supposed to like dirt. She rubbed the soapy washrag over her arm before whining an answer. "I reckon he's so big I gotta do like he says or he'll beat me."

Billie grinned at the sound of Lina's shocked inhaled breath.

"Oh, no, William. Grayson would never beat a young person."

A soft draft of air curled through the bathing chamber as Lina closed the door behind her.

Billie didn't want to be drawn to this kindhearted woman who rose to the defense of her family. Lina stood between Billie and Destiny. She was the enemy.

As much the enemy as the Yankees who had ransacked her home. Damn Yankees who paid no attention to a half-wit, crippled stable boy. Why monitor what you said in front of a half-wit? Gathering military information for Fletcher, whose traveling apothecary hid the most wanted Confederate spy in Tennessee, had been child's play.

She swished her right foot through the water. Outwitting the Yankees had been fun, but she missed being a woman. Her eyes drifted shut as she pictured herself settling one of those delightful new bonnets on curly, clean hair.

Hair she kept out of the water to avoid getting wet. How she hated greasing curls she hadn't even known she possessed until she'd whacked off her waist-length hair. But grease it down she must, because no one would take her for a boy with curls framing her face. And if she washed her hair, she would wash away the muddy brown hue that hid a distinctive auburn color.

Warm water lapped her chest. With a sigh, she closed her eyes and dreamed of frequent baths, clean hair . . . and the horse farm in Texas that would make it all come true.

Mixing Destiny's Morgan blood with the wild mustangs would produce the ultimate cow pony: nimble, good-natured, versatile. All she had to do was get Destiny to Texas, refurbish her uncle's ranch, catch some wild mares, and put them into a pen with Destiny. Within a few years, she would have enough money to buy back Vallata D'Angelo and furnish it as it had been before the Yankees came.

She would not think about Archibald Seyler and the auction. As sure as she knew Vallata D'Angelo would be sold for nonpayment of taxes, she knew Seyler would outbid everyone else to get it. She opened her eyes, refusing to picture him living in her beautiful home. *Concentrate on the plan.*

One or two days and she would have Destiny. Fletcher had given her a week to get the horse. As long as she signaled him each day, he would remain out of sight. He hadn't understood her determination to be the one to rescue Destiny, but he respected it.

The flexibility of their agreement gave her the room to become Lina's temporary protégé. It wasn't in her original plans, but flexibility had helped her survive the war, and now it would help her get Destiny.

Another knock on the door broke into her daydream. Brisk and firm, this one put her nose deep in the cooled water. To her relief, its grimy hue sheltered the clues to her sex. She should have known better than to dawdle in the tub.

The towel Lina had draped on a small table near the tub seemed miles away.

The door opened. "Are you almost finished, rapscallion? It would be a pleasure to get to bed sometime tonight."

Why on earth did the thought of the Yankee in a bed cause this odd tightening in her lower abdomen?

"Soon as I wash behind my ears."

"I have some clothes for you. Nightshirt, trousers, shirt. A pair of drawers."

Odd feelings tickled Billie's brain at the thought of wearing the Yankee's drawers. She squelched them.

"Miss Lina done put everything on a chair." Her voice seemed high-pitched, and the wood privacy panel that separated them seemed inadequate. She strained to pinpoint his location.

An overwhelming fear that he was going to come around the screen, take the towel from the table, and offer to help her out of the bath clamped her heart. The effects of this fear were as odd as the fear itself. Although she worried about the loss of her disguise, a tiny part of her wanted to see his reaction when he realized she wasn't a boy. Why she wanted to see his reaction, she didn't know. It was a dangerous path to follow. She slid quickly back into her role.

"What're ya waitin' fer?" Then she let a note of indignant youthful scorn coat her voice. "Are you one of them men what likes to look at nekkid boys?"

A smothered oath met her accusation. "Count yourself lucky, rapscallion. If I had my way, you'd be spending the night in jail. And you'd be wise to remember I'm the one who stands between you and Angel, not Lina. You should also be aware I'm a light sleeper—the merest creak of a floorboard and I'll be out the door with my gun."

"Well, you kin jump up and down all night long iffen you want, Yankee. You won't catch me doing nothin'."

"That's a wise boy. And when you wake up in the morning, why don't you come up with a good story to tell Lina about how you have to return home. If you leave tomorrow, I'll buy you a railroad ticket to Tennessee."

"Leave? Why would a pore crippled orphan like me wanna leave New York?"

Complete silence met this last announcement. Billie sank lower into the tub, wondering if she had pushed the Yankee too far.

"The jails in New York aren't a good place for a Reb to be, rapscallion. And if I catch you stealing my horse again, it's jail."

The door slammed shut behind the Yankee. Billie exhaled. The Yankee represented an obstacle, but she would think of a way around him. She wouldn't leave New York without Destiny.

There was a distinct chill to the small room now, and she hurried to dry herself and dress. It would have been nice to have a clean cravat to flatten her breasts, but she picked up the band of cloth she had hidden before her bath. Winding it tightly around her chest, she pinned the trailing end with her grandmother's brooch.

The rubies in the brooch winked red in the wavering light of the candles. It had been several centuries since a skilled craftsman of the Old World had created this elegant work of art. She rubbed her fingers over the brooch. This pin and Destiny were all she had left of her life before the war.

She found the clothes neatly folded on a chair beside the screen. On top lay the Yankee's drawers. Her fingers stroked the soft, worn long cloth before she stepped into the too-large drawers. Pulling them up her slender hips, she tied the tapes as tight as she could, trying not to picture the Yankee's lean body in these same drawers.

For some strange reason she was no longer chilled. As she lifted a flannel nightshirt from the chair, she unleashed a faint scent that brought the Yankee into her mind. Neither time nor washing eradicated the fact that he had once worn these clothes. She closed her mind to images of the Yankee in various stages of undress. No woman of her upbringing should have such thoughts.

Even as she fought the images, she buried her face in the soft flannel fabric. She inhaled one last deep breath and then jerked the nightshirt over her head before scooping the shirt and trousers off the chair. Limping, she crossed to the room and opened the door to her new, temporary life.

Billie awoke sprawled across a bed with her cheek rubbing against the case of a crisp, freshly washed pillow. The faint fragrance of dried lavender tickled her nose. She stared at a sloping wall. Turning her head, she searched for the canvas of Fletcher's wagon. A small, sparsely furnished attic room met her gaze.

She dropped her face back into the pillow. It was the Yankee's house. She had tried to get Destiny and failed.

Tossing aside the bed linens, she tested her bad leg before limping to a dormer window. She pushed aside the calico curtains and peered out. A sprawling white oak whose limbs reached past the roof of the house blocked her view of the barn.

She looked down. The ground was a long way away. She closed her eyes against the sensation of falling while a wave of dizziness vied with nausea. Her father had bullied her back onto horseback once her leg mended, but no one could bully away this horrible fear of falling. Over the years, she hid the fear from her father, but she had never conquered it. She lived with it.

When the time to escape arrived, she hoped she wouldn't have to climb out the window to get Destiny.

The aroma of coffee hit Billie's nose the moment her feet touched the top step of the well-worn oak staircase. Her steps slowed, her breathing deepened, and she filled her senses with the rich scent. Sometimes she had wondered which she hated more, the way the Yankees tore up her home or the way they had tossed cups of real coffee into the dirt at their feet.

She had gotten caught stealing coffee one time, and the fear of jeopardizing her masquerade had curtailed but did not erase her lust for real coffee. And even for the Confederacy she had never lied and said boiled parched peanuts tasted good.

"The dining room is this way, William."

Billie jumped. Engrossed in absorbing the aroma of coffee into every cell of her body, she hadn't heard Lina enter the hall.

"I jest as soon eat in the kitchen, ma'am."

"Family and guests eat together, William."

Billie found herself being ushered into the dining room, where the Yankee sat at the head of a large table. He rose as his sister entered the room.

"Billie might be more comfortable in the kitchen, Lina."

"Nonsense. William will do fine right here."

Billie slid into the closest chair. She widened her eyes into an innocent gaze and looked at the Yankee. "Whatever you want, Miss Lina."

"I want you to eat well."

Billie glanced at the groaning sideboard. An army could eat well for a month on the food she saw.

"I told Mary we had a hungry young man as our guest," Lina said, "and she has outdone herself. Go ahead, help yourself, William."

When Billie reached the sideboard, she couldn't concentrate on the scrambled eggs, pancakes, breads, or sausages. All she could see was the elegant porcelain coffeepot. The feel of the smooth, curved handle in her hand reminded her of breakfast at Vallata D'Angelo with her father.

The hairs on her neck tickled. She didn't need to turn around to know the Yankee stared at her. Damn! A young boy would have heaped food on a plate, not poured himself a cup of coffee. She set the hot coffee aside, picked up a plate, and scooped a spoonful of eggs on it.

By the time she finished with the plate, it took both hands to carry it to the table. Then she limped back to the sideboard for her coffee. The coffee's deep, rich aroma, not the savory smells curling off the plate, captured her taste buds. She yearned to taste its delicious warmth.

"When I was your age, William, I found putting sugar and cream into my coffee helped its taste."

Billie swallowed her dismay. Coffee was meant to be savored as it was, not to be fouled by sweeteners.

"No thank ya, Miss Lina. I ain't used to such as sugar and cream."

"Any more than you are accustomed to coffee."

She ignored the Yankee's quip. Setting her lips against the cup's rim, she closed her eyes and sipped. Earth's nectar flowed into her mouth.

"Speaking of age, rapscallion, how old are you?"

Billie choked, coffee spewed, and the cup clattered back onto the saucer. Lina pounded on Billie's back as if she had choked on a piece of gristle. To her dismay, brown coffee stained the pristine tablecloth between her and the Yankee.

As she struggled to breathe, she wished she had missed the tablecloth and hit the Yankee's white shirt. It would have wiped the sardonic grin off his face. And repaid him for the ungentlemanly question concerning her age.

As soon as she got a breath, she waved Lina away. "I'm just fine, now. Thank ya, Miss Lina."

"You see, William," Lina admonished as she settled back into her chair. "A dash of cream would have cooled your coffee and prevented an incident such as this."

Rather than admit the coffee temperature was perfect, Billie mumbled, "Yes'um." She submitted without a word to the indignity of Lina ruining a good cup of coffee with a dollop of cream.

"Perhaps you're too young to indulge in such a potent brew," the Yankee observed.

"I'm not young. I'm nearly fifteen!" Recklessly she stripped ten years from her age. She drew her face into the scowl that had teased her features since Lina poured cream into the coffee. Tension flirted with her spine as she prayed the Yankee wouldn't make any comment about her lack of facial hair.

To her delight, neither Lina nor the Yankee questioned her declaration. Fletcher was right—people saw what you wanted them to see. She wanted them to see a young male, and that's what they saw.

"Fifteen!" Lina said. "You'll probably outgrow those trousers this week. Remember how you and Darrell grew by leaps and bounds the summers you turned fifteen, Grayson? Why, Mother despaired of keeping you properly clothed."

Until this moment, Billie had never thought of herself as short. At five feet four, she thought her height acceptable for a woman.

For a woman. The phrase echoed in her mind. A boy would want to be taller. She sawed at the stack of pancakes on her plate while her mind looked for good reasons to be comfortable with her height.

"I ain't growed much since the accident, and Doc said I probably won't grow no more. And iffen I do, I'll have a worser limp because my left leg ain't never gonna grow no more. So, iffen it's all the same to you, Miss Lina, I'd as soon stay exactly as tall as I am."

A gasp swung Billie's gaze from her plate. Lina's hand covered her mouth, and she peered over it with a horrified expression in her eyes. A bright red blush stained her cheeks.

Billie's heart, hardened as it had been against Yankees by the war, softened in the face of such sincere distress.

"There ain't no call to be upset, Miss Lina. I'm used to being crippled." She kept her tone youthfully matter-of-fact. "As Fletcher says, it ain't the accident but what you make of it that counts."

"A solid piece of philosophical advice, if I have ever heard one. And who might this Fletcher be?"

Billie looked at the Yankee. The unexpected image of him as a growing adolescent distracted her. He hadn't stopped growing until he reached six feet.

"Fletcher?" She tried to remember the question.

"Your mentor?"

She kept the blank look glued on her face. She hadn't meant to mention Fletcher.

"Your adviser, your friend," explained the Yankee patiently. "Or is Fletcher a relative?"

"Oh, Fletcher. Jest a slave." Billie shoved a mound of pancake into her mouth, chewed a little but didn't swallow. "He run off right after the war started. I heered he was killed by Yankees for stealin' a rifle."

Out of the corner of her eye, she saw Lina open her mouth and then shut it. Comments on table manners would wait until she had recuperated from her faux pas over Billie's height.

The Yankee didn't share his sister's sensitivity.

"For future meals, rapscallion, it's impolite to talk with food in your mouth."

Billie tried, but she couldn't stop herself. The "Yes, sir" popped out, right around another mouthful of pancake.

The words no sooner left her mouth than she had the uncanny feeling he knew she talked with her mouth full on purpose. Her father had claimed he knew when she planned trouble because she got a mischievous light in her eyes before she acted. No one else had ever noticed the giveaway gleam—no one until the Yankee and his observant eyes.

"We have plenty of time to improve William's table manners," Lina said.

Billie grinned at the Yankee over the rim of her coffee cup.

Lina would have as long as it took for Billie to figure out how to steal back Destiny.

"Oh, I just had the best idea!" In her excitement, Lina waved a jam-smeared biscuit in the air. "We're having a small dinner party Saturday night." She paused to count on her fingers. "That will give us almost five days to polish your manners, William."

It took Billie and the Yankee several seconds to digest Lina's suggestion. Theirs was a simultaneous protest.

"Oh, no, Miss Lina."

"Really, Lina. Aren't you carrying this a bit far?"

"He's right, Miss Lina. I best eat in the kitchen that night. I wouldn't wanna embarrass ya in front of yer friends."

"William, you won't embarrass us. I shall personally take charge of your training. I think of you as a member of our family, and I won't have you shunted off to the kitchen when we have guests for dinner. Why, I was fourteen when Mother allowed me to attend my first small dinner." Lina stared dreamily over the Yankee's head at the painting of an English landscape hanging on the wall behind him. "Fourteen. It seems longer than eight years since I saw that birthday."

"I hardly believe twenty-two constitutes old age," the Yankee murmured.

Billie stared at Lina and then wickedly fell into her part of young boy. "Twenty-two years old!" She widened her eyes into huge saucers.

"Billie." There was a stern note of disapproval in the Yankee's voice that brought Billie's teasing to a halt.

"I'm sure twenty-two seems quite ancient to someone as young as William," Lina said.

"Keep in mind, young man, that my ancient, nearly thirty-year-old hand can beat quite a tattoo on that backside of yours if you don't learn some manners."

Billie couldn't resist swinging her wide-eyed gaze at the Yankee as if thirty years were quite beyond her comprehension. To her delight, he scowled.

"Please don't threaten William. His offense is not one that merits a thrashing. You know our parents seldom raised their hand against us. I would have you use Father as your role model when it comes to William."

"Billie is not my son."

"No, but William is an orphan. I thought you quite understood my plans."

Lina became the beneficiary of the Yankee's scowl.

"Plans? What plans do you have for this scruffy Reb?" The Yankee's snarl had no effect on his sister.

Billie remained quiet, watching the interaction between brother and sister.

Lina set down her coffee cup and smiled sweetly at her brother. "Why, I believe we should adopt Billie."

CHAPTER THREE

"Adoption makes perfect sense," Lina said. "The boy needs a home, and we have one. Why not share it?"

Women! Grayson could live to be a hundred and still be unable to fathom how their minds worked. No matter what Lina said, he never remembered any mention of anyone adopting the boy.

He tried logic. "Billie is not some stray animal. I'm sure he has family in Tennessee that wants him."

Billie, who originally appeared as shocked at Lina's suggestion as he, now had that annoying aura of repressed laughter. Rather than claim any family, he turned his green-eyed, guileless gaze toward Lina and shook his greasy head soulfully. Why hadn't the youngster washed that filthy hair when he bathed last night? Grayson had seen enough head lice to last a lifetime during the war; he wasn't interested in battling them in his own home.

"I ain't got nobody in Tennessee. Ma died of fever before the war, and Pa were killed durin' the war."

"Now you have no brothers and sisters, yet you claimed a

herd of them yesterday. How conveniently your family grows and shrinks, rapscallion."

"I made up them brothers and sisters yesterday, to make Miss Lina feel sorry for me and give me my horse."

"And today you need her to feel sorry for you, so you wipe out your entire family. *The family who needs you home in Tennessee.*" He gave Billie his best military stare.

It had no effect.

The rascal did not tell Lina he had to go home.

"I really had a brother, but he died in a duel, oh, years ago, when I were little."

The frown squeezed Grayson's forehead. Not only had the brat refused to go home, he had once again offered a snippet of a life at odds with the way he dressed and talked. These snippets painted a family comfortably situated in Southern society, but his manners and speech said otherwise. Four years of running loose with no parental supervision must have shorn the boy of the genteel side of life.

Across the table, Lina made *tsk*ing sounds that did not bode well for his scheme of ridding the Vanderlyn household of an unkempt Reb. Once she set her mind on a course of action, it was hard to deter her. With his luck, she'd have their older brother Darrell drawing up adoption papers by week's end.

Grayson felt his plan to send the young Rebel home on the next train slip through his fingers while his mind raced with options. He decided to act as if adoption were a possibility rather than contest Lina's plans. After all, the boy probably wouldn't be around next week.

In fact, he might let the boy steal Angel just to catch him and have the satisfaction of throwing the brat into jail. Imagine, accusing Grayson Andrew Vanderlyn of lusting after boys! A night or two in jail would teach the brat some manners.

He decided to defuse his sister's wild scheme without alienating her.

"Adoption is a serious business, Lina. We'll need time to

discuss all the implications with the rest of our family. And while Billie's immediate family is deceased, there may be other relatives."

"There ain't nobody left since Aunt Maria died last winter. And I doubt if she woulda minded you adoptin' me. She says I were a waste of the good Lord's time from the beginning."

"What a terrible thing to say to a child!" Lina cried.

Grayson didn't like Billie's uncanny ability to ignite the indignant, save-the-stray light in Lina's eyes. It boded ill for him.

"Now, we don't know what might have prompted this aunt's comment." For some reason Grayson felt a kinship with Aunt Maria. "Billie may have no relatives who will contest an adoption, but he needs time to think about the ramifications of adoption. For instance, it would mean living in New York permanently."

"It don't make no never mind where I live as long as I eat."

He could tell the initial shock had worn off and Billie liked the idea. Grayson would get no help from that quarter.

"Be careful of what you say," he said. "Lina plans to make you into a gentleman. You might not like the process."

There was that undefinable air of laughter again. And then a shrug.

"Long as she feeds me, I reckon I cain't complain about learnin' gentlemen things. But why would Miss Lina teach me? She's not a man."

"You're quite right," Lina said. "I can teach you many things, but Grayson will help, too. His education in the arts and sciences is excellent. Did you know he toured Europe before the war?"

Grayson wiped his mouth, folded the napkin, and placed it beside his empty breakfast plate. Lina's glowing picture of life as Billie's tutor made the railway's recent request for him to continue his wartime survey work an appealing idea. If he couldn't tempt Billie to leave by offering him a train ticket, he would have to devise another way to convince the brat to go home. Perhaps a few hours mucking out stalls would make Tennessee more attractive.

"Shall we begin your education in the stables?"

"I can show William the stables, if you wish to work on your book."

"I don't plan to 'show' Billie the stables, Lina. I plan to put him to work there. As for my book, I will be at my desk as soon as I discuss Billie's duties with Jacob." As if sitting at his desk had done him any good these past months. He'd published five novels about the colonial Indian wars, but he couldn't complete more than one page about the only war he had personally experienced.

"You're going to make Billie work in the stables like a common stable boy?"

"Billie *is* a common stable boy, aren't you?"

A noncommittal shrug met his question.

Grayson addressed his decision to Lina. "Until the family agrees to support your adoption scheme, the boy can work to earn his keep. He knows horses, and Jacob needs help— need I remind you of your latest rescue attempt gone awry? It left Jacob alone in the stables."

Lina, poised to argue her point, snapped her mouth shut.

Grayson swallowed a grin. Lina's attempt to help two local adolescents had ended when she found the pair entwined in the hayloft last week. Since Gerret had been the newest employee at the farm, he lost his position as stable hand, while Jennetje remained as a maid.

"If you are going to soil Billie's one set of clean clothing, I shall try and find him more. There should be some castoffs in the attic that will fit him."

Content with his victory, Grayson pushed back his chair and stood. "Ready, rapscallion?"

Billie had eaten a wonderful breakfast while the Yankee and his sister argued. Now she shoved a last forkful of sausage in her mouth. Lifting her arm to wipe her mouth on her sleeve, she paused when Lina shook her head slightly, then dabbed at her mouth with a napkin. Billie grinned and grabbed a napkin. After scrubbing her mouth, she threw the napkin on the table and followed the Yankee from the room.

As they headed for the barn, she made no excuses for her bad leg. She also made no attempt to keep up with the Yankee's ground-eating stride. He was halfway to the barn before he realized he would arrive there alone. Stopping, he turned and waited for her.

When she reached him, he sniffed the air as he shortened his step to match hers.

"Smelling a little sweet this morning, aren't you?"

"You made me take a bath, in case you fergot."

"For future reference, the rose-scented soap belongs to Lina."

Billie's step faltered slightly. It had been such a delight to soak in a tub, she had given no thought to the fact a young boy would find the scent of roses offensive. "I din't see nothin' else." She gave her tone a defensive edge.

"I'll make sure my soap is available for tonight. And you will wash your hair, unless you're planning a trip to Oregon and haven't told us."

She seized on the bath, not the hair-washing. "Another bath!" Inflecting her tone with a sheen of horror, she scowled up at the Yankee while her brain raced to come up with a valid reason for not washing her hair.

"After a day in the stables, some type of washing before dinner would make you a more pleasant dinner companion."

"I kin wash a little, I reckon, but I don't know about my hair. Pa said washing his hair's what killed his brother."

"That's an interesting theory. Would you care to elaborate?"

She took a patient breath. "Why, his brother washed his hair one night, took a chill, and died of the ague the next day."

"I see."

She pinned a puzzled look on her face. "And why'd ya think I wuz plannin' a trip to Oregon?"

The Yankee paused outside the barn. "You have enough Macassar oil on your head to keep a wagon axle lubricated for a trip to Oregon." He didn't give her a chance to deny the outrageous assertion before he pushed open the barn door.

"You seemed familiar with horses last night. Have you worked in a stable?"

Billie thought of all the hours she had spent with horses. "Do beaver pelts make good hats?"

"Morning, Master Grayson."

"Ah, Jacob. I have brought someone to help you." The Yankee's gray eyes studied her while he spoke. "Jacob is a little shorthanded this week, and I thought you might like to help him. To compensate us for your attempt to steal Angel, and your comfortable bed, and all the food you devoured this morning."

Billie bit back a retort; from the look in the Yankee's eye he was spoiling for another argument over Destiny's ownership.

"Do you want me to stop looking for a replacement for Gerret?" Jacob's question swung the Yankee's gaze away from her.

"Oh, I don't think Billie will be permanent. You'd best continue the search for another stable hand. There must be some young man in the area who needs a job."

"Oh, I can find the young men. Keeping them's the problem. It'd be easy if you fired Jennetje."

"Lina won't allow that." A rueful grin flitted across the Yankee's mouth. "We are, after all, saving Jennetje's soul."

Jacob snorted his disbelief.

"Go with Jacob. He'll show you what to do." The Yankee started toward the barn door, took three steps, and stopped. "Oh, and Billie, don't try and steal Angel. I know this county like the back of my hand. And I know plenty of men eager to chase one last Reb."

"And since you ain't gonna admit to 'em you stole my horse first, they'd come after me like a hound on a raccoon."

"You've grasped the situation well."

Since she had no intention of taking Destiny in broad daylight, Billie shrugged and followed Jacob toward the horse stalls.

By late morning, she knew the Yankee had been right. She would need another washing. The scent of roses had been obscured by the odors of horse manure, straw, and perspiration. Jacob had proved to be a demanding boss, but once he saw she knew her way around a stable, he had assigned her tasks and gone about his own chores.

Destiny's pleasure in seeing her helped ease the drudgery of the work. She was here to get him, and if currying horses and shoveling manure was the only way to get him, then she would do it. Hadn't she curried countless horses and carted away heaps of manure during the war? She scooped manure into a wheelbarrow while she whistled "Dixie" to herself.

With a grunt, she lifted the worn handles of the wheelbarrow and pushed the heavy load of manure toward the stable door. The load was balanced on one wheel, and it took all her strength and attention to keep the wheelbarrow moving across the loamy floor. She almost didn't see the slight figure that entered the door as she neared it. As it was, the girl startled Billie into losing control of the wheelbarrow, which slewed drunkenly onto its side.

"Holy Mary, Mother of God!"

"Don't you cuss at me, Reb."

The whiny nasal tones grated on Billie's ears, and she frowned at the girl. An attempt had been made to corral a head of wiry orange curls, but they fought against the pins and bun, springing out like a fuzzy halo around the girl's small face.

"It wasn't my fault you overturned the wheelbarrow."

Billie righted the wheelbarrow before limping back to where

she had left the shovel. Silently she began to scoop up manure again.

The girl pretended to be interested in a large gray gelding and rubbed its nose while she watched Billie.

"Gerret won't be happy when he finds out a Johnny Reb got his job—a crippled one at that."

Billie shoveled manure and ignored the girl, who addressed her remarks to the horse. It had to be Jennetje. The girl, who appeared to be about seventeen, had come to the stable to investigate the new stable hand. Billie hoped with all her heart Jennetje had the sense to dislike Southerners.

"He's gonna be mad," Jennetje told the horse. "And I don't think even a murdering, thieving Rebel would wanna face Gerret when he's mad."

Billie thrust her shovel into the soft loam near her feet and wrapped her hands around the handle.

"I don't see as how I coulda taken Gerret's job iffen he was fired afore I got here. The way I see it, you cost Gerret his job, not me."

Whipping around, Jennetje planted her hands on her hips. "Don't you try and blame me, you murdering Reb. Your kind killed my papa, do you hear? If the Rebels hadn't started the war, he'd be alive to take care of me and my ma. And I wouldn't haveta work for Miss Lina or anybody else."

Billie wanted to tell the girl the war had taken her father and dreams, too, but Jennetje slipped through the door, leaving the hatred in her words to swirl behind her.

Staring at the barn door, Billie rubbed her thigh. She was struggling to make her own world right, and there was no sense in wishing she had the power to right the world for a dead Yankee's daughter. Thrusting the shovel into the manure, she heaved another load into the wheelbarrow.

She groomed Destiny last because he was her reward for the morning's work. Her whole being delighted in the task as she brushed his dark coat, combed out his mane and tail, and cleaned his hooves. It was a joy to trail her fingers along his satin-smooth skin, to trace the familiar crooked white blaze that ran from below his ears to his soft right nostril. As for Destiny, he whickered softly, leaning his chin on her shoulder while she tickled his soft nose and whispered silly endearments.

A morning spent in manual labor freed her brain for tackling the problem of getting the horse safely away. She had watched the farm's routine for several days from the outside; now she had the opportunity to observe it from the inside. This time she would be patient. This time she would get Destiny.

Jacob had assured the Yankee that the horse suffered no ill effects from the attempted abduction, but Billie checked him again anyway. She was relieved to find Jacob was correct. It would have been painful to learn she had hurt her horse, but how was she to know that damn Yankee had taught Destiny to respond to a whistle.

Soothed by the familiar task of grooming Destiny, she pushed aside the present and daydreamed about their future in Texas. In a quiet whisper, she shared her dreams with Destiny. She never heard the Yankee enter the barn.

"Lina insists you stop work and eat."

She jumped at the sound of the Yankee's voice, jostling Destiny's head, which he had laid contentedly on her shoulder. How long had that damn Yankee been there?

"Holy Mary, Mother of God! Do you sneak everywhere you go, Yankee?"

"It was a useful trait during the war."

"That and hidin' in trees and droppin' down on unsuspectin' folks ridin' their own horse. Well, we ain't at war no more, so there's no need for you to sneak around."

"Aren't we?"

She wouldn't take the bait. She gave Destiny's gleaming coat a swipe and hoped no blush belied her embarrassment in being caught whispering to a horse.

"As I said, Lina sent me to tell you it's time to eat."

"I don't think Miss Lina'll want me in the dining room." Billie looked down at her sweat-stained clothing.

"Who said anything about the dining room?" The Yankee waved a basket above the stall door.

"Where we gonna eat?" she asked, looking around the barn.

"I know a good place for a picnic. We'd need to ride some horses."

Running her fingers through Destiny's mane, Billie wondered if the Yankee meant to let her ride her horse.

As if he read her mind, he said, "I thought you might like to ride Angel. Jacob says you worked harder than two Gerrets this morning. Think of this as a reward for good behavior."

Not even the prospect of the Yankee going with them could dim Billie's joy at riding her horse. She looked over Destiny's back at the Yankee. Elbows propped on the stall door, he watched her.

"What'll you ride?" she asked, distrusting the speculative glint in his gray eyes.

"As you probably noticed, there are several good hacks here. I usually ride the gray, Dinsmere."

"You named a horse after Captain Dinsmere?"

There it was again, the puzzled gleam in the Yankee's eye, triggered by something she said. Damnation, this Yankee kept her on her toes! Always looking for holes in her stories.

"You're acquainted with the Captain Dinsmere books?" His question sounded casual, but Billie knew he delved for personal information.

Turning away, she gave Destiny's gleaming coat another few swipes with the brush. How should she reconcile her supposed background with her real one? Her brain raced, looking for answers. A brash defense seemed the best path.

"Why shouldn't I be? And iffen you was awonderin' iffen I knowed you wrote 'em, well, I do."

"Smooth your bristles, Billie. I'm flattered my poor scribblings got an audience as far away as Tennessee."

As far away as Tennessee. As far away as lazy days spent reading books about Captain Dinsmere. As far away as her father's dream to raise the best horses in the state.

She ran the brush over Destiny's flank and kept her face hidden from the Yankee. It wouldn't do her image as a boy any good if he saw the tears that burned the back of her eyes. She hated these unanticipated bouts of grief, because it was best to keep thoughts of her life before the war snuggled tightly into the back of her mind. She had to deal with the present and the future; she dare not think of the past, or she might drown. She embroidered the truth.

"My pa read 'em to me. He liked Captain Dinsmere."

"It's not unmanly to grieve over the loss of a parent."

The gentle advice gnawed at her control. She tightened her grip on the handle of the currycomb and breathed deeply. One thing she didn't need was a Yankee's sympathy. If the Yanks had let the South go its own way, there never would have been a war. Her father would be alive, and Destiny wouldn't have left Tennessee.

To follow that line of thought led to despair. She ran the currycomb over Destiny's flanks one last time and gave him an affectionate pat. She was positive no sign of moisture gleamed in her eyes when she moved away from Destiny and asked, "Which saddle were you awantin' me to use on Angel?"

CHAPTER FOUR

Billie couldn't argue with the Yankee's choice of site for their impromptu picnic. After an exhilarating gallop, he led the way to a shady grove of beech trees. It was a natural picnic site—cool shade tinged with the sweet smell of spring.

She kicked her feet free of the stirrups, swung her leg over the saddle, and slid to the ground. Another time, another place, she would have been dressed in a riding habit and waited for the Yankee's hand to dismount. She pushed away the image because she couldn't afford to notice how handsome he was. To succeed, she had to maintain her hate of Yankees in general and this horse-stealing one in particular. If she let her hatred slip, if he once suspected she wasn't what she claimed to be . . .

"Mary forgot she was sending two males on a picnic. She included a quilt." Rather than spread the quilt, the Yankee tossed it toward Billie while he rooted through the basket.

The quilt, faded with time and washings, was soft in her hands when she caught it. She suppressed the desire to spread it on the ground. Nor did she smooth away its wrinkles when she laid it on the fallen tree trunk beside the food the Yankee was unpacking and lining up.

When he had emptied the basket, the Yankee grabbed several thick slices of roast beef and crammed them between equally thick slices of bread. He handed one of his concoctions to her before settling himself on the log and wedging his back against a sturdy beech. Without more ado, he bit off a mouthful.

Billie joined him on the log, keeping the picnic basket between them. She stretched her left leg out, trying to ease the ache. The peace of the glade gave her the courage to ask a question that had pestered her since their first encounter.

"You don't look nothin' like him."

"Like who?" The Yankee bit off a mouthful of sandwich.

"You know, Captain Dinsmere." She tried to imagine the fastidious young man opposite her sloshing his way through freezing rivers in pursuit of hostile Indians. She shook her head. She couldn't see him as Captain Dinsmere.

The Yankee stared at her, startled by her answer. Then he broke into unfortunate laughter. Unfortunate because he had a mouthful of beef and bread. His laugh ended in a spasm of coughing.

Frightened, Billie leaped to her feet. Her unstable leg wavered beneath her. She steadied herself by leaning on the Yankee's shoulder. Then she pounded his back. Several hard thwacks, and his coughing eased. He motioned for her to stop.

Right hand suspended in the air, she realized her left hand clutched his muscular shoulder. His body heat radiated warmth into every crevice of her hand. Muscles bunched and relaxed beneath her touch. Her breath hitched in her throat as she sucked his scent, a mixture of musk, tobacco, and male, into her nostrils. It filled her lungs and filtered into her heart to be pumped into every cell in her body.

She wanted to run her fingers along the ridge of his shoulder, up into the dark brown hair fringing his neck. He leaned backward, drawing in a lusty gust of air. She jerked her hand off his shoulder and stumbled in her haste to put distance between them.

She swallowed, searching for saliva to dampen her mouth before she spoke.

"Are you recovered?"

In her agitation, she forgot to be young Billie. The educated words hovered in the air between them. The Yankee whirled around to face her. Confusion flickered in his gray eyes.

Holy Mary, Mother of God! Billie could have kicked herself. Fletcher's advice echoed in her ears: *"Make them see what you want them to see."* Her mind raced. Then she relaxed. She reached down with her right hand and idly scratched her crotch.

Her action had its intended effect. It chased away the speculative gleam in the Yankee's eyes. A rueful grin curved his mouth. A mouth she dared not stare at too long.

"Thank you for your quick assistance."

Billie fell back into her role of impudent youngster with practiced ease.

"It weren't so quick. I had to weigh the idear of yer chokin' to death against yer sin of stealin' my horse."

"And what swayed the outcome?"

"I din't want Yankees doggin' me the rest of my life, sayin' I killed you."

"Yes. I can see where that would be a problem."

She limped back to her place on the log.

"Does your leg pain you?"

She shrugged. "I reckon it's fixin' to rain." Billie knew as well as the Yankee there wasn't a cloud in the sky, but she didn't feel like lying about her leg. It wouldn't hurt once she started wearing her special boot. Two or three more days and she would have Destiny, Fletcher, and her boot. What more could a young woman ask of life?

It was time to change the subject.

"Well, are ya gonna tell me why you don't look like Dins-mere?"

"Dinsmere is a fictional character, as are his actions. Both are larger than life."

The touch of asperity in the Yankee's voice surprised her. How many other folks had compared him to his book hero? Did the Yankee write about a man he couldn't be? She chewed that thought along with a mouthful of bread and meat. Fletcher had taught her to know the enemy. Now was as good a time as any to take this Yankee's measure.

"Miss Lina said how ya was on a scoutin' mission when ya stole Angel. Was ya a scout during the war?"

"Not exactly—I'm a topographical engineer."

At her blank look, the Yankee elaborated. "It's similar to a cartographer."

Billie knew what a cartographer was, but she preferred to wrinkle her nose in confusion. "Car-to-grapher?"

"I draw maps."

"You drew maps for the army?"

"Yes."

"Ain't this country been mapped already?"

"Most of the nation has been, but it wasn't mapped for war. It was mapped for travelers, for businessmen, for tax collectors. Military leaders need a different sort of map."

"Different how?"

"More detailed."

This time her confusion was real, but she had to admit Lina was right—the Yankee would make a good tutor. He didn't mind her confusion.

"A general moves an army from one place to another," the Yankee said. "To do that, he needs to know all the man-made and natural features of the land. Take a bridge, for example. How many bridges are there between where the army is located and where he wants the army to be? Can he use the bridge? Is it strong enough to support his artillery? If there's no bridge, is there a safe ford? That's the kind of information I collected. Then I put it on a map."

It didn't take a large leap of the imagination to realize that in order to draw these accurate maps, one had to see the land, even walk it.

"Were ya gatherin' information for a map the day ya took my horse?"

"I was. General Rosecrans had us mapping most of the state."

Billie looked at her Yankee with new respect. "Did ya always scout land miles from the army?"

The Yankee shrugged. "It was my job."

Billie loved maps. Geography had been one of her favorite subjects at Clarksville Female Academy, yet she had not once thought about the people who drew them. If she closed her eyes, she could see the map of North America she had studied before she left Tennessee. If she couldn't imagine traveling into a strange land without consulting a map, how much more difficult it must be to wage battles over land that had not been well mapped. And how difficult to be the one to go ahead of the army and map the land, knowing lives might be lost if your work was inaccurate.

"You were miles from the Yankee lines the day ya stole my horse. What happened to yers?"

"A black bear startled him a few hours before I saw you. He ran for miles before he knocked me off with a tree branch." The Yankee chuckled. "I doubt that horse stopped running until he hit Canada."

Billie smiled, as much in response to his story as to his deep, warm chuckle. She liked the laugh lines skirting his mouth and eyes. Her father had been too serious after her brother died, and she sometimes wondered if it had been Stephen's sense of humor that had captured her fancy when they first met. Regret squeezed her heart as it always did when she thought of Stephen. Too many "if onlys" peppered her past, and "if only she'd married Stephen" headed the long list.

The Yankee grabbed the picnic basket, fished around in it for a moment, then said, "Ah-ha! She didn't forget." He tossed something at Billie.

"Try one of these. Mary is noted throughout the county for her tarts."

The pungent aroma of sweetened apples rippled into Billie's nose as she caught the tart.

"If you choose to stay here, you realize you won't find all New Yorkers as kind to Southerners as my sister."

Billie thought of Jennetje. "I kin take care of myself."

"If cockiness and belligerence can win battles, then I expect you can take care of yourself."

For once she didn't bristle back. She couldn't argue with a mouthful of apple tart. She hadn't tasted such a sweet, succulent treat in years. Her mouth rejoiced as flaky crust crumbled into the warm, juicy, sweet filling. And she was free to eat as many as she wanted, because she was a boy.

Grayson watched Billie's eyelids drift downward while a blissful, sensuous expression crept across the boy's face. Sunlight caught in the thick eyelashes that curled above a smattering of freckles. His eyebrows reflected a brilliant mahogany color that was quite at variance with the muddy brown hair plastered to the boy's skull. While Grayson watched, a small pink tongue flicked out to capture a crumb stuck to the edge of his mouth.

The oddly sensual quality about the action startled him into a physical reaction. An immediate wave of self-disgust doused the reaction, but Billie's jeering accusation of the previous evening echoed in his ears.

"Are you one of those men what likes to look at nekkid boys?"

What a disgusting notion. He had never harbored such vile thoughts until he met Billie. Why, the rapscallion had him doubting his manhood! And probably laughed the whole time. Grayson shoved Billie's allegation into the deepest recesses of his brain. He had more important topics to discuss with Billie.

"My sister's quite serious about adopting you. What do you think about the idea?"

Billie's eyes snapped open. The boy gulped the last of the tart, wiped his mouth with his sleeve, and stared at Grayson.

"What do I think? I think I ain't got nowhere else to go. And it would keep me close to, uh, Angel."

"Close enough to try to steal him again?"

The question hung in the air between them, and Billie's hesitation in answering gave him his answer.

"Let's not play games, Billie. You came here to steal my horse."

"He belongs to me. You stole 'im. And I don't care what ya say about it being a government comandeering. Ya took what's mine."

"Billie, wars are not nice, and the things people must do sometimes during wars are not nice." He saw Billie's jaw tighten. "I was on foot in enemy territory with important information I had to get back to my commander. You happened to be in the wrong place at the wrong time."

"Well, the war's over and y'all don't need Angel no more. Why cain't I have 'im back?" An irritating whine edged Billie's voice.

"Because you tried to steal him instead of coming to my front door and asking."

The young boy snorted his disbelief.

"I will not countenance trespassing and thievery. You weren't hauled off to jail, because my softhearted sister wouldn't let me. A night in jail would probably do you some good."

"Ain't that just like a Yankee. Hang a person fer takin' back what's theirs."

"The State of New York does not hang horse thieves. Horse stealing is no longer a crime punishable by death."

"I reckon folks in Tennessee think more highly of their horses. We still hang horse thieves."

"And I 'reckon' you are full of moonshine, Billie Angel. Whether or not you should hang is not the problem we need to discuss. We need to discuss the foolish notion of adoption Lina has buzzing around in her head. An idea which appeals to you as little as it does to me. But it does give you a reason to remain at our farm until you can devise a new scheme to get Angel."

Billie's eyes rolled heavenward. "I cain't stop ya from thinkin' what ya want. Being adopted by a couple of Yankees ain't my idear of a perfect life, but then my idear of a perfect life was tore up by a passel of Yankee soldiers."

"What if I told you to leave, now, this moment?" Grayson kept his tone noncommittal and his gaze on Billie.

The boy jumped to his feet and started toward Angel. Grayson frowned when he saw the boy's pronounced limp. Was this a manufactured bid for sympathy or the result of a real childhood injury?

"With pleasure. Thanks for the food, Yank."

He waited for Billie to grab Angel's reins before saying softly, "I don't remember mentioning the horse."

His words froze the boy midstep. When Billie turned, the gold flecks in his green eyes seemed to spark fire.

"If you were any lower to the ground, Yank, a salamander couldn't crawl under your belly."

There it was again, the perfect diction. Nor did the voice hold any hint of deference. Billie spoke as if he were addressing an equal, and respect had never tainted the boy's tone when he talked to Grayson. It was a nagging puzzle he knew the boy would not willingly unravel.

"Purely for information's sake, I don't fight children even when they insult me," Grayson said. He liked the feel of his anger; it smothered his earlier, unacceptable physical reaction to Billie.

"I ain't no child!" Defiance crackled in Billie's voice and posture.

Grayson had at least fifty pounds on Billie. The boy bristled with the bravado of youth, not the common sense of age. Grayson felt his own bad temper ooze away.

"As I said, I don't fight children. Now, we better return home. My sister thinks to make a gentleman out of you, and she plans to begin the task this afternoon."

"Being a gentleman cain't be too difficult a task." Billie's eyes glittered with contempt. "You claim to be one."

Grayson liked to think of himself as calm and sensible. He had often been in situations during the war where those qualities had kept him alive. Now it seemed his pride in his ability to remain cool in the face of difficulty had been misplaced. This mere slip of a boy had the uncanny ability to jar his self-control.

And it was taking what little self-control he had left not to pick Billie up by the scruff of his soiled shirt and shake the boy until his teeth knocked together. Straight white teeth that didn't belong in the mouth of a poor boy. Teeth that should flash in a smile and not be constantly distorted into a snarl. He let go of the anomaly and reminded himself Billie would soon be gone. The question was whether the boy would take Angel in the process.

He had better establish some ground rules.

"I want you to know one thing, Billie. If you leave here with Angel and I have not given him to you, I will find you. Make no mistake about that. Wherever you go, I will find you. Not only because you stole my horse, but because you also hurt my sister. I will not tolerate either situation."

His warning sliced the air between them. Billie gave him a quick, hard look before swinging onto Angel.

"Thanks for the lunch, Yank. I believe yer sister's waitin' for the chance to make a gentleman outa me."

The boy chirruped to the horse. Without a backward glance he rode toward the house.

Grayson watched the boy ride away. He doubted his threat would change Billie's plans, since the boy had traveled all the way from Tenneesee to steal Angel. The boy had spunk, no doubt about it.

With a grin, Grayson scooped up the quilt and gave it a sharp snap. As the faded blue, brown, and white cloth billowed in the air, he wondered how much trouble Billie's spunk was going to cause both of them.

CHAPTER FIVE

Billie stabled Destiny, washed up as best she could in the rain barrel, and went looking for Lina. She found the Yankee's sister in the attic.

"Oh, William, there you are! I've had the most delightful morning rummaging through these old chests." Lina scrambled to her feet and headed toward a pine cupboard. "And look what I've found. I'm sure some of these will fit you." As she spoke, she pulled clothing from the shelves.

Billie wrinkled her nose against the discordant mixture of scents filling the room. Dried herbs dangled in bunches from the rafters above them. Drying had muted but not extinguished their aroma. One bunch of herbs drew her. She touched it, unleashing the heady bouquet of lilac, which reminded her of her mother.

"I even found one of Grayson's old frock coats that is too small for him." In quick order, Lina held up several shirts, a pair of trousers, and then a frock coat for Billie's inspection. "What do you think?"

The triumphant pride in Lina's voice made Billie grin.

"I think, Miss Lina, I'll have more clothes than I kin wear."

"If they don't fit, I can alter them."

Billie swallowed the offer to make the alterations herself. Such a suggestion would seem odd for a boy who was not tailor-trained.

"I reckon I better wash off the stables afore I try 'em on." She glanced around the attic. "First, I'll help you put the attic back to rights."

Lina's search had led her through generations of castoffs. It looked as if she had jumped willy-nilly from one chest or cabinet to another, pulling out anything that had struck her fancy and tossing old clothes, bedding, papers, and dust here and there.

Lina followed Billie's gaze. "My, my. It looks as if a tornado has whirled through here, doesn't it?"

"Yep, it shore does." Billie set to work righting the mess.

A cashmere shawl, tossed aside in Lina's quest, spilled off a rough-hewn kitchen cupboard. When Billie's fingers pulled at the soft fabric, a corner of the shawl caught on a splinter of white pine. With delicate care she worked the fabric loose, trying not to snag it. Freed, the shawl spilled into her grasp.

Without thinking, she brushed the fabric along her cheek. If she closed her eyes, she could make the present disappear and the past take its place. A past devoid of war, death, and destruction; a past filled with pretty silk dresses and cashmere shawls. But try as she might, she could not imagine a future in which she married Stephen.

Would she ever forget the expression on his face the day he asked her to marry him? Their predictable world had been torn asunder. How could she refuse his engagement ring? How could she tell him she loved him as a friend when he was going away to fight a war?

But if she had known how he would die . . .

Then she would have insisted they marry, and she would

have lied, cheated, stolen, perhaps killed to give him whatever happiness she could for those few months he had left.

The faint gong of the Swedish tall-case clock brought Lina to her feet and snapped Billie into the present. The cashmere absorbed the tear that trickled down her face before the shawl flowed through her loosened grip to fall on the floor.

"Dear me, I lost track of the time." Lina brushed at the dust on her skirt. "I need to check on our meal. Jennetje doesn't always help Mary the way I could wish." She glanced around the attic and frowned.

"Don't you worry none about the mess." Billie bent to retrieve the shawl, hoping Lina couldn't hear the rasp of sorrow in her voice. "I'll be glad to straighten up fer you."

"Especially if I offer to postpone our first etiquette lesson until tomorrow?"

It wasn't hard to hide one's feelings when one had been doing it for an eternity. Billie tossed the shawl into an open drawer, put a jaunty grin on her mouth, and turned.

"Sounds a mite fair to me, Miss Lina."

"I had Jennetje freshen the water in your room. And I laid out some of Darrell's old clothes. Ones I thought would fit without too much alteration. We meet in the drawing room in an hour."

"Yes, ma'am."

In a flutter of skirts, Lina left Billie alone in the attic. Billie smiled. For a brief time, she could indulge in sliding her hands over silks and satins without having to worry if anyone saw her. Humming softly, she folded clothing and packed them into the various trunks and cupboards.

She saw the handmade cradle after she closed the lid of the last trunk. The workmanship wasn't the finest, but she ran her fingers across the satiny finish. A wave of sadness washed over her. She had once dreamed of children. The war had killed those dreams along with so much more.

Her fingers set the cradle rocking, but it whomped to a

sudden stop. One of the curved runners had caught on a metal ring fixed to a trapdoor in the floor. She moved the cradle aside and pulled on the ring. The door creaked open, protesting her curiosity the whole time.

She peered into the opening. A set of stairs had been worked into the brick interior of the huge chimney. She leaned back on her haunches. She was no architect, but she knew the Vanderlyn house was old. It doubtless dated back to colonial days, when Indians were a threat in New York. The trapdoor and the stairs provided a secret exit from the house. Did it lead to the outside?

Escape. Escape. Opportunity summoned. The idea sent her blood racing through her body, roaring into her heart and dulling the tall-case clock's chime from downstairs.

Doubts assailed her. Could she maneuver her leg down the crude staircase? Would the aging bricks support her weight? She pushed against the top bricks. They seemed firm.

There was no time to explore before supper. But she would explore her discovery as soon as possible. She could no more resist the temptation than she could resist a cup of real coffee.

A movement by the drawing room door caught Grayson's eye. Billie hovered by the entrance, looking uncomfortable in an unbuttoned frock coat.

"Oh, William, how handsome you look." Lina ruined her compliment by crossing the room to finger the sleeve of the frock coat. "I shall have to shorten the trousers a bit, but the coat seems to fit."

"Do ya want me to take 'em off right now?" Billie started to shrug out of his frock coat.

Lina jumped backward.

"Oh, no. I meant later. After dinner. Tomorrow morning. When you aren't in the trousers."

Grayson hid his smile in a sip of wine.

"Ya want me to bring 'em down to breakfast? You ain't gonna make me learn how to sew, are ya? That's not anything I heerd tell a gentleman has to do."

Billie's whine grated across Grayson's nerve endings. Then he remembered the melodious tones of Billie's voice when he didn't whine. Perhaps the boy whined to keep his voice from sounding too feminine. Grayson remembered a few ploys he had used when younger to mask the fact his voice hadn't deepened.

"Breakfast will do nicely." Lina turned to her brother. "Doesn't William look nice?"

A wary green gaze slid in his direction. Good. He wanted the boy tense. Nervous. Prone to mistakes. He set his wineglass on a side table and strolled across the room.

The boy swiped a palm against his thigh.

Grayson circled Billie. He recognized a coat he hadn't worn since his youth.

"Compared to what he looked like last night, I would have to agree with you."

When he stopped in front of Billie, he saw the braces. They appeared to be holding up trousers too large for Billie's small waist.

"I can hardly believe my eyes." He leaned closer to Billie. "I thought someone burned these years ago."

He reached out and looped two fingers beneath the left brace, plucking it off Billie's chest. Grayson felt the fine weave of cotton when the backs of his fingers brushed Billie's shirt. The boy stilled as if he had stopped breathing.

"Are those dragons running up the edges?" Grayson bent his head to better examine the dragons. Tonight Billie smelled of freshly laundered clothes, but he hadn't yet washed his hair.

"You sure are quick to burn perfectly good clothes." Righteous indignation edged Billie voice. The boy eyed him up and down. "But then, you ain't never been without, have ya?"

Grayson used the brace to tug Billie closer until they stood toe to toe. He looked into the hot challenge sparking Billie's green eyes. An odd thrill raced down Grayson's spine. He squelched it.

"Winners seldom do without. It would behoove you to remember that."

With a snap, he released the brace and stepped away. He knew better than to turn his back on Billie. His words had caused the boy to ball his fists. Grayson felt an eyebrow edge toward his hairline as he stared Billie down.

"There's the dinner bell," Lina announced, relief plain in her voice.

The moment ended. Billie's hands eased open; he relaxed his stance.

In the dining room, Grayson seated Lina. Across from them, Billie slouched into a chair. He placed his arms on the table, framing the place setting before him. Clean, well-shaped nails crowned the fingers of two tanned, callused hands now resting on a snow-white damask tablecloth.

The effect jarred Grayson.

"Are you ready for the soup, Miss Lina?"

"That would be fine, Jennetje. My, it smells delicious, doesn't it?"

Jennetje set a tureen on the sideboard and removed the lid. Grayson recognized the smell of Mary's hearty vegetable beef soup. He smiled. She had bowed to the pressure of cooking for two males.

Jennetje ladled soup into three bowls, serving Grayson and Lina before she slapped a bowl in front of Billie. Her thin lips squeezed together, telling everyone she wasn't happy to serve a Rebel. Soup sloshed over the side, staining the tablecloth.

"Jennetje." Patience laced Lina's voice. "You will have to remove the stain and wash the tablecloth after we have dined. You must learn to be more careful when serving soup."

"Yes, Miss Lina." Jennetje glared at Billie before she stalked from the dining room.

Jennetje's behavior didn't appear to bother Billie. The boy picked up a spoon, dipped it into the bowl, and slurped up a mouthful of soup.

Lina's head shot up, her fingers stilled in the act of smoothing a napkin on her lap.

"I take it there was no class in soup-eating today?"

Lina's tone seethed with aggravation when she answered him.

"How could we have time for a class when you put William to work in the barn and ruined his one set of clothes? And then you take him on a picnic until late afternoon."

"I sent him home in plenty of time for your lesson."

"Did I do somethin' wrong, Miss Lina?" Billie assumed the fake air of innocence Grayson had come to detest.

"Well, William . . . when one eats soup, one doesn't, uh . . ."

"Lap it up like a dog."

"Yes. Thank you, Grayson, for that vivid description." Lina turned back to Billie. "Perhaps if I show you how one eats soup?"

Grayson watched Billie watch Lina. The clean fingernails bothered him. Why would a boy take such care with his fingernails?

Then Billie picked up his spoon. Carefully, he mimicked Lina's instructions. Too well, too fast. Grayson knew Billie had been taught good table manners.

He kept an eye on the boy during the meal, looking for proof.

"Very good, William. I can see you are eager to learn. Don't you think he did well tonight?" Lina asked her brother. "I think he should forgo working in the barn while I prepare him for our dinner party."

"Since Billie came all the way from Tennessee to get Angel, I don't see how I will be able to keep him out of the barn. And Jacob is counting on the boy's help." Grayson wanted Billie working hard in the barn, too exhausted to steal Destiny.

He looked at Billie. "It seems you have impressed Jacob with your knowledge of horses. 'Course, he says you're a little on the thin side for a stable hand, but he feels his wife's cooking will soon remedy that."

The dining room door opened. A sweet apple smell followed Mary into the dining room.

"Ah, Mary," Grayson said. "You read my mind and made apple pudding."

When Billie took a bite of the dessert Mary placed in front of him, Grayson was treated to a repeat of the afternoon performance. Once again Billie's eyelids drifted downward while a blissful, sensuous expression crept across his face. Once again Grayson experienced a physical reaction. Once again he questioned his manhood.

What was wrong with him? He shied away from the possibilities, but he was unwilling to test himself if Billie's tongue emerged to grab an errant speck of pudding.

With a silent curse, he glared at his dessert.

"I been wonderin' why y'all don't have no dogs. What with this bein' a farm and all."

Billie's question ripped through Grayson's troubled thoughts. He welcomed the diversion.

"Don't worry, Billie." He waved a spoonful of apple pudding. "There won't be a dog to sound the alarm when you try to steal Angel again."

"I—I—I don't know why you keep harpin' on me takin' Angel."

Billie's agitation surprised Grayson. Was that a blush staining the boy's cheeks?

"We stumbled into a good life here." Billie opened his arms wide. "We have a chance to eat better'n we could in Tennessee. It seems a fool thing not take ya up on yer offer. 'Less'n you was havin' second thoughts?"

"Always second thoughts where you are concerned." Grayson wondered why Billie wouldn't meet his gaze.

"When we were children," Lina said, "we had all sorts of animals around. Dogs, cats. Grayson was forever dragging home sick or injured animals. Once we had two raccoons, a fawn, and a fox. We expected him to become a doctor when he went off to school."

"Sorry to disappoint you, my dear." Grayson wasn't sorry. He had never wanted to become a doctor. Plant and animal biology interested him, not healing people. Too bad his father hadn't realized the difference. "But a doctor would have rounded out the professional list, wouldn't it?"

" 'Acclaimed author and war veteran' have added welcome new dimensions to our family."

Lina's gentle reminder of his current writing difficulties soured the taste of apple pudding lingering in his mouth.

"Such accolades fade with time." He drained his wineglass, trying to wash away the taste of frustration.

"Now, Grayson," Lina said, "you'll think of another Dinsmere book. Give yourself time to put the war behind you."

He set the wineglass on the tablecloth; his fingers loosely draped its stem.

"And I know just the thing to get your mind off that pesky book your editor is always harping about." Lina leaned over to pat his hand. "You can come to the city with Billie and me."

"City? What city? Why ever would ya be awantin' to take me to a city?"

"New York City," Lina clarified. "I'm sure there will be a specialist there who can correct your limp."

Billie's familiar whine crawled up Grayson's spine. He hoped elocution lessons topped Lina's lesson list.

"Wait a minute, Miss Lina. I don't see no need to go traipsin' off to New York City. My pa took me to a doctor in Tennessee, and he said there weren't nothin' could be done."

Lina sniffed her disdain. "Really, William. I doubt if there's any doctor in Tennessee who can diagnose better than a city doctor. Anyway, it won't hurt to have another doctor look at your leg."

When Billie glanced at him in mute appeal, Grayson could only shrug. The boy should be able to read the stubborn gleam in Lina's eye by now. That same gleam had gotten him a room and possible adoption.

"I don't know what you think kin be done. The doctor said sometimes iffn you break a leg when you're still agrowin', the broke one stops while the other leg keeps agrowin' to where God intended both of 'em to be. There ain't much can be done about that. I were lucky. I were almost growed when the accident happened."

"I know you don't want a doctor probing your leg, but it would make me feel better to have someone look at it. Perhaps you will do this for me?"

Ah, thought Grayson. How could Billie refuse such a plea?

He couldn't.

"Oh, aw right. Iffen you think it's a good idear."

"And a trip to New York City will be such fun. There's so much to see, and we won't spend the whole time in musty old doctors' offices. Why, we can secure you a new wardrobe while we're there. Of course, we shall have to go to Albany first, where you will meet the rest of the family."

"Albany?" Billie shook his head. "Ain't Albany north and New York City south?"

So the boy knew something of geography! Yet another odd piece to the puzzle sitting across from him.

"My sister's geography isn't at fault, rapscallion. I think she wants to share her new protégé with our family before she takes you to the city. Since they're in Albany, we must go north, then south."

Billie set down his spoon, rubbed his stomach, and then

leaned back from the table. When he opened his mouth, Grayson anticipated the boy's intentions.

"Before you shock my sister's tender sensibilities again, it's considered gauche to belch at the table."

Billie scowled. Grayson grinned. In a flash of insight, he realized he enjoyed second-guessing the boy as much as the scruffy little Reb hated it.

CHAPTER SIX

"I will not have William mucking out stalls this morning," Lina decreed at breakfast Saturday. "And I want both of you out of the way today."

Billie welcomed Lina's announcement. The past few days had settled into a routine. Lina tutored her on dining etiquette in the morning, and she spent her afternoons in the stables, capped by a brief ride on Destiny. The Yankee always accompanied her, but they didn't have another picnic.

"Not to worry," the Yankee said. "I promised to survey a piece of land for Tom Bullard today. The boy can help me."

The "boy" had other plans for her morning; helping the Yankee survey land wasn't one of them. Billie pushed back her chair and limped over to the sideboard for another helping of eggs.

"Does your leg pain you, William?"

Concern threaded Lina's question. Billie brushed off the guilt. She couldn't go surveying with the Yankee when she needed to explore the staircase. Whether it offered an exit or not, she had decided to leave tonight.

"A little mite more than usual, Miss Lina. It'll be all right. I kin help . . ." She hadn't called the man seated at the table anything out loud. In her mind, he was simply the Yankee.

"Oh, dear. It's my fault. I had you practice the correct method of sitting in a chair too many times. You should have said something."

"I'm sure riding over to the Bullard's farm and helping me won't kill the boy. And he'll be out of your way."

"Do you think he'll be all right? We don't want William unable to dine with us tonight."

Afraid the Yankee would win the argument, she exaggerated her limp as she returned to the table. She eased herself into the chair as if the movement pained her.

"It ain't yer fault I got a bum leg, Miss Lina. I kin go help survey, honest."

"No, Billie. You shall stay here. You can rest in your bedchamber, there won't be any reason to clean up there. And Grayson can lend you some copies of his Dinsmere books. You'll enjoy reading them. Won't he, Grayson?"

"Why do I have the feeling you won't spend the day reading, rapscallion?"

Looking at the Yankee wasn't an option. Billie shoved a forkful of scrambled eggs into her mouth; this might well be the last good meal she ate in a long time.

"And William. We are having company. You will wash your hair before dinner."

A mouthful of scrambled eggs and the determined look in Lina's eyes kept Billie from arguing. With a careless shrug, she surrendered.

Thirty minutes later, she eased open the trapdoor. The smell of musty, closed-up air bathed her face. Lying on the floor, she tested the closest bricks. The edges disintegrated at her touch, but the bricks themselves felt solid.

There was only one way to discover if the stairs were stable. She picked up her candle and swung her legs over the entrance. As her feet settled onto the stairs, crumbs of brick showered into the blackness below, but the stairs took her weight. Stepping down into darkness, she crouched low and pulled the trapdoor closed behind her.

The door fell into place, and the draft of its closing played havoc with the slender flame of her candle. The tiny light flickered into nothingness for one heart-stopping moment while she cringed in the velvety darkness. Then the candle flame danced back to life.

As she gathered her courage, small scurrying footsteps told her she was not alone. She had no choice; she began the descent. In the dim light, she lost any sense of time and distance. She feared looking upward. Her small circle of light would not shine to the trapdoor. And she couldn't look up to a ceiling of blackness even if logic told her the trapdoor was there. To keep her anxiety under control, she counted the steps.

"Seventeen. Eighteen. Nineteen." She stopped. The candle-light showed the top of a wooden door. If the steps led to an entrance on the first floor, the door opened into the Yank's library. She racked her memory for a door but couldn't remember one. Was it hidden by bookcases? She hoped the door opened unblocked into the basement.

The only way to discover where the door led was to grab the iron ring embedded in its thick oak panel. Even as she wrapped her fingers around the ring, a muffled knock on the other side of the wall stopped her.

She leaned forward and pressed her ear against the door. "Come in."

Holy Mary, Mother of God! The Yankee was supposed to be off surveying. Well, now she knew where the door led.

"There's a gentleman to see you, Mister Vanderlyn."

"Did you by any chance get a name, Jennetje?"

Billie grinned at the resigned tone of the Yankee's voice.

"Seyler," boomed a deep voice. "Archibald D. Seyler at your service, Colonel Vanderlyn."

Billie's heart skidded to a halt at the sound of a voice she never expected to hear again.

"No longer Colonel, Mr. Seyler."

"I understood your removal from military life to be a temporary matter, sir. Or do you prefer the offer made by the Union Pacific Railroad Company?"

Seyler! What was he doing in New York? A glob of hot wax slid out of the candle holder and seared her thumb. She jerked the tilting candle upright. Switching hands, she sucked the injured digit while straining to follow the conversation in the library.

"Strange, I have never heard of you, yet you seem intimately acquainted with the details of my life."

"I applaud your modesty, but your exploits during the war did not go unnoticed in Nashville. Or anywhere else. Your talents are highly prized by both the government and private companies. I understand the railway company is so anxious to have you join their endeavor that they're giving you several months in which to make your decision."

Billie felt the Yankee's raised eyebrows through the door. She also heard the jovial attempt at camaraderie in Seyler's tone.

"Your ability to obtain accurate maps of contested areas was well known in official circles. Too many commanders praised your talents for you to remain unknown in Tennessee. As for your future prospects, I'm a man of business. It makes good business sense to know as much as you can about anyone you wish to do business with. May I have a seat?"

Billie had no idea how long Seyler would be with the Yankee, but she wasn't leaving until he left. Taking care not to put much weight on her leg, she lowered herself to the ledge. With a small sigh, she blew out the candle stub, closed her eyes against the darkness, and pressed an ear against the door.

Although she couldn't see Seyler, it was easy to picture

him in his well-tailored suit. He had returned to Tennessee a wealthy man, whose fortune had grown when he hitched his horse to Truesdail's wagon. It had been a partnership made in hell. Seyler provided the Federal officer in charge of the secret police with information about Tennessee's Confederates; Truesdail ensured Seyler made a fortune in cotton.

When Fletcher had asked her to spy, Billie had agreed to help because she'd needed to avenge Stephen's murder. When she discovered her new role also thwarted Archibald Seyler, it became a double pleasure to spy for the Confederacy. A pleasure heightened by the fact Seyler overlooked her as his men scoured the countryside for Rebel spies.

"I'm not a man to beat around the bush, sir. I believe you obtained a horse during the war that belongs to me. I wish to buy the horse back."

D'Angelo's Destiny belong to Archibald Seyler? Never!

"I presume you have proof of this alleged ownership."

Papers rustled.

"As you can see," Seyler said, "the bill of sale was signed by the owner during the war."

Billie jerked back as if the door had stung her. A bill of sale from her father? Impossible! Her father would never sell Destiny to the man who had goaded his only son into a duel. The bill of sale was a forgery.

"This looks legal enough, but what makes you think I have this horse, D'Angelo's Destiny."

At the Yankee's voice, Billie jammed her ear back to the door.

"Why, Billie told me. I believe you wrote a letter. . . ."

How had Seyler known about the letter? Billie knew the answer as soon as she asked the question. A letter from New York to her father would have been noticed by Postmaster Mingleton, who owed his job to Seyler. A word here, a question there. Seyler had become a master of espionage during the war. Finding out about Destiny would have been child's play for the man obsessed with destroying her.

"Billie begged me to buy back the horse. I'm afraid I didn't act quickly enough. Billie ran away."

Billie's heart rammed against her rib cage. Pressed as she was against the door, she feared the echo would vibrate through the door and alert the men to her presence. Would the Yankee admit she was there?

She! Oh, God, Seyler knew she was a female! The Yankee thought she was a boy. When Seyler told him . . . She squeezed her eyes shut, trying not to imagine the Yankee's reaction.

"What makes you think Billie came here?"

"Your letter. It gave the exact location of the horse. Billie will do anything to get that horse back."

"Before we continue this discussion, I'm curious as to your relationship with the young man."

Young man! Perspiration frosted Billie's upper lip. She tucked a breath into her lungs, flattened her ear on the door, and tried to listen over her pounding heart. Seyler knew she had played the part of a young man well enough to fool his men. Would he surmise she had chosen to hide behind the old disguise while in enemy territory?

And if he revealed her identity, could she escape both him and the Yankee? Her brain seethed with solutions, then grabbed the first one. She could hide in the wall until nightfall, hope the stairs continued down to a basement door.

"Ah, so I was correct. He's here."

Billie slumped in relief. For whatever reason, Seyler had gone along with the masquerade. Nerves stretched taut, relaxed. She hated to think how frayed they would be if she had to stay here in pitch blackness. How would she know it was night if she stayed here? A hysterical giggle bubbled into her throat as she imagined a future owner discovering her bones.

"Perhaps. Perhaps not. As I said, I'm curious as to your relationship with the young man. He's a war orphan, isn't he?"

Billie hugged the door again.

"Why, didn't Billie tell you?"

Billie frowned. Tell the Yankee what?

"I'm his guardian. His father died during the war."

Billie gasped. *Liar!* Her guardian, indeed. As if she would allow that disgusting piece of slime to have any say over her life. Ah, but right now he did have say over her life because he knew her true identity. And he knew her well enough to know she'd not go crawling to a Yankee for help. Not after what they did to her family and home.

"Billie's guardian?"

She blotted her upper lip with the back of her left hand, hoping the Yankee wouldn't consign her to the devil's spawn.

"I presume you have documentation."

The hand stilled. The Yankee wasn't fooled by Seyler!

"Well, no. I didn't think I needed proof. What use could you have for the scamp? And Billie is too attached to the horse not to follow wherever it goes."

"You are Billie's relative, then?"

"Oh, no. Just a dear friend of Billie's father."

Nausea welled up in Billie's throat. As far as her father was concerned, Seyler had broken any bond that held him to the human race when he shot Karl in that rigged duel.

She didn't hear the door open, but she heard Lina's gentle voice.

"Jennetje said Mr. Bullard postponed the survey . . . Oh, excuse me. I didn't realize you had a guest."

"Come in, Lina. I believe you'll want to hear what this gentleman has to say. Mr. Seyler, I'd like you to meet my sister, Miss Vanderlyn. Mr. Seyler is visiting from Tennessee. It appears Billie failed to mention a guardian."

Billie imagined Lina's soft hand fluttering to her mouth even as the younger woman's faint "Oh, my" penetrated the wall.

"As you can see, Mr. Seyler, your news is upsetting to my

sister. We have already set into motion the paperwork to adopt Billie ourselves. I cannot disappoint my sister by sending the lad away when you offer me no legal proof of your claim. I will need some documentation before I can release him into your custody. As for the horse, Angel—or Destiny—is not for sale."

"The horse and the . . . uh, boy belong to me, Colonel Vanderlyn."

Billie heard anger in Seyler's voice. She wiped her damp hand on her chest. The Yankee didn't know how dangerous Seyler could be.

"If you will not take the word of a gentleman that they belong to me . . ."

Gentleman! Billie wanted to scream out a protest. Archibald Seyler was not now and had never been a gentleman. Like the expensive tailored suits he loved to wear, the designation "gentleman" was new and Yankee-made.

". . . I have no choice except to go to Albany."

"Mr. Seyler, I regret you think I'm questioning your honor. That's not my intention. But I cannot feel comfortable releasing Billie into a stranger's care. He has come to mean a great deal to my sister. We are in the midst of filing paperwork to adopt him. As for the horse, he's mine, purchased legally from the United States government. I do not wish to sell him."

"I disagree. I believe my prior claim takes precedence. I also believe your governor will agree. I will go to Albany and seek an audience with him immediately. Let me add, I will be armed with a telegram from Governor Brownlow of Tennessee. It will confirm my claim to the horse and the boy."

"You must do what you believe best, Mr. Seyler, as must I. Now, if that is all?"

A chair creaked. Billie could imagine it being relieved of Seyler's overweight bulk.

"I shall be frank with you, Colonel Vanderlyn. I won't leave New York without the horse *and* the boy. And I warn you, keep an eye on Billie, I shall expect to collect . . . him when I return. Good day, Miss Vanderlyn."

CHAPTER SEVEN

Several moments of silence followed Seyler's departure.

"No wonder William left Tennessee! If that man were my guardian, I would run as far away as I could, too. I can't like him. His eyes hold a false sense of amiability."

"What an odd way to describe someone."

"I don't know how to explain it, but his eyes . . ."

Billie heard Lina stutter into hopeless silence as she tried to put her impression into words. But she knew what Lina was trying to say. Archibald Seyler exuded jovial friendliness, but closer inspection revealed a sense of discordance between eye, manner, and expression.

"Show few signs to match the illusion of friendliness in his manner?" the Yankee said.

"That's it," said Lina. "How can William thrive as he should in such an atmosphere?"

"I agree with you. I don't feel Billie should be released to that man. If he's the boy's legal guardian, though, I doubt I can stop him."

"Oh, Grayson. There must be something we can do to stop him."

If she pressed any harder against the wood, Billie felt sure she would leave a permanent outline of her ear.

"I didn't like the man's interest in Angel, either." The Yankee's concerned tone warmed Billie's toes. She and Destiny might not need his protection, but she liked knowing he had read Seyler so well.

"A man unfit to care for a child would be unfit to care for a horse."

"True," the Yankee agreed. "But I got the distinct impression he wanted the horse more. As if having the horse ensured Billie would go to Tennessee."

Billie nodded. Seyler knew exactly what would draw her back to Tennessee.

"What, pray tell," the Yankee continued, "has Billie done to warrant such a man's interest? I should be jumping with joy at the prospect of a guardian taking him off our hands. Yet I recoil at the mere suggestion of sending Billie to Tennessee with that man. And the horse. What prompted me to refuse to make a profit off that horse when one horse can easily be replaced by another?"

Billie bristled. The Yankee was wrong. Destiny could not be replaced by any horse—not in her heart, anyway. When his dam died, she hand-raised him. Then for three years she'd hidden him from soldiers—a difficult task in an area overrun with soldiers from both sides. It had been easier to play the half-wit and supply Fletcher with information about Union movements than to keep Destiny out of military hands.

Destiny was one horse in a million. She knew it. And her father had known it. Why else would he entrust the horse's welfare into her hands? Why else would he claim this horse would salvage the D'Angelo fortunes after the war?

She had come to New York to take back her future. Neither the Yankee nor Archibald Seyler would stop her.

"No matter how I feel about the boy or the horse, I won't give them over to that man without a fight."

Tempered steel ran through the Yankee's words. Billie smiled her relief.

"You're too harsh with William. Granted, he's a little rough around the edges, but it's nothing that a little guidance won't refine."

A soft snort of disbelief met Lina's declaration. Then the Yankee said, "I think I shall go to Albany myself. It might be a good idea to apprise Darrell of the situation. Although I can't promise he'll welcome your idea. You know he's had his eyes on Washington for a long time."

"And adopting a Confederate orphan is not politically wise?"

"Think with your brains instead of your heart and you'll answer your own question."

Billie hadn't known the Yankee's voice could sound so tender and caring. For all his many faults, the man loved his sister. And he was right—Lina's kind soul didn't always face reality.

"You think Darrell will refuse to help us?"

"We won't know until we ask him."

"If he refuses, will you get Uncle Morrison to do it?"

Bravo, Lina! Billie grinned to herself. Kind but stubborn as a quartermaster mule. That was Lina Vanderlyn.

The Yankee's chuckle tickled its way through the wall. "Yes, dear. If our brother refuses to help you adopt a Reb orphan, I shall approach Uncle Morrison. How can the black-sheep uncle balk at adding an orphaned Reb to our family? One way or another, I will have someone file paperwork on Billie's adoption."

"Thank you. Your promise sets my mind at ease. I realize you thought adoption a bad idea, but I think you've changed your mind."

"Events forced a change of heart, Lina. I don't trust your

orphan to stay. But I can't have Mr. Seyler think I don't tell the truth, can I?"

"I'm glad it's settled. Do you leave this afternoon?"

"I shan't leave you to deal with our guests and Billie's social debacle alone. Even if Mr. Seyler went straight to Albany this afternoon, I doubt he would obtain an immediate audience with the governor. I'll take the first train tomorrow morning."

"Do you think we should tell William about that dreadful man?"

"Not immediately. I have no desire to give him more incentive to steal Angel."

"I know you think me foolish, but I truly want our family to adopt William. I realize he's the son of a former enemy, but he lost everything in a war not of his making. And I can't in clear conscience send him to Tennessee with that . . . that man."

"I'll do my best, but you must be prepared for him to run away once I'm gone. Jacob's no longer a young man, and Billie will probably take advantage of my absence to attempt an escape."

The Yankee's pragmatic words sent a rush of moisture into Billie's eyes. Her departure would cause Lina pain, but she couldn't stay.

Lina's sigh was audible through the wooden door. Several moments of silence ticked past, measured by a clock on the other side of the wall.

"Well, one must hope for the best. I believe William is beginning to feel he has found a home with us."

"There's no reason to believe he'll abandon his scheme to steal Angel. If Seyler awaits him in Tennessee, he may prefer to stay here. After all, he eats regularly, rides his horse every day, and is learning table manners. What more can a young man want?"

Billie heard the forced optimism in the Yankee's voice.

"Oh, dear, that reminds me of why I bothered you. Sophronia wishes to invite two acquaintances to join us for dinner. It's short notice, but two missionaries arrived from South Carolina yesterday. She thought we might enjoy hearing about their work. They teach the freedmen in South Carolina, and I think your betrothed is anxious for you to meet them."

Betrothed! Why did the news knock the air out of her lungs? Billie reached for the crumbling wall to steady herself and sent a fragment of brick skittering into the darkness below.

"It's your dinner. I'm not the one who has to deal with two more mouths to feed."

The Yankee was engaged to marry! Billie stared at the faint outline of the door between her and the Yankee. Distant pings followed by silence told her the fragment had reached the floor below. She hoped no one heard, but she didn't care.

"Well, it shall throw the numbers off slightly with two single males . . ."

"Why, sister, your marriage hooks are showing."

"Grayson!"

Neither Vanderlyn heard the piece of brick she had dislodged, because the sibling banter continued. It faded as Lina dragged her brother out of the room to get his opinion on the new seating arrangement.

Sophronia! The beautiful, feminine name echoed in her head. Sophronia. The Yankee was engaged. She hugged her knees, balanced on the edge of an abyss, and tried to figure out why this information hurt.

The Yankee had stolen her horse.

And she wouldn't allow this tiny bud of affection for him to remain in her her heart. With Seyler breathing down her neck, she had to yank it out, throw it on the ground, and stomp it into tiny pieces.

Sophronia. He was to marry a woman named Sophronia.

By tomorrow she would be out of his life forever. And he would marry Sophronia, have children, and go to his grave never knowing she was a female.

She could not let it matter. Grabbing on to the iron ring, she pulled herself up, opening the door at the same time.

The back of a picture frame and a cabinet greeted her. Someone had hidden the entrance in plain sight. She'd have to push aside the picture and crawl over the cabinet, but she had a way to get from the attic bedchamber to the library without awakening anyone.

She closed the door. The faintest whiff of tobacco mixed with a cloying cologne sifted its way through the tiny cracks. She smelled her reality: Seyler.

He would go to Albany and see the governor of New York. He would get the documents he needed, because the governor of Tennessee would convince the governor of New York to do it. If Governor Brownlow had not already put her in Seyler's custody, he would do it now. She and her father had been Confederates. Seyler and Brownlow were Unionists. It was as simple as that.

Both men had sworn to make all Confederates pay for their part in the war. Once Seyler had learned the extent of her spying activities, she became a Confederate who must be punished.

Her guardian! How ridiculous. She was twenty-five years old, not some mewling babe. But she had played the part of a half-wit. It would be easy for him to get her declared incompetent. With her friends denied access to the political process, she would she unable to contest his claim. If she returned to Tennessee, she would be his to do with as he wished.

And she knew what he wanted to do with her. He hadn't minced any words that brisk February morning six weeks ago when he tooled his handsome maroon gig down her rutted, overgrown drive. Two glossy black dogs had been seated on either side of him.

The war had been kind to Archibald Seyler.

She had met him in the front yard, unwilling to have her father's enemy cross the threshold of her home even though the house was but a shell of its former self. Nor did she offer Seyler her hand in greeting when he stepped from the carriage, signaling his dogs to follow him. Upon reaching the ground, they obediently resumed their positions on either side of him.

He matched her small act of defiance by not doffing his hat, nor did he waste time on pleasantries. Lifting a chubby finger, he admonished her with counterfeit gentleness.

"My dear Miss D'Angelo, you should have spent the war in Gallatin with your aunt."

"Why, Mr. Seyler, I'm sure I don't know what you mean." She was all innocence and Southern-toned honey. "Of course I spent the war with dear Aunt Maria."

"I'm sure you spent part of the war there, as I'm sure you spent part of it here, masquerading as a young half-wit." His hand dropped to caress a black head near his knee. "Quite the disguise, my dear. I applaud your creativity."

"You think I played the part of a boy?" She ran her hand along the curve of her waist. "You do take the funniest notions." Careful to hide her pleasure at having fooled him, she rested her hand on her hip.

"You have upset my plans, dear." Silkiness threaded his voice. "I planned to force you from your childhood home into genteel poverty with your aunt. Now . . ." He shook his ponderous head; not a pomaded hair moved. "Now, your activities during the war change everything. Activities, I might add, that have been brought to the attention of our new governor. You know how Governor Brownlow detests Confederates."

Oh, she knew. He'd ranted and raved in print before, during, and after the war about how he would treat anyone who supported or fought for secession. His desire to erase them from Tennessee was well documented. Oh, she knew.

"I care this," she snapped her fingers at him. "For you and your precious Parson Brownlow. I did nothing wrong during the war. Unless you plan to imprison all the women who made shirts or knitted socks for their soldier menfolk."

"Tsk, tsk. Thus speaks impetuous youth. You're a woman alone in a battered land. You'd find life easier if you had a male protector. . . ."

A male protector! The idea of Seyler offering himself as a marriage prospect repulsed her.

Her answer tumbled out too fast. "I'd marry a lowdown Yankee carpetbagger before I married you."

"Marry? What a droll idea. Marriage wasn't what I had in mind." He stared at her for several long moments; his blue gaze sent frissons of fear dancing up her spine.

She didn't let him see it. But the drizzle of honey was replaced by a hard, matter-of-fact tone. "What do you want from me?"

"Why, your complete humiliation and degradation. That's what I want." He ran his gaze insolently up and down her figure. "With perhaps a little bit of begging first. Yes, I'd like to hear you beg to be my mistress. A D'Angelo on her knees to a Seyler."

"I would sell my soul to the devil before I allowed you to touch me, Archibald Seyler."

"But, my dear, didn't you know? You sold your soul to the devil when you agreed to help Fletcher Darring. And now you must pay the price."

His blue eyes took on a zealous glow; fear nipped at her composure.

"I confess, you're a mite thin for my taste. I prefer my women a bit more robust, but one has to take one's pleasure where one can when seeking revenge."

He looked past her to the house she defended. "I think I shall take my fill of you here. Yes, that would be fitting. The last of the haughty D'Angelos humiliated in the ancestral home. So it will happen before the auction."

She had cultivated self-control during the war because it had been the only barrier between her and death. Now she kept her expression neutral, denying the fear. It dried her mouth and tossed her heart into a pounding tattoo, but he wouldn't know it.

"Auction?"

"When the taxes come due this spring, you won't be able to pay them. You have nothing left to mortgage. Angel's Valley will be mine."

Her mind flooded with all the vile names she had learned from the Union soldiers. She chose silence. Bullies had trouble dealing with silence. They preferred fear and groveling.

He pulled his leather driving gloves over his plump, soft hands. After he flexed each finger, ensuring a tight fit, he looked up at her.

"When I'm finished with you, my friend Rosemary wants you. She'll keep you busy. She has a large clientele of Union soldiers that need constant servicing."

His words warred with the well-modulated, cheerful tone. If she listened to the voice inflection and not the words, he could have been inquiring about her health. But he wasn't, and the sinister words underlay the aura of amiability.

Fear trailed its way into the sunny morning and dug its tendrils deep into her soul. She refused to allow him to see it.

A gloved finger touched the brim of his bowler as he turned to haul his heavy weight into the gig.

"Don't think to slip away before the auction. My men are guarding your farm. I've told them you like to dress as a young male."

How she detested his eyes. The amiable blue masked a black soul. He ordered the dogs into the gig. They obeyed him; she wouldn't.

Shaughnessy had trained her well to the role of boy. Without a flicker of embarrassment, she spit her disgust onto his well-polished boot as he lifted it to step into his gig.

CHAPTER EIGHT

Grayson complimented Lina on the seating arrangement for dinner and approved her choice of centerpieces. His duties performed, he escaped to the library. The sweet smell of Seyler's cologne pervaded his sanctuary.

Damn. The man had worn enough cologne to last a brigade a week. He opened the window behind his desk and let in fresh spring air. The smell of the cologne faded, but Grayson's dislike of Seyler didn't. He didn't like the way Seyler's eyes shifted when he talked, and he didn't like the extra pounds the man carried. Like all the Southern states, Tennessee had suffered food hardships during the war. Yet Seyler had eaten well for a long time.

The bill of sale Seyler offered for his examination bothered him, too. The paper was too new, the ink too fresh. Billie had said his father had died three years earlier.

D'Angelo's Destiny. No wonder Billie had followed the horse to New York. Grayson had suspected that Angel came from excellent bloodlines; the bill of sale confirmed it.

Seyler threw a new piece into the puzzle of Billie D'Angelo. Grayson smiled. Or Billie Dwight Angel, if you were trying to think of a new name quickly.

Eschewing his comfortable chair, he propped his hip on the desk and grabbed pencil and sketch pad. His pencil skimmed over the paper as his thoughts circled around Seyler and Billie. It appeared the Vanderlyn family was stuck with a war orphan.

A horse, a boy, next a wife, then a house. He frowned at his pad. He wondered how Sophronia would feel about adding Billie to their family. He couldn't leave the rapscallion in Lina's hands. The boy needed the guidance of a man.

He would have to tell Sophronia about Billie. If she didn't like it, she could end the engagement. And then he would accept the railway company's offer, take Billie, and head west.

His rapid pencil strokes stopped midair. Perhaps there was a reason he and Sophronia had yet to discuss what type of house would please them. Perhaps she couldn't imagine their marriage, either. Perhaps returning from a war and asking your best friend's fiancée to marry you wasn't the best idea of the century.

He grinned, then looked down at the sketch pad. While his thoughts played with his future, his hand hadn't sketched either the fence or apple trees outside the window. Looking back at him was a reasonable likeness of Billie. His artist's eye saw the amateur qualities, but it wasn't bad, considering his speciality was terrain and plants. Odd, he hadn't noticed until now how fragile the boy's bone structure appeared. Billie needed more meat on his skinny bones.

He tossed the sketch pad onto his desk. A horse, a wife, a boy, and a house. What else was there to get out of life?

With sincere apologies, Billie D'Angelo.
Billie stared at the signature scrawled at the end of the

letter. How she despised this coward's way of confessing to Lina, but she had no choice. She wished she had met Lina under different circumstances.

A knock sent her scrambling to tuck the letter between two books. When she cracked the door and peered out, Jennetje scowled back at her.

"Miss Lina wants to see you."

"Soon's I put my books away, I'll be there."

Jennetje frowned. "Be quick. Miss Lina doesn't like waiting on Rebel trash."

Billie didn't rise to the bait. "Where'd Miss Lina be found?"

"In the kitchen." Her message delivered, Jennetje flounced down the stairs.

Billie slipped the letter into her waistcoat pocket and followed Jennetje to the ground floor. Instead of turning toward the kitchen, she went to the parlor, where cheery sunlight spilled through dimity curtains to caress the worn oak floor. As her gaze skimmed the room, she saw Lina's sewing table in the corner.

Ah. The perfect hiding place for her letter.

When she ran her fingers over the carved wood, she didn't see fond scenes of her mother's head bent over a similar table. No, she saw the hateful pleasure on Lieutenant Adams's face when he ordered a soldier to chop the table into pieces and burn it. Adams had decided General Paine wouldn't want a sewing table. And the Yankee wagons were full to bursting with better furniture looted from Vallata D'Angelo.

She would never forget Lieutenant Adams. The man had ordered the systematic destruction of her home and enjoyed every moment of it. To watch the physical ruin of her family's farm had strained her ability to play the half-wit. Not by one shimmery eye did she reveal her anguish.

The tear struck her hand where it rested on the sewing table. She watched it slide between two fingers. Then she took a deep breath and blinked back any other tears that might lurk in her eyes. It did no good to dwell on the past.

She stashed the letter in Lina's sewing table, hoping it wouldn't be found until she and Destiny were hours gone.

Lina's cheerful but strained smile met Billie when she wandered into the kitchen a few moments later.

"Ah, there you are, William. I need someone to take this to the stables." She waved a piece of paper under Billie's nose. "Would you mind? Jacob won't be happy to make another trip into town. Perhaps you could go with him, keep him company?"

"I'll be happy to do that, Miss Lina. Iffen it would help you."

Lina looked over Billie's shoulder. "No, Jennetje. Not those serving dishes. I distinctly told you . . ." She stuffed the list into Billie's hand before she rushed after Jennetje.

Billie found Jacob in the harness room, hanging up a harness, which he wearily pulled off the wall when he saw what she held. "Miss Lina and her dinner parties are enough to drive a man to drink. I might as well move into the village, as many trips as I've made this week. I knew I should've left the horses hitched to the wagon when I returned an hour ago."

Billie followed the grumbling groom into the barn.

"I'll be glad to help ya with the team. And go to town with ya, iffen you want."

Jacob grunted his agreement. "Go get Stockings and Clara while I get the harness ready."

Her thoughts weren't on the horses as she led them out of the barn and helped hitch them to the wagon. The air of excitement at the house made her think of her childhood, her mother, and long-ago parties. She remembered peering through the banister at the beautiful men and women swirling through the rooms below.

"You coming or not?"

Jacob's brusque question shattered the images. Billie gave the bridle check rein one last tug, stuck her head around Stockings, and said, "Yes, sir."

She joined Jacob on the hard wooden seat. For the next few hours, she would put aside her escape plan and enjoy the spring afternoon. The road followed the river to the town nestled about five miles north of the Vanderlyn farm.

At the edge of town, the wagon rumbled over a railroad crossing. Billie could see the train station half a block away. A gaggle of boys loitered around the small building.

"Wo, horse!"

When the horses stopped beside the general store, Billie climbed off the seat. She led them to the water trough.

"You wanna wait out here?" Jacob said. "I doubt if Chaucey's got any news different from what he told me this morning. I won't be long."

"Sure."

Stockings lifted his dripping nose from the trough and snorted water bubbles at her. After Clara finished drinking, Billie tied them to the hitching post. She walked around the wagon to the right rear wheel, which she and Jacob had fixed the previous day.

With her back to the small alley, she didn't see anyone, but she heard a loose stone roll behind her. A frisson of fear rippled the hairs on the back of her neck. As she turned, two boys grabbed her arms and dragged her into the alley.

Twisting and kicking, she silently fought them every inch of the way. Alone they outweighed her; together they overwhelmed her. They sent her sprawling on the ground when they released her.

"Here's the thieving Johnny Reb what stole your job, Gerret."

The first thing she saw as she scrambled from the ground were the boots. Huge, heavy work boots. Cracked leather boots that encased a pair of the largest feet she had ever seen. Her gaze traveled upward to cheap homespun trousers tied with a rope around a waist whose girth matched Destiny's barrel, and a soiled muslin shirt with half the buttons missing.

Holy Mary, Mother of God, the boy was huge! He wasn't

all muscle and would slide into obesity with age, but in any shape he posed a threat. Too bad he hadn't been old enough to fight in the war—he would have made a large target for Confederate snipers.

"You think you can take my job without paying a price, Johnny Reb?"

"Like I told yer sweetheart, I din't have nothin' to do with you losin' that job." She wrestled to keep her voice an octave lower, when it wanted to warble with fright.

"Don't you mention Jennetje, dirty Reb, or I'll smash your face."

"Din't you plan to do that, anyway?" She couldn't stop the eyebrow that rose in a supercilious way bound to incite the bully. Gerret had at least a hundred pounds on her. He was also taller, nearly six feet. And she refused to look at the huge, meaty hands he had rolled into fists. She'd seen smaller hams at a church picnic.

God, she was scared. Underneath the nonchalance, the blood sluiced through her veins like sleet washing down from a cold December sky. She clenched her teeth together to keep them from chattering, because she'd die before she let these Yankees see how scared she was.

A hysterical giggle bubbled against her throat.

To keep her thoughts from death, she counted the boys who circled her. Five to one. Stephen had gone down against a dozen. And they had used their superior numbers, guns, and knives to hog-tie him before they tortured him. There hadn't been much left for old Jefferson to fetch home for the burial.

A wave of red-hot hate roiled into her veins and washed away the freezing fear. Stephen's hands had been tied, and he'd been unable to offer much resistance. She might be beaten to death, but her hands were free and she was going to use them. Without warning, she charged Gerret while a wild, primeval scream containing as much fear as bravado tore from her throat.

Her attack caught Gerret as much by surprise as it did her. She slammed into a rock-hard chest that smelled of unwashed male sweat. Her lunge did no more than rock him gently backward while her fists, possessing no knowledge of the art of fisticuffs, pummeled his torso like two bothersome mosquitoes.

His first blow came between her flailing fists and caught her jaw, slinging her head backward so hard she thought it would snap off her spine. The blow lifted her off her feet. When she touched ground again, she came down on her left leg. It couldn't support her weight. Her head reeling, she buckled to her knees. The tiny stones of the alleyway ground through her wool trousers while the coppery-sweet taste of blood was on her lips.

"That's it, Gerret! You got 'im now!"

"What a punch. I betcha that Reb's head will be hurting for days."

Before her hand could touch her aching jaw, Gerret's boot swung for her chest. Something made her reach for his foot and heave it upward with all her strength. Once again Gerret was caught by surprise, but this time her ploy had the advantage of using his own weight against him. Thrown off balance, he landed with a lung-emptying thump. Billie grabbed the moment to stagger to her feet.

"Come on, Gerret! Get up!"

"Don't let that Johnny Reb do that! You're bigger than he'll ever be."

She stood while he was on the ground, but the ugly look on his face told her she had made him madder. In spite of his bulk, he moved quickly. He jumped to his feet and smashed his fist into her face before she had time to enjoy seeing him down.

"That's it! Give the Johnny Reb what for."

Once again she hit the ground hard. Gerret gave her no chance to grab his foot. His heavy work boots slammed into her side, one after the other. She heard a rib crack. Nausea squeezed her stomach. Bile rose in the back of her throat. She refused to humiliate herself in front the Yankee boys.

Instead, she curled into the fetal position and tried to protect herself as much as she could. It seemed as if Gerret had a dozen feet. No, she realized from the jeers and shouts, all the boys were kicking her.

"Get up, you yellow Reb!"

"Get up and fight!"

"You're a loser like all the other Johnny Rebs!"

"What's this?"

Billie had never been as pleased to hear a Yankee accent as she was to hear Jacob.

"Get away with you, boys! Five against one ain't fair in any part of the country. And you, Gerret Midland, beating up someone half your size. Get away with you now."

At the sound of Jacob's voice, the kicking stopped, but she couldn't find the strength to uncurl. Her body continued to resound with pain, unable to comprehend that the kicking had ended. Each inch of skin screamed its outrage over the way she had allowed herself to be battered. Scattered along the edges of the agony was the crunch of footsteps. They faded from her universe; her tormentors were gone.

"Billie, can you hear me?"

Slowly, painfully, she forced her body to uncurl and she turned her face toward the voice. A callused hand brushed against her left cheek. It smelled of leather and tobacco.

"You'll have a shiner, boy. Is anything broken?"

With great effort, she opened her eye and peered up at Jacob.

"Dunno." Her lip was swelling, and she had trouble talking. With infinite care, she worked each part of her body. Pain rewarded her movements, but there didn't seem to be any broken bones.

Jacob hovered over her. "Can you walk to the doctor's office? He ain't far."

"Beat up before," Billie lied. She wouldn't need to confess this lie, because the pain in her jaw when she spoke was more penance than any priest would give her. "Don't need no sawbones." The mere thought of a doctor got her into a sitting position. She squinted up at Jacob. "Farm."

Jacob hesitated, then nodded. "I'll get the wagon."

While he fetched the wagon, Billie pushed her tongue around her mouth. She tasted blood, but no loose tooth met her probe. The wagon rattled into the alleyway.

Jacob jumped down and took her by the arm. "Up you go now."

She found herself on her feet. Jacob was strong for all his wiry build.

The height of the wagon seat stopped her stumbling walk.

"Get a good toehold, and I'll be back here to keep you steady."

She grabbed the wagon and hauled herself up. Pain stabbed her chest; her muscles threatened to collapse, but she could not faint. If she fainted, Jacob would take her to the doctor. Her masquerade would end. She would never get Destiny.

Somehow, she reached the seat. Jacob climbed up beside her.

"Miss Lina . . . not gonna . . . like." She wondered if her smile made it to her mouth.

"It wasn't your fault."

She tried to chuckle, but it was too painful. "More . . . birthplace."

Jacob nodded and clucked to the horses. Billie locked her hands onto the wagon seat. If she tumbled off, he would drag her to the doctor no matter how loudly she protested.

Each step of the trip hurt. She dulled her mind to the pain, filling it with past images: rolling Tennessee hills, paddocks filled with spirited horses, whitewashed fences. Cocooned by memories, she still had never been so glad to hear Jacob say, "Wo, horses," and know they had reached the Yankee's farm.

With Jacob's help, she climbed off the wagon. To her dismay, they were in the stable yard and nowhere near the house.

He took her arm and steered her into the barn. "I don't see you climbing stairs this afternoon. We've got a fine room right here. Even Master Grayson'll know you ain't in any condition to steal a horse."

Oh, but opportunity dangled within her grasp. It was the night of the dinner party, and she would spend it near Destiny. All she had to do was find the strength to take him. First she had to die; then she would think about getting Destiny.

"Here we are."

Jacob eased her down onto a small cot. He plumped the pillow before helping her lie back and lifting her feet onto the cot. "I'll get Miss Lina."

As Jacob's footsteps faded, she closed her eyes and proceeded to die. She wasn't allowed a long death. Lina's horrified voice brought her back from the peace of the grave.

"Dear Lord! What on earth happened to you?"

"Like I said, Miss Lina. Gerret Midland's fists and feet happened to Billie."

"You have to bring the doctor."

"Well, rapscallion, what have you done now?"

Billie opened her good eye. The Yankee stood beside his sister, and for the first time since she had met him, Billie found his gray eyes filled with concern for her. The notion gave her an uncomfortable feeling she didn't have time to explore. Lina wanted to fetch a doctor.

Billie marshaled all her resources. She had to be more stubborn than Lina, and she wasn't feeling stubborn. She was feeling battered, bruised, and ready for the last rites. But she was in the wilds of New York; there wasn't a priest within miles. No, death would have to wait, as would the doctor.

"Don't need no . . . doctor." It hurt to talk, but Billie was in no condition to hide her sex from a doctor. "Pa said . . . sawbones kill ya . . . only bruises. Better . . . soon."

"You might have some broken ribs." The Yankee leaned over her.

Pain hazed Billie's brain, but she had to watch the Yankee. He seemed intent on examining her chest. She pushed at his hand when it neared the top button on her shirt.

"Worry about yer . . . guests . . . leave me." Talking was hell. Her whole jaw screamed with each movement, and her swollen lip kept getting in the way. But there could be no doctor. "No doctor . . . rest."

"And a beefsteak for that eye," the Yankee said. "All right, we'll leave you to nurse your wounds tonight. But if you're unable to move without pain by tomorrow morning, we'll have the doctor here to check those ribs no matter what your father said."

Billie hurt too much to argue, and she didn't plan to be here in the morning. Gerret had given her the perfect opportunity to get Destiny.

"After you've recuperated," the Yankee said, "we'll strip down and I'll give you a few tips on self-defense. We wouldn't want you to lose all your encounters with Gerret."

Shock drove Billie's swollen eye partway open. The image of the Yankee without his shirt vied with the idea of facing Gerret again. She wasn't sure which shocked her most.

The Yankee grinned. She moaned, hoping to lull him into believing her incapacitated.

Destiny. She would wait until the dinner party was in full swing. He wouldn't be in his stall. Jacob planned to put most of their horses in the near pasture to leave stalls free for the guests' horses.

Rest. A few moments and she would be all right. . . .

Billie tried to drag Destiny after her. She had to hide him, but they were caught in a sea of mud. *Hurry up! The Yankee's coming. We have to move.*

So much heaviness. Her arms were heavy; her legs were heavy; her head was heavy. Sluggish. She couldn't move. Even her eyelids were heavy. She dragged open one eye.

There was no mud, no Destiny, no Yankee. She was lying on a cot in a small room that smelled of leather and horse liniment. She licked dry lips, tasting a familiar bitterness. Laudanum.

Jacob had been wrong. The Yankee hadn't trusted Gerret's work to keep her from stealing Destiny. He had added drugs.

Although the laudanum had helped her sleep, its effects had dissipated. Now she hurt. The tiniest motion reminded a hundred points in her body that she had been beaten. She needed to run, to hurry, to escape, but she couldn't.

She pushed herself upright, pausing to deal with the nausea. One of the boys had managed to land a kick on her bad hip, taking the familiar ache to new heights of agony. She swung her legs off the bed, then limped across the small room to look out the window.

Gripping the windowsill, she searched the sky. Night was tipping into dawn. She had lost the hours of darkness. Panic welled in her throat, but she had no time for it. *Don't worry whether or not Fletcher's waiting; get to the rendezvous and then worry.*

Dinsmere's soft whicker greeted her when she passed his stall. Good, the Yankee's horse was in the barn. There would be no need for him to go to the pasture to get a mount if he left for Albany this morning.

She grabbed an old bridle Jacob didn't use. Outside the barn there was a vast stillness to the early morning air, as if every living thing had settled down to sleep. The scent of dew-laden grass skimmed past on a playful breeze.

The horses were large, dark bulks in the gray morning. Destiny saw her painful shuffle long before she reached the gate, and he met her there. She scratched the head he offered in greeting.

"I don't have any carrots."

The horse satisfied himself by snuffling her hand and shirt. The bridle jingled as she opened the gate. Several other horses joined them at the fence, but they were uninterested in an early morning ride.

"Time for us to leave, big boy."

In response, Destiny lowered his head. She raised battered arms, gritting her teeth against the pain. Stiff fingers worried with the halter's straps and buckles. While she worked with them, she talked to the horse, soothing his early morning friskiness.

"We're going to Texas, like I promised you. Remember all those mares I told you about?"

"There will be other females, you know. There always are. And between you and me, one female's as good as another."

She brushed the Yankee's voice out of her head. His estimation of women wasn't her problem. His opinion belonged to his fiancée.

A final tug on the halter; Destiny was ready. Should she lead him to the rendezvous? Above them the pinkening sky in the east warned she had little time. Her slow walk would never put enough distance between them and the Yankee. But she wasn't sure she could mount the horse.

She should have practiced his tricks, but she hadn't wanted the Yankee to learn them. Now she would have to hope Destiny remembered. She drew her right hand down across her chest.

"Destiny. Kneel."

The horse stared at her, his gaze on her hand, his ears cocked forward.

She looked into the dark brown eyes and repeated the hand signal. "Kneel."

Destiny shook his head, then bent his front legs until he knelt on the damp ground.

"You remembered! Good boy. Good boy." She hugged his head.

"Carrots, lots of carrots. I promise you a bucketful when we reach Fletcher."

She slid her right leg over the horse's back. Bruised muscles weakly clenched his bare sides. She laid her head against his neck, breathing in the sweet scent of her Destiny.

"Good boy. Up, Destiny. Up."

The horse rose. His earlier inclination to prance had evaporated. He seemed to sense she needed help to stay on his back. With a soft cluck, she urged him forward. His gentle walk kept her in place; she dare not risk a trot. Looking behind them, she prayed the Yankee would not whistle for Destiny.

Relief oozed through her body when they reached the shelter of the forest. Each step took them farther from the Yankee. Closer to Fletcher. She could barely breathe around the pain in her chest. Blackness tickled the edges of her mind. So easy to slip away, to relax, to let Destiny have his head.

When Fletcher materialized out of the woods beside her, she feared she'd dreamed him. "Fletcher?"

When he smiled, happiness raced through her. She had found Fletcher.

"Well, Billie darling, I see you've saved me a trip to the Yankee hellhole farm to rescue you."

"Oh, Fletcher." Relief poured through her. She fell off Destiny into a pair of strong arms. Fletcher cradled her against his chest. For the first time in many days a sense of security enveloped her. Then raw triumph surged into her heart, obliterating the racking pain, the fear of discovery, and even the warm security of Fletcher's embrace.

She had Destiny. Everything was going to be all right.

"My God!" Fletcher's voice rumbled in his chest, close to her ear. "What'd that damn Yankee do to you?"

CHAPTER NINE

Although Grayson glanced at the lump that was Billie before saddling Dinsmere, he didn't wake him. No sense giving the boy any more laudanum until the doctor saw him.

Five against one. Grayson shook his head as he led Dinsmere out of the barn. And Jacob swore Billie had not uttered one cry. The boy had an impertinent mouth but plenty of courage. And every boy should know how to handle his fists as much as he should know which dinner fork to use. Tutoring the rapscallion in the art of self-defense would prove interesting.

As he urged Dinsmere into a canter, his thoughts went to Sophronia and the unexpected invitation to breakfast. She was correct—they needed to talk. He was en route to arranging an adoption that would affect her life as well as his.

Perhaps Sophronia wanted to set the wedding date. He mulled over the finality of setting a date, but it might convince Darrell to handle the adoption process if his brother arrived in Albany practically married.

Married. He toyed with the word, wondering why the prospect of setting a date depressed him.

Dinsmere shied at the call of a mourning dove, breaking into Grayson's thoughts. He reassured the horse and gave his attention to the ride. Above them, the sun cleared the horizon and spilled its rays onto the new life budding below. He drew in a breath of crisp spring air, pleased with how well he had mapped out his life.

Within the hour, he guided Dinsmere to the hitching post in front of Sophronia's house. To his surprise, she rose from the porch swing.

"Good morning, Grayson."

"Morning, Sophronia." After looping Dinsmere's reins over the post, he opened the decorative gate. If Sophronia hadn't been watching him, he would have stepped over the silly little thing.

She stood at the top of the steps, her hands clasped in front of her. He never felt comfortable with women, but Lina had drilled him on social pleasantries.

"You look charming this morning." As his foot touched the bottom step, he realized he had lied; she didn't look charming. Dark shadows smudged the fragile skin beneath her light blue eyes while strands of brown hair escaped the braided coronet she wore—the same braided coronet that had looked quite fetching the previous evening.

He swept off his hat and bowed, trying not to stare. Unless he was mistaken, she had not changed her dress since last night, either. As he raised his head, he realized she wasn't clasping her hands—she was wringing them.

"I know you're wondering why I invited you here." Her hands fluttered to smooth the wrinkles in her skirt.

A sense of misgiving settled in Grayson's stomach. "For breakfast?"

"It's about our betrothal. I hope you understand how honored I am by your marriage proposal, but I fear I acted hastily."

"Hastily?" It had taken her weeks to agree. He wanted to protest her use of the word "hastily" but didn't think she'd hear it. She had fixed her gaze on something behind him—he guessed Dinsmere.

"Pride, I'm sure, was at work," she continued as if he hadn't spoken. "You're a handsome man, and it was quite a coup to have you as a fiancé."

He was a coup? The thought startled him. He'd spent his life in Darrell's shadow. His brother had wooed the women, while Grayson watched. His preference for drawing maps and writing books kept most women out of his sphere.

". . . so many killed during the war, the county wasn't exactly littered with men available for marriage. And I thought, perhaps, with time . . ."

Her voice dwindled to a whisper.

He leaped into the silence, unwilling to lose his chance at the life he had mapped out.

"You're having second thoughts. And it's my fault. I haven't pressed you for a wedding date. You must feel I am not sincere in my wish to marry you."

"I'm going to South Carolina with Mr. Espey." Now her wide blue eyes fixed on him. "To work for the American Missionary Society. To teach in his school for former slaves."

Her announcement speared his heart; he latched on to the only part that made sense. "You and Mr. Espey?"

"No, silly man. Well, possibly, maybe." A fiery blush burned her cheeks. Then she drew a deep breath as if to rally her thoughts.

"My feelings for Mr. Espey made me realize how wrong it would be to marry you." She reached out to cup his cheek with her right hand. "Grayson, you are the best of friends. You were John's best friend."

He felt as if her blue eyes drilled into the deepest recesses of his soul.

"I think you feel guilty John died but you didn't. And you

proposed in his place. Because he couldn't marry me." Her eyes closed against an old pain they both shared. "Thank you for loving him enough to try and love me."

He took her hand in his. "Oh, Sophy. I miss him so much. He was my one true friend."

"I know. And I love you for being his friend."

The aroma of coffee wove its way into Billie's dreams and tugged her gently into consciousness. She opened her eyes. Fletcher held a battered tin cup filled with coffee beneath her nose.

"I knew this would get your attention." He grinned.

She blinked, bringing his dear face into focus. Behind him was the mahogany cabinet that held the elixirs he sold.

"We need to make some plans, Billie darling. After you tell me whether I should smuggle the horse out of the county or challenge someone to a duel."

She tried to smile, but the effort was too painful. "Morning?"

"Afternoon. You've been asleep about eight hours." Fletcher slid his arm under her neck and helped her sit up. After he secured the cup in her hands, he settled himself at the foot of her bed.

"You don't appear to have any broken ribs."

With a nod, she accepted his diagnosis. Clutching the hot tin cup with both hands, she refused to ask how he knew. The fact she no longer had her father's old cravat tied around her chest told her. Instead, she sipped the coffee and let the magic brew give her a reason for joining the rest of the world.

"Now, Billie darling, can you tell me what happened?"

"Not Yankee."

"Last time I took a look-see, we were surrounded by Yankees."

"I mean . . . Vanderlyn—no touch." Even as she spoke, her thoughts skidded to that first night when he had grabbed Destiny's reins and his hand had brushed her shoulder.

"Well, somebody beat the tar out of you. And why that damn Yankee didn't protect you, I'd like to know. I thought even Yankees looked out for their womenfolk."

Billie rolled her eyes.

Fletcher chuckled. "Well, if that wasn't a darn fool statement. Had anyone suspected you were a female, you'd be dressed proper."

If she held her mouth a certain way when she talked, it kept her lip and jaw from hurting too badly.

"Yankee not bad. Sister kind. Took me in." She paused.

"Bruises . . ." she dismissed them with a wave of her hand. "Bully. Yankee didn't know. Not the problem. Seyler here."

Her last sentence shattered Fletcher's indolent posture. He sat up and leaned toward her, his body tense. "What the devil! Seyler's in New York?"

"Yes."

"You saw him?"

She gave a tiny nod.

"Where?"

"Vanderlyn house."

"Oh, God, did he see you?"

"No. Hiding."

"Ah, but you saw him?"

"Yes."

"Damn, I wish your jaw wasn't hurt. Let's see if I can get the facts with the least amount of pain for you."

She saluted her gratitude with the coffee cup.

"First of all, Seyler's in the area, but he didn't see you. You were hiding. Did you hear anything he said?"

She nodded again.

"Can you give me a clue?"

"Owns Destiny."

"What? He's claiming to be Destiny's owner?!"

She stayed his outburst with her hand. "More. Pretended"—she patted her chest—"boy."

"Ah." Fletcher leaned back on the bed. "He didn't tell the Yank you were a female. I wonder what that scoundrel has up his sleeve."

Billie fluttered her fingers to get Fletcher's attention. "Worse." Her mouth ached from talking, but she needed to say this as clearly as possible. She didn't want him to misunderstand the magnitude of their problem. "Said . . . he is . . . my . . . guardian."

"Your *what?*"

She opened her mouth to repeat herself, but Fletcher raised both hands.

"I heard you the first time. I just can't believe it. You're a twenty-five-year-old woman. What did that son of Satan hope to achieve by claiming to be your guardian?"

She had given Seyler's declaration a lot of thought since she heard it. "Gets Destiny. Gets me."

"Which is all he's wanted since he learned you worked for me during the war. Damn the man." Fletcher surged to his feet and paced the small confines of the wagon.

"How did he know you were in New York?" he said.

"Letter."

"Oh, God. I never thought about that. Old man Mingleton probably takes the mail to Seyler first."

He smacked his fist into the elixir cabinet. Bottles rattled in response, drowning his disgusted sigh. "I'm sorry, Billie darling. I had no idea your war masquerade would come back to haunt you like this."

Nestled in the bed, with Fletcher standing guard, she felt safe from Seyler. She trusted Fletcher to get them out of New York, and then Seyler wouldn't know where to find her. She had told no one about the ranch in Texas, not even Shaughnessy. She sipped her coffee, looking across its rim at Fletcher's troubled expression. Something about Seyler worried him. Something that concerned more than her recent escape.

"Not telling me?"

Fletcher massaged the back of his neck as if weighing whether to share his worries with her. Decision made, he dropped his hand to the wool blanket on the bed.

"Seyler's out to destroy anyone who worked with me during the war. Max and Quincy are dead. That leaves you, me, Angie, James, Warren, Sam, and Angelica."

Billie only recognized one of the names: Warren Maples had been her emergency contact. Jealousy flickered briefly. Silly to think she had been the only female spy in Tennessee.

"Angie should be safe. She married an ex-soldier and went to Texas. He's promised to protect her. I've got Warren searching for Angelica. We think she's in New Orleans. Sam and James decided to go to California. I was to join them there."

He rose to pace the small cabin again. "We need to decide where you'll be safe. Tennessee is out of the question. If Seyler sticks with his guardianship idea, he'll have you declared incompetent. Damn! I never thought your disguise would lead to this."

He dropped back on the end of the bed. "I'm sorry, I never intended—"

"No matter. Got plans."

Fletcher didn't seem to hear her; his forehead creased with worry. "We're lucky your Yankee didn't turn you over to Seyler."

"No like Seyler."

That won her a smile. "What an intelligent reaction for a Yankee."

Billie grinned and then winced. Damn Gerret and his fists. Her jaw throbbed, but she had more to tell Fletcher if they were going to make plans.

"Yankee refused sell. Wanted papers . . . for guardian. Seyler mad. Went to Albany. Governor."

"Seyler's a bastard and that's all there is to it."

"Leave New York now."

"Don't worry, we will. And if Seyler's in Albany, we'll do it right under his nose." Fletcher rubbed his hands in glee, his speculative glance studying her. "You'll be easy to disguise. Now, Destiny poses something of a problem. But," he added as a new thought hit, "Seyler hasn't seen the horse in years. And he won't be looking for him or you in Albany."

"Albany?"

"Now, who slipped in and out of the Yankee garrisons for four years? You or Fletcher Darring? Are you insinuating I can't smuggle one female and one horse out of Albany with no one the wiser?"

"No! Yankee in Albany!"

"Wait a minute. Are you saying your Yankee went to Albany, too?"

She nodded. The motion set her head spinning. Closing her eyes, she willed the wagon level. She opened her eyes, determined to make Fletcher understand their dilemma. "Adopt me."

After one long, incredulous look, Fletcher started laughing. Billie wondered if he had survived the war only to laugh himself into the grave.

Wiping the tears from his eyes, he shook his head. "Adopt you!" he gasped. He drew a steadying breath. "Can you imagine the look on their faces when they discovered who they adopted?"

The image pushed him into another laughing fit. He finally corralled his laughter enough to say, "It'll be all right. Albany's big enough. We probably won't even see Seyler or your Yankee."

"Albany north. Texas south."

"Texas?"

"Yes, Texas."

"Oh, you weren't planning to return to Tennessee? You have family in Texas?"

Relief tinged his question. She knew she had to lie because Texas wasn't his future—it was hers. If she didn't reassure him, he might dump his future and stay with her. She had stolen enough time from him. He had a new life to shape, and so did she.

"Uncle." She spoke the truth. Her uncle had lived in Texas until he was killed in the war. Now his ranch was hers.

"Texas it is, then. But we go to Albany first, Billie darling."

She widened her eyes and raised her hands, not liking his firm tone.

"Think about it," Fletcher said. "What did I always tell you during the war?"

When she tapped her mouth in frustration, he answered his own question. "Think like the enemy and then do the unexpected. Seyler won't expect you to take Destiny north. He'll expect you to go south, to Tennessee."

"Texas," Billie corrected.

"Texas. Tennessee. Alabama. Whose transportation system is in a shambles? Ours or theirs? Does it make sense to go overland through a country recovering from war, or north on nice roads and then west on a canal boat with plenty of fools waiting to be plucked of their greenbacks? Soon as we reach the Mississippi, we'll catch a steamboat south. More fools waiting to gamble."

"Sorry." Weariness numbed her brain. Her eyelids drifted down.

"It's all right. That Yankee bully probably knocked your usual agreeable self right out of you. Now, don't you worry. I've planned everything. When your Yankee starts looking for you, he won't find you, because he won't think to look north on the canal boats. Remember, Billie darling, the unexpected. Always do the unexpected."

She felt Fletcher shift his weight off her bed and take the cup from her loose grip. A few minutes later, harnesses jingled and the wagon lurched forward. She was asleep before the wheels made their first revolution. The last whisper of thought that trailed through her brain echoed Fletcher's tendency to call the Yankee *her* Yankee.

But he wasn't her Yankee any more than she was a boy.

CHAPTER TEN

"Adopt a Rebel orphan! Have you and Lina lost your minds?"

Grayson settled himself more comfortably into the leather chair in front of his brother's desk. Rolling the Conestoga cigar Darrell had given him between his fingers, he watched smoke curl off the end. His brother paced his way to the far side of the room.

"You know how Lina is when she's settled on a course of action," Grayson said. His mouth closed around the tip of the cigar, eager to taste the strong tobacco mix.

Darrell stopped midstep, swinging around to face his brother. "I know she can be stubborn. But if anyone can change her mind, it's you."

Grayson unleashed a puff of smoke. A lazy spiral drifted toward the ceiling. "In this instance, I happen to agree with her."

"What does Mother think of this insane idea?" His brother's stiff-legged stride back to his desk would have done an infantry unit proud.

"Her feelings mirror your own." Grayson hadn't liked Darrell's smug expression of superiority when they were children; he didn't like it now.

"Just out of curiosity, how does Sophronia feel about instant motherhood?"

Resentment climbed into Grayson's mind at Darrell's question. But satisfaction trailed in its wake. He smiled, pleased he could aggravate his brother's life further.

"Her feelings on the matter have become a moot point. She broke our engagement two days ago."

Two days Grayson had spent cooling his heels at his mother's house while Darrell fished. Since the governor had accompanied Darrell on the out-of-state fishing trip, Grayson figured Seyler hadn't made any headway, either.

His brother sank slowly into his chair, placed his elbows on the desk, and rested his head in his hands. He drove his fingers deep into his thick brown hair and massaged his temples. After several moments, he folded his arms on the desktop and looked at Grayson.

"Since you're smiling, am I to felicitate you on a narrow escape?"

"You're correct." Grayson stared into a pair of eyes whose brown hue spoke of their father. "Sophronia's decision hasn't rendered me heartbroken. Relieved, I think." He didn't mention Sophronia's insight as to why they shouldn't marry. It was too raw to share with Darrell.

"Does Mother know about Sophronia?"

"Yes, which only added fuel to her fire of disapproval."

Darrell's fingers drummed the desk. "I doubt the court will award custody of the boy to a single male and female."

"We won't know unless we try."

"It's going to be a waste of time and money. Why don't you give the horse back to the urchin and let him return to where he came from?"

Grayson detested his older brother's tendency to think his solution to a problem was the best one. "The horse you're so eager to give away is a blooded Morgan worth a great deal of money. The urchin doesn't have the means to feed a donkey, much less a quality horse. Besides, the horse is mine."

"Much as I dislike the idea, I think the only solution is for Margaret and me to adopt the boy. As a married couple we'd have a better chance in court. You and Lina would have the care of him, of course."

"The boy is mine." His vehemence surprised him as much as it did his brother. Yesterday he would have leaped at the idea of Darrell taking responsibility for Billie. Yesterday he hadn't known about Seyler.

Leaning toward the desk, he tapped the ashes off his cigar into an ashtray. He slanted a look toward his brother. "Either you petition the court in my name or you don't petition at all."

He infused his tone with steel because Darrell liked to take what belonged to Grayson, be it things, ideas, or people. It had started with toys and ended with Margaret.

Darrell frowned. Grayson didn't let him begin his objections.

"If you don't think it's worth your time to petition the court for me, I'm sure Uncle Morrison will be glad to do it."

Darrell spread his hands apart in surrender. "There's no need to drag Uncle Morrie into this. I'll petition the court in your name." He folded his hands on his desk. "Before I let my heart settle into its complacent rhythm again, have you any other bombshell you wish to drop?"

Grayson let his brother's question drift through his mind as quietly as the cigar smoke drifted toward the ceiling. He decided not to discuss his surveying plans with his brother until they were firm. However, the news he planned to take the Rebel orphan with him to Colorado would cheer Darrell, who wouldn't run for office until next year. By then Billie would be halfway across the continent.

"I can't think of anything right now, but I'll be in Albany a few days. Perhaps I can think of something before I leave."

Grayson grinned as he rose. "Mother said to tell you dinner will be served at seven. She hopes you won't be late. Company, you know."

"You, brother dear, aren't company."

Outside his brother's office, Grayson took a deep breath. It hadn't gone too badly. Darrell had consented to file the necessary paperwork to block Seyler's attempt to remove Billie from New York. There would be no need to tell the story yet a third time to Uncle Morrison. Yes, he thought as he scanned the busy street before him, things were going well.

His mind on his future, he barely noticed the ramshackle wagon rumbling toward him. His gaze skimmed the elderly couple perched on the seat, his eye caught more by the gaudily painted side of the wagon than its occupants. *Dr. Fletcher's Traveling Apothecary Shop* announced itself in white, gold, and green lettering.

But the green in the apothecary's letters was no match for the shiny green runabout that took advantage of a break in the traffic to scoot around the decrepit wagon. He knew Miss Heatherstone well enough to know that the green of the runabout had been chosen with care to match her emerald eyes. Perhaps he should stay in the capital a few more days. He could keep an eye on Seyler and be available if Darrell needed him.

He could also pay a call on Miss Heatherstone. After all, he had it on good authority that not only was he a handsome man, but he was quite a coup.

"Holy Mary, Mother of God! Don't look now—it's the Yankee!" Without thinking, Billie grabbed Fletcher's arm, her viselike grip ripping another hole in the worn fabric encasing it.

"Please, Billie darling," said Fletcher as he unlocked her fingers, "this old coat won't take such abuse."

"Shush! He might hear you."

Swathed from head to foot in patched and faded clothes, Billie still felt vulnerable. The flimsy black veil attached to her bonnet hid her bruised face from prying eyes, but right now she wished it were thicker. Opaque. Anything to hide her from the familiar figure waiting for a break in the traffic to cross the street. With Fletcher holding Destiny to such a slow pace, the break would occur between them and the wagon ahead.

"Oh, dear, you've got to make Destiny go faster."

"That would draw his attention to us. A horse racing down the street dragging an ancient wagon and two old people. You have to trust me on this, Billie darling. Remember, people see what we want them to see if we don't panic. And stop staring at him."

She jerked her head forward. "What if Destiny recognizes him? And does something?"

"Well, now, that won't be good, will it?"

Billie couldn't respond to Fletcher's bantering. Step by step, Destiny closed the distance between them and the Yankee. She worried about Destiny. The horse couldn't bear close scrutiny even though Fletcher had dyed his distinguishing white marks brown.

Then they were abreast of the Yankee.

Her gaze shifted to him, then to Destiny. Her body tensed, willing Destiny not to notice the Yankee. She could tell when the Yankee decided to cross the street in front of them. He glanced at them, eyeballed the distance between wagons, and stepped off the sidewalk.

Destiny stretched his head toward the Yankee, rattling his harness.

Fear swabbed Billie's mouth dry, but she resisted the urge to lick her lips. In fact, she probably couldn't have gotten her tongue to move. Fear convinced her that if she moved, the Yankee would recognize her and Destiny.

Destiny opened his mouth. Billie braced herself for a whicker of recognition. The Yankee looked at Destiny, frowned, then smiled, his attention kidnapped when an emerald green runabout dashed past the wagon.

The carriage, driven by a young female attired in a deep russet dress with a saucy bonnet perched on her blond hair, grabbed the gazes of all the males on the street. For some wild reason, Billie wanted to punch the Yankee. She had to settle for Fletcher.

Digging her elbow into his side, she hissed, "Stop drooling over that hussy."

"Ow!" Fletcher glared down at her.

"You're supposed to be an old man! Stop staring and get us out of here."

"Age has nothing to do with appreciating loveliness." She elbowed him again.

"Umph! That hurts."

"I told you to shush. He'll hear you."

"That I doubt." Fletcher's gaze skimmed past her to the Yankee. "His attention appears fixed elsewhere."

Billie locked her teeth together and denied that jealousy had shafted through her soul when the Yankee looked at the other woman. These odd feelings she harbored for him meant nothing. With each step Destiny took, the Yankee took a step into her past. She would never see him again.

And she refused to explore why the idea made her unhappy.

Twenty minutes later, the Yankee eased back into her thoughts while she waited for Fletcher to buy them passage on a canal boat to Buffalo. She found herself wondering if he would have stared had *she* been the fashionably dressed driver of the runabout. The color of the runabout matched her eyes, and with her long, dark red hair, it would have formed a dazzling backdrop.

Except she no longer had long hair.

Still, she could imagine herself in the runabout . . . with the Yankee seated next to her . . . his leg brushing against hers. Billie fanned her face. Shifting on the wagon seat, she looked around, pleased no one could see her features clearly. The blush suffusing her cheeks was hot enough to scald, had she the courage to put a hand to her cheek.

The old wagon protested as Fletcher hauled himself onto the seat. Billie welcomed the distraction.

"It's a good thing I didn't sell the wagon yet, Billie darling. It seems if we take the canal boat from Albany and follow the river, it will take us twenty-four hours to reach Schenectady. If we go by wagon, Schenectady is only a couple of hours away."

"I felt sure the Yankees would have straightened any river that didn't run as they wished."

"It's kind of nice to know the Yankees don't get their way in everything, isn't it?" Fletcher flashed her a cocky grin as he unwrapped the reins.

They spent the night in a Schenectady hotel. Billie stayed in the room while Fletcher sold the wagon and arranged passage on a canal boat. She spent most of her time pacing around the small room, with frequent pauses to examine her bruises in the cracked mirror over the washstand.

"Billie darling, are you decent?"

The cheerful question interrupted her tenth inspection. She opened the door to Fletcher, who waved a few greenbacks under her nose.

"These damn Yankees drive a hard bargain when they know you're anxious to catch a boat out of their fair city."

"You didn't get what you expected for the wagon?"

"Let's just say I got what the Yankees thought a Reb deserved." He tapped the money under her chin. "Now, don't frown. We have enough to get started. Once we're on the Mississippi, I'll find plenty of fools eager to part with their money."

"You didn't have any trouble getting passage for Destiny?"

"As for that," he said as he came into the room and closed

the door behind him, "I have a little proposition to make you."

She backed into the room, a flicker of unease tickling her spine at his expression. "I won't leave Destiny even if I have to stay in New York."

A grimace of injured dignity flitted across Fletcher's face, making her regret the hasty words. Impulsively she touched his arm. "That was thoughtless of me. I guess I'm worried Seyler will find us."

"It's all right, Billie darling." He patted her hand where it rested on his arm. "You've endured a lot these past weeks. And I've more to ask of you."

"I promise I'll try and do my best."

"That's my girl." He paused, as if searching for the right words. "It seems canal boats are designed more for the shipment of goods and people than stock. They have stalls on them, but they're for the mules and horses that pull the boats. I had to do some fast talking to secure a place for Destiny."

"Oh, dear, you did have trouble getting passage for Destiny."

"In a way, but I got him passage in exchange for . . . services."

She jerked her hand off his arm. "Services! Surely, you didn't arrange for him to pull a canal boat!"

"Not Destiny's services. Yours."

She backed away from Fletcher as if he had just announced he had yellow fever. "You offered my services to a canal boat . . . captain?"

"Billie darling—"

"Don't 'Billie darling' me! Of all the vile, disgusting, horrid, lecherous . . ." She sputtered to a halt while she racked her brain for another adjective.

Fletcher seized both her hands, his dark eyes velvet with reproach. "I can't believe you'd think such a thing of your best friend."

She watched mischief bloom in his eyes.

"To be blunt, the captain needs a cook, not a hooker. I know I stretched the truth a little when I told the captain you could cook, but I thought you'd agree since it meant getting Destiny on board."

She almost sagged against him with relief. Cook! He had told someone she could cook. She mustered a feeble smile of apology. "Perhaps we should try this conversation again."

The captain needed a cook because his wife had taken ill. He had to leave her with relatives while he made the run to Buffalo.

"I told the captain we're from Missouri and came east to see your poor ailing father, who just died. He didn't leave you much except the horse, and you couldn't bear to sell it."

"And he believed you?"

"He needs a cook."

"Then he won't be too pleased when he discovers I can't cook."

"Haven't you been cooking these past three months?"

"I wasn't aware you considered what I did cooking, from the comments you made while eating it." She tilted her head to one side as if concentrating. "Let's see, terms like 'hog swill'—oh, and 'shoe leather,' and I believe you compared my biscuits to charred wood."

"You do have an interesting way with biscuits. But I figured I could help you cook, and Captain Borgus agreed to take Destiny, which is a sight more than anyone else offered to do. A shortage of funds hampers a man's style of travel." Then he grinned, pulled her into a bear hug, and swung her in a circle off her feet.

"Fletcher! Put me down this instant! You're crushing my poor ribs."

He set her back to her feet. "Is that better?"

"Much, thank you."

Scant inches separated them, and the scent of whiskey tinged the air he exhaled. It was easy to picture him sharing a glass with the canal boat captain while he persuaded the man to accept unplanned passengers. Fletcher had a way with people. It had kept him alive during the war and would help him succeed in California.

Laughter lingered in his eyes. "Isn't this where you thank me and tell me what a resourceful man I am?"

She patted his bearded cheek and gave him a smile. "You're a resourceful man. Now feed me one good meal before I'm forced to eat my own cooking again."

Billie's pleasure ticked away with the passing hours. By the following morning, she no longer felt the sweep of excitement about securing passage on the canal boat. She didn't know what bothered her. They had some money, she was on her way to Texas, she had Destiny, and Seyler didn't know where she was. And neither did the Yankee.

Scowling at herself in the pitiful excuse for a mirror, she plopped the ancient bonnet on her head and tried to shove her muddy brown hair underneath. At least she no longer had to grease her hair, and the temporary dye was fading.

"I know it's an abomination to hide such a fetching face, Billie darling," Fletcher said as he turned her around to face him. "But we haven't much choice until your bruises heal. You don't want people to think I've beaten you, now, do you?"

"I don't mean to sound peevish, but it's been a long time since I've been me and not a crippled boy or an old hag."

He straightened the unfashionable bonnet on her head. "I know. It seems forever since I saw that pretty auburn hair of yours." His hand grazed her hip as swiftly as a hummingbird sipping nectar from a flower. "Didn't it used to hit about here?"

His hand came and went so quickly, she wasn't sure he had touched her. Nor did it seem worth a protest when he continued talking as if nothing had happened.

"Marianne always said you had the prettiest hair." He squinted as he tied the ribbon squarely under her chin. "You know, we could get off the boat in St. Louis and head west. You might like California better than Texas."

He tugged on the finished bow, tilting her head up. She stared into his dark brown eyes. His pupils widened slightly before he bent his head and kissed her. His lips brushed against hers as quickly and lightly as his hand had grazed her hip.

The kiss reminded her of Stephen's kiss. Chaste. Nice.

"And don't look so wide-eyed. I meant marriage." He laid his fingers against her mouth. "I know I'm no longer a man of property, but we'd have each other. You're a special woman, Billie darling, and it would be an honor to have you beside me."

Warm affection glowed in his eyes. His kiss and offer stunned her. She had known Fletcher most of her life and always counted him as a friend.

"I, uh, don't know what—"

"I realize my proposal caught you by surprise," he interrupted gently. "You don't have to answer me right now."

She smiled, relieved he didn't want an immediate answer. Marry Fletcher? Change him from friend to lover? Her mind balked at the idea because he belonged to Marianne Darring. His wife might have died during the war, but they had been the perfect couple. They had loved each other, and she didn't think Fletcher would ever love like that again. Not that he had mentioned love when he proposed.

And Billie, perhaps a romantic fool, wanted to be loved by the man she married. Not that she planned to marry. The war had chased that fantasy out of her head.

But when she had dreamed of marriage, she had dreamed of kisses that made her insides melt. And pleasant as Fletcher's kiss had been, it didn't make that happen. She frowned. Would the Yankee's kiss make her insides melt?

"I thought to make you happy. Not sad."

She blinked and banished the Yankee to perdition. "I'm not sad. Your proposal caught me off guard. So much has happened, I don't want to make the wrong decision."

"Not to worry, Billie darling. We'll have plenty of time on

the boat to discuss it." Fletcher picked up the carpetbag filled with their meager possessions. "We'd best go."

She flipped the veil down, pulling and adjusting the gauzy fabric to hide her face. The hotel room assumed a black hue.

Her gaze skimmed over the small room, pausing at the bed where she had spent the night. It was jumbled with the linens Fletcher had used to pad the hard floor. Marriage would mean sharing the same bed.

Her thoughts flitted back to the morning after she took Destiny. Fletcher had checked her bruised and crippled body for injuries. She blushed at the idea he had seen her naked, but realized her leg hadn't deterred him from asking her to marry him.

Security. Affection. Companionship.

She wondered if they needed good cow ponies in California.

CHAPTER ELEVEN

"Ayumph, you're home," said Jacob. The aging retainer waved a hand toward the hitching post where Dinsmere stood.

Grayson offered the horse a bit of the apple he had saved for him. "How did things go while I was gone?"

"You'll see."

"Damn!" Grayson tied his carpetbag to Dinsmere's saddle. "What did that rapscallion do? I was only gone four days."

His question went unanswered; Jacob was too far away to hear him. Grayson mounted Dinsmere and trailed Jacob out of town. If he hadn't been so sure Billie's ribs would keep the boy immobilized for a week, he wouldn't have dallied in Albany. But the need to prove Sophronia's compliment had eroded his common sense.

After mustering his courage to invite Miss Heatherstone for a ride in Darrell's carriage, he had discovered the poor woman lacked intelligent conversation. He may as well have stayed home. At least Lina and Billie could converse on topics other than hats and gloves. Grayson urged Dinsmere to catch Jacob.

"Did Billie steal Angel?"

"Miss Lina wants to talk to you."

From Jacob's pursed lips, Grayson knew the old man wouldn't tell him anything. He could also tell the groom blamed him for whatever the rapscallion had done. If Billie had stolen Angel, it would have been a slow and painful escape. Finding him shouldn't prove difficult.

He patted the papers in his frock coat pocket. Darrell had worked fast to secure temporary guardianship of the Rebel orphan. And their mother, who had decided she couldn't sway her younger son from his chosen path, was going to be upset when she came to visit and there was no orphaned ward there to meet her.

Lina waited for him in the parlor. Rising hastily when he entered the room, she thrust something behind her back.

"Thank goodness you're home."

Jacob's reticence, the worried look on Lina's face, and the fact he hadn't seen Angel in the barn told him what he needed to know. He wasted no time on amenities.

"How long has he been gone?"

"Jacob believes, uh, he left the night of the dinner party."

"Why didn't you telegraph me immediately?"

"I didn't know what to do. I was afraid if I telegraphed you, Darrell would find out. That he might not file the paperwork. You do have something legal, don't you?"

"Yes, yes. I have temporary guardianship." He massaged his temples with his right hand. "Billie was in no condition to steal the horse. His ribs were bruised, perhaps fractured."

"He didn't have to ride far."

Grayson dropped his hand from his forehead and looked at his sister. "What do you mean?"

"Jacob found William's tracks and followed them. Jacob thinks . . . William fell off the horse."

"Little idiot. What made the boy think he could ride?" A

scowl tightened his face, complementing the headache now pounding behind his eyes.

"I'm sure William believed he had a compelling reason. But that's not all Jacob found. He says William never hit the ground because someone caught him and carried him to a wagon."

"Seyler?" Worry speared him with an unexpected intensity. Billie was in no condition to defend himself from Seyler. But the man had been in Albany; Grayson had seen him several times.

Lina's strained voice interrupted his wayward thoughts.

"Not Seyler. Jacob tracked them to a camp site about three miles from here. Then he questioned the neighbors. Several of them remember an apothecary wagon in the neighborhood for over a week. Mr. Carmington spoke with the man." Her voice faltered. "He claims the man had a Southern accent."

Apothecary wagon. He should have known. "Dr. Fletcher's Traveling Apothecary?"

"Yes, I believe that's the name Jacob mentioned," Lina said. "Did you see the wagon, too?"

Oh, yes, he had seen the wagon. Catapulted from the fringes of his memory came the vision of a creaking wagon pulled by a dingy brown horse. With amazing clarity, he recalled the old lady on the front seat, clutching in fear on to the arm of the driver. The elderly man had given Grayson a grin that exposed several missing teeth before they both looked at the lovely Miss Heatherstone.

Disguising Billie as an old woman made sense. Gerret's beating would have forced him to move with the sluggish, painful movements of age, while the heavy black veil hid his purpling bruises from prying eyes.

Miss Heatherstone had proved a fortunate diversion for Billie and Dr. Fletcher. But, he admitted to himself, he probably wouldn't have scrutinized the wagon if Miss Heatherstone hadn't driven past. He'd had no reason to suspect its occupants were other than they appeared.

The anger growing in his soul was slow to heat but would take a long time to quench. "Why Albany?" he muttered.

"Albany? What's Albany got to do with William's disappearance?"

"I saw the wagon in Albany."

"Why in heaven's name didn't you tell me? Here I've been going mad with worry."

Before she could get up an indignant head of steam, he lightly put his hand over her mouth. "Hold on! Give me a chance to explain. I didn't know it was Billie when I saw him, because the rapscallion was dressed as an old woman."

Lina's soft gray eyes widened in surprise above his hand, and it felt as if her mouth struggled not to smile.

"Billie wasn't alone," Grayson continued. "I'm guessing the man beside him was Fletcher, although I would say this Fletcher is neither dead nor a former slave."

She pushed his hand aside. "Why Albany?"

"Possibly the railroad. Our railroads are in better shape than theirs." Even as he spoke, his mind calculated possible routes to Tennessee.

"Oh, dear," said Lina, "what if sh—uh, Seyler finds out?"

"I hope to reach Master Billie D'Angelo before Seyler does."

"You're going after William?"

"Oh, yes, sister dear. I have a little score to settle with Master D'Angelo, and he has my horse."

"Oh, my . . ."

He almost laughed aloud at the anxious expression his words brought to his sister's face, but the letter she had clasped to her breast captured his attention.

"A farewell note from Billie?"

Lina stared at him blankly, blinked, then followed his gaze downward. With a tiny gasp, she thrust the letter behind her back.

"Let me see Billie's note. He might have left a clue as to where he was going."

"No!" She stepped backward from his outstretched hand. "This letter isn't from William."

"Then why were you hiding it?"

His reasonable question caused her to blush, but she kept the letter behind her back. With a big sigh, she lowered her head. "It's a letter from Sophronia. I was afraid it might upset you to see her handwriting."

He doubted he would be able to identify Sophronia's handwriting; he hadn't seen it over two or three times. "I guess she told you we're no longer engaged to be married."

"Uh, yes." Lina's head snapped upward. "As a matter of fact, that's exactly what she wrote."

Why did he have this feeling a thread of deceit ran beneath her words? "You're not disappointed to learn she won't be your sister-in-law?"

"Are you disappointed she won't be your wife?"

"I think I'm relieved she had the sense to break the betrothal. It helped me realize I'm not ready to marry yet."

To his surprise, she patted his arm and gave him a sly smile, as if she knew something he didn't.

"Oh, I'm sure when you find the right person, you'll be eager to marry. In fact, I shouldn't be surprised if you aren't married within the year."

He stared at his sister as if she had gone mad. "Married within a year! I doubt that will happen. As soon as I find Billie, I'm headed west to Colorado. From all accounts, there's a decided shortage of women in the West."

"Colorado?"

"I took the railway position. They gave me a few weeks to wind up my affairs in the East. I guess Billie's now my affair. Once I find the rapscallion, I'll take him with me to Colorado." He flexed his fingers. "Soon as we come to an understanding."

A gurgled sound came from Lina.

He ignored her. "He can assist me and learn surveying. I

doubt Seyler will follow us to Colorado. By the time we return, Darrell should have completed the adoption proceedings."

"Oh, my." Lina's hand clutched her throat.

"Why are you staring at me like I've grown another head?"

"Perhaps," she said faintly, "I'd better go with you to find Billie."

"Bridge! Mind low bridge!"

Billie flattened herself on the deck of the *Betsey* for what seemed like the thousandth time. The aroma of frying potatoes and onions vied with the smell of damp wood as she pressed herself against the planking. The shadow of yet another ramshackle bridge flitted over her head before she pushed herself to her feet, grateful her bruised body had had several days to heal before they began the canal trip.

Fletcher shot her a cocky grin. She stuck her tongue out. He had reason to grin; he was enjoying himself. Captain Borgus had taught him how to steer the boat. She, on the other hand, got to prepare all the meals over an open stove on the deck, wash clothes, and break the monotony of those tasks by ducking the innumerable bridges that crossed the canal. But Destiny was on board, and they were headed to Texas. All she had to do was convince Fletcher he could go to California without them.

She scooped well-browned potatoes and onions onto a platter beside a slab of ham. "Food's ready," she called. "Joseph! Ready to eat?"

In response to the captain's bellow, the twelve-year-old hoggee who drove the four horses along the towpath turned. He saw the food, and a big grin split his skinny face.

Billie watched Fletcher bring the canal boat close to the towpath. Captain Borgus jumped ashore and took control of the horses. Then Joseph came aboard to shyly hold his plate

134   *Ginger Hanson*

out for her to fill. Once the hoggee had finished eating, he would return to his post while the captain ate. After the captain finished, Fletcher would be free to join Billie for their quick dinner.

By the time she had cleaned up after the meal, the wail of the boat horn announced their pending arrival at the lock tender. As usual, other boats crowded around the lock.

"It looks like quite a wait," Fletcher said as he joined her on the stern. "Want to take a walk?"

"I'd love to." She grabbed her bonnet, grateful her bruises had faded.

Fletcher jumped the two feet from the boat to the towpath. When she mimicked him, her toehold didn't prove as solid in the damp clay-lined bank. Her feet slipped toward the water.

"Fletcher!" When she gasped out his name, he grabbed her waving hand and tugged her up the bank and into his arms.

"We wouldn't want you falling in the canal, Billie darling, even if it is only four feet deep."

She clung to his arms, enjoying their muscled strength. Tipping her head back, she grinned up at him. "If I'm going to fall off a boat, I'd rather it be a canal boat on the Erie than a steamboat on the Mississippi. At least here I can wade out of the water."

"Are you telling me you can't swim?"

She nodded.

"I recruited you to play the part of a young man, and you lack knowledge of this manly art?" Mock horror vied with amusement in his brown eyes. "Another reason to marry me and go to California. I'll teach you to swim."

She slipped out of his loosened grasp. Too many interested gazes watched from the surrounding canal boats. Keeping her voice light, she said, "I've survived this long without knowing how to swim. I doubt I'll ever need to know."

Before she took two steps, he came beside her, left arm

extended. She placed her hand there, ignoring her broken nails and callused palms. He covered her roughened hand with his and guided her along the towpath as if they strolled around the ballroom of his beloved Fairmount.

"In case you do fall off a steamboat, Billie darling, here are a few tips on staying afloat. First of all," he looked down at her skirts. "Get rid of as much clothing as possible. Water-logged clothing pulls one down. And remember, everything tries to float. If you stay calm and don't fill your lungs with water, you should float, too."

"How in the world could I stay calm if I fell in the water and thought I was about to drown!"

"Did you ever see old Cato swim?"

"Father's hound dog? Why, yes, I'd forgotten how much he loved the water."

"Think about him. Four paws, no hands, no arms, and yet he could swim all over the place. Or paddle. That's all you have to do. Relax, keep your nose out of the water, and paddle like Cato."

He stopped. "What do you do if you fall in the water, Billie darling?"

"Relax, keep my nose out of the water, and paddle like Cato. Or walk out if it's the Erie Canal."

"Minx!" Fletcher resumed walking toward the lock. "I'm surprised Karl never taught you to swim."

"He was ten years older than me," she said. "He thought himself much too old to pay attention to a child."

Her memories of her older brother were entwined with the legacy he'd left her. His duel with Archibald Seyler had ruined her mother's health and forced her father to put his life's work into a pair of hands he'd believed too weak to hold them.

"It's probably as well he didn't try to teach you to swim; Karl didn't have the patience to teach anyone. He had the devil's own temper. If he hadn't died in a duel before the war, he would have died in one during the war. Or rode into a company of Yankees, positive he could outride and outshoot them all."

"I grew up believing Karl the best shot in the county. And I know he could ride anything with four legs."

Fletcher smiled down at her. "He could outride and out-shoot everyone in middle Tennessee."

"Then how did Seyler kill him?" This question had haunted her since Karl's death.

Fletcher paused, his gaze captured more by the past than by the packet boat that slid slowly through the water down-stream.

"Your brother could charm the skin off a snake when he wanted. When he didn't, he had a temper I tried not to rile. Seyler knew if Karl's temper was mixed with liquor, it would even the odds. Seyler's a decent shot, but Karl sober was the best shot in a dozen counties. And Seyler knew that. He got Karl roaring drunk and then insulted him. We were so drunk, we barely got ourselves to the meeting place on time."

"You were there?"

"I'm afraid so. I was Karl's second."

Grayson yanked the auction notice off the wrought-iron gate that swung drunkenly ajar beneath an arch. The horse he had rented in Nashville shifted beneath him as he read the proclamation. Angel's Valley would be auctioned tomorrow morning at ten.

Stuffing the notice in his pocket, he urged the horse through the entrance. They followed a winding dirt road between overgrown fields no longer sliced into neat pas-tures by whitewashed fencing. When he rounded the last curve in the rutted drive, he saw the house. Even with missing and broken shutters, dingy woodwork, and shat-tered windowpanes, the two-story Greek Revival house was impressive.

The stables and paddocks sprawled behind the house for several acres. Angel's Valley had once been a thriving horse farm, and its horses would have drawn soldiers like ants to a dollop of spilled honey—until there was nothing left to take.

Grayson dismounted, tied his horse to an iron ring, and went up the stairs. When he knocked on the front door, it opened of its own accord. Torn between trespassing or warning Billie of his presence, he chose trespassing. He doubted anyone would be in the house; it exuded abandonment. Leaving scruples behind, he stepped into the foyer.

The morning sun streamed though the two long windows on either side of the front door, bathing the walls with a golden hue. The rays highlighted the work of an itinerant artist whose colorful pastoral scene had been wined and be-grimed by a horde of heedless men.

Crossing the foyer to the first room on his left, his booted feet echoed against oak flooring scarred by careless spurs. The soldiers had been at work in the parlor. Someone had taken a saber to the wainscoting that encircled the room. He ran his fingers along the splintered wood, dismayed at the destruction.

The aroma of wealth lingered in the walls of the elegant house, but its furnishings had been sacrificed on the altar of war. Room after empty room bore mute testimony to the sac-rilege of pillage. Whoever had ransacked this house had left nothing portable behind.

Only one small room off the kitchen showed any sign of recent habitation. He nudged the door open, his hand draped over the butt of his gun, but no one waited in the tiny room. A neatly made cot graced one corner, while books lined an uneven desk in the other.

Running his finger over the books, he freed dust motes to dance in the thin square of light offered by a small high win-dow. He scanned the familiar titles. Three of them were his. He pulled *Final Fury,* his favorite of the Dinsmere books, from the row. When he flipped open the cover, the name *W.*

Constanza D'Angelo flowed across the bookplate in impeccable cursive.

"Constanza." The syllables ran across his tongue like sweet molasses. A good name for a character in the book he wasn't writing.

He closed *Fury,* slid it back into its slot, and pulled open the top desk drawer. It was empty, but the sound of paper crinkling made him tug the drawer free. His search netted a gold pocket watch and a folded piece of paper.

Flipping open the scarred metal lid, he stared at the portrait of a young woman. His artist's eye traced the similarities between Billie and the young woman. The nose, the eyebrows, and the mouth clearly marked her as Billie's relative. Perhaps Constanza of the book flap?

He snapped the watch shut and tucked it in his pocket. With the house set to be auctioned off tomorrow, the watch would be safer with him until he could give it to Billie. He picked up the folded paper. A lock of mahogany hair long enough to tickle the bare derriere of its owner with each step she took fell into his hand. The faint scent of lavender drifted into the air.

Constanza.

He couldn't believe a name, a lock of hair, and a miniature could play such havoc with his body. Curling the hair around his finger, he put it on the desk while he smoothed the paper. No, not paper. A letter. Written in Italian.

A floorboard in the kitchen creaked. The hairs on the back of Grayson's neck stirred. His hand crept down to his gun while he slowly pivoted toward the door.

A wiry, gray-headed man stood three feet away. His gnarled right hand held a flintlock pistol old enough to have helped clear Jamestown of Indians. A large splayed thumb cocked back the hammer.

"And what would a fine young bucko such as yourself be doing in this house? If you're after thinking to steal what little the Yanks left, I warn you I'll be angry as a leprechaun whose gold's been stolen."

With that pronouncement, he turned his head and shot a stream of tobacco into a spittoon near his left foot.

The acrid smell of damp, burned wood hung over the St. Louis harbor the morning Fletcher said good-bye. Five steamers, stocked with supplies for fur-trading posts, had burned the previous day. The bustling river port city paused to witness the fire, then resumed its frantic spring pace of shipping people and goods up and down the river.

"I thought to have more funds for you, Billie darling." A tiny spray of sparks sprinkled the air as Fletcher lit the cigarillo he had pulled from his frock coat pocket.

"The freedmen working these boats are the poorest humans I've ever relieved of greenbacks," he continued. "Are you positive you won't give me a week in St. Louis? I know I can find rich men anxious to part with their money."

"You've already done more than enough." Billie touched her shirt; beneath it lay the money belt Fletcher had cinched around her waist earlier. "I have the money to pay our passage to Galveston, and I can ride Destiny from there to the ranch."

"You could go with me to California."

"I could, but I won't." She gazed steadily into his eyes, knowing she had to be realistic for both of them. It had taken her days to convince him they should part in St. Louis.

"You know how much I value your friendship. How much I appreciate your help in rescuing Destiny, but—"

"Ah, the proverbial kiss of friendship." He leaned toward her but didn't get too close. "I'd prefer a real kiss, but mustn't ruin your disguise. Are you positive you won't marry me?"

"For the hundredth time, I adore you, but I'm not interested in marriage right now."

"Not even if your Yankee asked?"

His nonchalant question stunned her. Marry a Yankee? Why did her heart squeeze at the thought? She dodged the feeling and raised her eyebrows and voice in surprise.

"Have you lost your mind? Me, marry a Yankee after what they did to my home?"

"Ah, but this Yankee had no hand in destroying your home, Billie darling."

"He stole my horse." Her words slapped the air with a flat, uncompromising ring.

"And probably saved Destiny's life."

Fletcher had an uncanny knack for telling the truth when she least wanted to hear it. She wasn't about to let him know he had hit a raw nerve.

"I have things to do before I will be free to think about marriage to anyone."

"I'll go to Texas with you, without marriage, if that's what you want." He flicked an ash off the tip of his cigarillo, watched it arc over the side of the boat and disappear into the Mississippi River.

Their island of silence was buffeted by the voices of men loading and unloading steamboats drawn up to the levee like so many ducks swarming around a handful of bread crumbs.

Honesty nagged Billie into speaking. "I have no desire to compete with a memory."

"Ah, sweet Marianne."

When he looked at her, Billie saw the mischievous twinkle in his eyes had dimmed.

"I can't lie about Marianne—she'll always be with me—but I thought you'd understand. You lost Stephen."

How to explain to Fletcher something she had never explained well to herself? "Stephen was my dearest friend, but we never loved each other the way you and Marianne loved each other. If he hadn't been going to war, I would have refused his proposal." There, it was said, and she felt a great weight lift off her shoulders.

"So you see," she added softly, "you can't compare my loss to yours. I lost a dear friend, but you lost a beloved wife. And I know how much you loved each other. Sometimes when I saw you together, it was almost painful . . . to know I would never have what you had."

Fletcher moved to touch her, but she stepped back. She had to finish this with dignity. She hoped her lips wouldn't tremble. "I couldn't bear to be your wife and know you loved her still."

"Oh, Billie darling. I am a fool to let you go to Texas without me."

She swallowed, trying to rid her throat of the tight feeling. "I will be raising horses. You don't even care for the animals."

"True enough, but I thought I'd try for your sake."

She wanted to hug him. "You know I love you."

"Like the brother Karl should have been."

Tears raked the back of her eyes, and she had trouble relaxing her throat enough to talk. "Are you sure you have enough money?"

"I have enough. And I'm in St. Louis. If an enterprising man such as myself can't make enough money off these yokels to get to California . . ."

Around them were the sounds of a boat preparing to cast off. She forced a grin onto her face. "You'll be in New Orleans if you linger much longer."

He grabbed his carpetbag and headed toward the gangplank. Halfway down, he turned and waved.

She waved back. "If you don't like California, come to Texas. You know where to find me."

He ran back up the gangplank. "I hear the sun's bright in Texas, Billie darling. You'll need this." He pulled the battered hat off his head and plopped it on hers.

She wanted to throw her arms around his neck and kiss him farewell, but she had to settle with shaking his hand. Then she released her grip on her last human tie to Tennessee.

Within moments Fletcher disappeared around the corner of a warehouse. Loneliness and fear of the unknown crept into Billie's soul. She had been an idiot not to accept Fletcher's offer of marriage. Their friendship could have blossomed into love. Eventually.

Deep within her heart she knew he wasn't ready to marry. Marianne's death had unleashed a side of him that played a dangerous game. A woman couldn't marry a man who taunted death because it had taken his beloved and left him behind.

Life wasn't a game to Billie. It was a matter of getting up each day and doing what she had to do to get Destiny. Only with Destiny could she build a future that would give her back her past. Ah, yes, her father would be proud of her when she owned Angel's Valley again. Proud he had rested all his hopes for the future on her shoulders.

She watched the last-minute scurry of activity as the crew prepared to cast the boat back onto the mercy of the Mississippi. The banks of the river slid past with increasing speed, but she didn't see them. For some reason, that damn Yankee haunted her thoughts.

What had he done when he found Destiny gone? Would he come after them? If he did, he'd find the trail ended in Tennessee. Shaughnessy knew her plans to breed horses in Texas, but she'd never told him the location of the ranch. But why worry? The Yankee was in New York. He had a house to build and a fiancée to marry. Why leave his future to follow her? She had left a letter that explained everything.

But deep in her soul, a restless hope simmered. She wanted him to come after her. To keep his promise. And if he found her, then what?

Reality quenched hope.

The past would always lie between them.

Her espionage had killed his friends. His maps had killed her friends.

For several long moments, she watched the wake of the steamboat trailing behind her like the past she couldn't forget. With a deep sigh, she trudged along the deck to the only friend she had left.

CHAPTER TWELVE

Three weeks later

Grayson plastered himself against the side of the cabin, hoping Billie wouldn't notice his shadow through the widely spaced logs. His nose twitched at the mouthwatering smell of rabbit stew curling through the logs. Above his gun belt, his stomach grumbled with hunger.

Damn! He hadn't spent the day in the hot sun hiding among bluebonnets and tarantulas to have his stomach give him away. He pressed his eye to a gap in the wall, but he couldn't see Billie. With any luck, the boy had passed out after his attempts to build a corral that would fall over when the first wild horse slammed into it.

"Oh, I wish I were in the land of cotton, old times there are not forgotten . . . look awayyyyyy, look awayyyyy . . ."

The off-key high-pitched singing replastered Grayson to the cabin wall. The words degenerated into a whistle mingled with the sounds of splashing water. He grinned. Lina would be happy to know Billie had adopted the practice of bathing.

Grayson took a chance. With one fluid motion, he pulled aside the deteriorating deerskin that served as a door, and entered the room. Then he came to a boot-grinding halt.

A slender naked woman was toweling her hair dry.

Enthralled by the vision, Grayson didn't even look for Billie. The boy could have held a gun at his head and threatened to kill him and Grayson wouldn't have noticed. His attention was riveted by a pair of swaying breasts. He couldn't stop the rising in his groin any more than he could stop his lazy grin.

The woman paused as if she sensed she was not alone. Slowly her hands lowered. The towel came with them.

His grin faded as he stared into familiar features. Then his gaze flitted from the woman's face to her breasts.

"You have breasts!"

His heart slammed against his chest as if an enemy sniper's bullet had come singing through the cool evening air and blown his hat off.

"Holy Mary, Mother of God! What in blue blazes are you doing here?"

"You have breasts!"

"Damn! Damn! Double damn. You are the sneakingest Yankee I ever met."

He watched Billie struggle to cover himself—no, herself—with the towel. It wasn't large enough.

"You have breasts." His brain couldn't absorb what his eyes told him. A puckered nipple peeked through one of the numerous holes in the worn towel she tried to wrap around her midsection. Grayson licked his lips. He could taste its dewy freshness.

"Of course I have breasts, you ignoramus! You'd have to be blind not to have noticed. Shaughnessy told you where I was, didn't he?"

"You're a girl." No, she was a woman. A curvaceous, beautiful woman. Constanza of the watch.

"I'll have his worthless, black-hearted Irish hide for this." She fought to make the towel cover her body. It was a losing battle. "You got him drunk, didn't you?"

"You have freckles." They dusted her shoulders, breasts, and arms.

"No, Shaughnessy wouldn't betray me. Drunk or sober. And I never told him where I was going. Did I?" She frowned.

"Your hair looks different, too. Better. No grease." Dark red hair curled in a wet riot around her face—and matched the lock of hair he carried in his pocket.

"No, Shaughnessy couldn't have told you. He doesn't know where I am."

D'Angelo. She was the angel, not the horse.

"You lying Yankee scoundrel, how did you find me?" She scowled at him, giving up on the towel, which could protect either her chest or the thatch of copper hair at the juncture of her legs, but not both at the same time.

Two lovely, bare legs. He marveled at their perfection, delighted by the bare feet tipped with dainty toes splayed against a rough-hewn scrub-oak plank floor.

"A gentleman wouldn't stare at a lady like that."

He frowned. Not perfect legs. There was the merest of cants to her stance. Near her left foot rested a pair of boots, one of which sported a thicker heel than the other.

"You didn't have those boots at the farm, did you?"

"I told you the truth about my leg."

"One truth in a web of lies."

"We've established I lied about my gender. Now will you tell me how you found me?"

"How old are you?" He ignored the urge to plunge his tongue into the sweet indentation of her navel, which the towel failed to hide. What a sweet, joyous package of womanhood had been hidden beneath the grease and impudence.

"Gentlemen don't ask a lady's age any more than they stare at them. I had gotten the impression you might be classified a gentleman. Your dear sister is certainly a lady."

The vision was Billie, all right. The refined, genteel language went with the body, but the tone and drawl were Billie's tone and drawl. The abrasive edge that had made his ears cringe each time Billie opened his—or rather her—mouth was gone.

"How old are you?" His breath was harsh in his throat, and he felt as if he had run on foot from New York to Texas.

She blew at a tendril of hair that feathered across her right eye. Her hands were locked on the linen she held to her chest.

"I will be twenty-five tomorrow."

The pink tongue that had licked a crumb of Mary's apple tart from the corner of her mouth came out to torture him. He could feel its wet, slick softness as it darted across her lips. He wanted to feel it on his mouth. And elsewhere.

"I don't understand. I left Lina a note explaining my disguise."

Now he understood Lina's sly smile when he had raged into the parlor and threatened Billie with dire consequences once he caught up with the miscreant. Grayson tried to corral his rampaging thoughts and stay with their conversation.

"My sister failed to share your letter with me." He had so many questions to ask her. "Are you always called Billie, or were you once called Constanza?"

If his question surprised her, she hid it.

"After I was three years old, I wouldn't answer to any name except Billie."

"Constanza is a beautiful name."

"My mother preferred Wilhelmina, my first name."

"My vote goes with your choice. And such a convenient name to use when one masquerades as a boy."

Billie's taunting question echoed in his brain. *What're ya waitin' fer? Or are you one of them men what likes to look at nekkid boys?*

God, how she had enjoyed her deception. With startling clarity, he recalled the flashes of amusement he had caught dancing in the depths of her intelligent green eyes.

"I am tired of asking the same question," she said, "but I want an answer. How did you find me?"

He reached into his trouser pocket and pulled out a crumpled piece of paper. He was going to enjoy this. "You left directions in your desk."

"I never!"

He shook it open and began to read. *"Caro Fillipo."* He glanced over the edge of the letter, arcing his eyebrows upward. His ability to translate Italian outweighed his ability to speak it.

"You read Italian?" Her eyes widened.

He had never seen such expressive eyes. Until this moment, he had not realized how much he had ignored their beckoning depths. And her mouth, with its slightly fuller lower lip that two white teeth nibbled anxiously, further aggravated the exquisite ache that filled his loins.

"Well enough to figure out your uncle had a ranch in Texas. This seemed the logical place for you to go." He let his gaze roam her body; his hands itched to follow. When she blushed, it tinged her whole body pink.

She clutched the ragged towel to her chest with white-knuckled intensity. "A gentleman," she said with cool dignity, "would turn around while I dress."

"And have you hit me over the head once my back is turned?" He shook his head sadly. "I'm afraid you've used up your share of my trust, Angel."

She frowned. "I am not your angel, Yankee." Her glance swept the sparsely furnished room. "And I have no idea what you think I could use to hit you over the head."

"I admit your new lodgings are rustic, but with your ingenuity, I'm sure you could find something. Isn't that a skillet near the fire? Or the pot of rabbit stew, perhaps?"

"There's a hole rusted in the bottom of the skillet," she admitted crossly, "but I suppose the sides are intact and would render you senseless." The image seemed to intrigue her, but he gave her no time to pursue it.

Unable to stop himself, he stepped toward her.

She stepped back. "And I would risk wasting my dinner if I used the stew pot." She scowled, either at herself for stepping backward or at him for general reasons. Her right hand released its death grip on the towel to grab her shirt, or rather his old one, off the table beside her.

A sweet whiff of lavender femininity stirred the air, telling him he liked this Billie a lot more than the other Billie. This one was clean, beautiful, and shapely. And utterly desirable.

"You may as well leave, Yankee. Destiny is mine." She struggled to put her arm in the sleeve without dropping the towel.

He watched her, wishing he were the shirt that would hug that delectable body in a few short seconds. The right words might slow her attempt to clothe herself.

"You're wrong, Billie. I bought Destiny from the federal government. I own him. It's all perfectly legal."

"Legal!" As he'd hoped, she quit fighting the shirt and looked at him. "I have the papers to show Destiny was born on my family's farm and belongs to me. No bill of sale signed by my father or myself has ever—and I repeat, *ever*—been issued. There isn't a court of law in Texas that will side with you. Destiny belongs to me."

He knew the moment she realized he wasn't paying attention to her tirade. Glassy-eyed delight gave him away. She stopped talking, glared at him, and then stuffed her left arm into the shirt. Without trousers and a frock coat to hide its size, he saw firsthand how much too large the shirt was for her.

She buttoned the top button. He frowned. The show was over.

"Isn't that just like a Yankee. . . ." Her voice stumbled to a stop. Eyes wide in surprise, she stared over his shoulder.

"Dewey Perkins, what are you doing here?" Her gaze swung back to Grayson. "Holy Mary, Mother of God, Yankee! Did you issue engraved invitations?"

"Almost as good, Miz Billie. He done sent a telegram to his sister saying he knew where ya were. It weren't that hard to follow 'im."

At the gravelly Southern drawl, Grayson's hand went for the gun strapped around his waist.

"I wouldn't be doin' that iffen I were awantin' to live a little longer."

Unable to protect Billie with his gun, he shielded her with his body. "Button your shirt," he ordered as he turned to face their unwanted visitor.

"Wait'll the boys hear how I caught Miss High And Mighty nekkid with a Bluebelly. Maybe yer Rebel friends won't be so impressed with yer spyin' iffen they knew how you did it."

"What do you want?"

"Nothing with you, Bluebelly. My business is with Miz Billie, and she can quit hidin' behind ya."

Billie stepped from behind him. She may have been wearing only his shirt, which stopped inches above her knees, but no one would have guessed she was not in the drawing room of her home in Tennessee when she spoke.

"What does Seyler want?"

"Why, Miz Billie, Mr. Seyler don't share his secrets with the likes of me. I don't know what he wants exceptin' the horse. Oh, and he said somethin' about you would know what ya gotta do to get the horse back."

Dewey shot a stream of tobacco juice into the hard-packed dirt at Grayson's feet. " 'Course, he probably won't be so eager to have ya onct I tell him about the Bluebelly." A grin revealed teeth tarred with tobacco and decay. "But he'll have a prime horse."

"I won't—"

"Don't argue with him." Grayson laced his warning with a hint of steel. Only Billie would argue with a man who was pointing a Henry rifle at her heart.

"That's good advice, Bluebelly. Now take yer gun out of

its holster real slow-like and slide it acrost the floor towards me."

Grayson followed Dewey's directions.

When the gun slid to a halt near his feet, Dewey scooped it up and slipped it into his waistband. Then he pulled a length of rope from his coat pocket and waved it in the direction of the cabin's one chair.

"You, Bluebelly, sit in that chair, and you," he threw the rope at Billie. "Tie his hands behind his back and tie his feet to the chair legs. And remember, I know ya kin tie a good, tight knot."

Billie watched the Yankee ease himself down into the aging chair and hoped the frayed seat would hold his weight. She hovered next to him, twisting the rope in her hands. Reckless escape plans raced through her head. As if he knew her thoughts, the Yankee looked up at her and smiled. He also gave his head an infinitesimal shake.

"Go on, now. Tie 'is hands real tight-like."

Another glance at the rifle Dewey pointed at them decided her. She went around behind the Yankee and tied his hands—a difficult feat since she also had to keep herself decently covered. She had no wish to get Dewey's slow brain going in another direction. Her wartime experiences had taught her how easily men got aroused.

Dewey surveyed her handiwork. "You've done such a good job, I'm gonna reward ya."

Her hands stilled above the rope. She had tried hard not to incite any notions in Dewey's head, but the Yankee's old shirt wasn't long enough to cover her legs.

"Folks don't know it, but I've got a romantical streak for lovers, so I'm gonna tie y'all together. Go ahead, Miz Billie, climb aboard yer Bluebelly."

"Wh . . . What?"

"You heard me." Dewey waved the gun impatiently. "Sit on the Bluebelly."

"Straddle him?" Unmitigated shock vibrated in her voice.

"Do as the man says, Angel." The Yankee's tone of velvet-wrapped steel demanded obedience.

She fought the urge to obey. "You can't tie us up and leave us here."

"Yes, I kin. Mr. Seyler only tole me to get the horse. He din't say I had to drag a Yankee's whore with me. Hell, not even Stephen'd want ya now."

She wanted to scratch Dewey's eyes out. Her desire must have been written on her face, because he pressed the gun muzzle to her temple.

"Mr. Seyler said not to hurt ya . . . if I could help it." Dewey's muddy eyes challenged her to defy him.

Billie slid her leg across the Yankee's thigh and settled gingerly on his lap.

Dewey slipped his gun into his coat pocket and pulled out another length of rope. Jerking her hands behind her back, he wound the rope around her wrists. The rope bit into her flesh. From the immediate tingling sensation, she knew her hands would soon be numb. Bending down, he tugged her right leg back until he could tie it to the Yankee's leg. Then he repeated the process with her left leg.

She had never felt so vulnerable and exposed. Her legs were spread in such a way as to press her lower body intimately against the Yankee's worn trousers while her tied hands arched her back and brought her breasts within inches of his face. It was only by supreme effort she kept any space between his nose and her breasts.

Why, if the Yankee turned his head either way . . .

Dewey stood, briskly brushing his hands. His mud-brown eyes swept her arched chest, and for the first time since he had entered the room, she panicked. Dewey had *that* look in his eyes, and it chilled her blood.

To her horror, he leaned toward her. As he neared, she thought she would gag at the odor of his rotting breath. His dirt-stained fingers contrasted sharply with the stark white of her shirt. He slid a hand into her shirt and squeezed a handful of breast.

Mind-crushing fear stopped her heart.

"Maybe I oughter untie ya fer a few minutes. . . ."

"You'll like it, Reb." The Yankee's voice slid like warm liquid into her panic. "She's still wet from me. I always said, a Reb's only fit to drench his cock in Yankee leavings."

The force of the blow to the Yankee's jaw would have tumbled them backward, but Dewey used his free hand to keep them upright.

"She's all yers, Yank. Dewey Perkins don't take no Blue-belly's leavings. But I'll take that money belt y'all got wrapped around yer middle."

CHAPTER THIRTEEN

"For God's sake, woman, be still! I can't think with you rubbing yourself all over me." Not that he wanted to think—not with Billie tied to him in such an intimate fashion. What he wanted to do was turn his head an inch to the right and nuzzle aside the fine lawn cloth of her shirt and suck one of those lovely nipples into his mouth.

She must have read his thoughts. Her blush started somewhere below the V in her shirt, swept up her neck to her temples, and clashed into her auburn curls.

"Forgive me if I don't behave how you think a woman should behave when tied to a man—"

A distinctive neigh of unhappiness cut into her rebuke. Her body tensed. He tried to distract her with conversation.

"Who's Stephen?"

She ignored him, her gaze locked on the ragged door. Dancing hoofbeats punctuated the air.

"Damn yer hide!"

At Dewey's harsh words, she tried to rise. Her attempt

swayed a breast into his cheek. Soft temptation caressed his his cheek. All he had to do was turn his head.

She tugged at the ropes holding her arms. "Holy Mary, Mother of God, Yankee, do something. Get us free!"

Free himself of this sweet agony? Not in this lifetime.

A neigh of displeasure. A flurry of hoofbeats. Then silence.

Billie gave one last feeble tug at the rope holding her left hand before slumping in defeat. Her lips, so close to his, trembled.

"Who is Stephen?" The need to have this man identified ate at him. He had to know what manner of man would not want this woman.

She took a deep breath, pushing her breast against his cheek again. He could feel the puckered, cloth-encased nipple against his skin. He licked his lips, quashing the urge to turn his head and taste her.

"Stephen . . . was my fiancé. He was . . . killed during the war."

"For what it's worth, I'm sorry."

She straightened, as if suddenly aware of his cheek pressed into her breast. Unshed tears shimmered in the depths of her green eyes. How he wanted to reach up, cup the back of her neck, and pull her quivering mouth into the comfort of his.

Her mouth tightened; the eyes blinked back the tears. She looked down at her right ankle.

"Thank you, Yankee, but I've learned not to dwell on the past. It can't be changed. I prefer to think about the future." She wiggled her leg. "And unless you plan for us to starve to death . . ."

He shifted his hips. It was an honest attempt to position himself so he could kick at the chair leg, but his movement stretched Billie's legs farther apart. She was spread open, pressed against him in an intimate way with his worn, soft trousers between her and his hard manhood.

The pleasure of their position was excruciatingly delightful, but every cell in his body sang with tension as well as caution. Would it be possible to pleasure her in this position? He wanted to try.

Slowly.

He would go slowly.

Slowly.

He moved his hips.

She no longer wiggled on his lap. Her eyes, grown wide with astonishment, stared at him. He could feel her heat through the buttoned closure of his trousers, and the unmistakable scent of feminine desire wafted into his nostrils. It pleased him to know her body wanted his.

Without a hint of remorse, he shifted his hips. There was no rush. They had all the time in the world.

He moved his hips again.

And again. And yet again, until he had set up a gentle rocking motion.

The green in her irises receded before the dilating pupils as her gaze became unfocused. She relaxed against him with a soft sigh.

Her chest pressed into his face, and he kept up the slow rocking while nuzzling at the V in her shirt. She moaned softly and arched into him. He felt his erection pushing against his trousers, seeking the hot center of her being. The fabric rubbed against his sensitive tip each time he rocked.

He thought he was going to explode.

Using his teeth, he pulled two buttons free of their buttonholes, causing the shirt to gape open. Although his hands itched to cup her breasts—how could he have ever mistaken her for a boy?—he contented himself with taking a nipple into his mouth and suckling it.

Her response made him smile. She began moving with him, her inarticulate murmurs escalating into delicious moans. He licked his way beneath her breast, inhaling the heady combination of lavender scent mixed with the sweet smell of woman.

Sweat beaded his forehead as he rocked his hips back and forth. She sounded ready to tip over the edge, and he wished his arms were free. He wanted to pull her close the moment she shuddered into a climax, but the ropes prevented that.

"Come on, Angel. Let it go. Feel it."

At his soft words, her eyes widened in surprised confusion. She stared at him, but he didn't think she saw him. A beatific smile lit her mouth.

"Oh my." The words whispered from her lips.

With a whimper that stole his heart, she collapsed into his lap. Her head fell against his shoulder as if she lacked the strength to hold it upright.

The scientific side of his brain wanted to catalog all her reactions for further study; the cheering in the male side of his brain drowned out logic. He had never thought to give a woman pleasure without taking his own. Watching Billie had been the most erotic experience in his life.

A shuddering shriek rent the air.

"Damn!"

The aging chair, of poor craftsmanship, could take no more of their combined weight. First one leg buckled, then another, tumbling them to the floor. Grayson took the brunt of the fall. He landed on his back with Billie flattened against his chest, and the chair back punched into his spine.

In the unexpected quiet that followed the chaos of the previous moments, their thundering heartbeats seemed to fill the void. With a small cry of dismay, she rolled off him and struggled to her knees. Hands still tied behind her back, she seemed unaware that her shirt was open. His mouth was sweet with the taste of those breasts.

She stared down at him. "Holy Mary, Mother of God! What did you do to me?"

"Only what you wanted, Angel." He shook his hands free of the loosened ropes and reached for her, lacing his fingers in her soft hair and pulling her mouth down to meet his. He pushed his tongue against her lips, seeking entry.

Now she would satisfy him.

Her mouth parted slightly. His triumph was short-lived when she nipped his tongue. He jerked backward. "Damn, woman! Why'd you do that?"

She scrambled out of his reach, freeing her hands as she went. "How dare you do such things to me!"

He checked the finger he had pressed against his tongue, searching for blood. There was none. He looked at Billie. She was on her knees a few feet away with her hair tousled, her hands clutching the shirt closed, and her chest heaving in indignation. She was the picture of outraged innocence. Another role or the truth?

"How dare I not? And you can rant all you want. You're not going to convince me you didn't enjoy what I did."

She wiped her sleeve across her mouth with careful dignity, but the action pulled the shirt up and revealed most of her legs. Following his gaze, she smothered a most unlady-like oath and tugged her shirt down.

"If you don't mind, I would like to get dressed now."

He settled himself cross-legged on the floor and began loosening the bonds that wrapped his feet. "Good idea."

"A gentleman would turn his back."

"And have you knock me out? We've been over that plan already." He watched her cross the room with her now-familiar limp.

She snatched something off the pile of clothes. Holding the article of clothing to her chest, she glared over her shoulder at him. Tossing aside the rope, he met her angry look with a smile and a shrug. When she bent over to step into a pair of his old cotton drawers, her shirt rode up to fan the curve of her sweet bottom. Grayson's mouth went dry, and his heartbeat jacked up into a gallop. How he envied his drawers as they slid up her long legs, over her lean hips, to cuddle her warm derriere.

Over the drawers went the trousers Lina had given Billie in New York. Without the frock coat to hide everything, he saw the piece of cord that kept the trousers hitched to her oh-so-tiny waist. Sitting on the floor, she tugged on her boots, and the limp was gone when she walked past him. By the door, she stopped long enough to grab a battered hat he had last seen perched on Fletcher's head, before pushing the deer-skin aside.

Grayson jumped to his feet and followed her. Stopping outside the cabin door, he let the evening breeze cool his pounding blood. Billie had disappeared into the barn. They both knew what she would find, but he respected her need to see with her own eyes that Destiny was gone.

Destiny's empty stall awaited her in the barn. She stood at the stall door and stared into its dark depths. Her breath came in great gulps of air tinged with horse and fresh straw. Desolation swept her soul. Once again she had lost her best friend.

And she knew where to place the blame. That damn Yankee had led Dewey right to them.

Sweet Jesus, the Yankee had seen her naked! He had kissed her breasts! She sagged against the stall door. He had used his mouth to unbutton her shirt and kiss her breasts, all the while rocking his hips and rubbing her down there and making her body feel things it had never felt.

Things she would be too embarrassed to admit to a priest in confession if she lived to be a hundred years old. Surely, these feelings were sinful. But it wasn't her fault Dewey had tied them together in such an intimate fashion.

God in heaven, she had opened to him as readily as any mare in heat for a stallion. He had been as hard as any stallion she had ever seen, and she had been as willing as any mare.

She hit her head on the stall door. What had that Yankee done to her? Without using his hands, he had made every fiber of her being quiver with ecstasy. He had rocked his hips and rubbed his manhood against the most intimate center of her being. And to her dying shame, she had liked every minute of it. She'd joined in his motion, driven wild by the sensations flooding her body.

And his mouth. She could still feel his tongue licking her nipples into hard excitement while his day-old beard roughed her tender skin. Her knees wanted to buckle with the memory of his hips rocking and rubbing her until every cell in her body exploded. And then she had melted into him like a handful of Mississippi River mud. Lord knows what she would have said or done if the chair hadn't collapsed.

But the chair had collapsed, and he had begun reweaving the shattered spell with his mouth on hers. Nipping at his tongue had seemed the only way to rescue herself. From what? An experience she never wanted to end but could not let continue?

Just thinking about what he had done to her sent a hot, sweet, throbbing sensation through her abdomen. She could feel the warm dampness between her legs again.

Holy Mary, Mother of God! He was the enemy. Destiny was gone because of him.

She fingered a fresh gouge in the stall door. Destiny had not gone quietly. Her fingers squeezed the wood beneath them. This time she faced Seyler alone, but she would get Destiny back.

A boot scuffed the dirt behind her. She whirled. The Yankee stood in the doorway of the barn. She shot him one angry glance, then stalked past him toward the rickety gate that marked the entrance to the ranch.

The irritating man was beside her in three long strides.

"Where do you think you're going?"

When she ignored him, he grabbed her arm and spun her around to face him.

"Let me help you."

"Help me!" Disbelief colored her high-pitched voice. She brushed his hand away. "Help me? How can you possibly help me?" With each word she spoke, she heard another note of hysteria creep into her tone. "You've done nothing but bring me despair. You stole my horse during the war; you followed me to Texas; you led Dewey straight to me so he could take my horse, and now . . . now you say, 'Let me help you.' How in the world can *you* help *me?*" Her question didn't sound as she had planned. It wobbled into the evening air like a broken rocking horse. She clamped her mouth shut.

Night had nibbled at the edges of dusk until the Texas sky was filled with a panorama of stars blurred into shiny bits of spiky fuzz. Damn the Yankee for making her cry!

"You're crying." Surprise rippled through his accusation.

"I am not crying." There was no wobble in her voice, either.

"Oh, yes, you are."

The Yankee's finger reached out and caught the tear whose existence she denied as it slid down her cheek. When he pressed his finger to his lips and licked the moisture off, a shaft of hot desire ricocheted through her body.

"No!" Knotting her hands into fists, she went after the man who'd led her into uncharted emotional depths and epitomized all her troubles. "I am not crying! I am not crying!"

She beat against his chest in rhythm with the words. "I'm mad, mad, mad! It's all your fault Dewey got Destiny. You ruined everything!"

And then she was in his arms. Huge, heaving, convulsive sobs spilled from the depths of her soul. Sobs for more than Destiny. She cried for the loss of a world that had protected her, sheltered her, and fed her. A world that had been turned upside down and then disappeared while she was left alone to make sense of a new world.

She clung to the Yankee, her head buried against the chest of the author of all her problems. Yet she didn't move. The rush of anger collided with a grief denied for too many years. For this brief time, she would be weak. Then she would reach down into the deep well of her being and find the strength to continue living. Somehow she would get Destiny back. But right now she was tired of pretending she could survive without the world she had always known.

Just for a moment, she would let this man hold her. Just for a moment, she would revel in the feel of his chest beneath her wet cheek and let the steady beat of his heart soothe the tempest in her soul while his hands smoothed down her hair and back. Just for a moment, she would be close enough to breathe his male scent, which was tinged with bluebonnets and caliche.

"Ah, sweet Angel, don't cry. I'll get Destiny back for you. I promise."

Her sobs gurgled into tiny mews. Then silence. She clung to the Yankee for a few more heartbeats. Then, with a loud sniff, she released him. Stepping back, she raised her sleeve to wipe her running nose. The Yankee thrust a handkerchief into her hand. For one wistful blink of time, she wished this man could see her as the lady she had been trained to be rather than a dirty ruffian.

"Thank you." She blew her nose, folded the handkerchief into a smaller square, then wiped her eyes.

"I tied my horse about half a mile from here," the Yankee said. "Maybe Dewey didn't bother with it. If you'll warm up that rabbit stew, I'll get the horse. We can ride double into town tomorrow morning."

She wadded the soggy handkerchief into a ball. Staring down at her hand, she tried to figure out how to get Destiny back, but her brain wouldn't cooperate.

The Yankee kept talking. "There really isn't much sense in following Dewey tonight. Neither of us knows the countryside well enough. And it's not as if we don't know his destination."

He was right. Going after Destiny now would be foolish. Exhaustion seeped into every pore of her body. She had spent the day digging holes in the brick-hard caliche. Her exhaustion wasn't only physical. The past hour had extracted a high emotional price, too. She needed to rest. To plan her next move. To figure out how to get rid of the Yankee.

She stuffed his handkerchief into her pocket. "Do you think we can catch Dewey before he leaves Texas?"

"We can try, but we don't know how he'll get Destiny back to Tennessee. Steamboat would be my guess, but plenty of them ply the Mississippi. Since we know where he's going, we might do better to get to Gallatin as soon as possible and then worry about getting Destiny when Dewey shows up with him."

"You're right, Yankee. It's too dark to follow Dewey tonight. Fetch your horse while I heat up the stew." She headed for the cabin, then stopped and turned back to face him. "I appreciate the ride to town, but you don't need to come to Tennessee. Destiny is mine."

CHAPTER FOURTEEN

"Ah, sweet Angel, don't cry. I'll get Destiny back for you. I promise."

What had he been thinking? Grayson kicked at the ground, and his booted right toe rammed into a half-buried rock he hadn't seen in the dark. "Damn!" He hopped a few steps on his left foot, willing the pain to ease.

Billie was a woman. A beautiful, intelligent, but deceitful and manipulative woman. She had come into his home disguised as a boy and stolen his horse. If he was wise, he'd do as she asked and take her into Seguin and then take himself to Colorado. Lowering his right foot back to the ground, he tested his weight. With a slight limp, he resumed his walk.

The night air hit the damp splotches on his shirtfront, cooling the skin beneath. He could feel her face burrowing into his chest and smell the sweet scent of her freshly washed hair. The desire to right her world had welled from deep within him. His knees had grown weak at the sound of sobs that scrambled his brain while his mouth whispered a rash promise to get her horse back.

Had he gone temporarily insane?

And if he accompanied her to Tennessee, he didn't want to think about the consequences. How would she react when she discovered who owned her beloved home? Worse than that, if she demanded to know why he had bought it, he wouldn't be able to give her a rational explanation. He didn't know why. He had gone to the auction to look for her; he left it as the owner of a horse-breeding farm.

Nothing had gone right in his life since Billie entered it. A simple trip to Texas to find an orphan had disintegrated into chasing a horse thief back to Tennessee. Instead of dealing with an adolescent boy, he had to deal with a beautiful young woman. His twinging toe warned him not to kick out in the dark again, but he wanted to hit something. If any man was ill equipped to deal with a young woman, it had to be him.

Talking with a female other than his sister usually left him tongue-tied and miserable. He doubted he would have had the courage to ask Sophronia to marry him if John hadn't died. Their mutual grief had brought them together, and it seemed logical to propose.

Logic. A commodity in short supply in his life since Billie tumbled into it. He had never argued with or teased a woman the way he had Billie. He supposed her masquerade had helped. Yes. That was it.

He stopped, unaware of the chirruping night sounds around him. If he applied a little scientific method, his ability to converse with Billie without his usual awkwardness became logical. He had believed her to be a boy, and conversation with her had not suffered from being filtered through the worry that she was a female and misunderstood him.

Pleased with his reasoning, he scanned the starlit countryside for landmarks. A slight breeze carried his scent to the horse, who neighed a soft greeting. Boots crunching on the rocky soil, Grayson adjusted his direction and headed toward the large, dark shape.

As for this desire to right her world, biology offered a simple explanation. His response stemmed from the natural tendency of males to protect the weaker females.

Another natural tendency popped into his head.

Mating.

Logic collided with the image of Billie struggling to cover her body with the too-small towel. It didn't take too much effort to see her half-closed eyes as she'd climaxed in his lap. His fingers ached to feel the satiny skin they had not had the chance to explore. He licked his lips, searching for the merest hint of the breasts he had suckled.

The horse whinnied a welcome, shattering the moment. Grayson frowned. How could he think of seducing Billie? Contrary to her accusation, he was a gentleman. A man of honor. And men of honor didn't go around seducing young women whose world had been destroyed by a war. No, a gentleman would keep his promise to help her get Destiny back, while keeping his hands to himself.

"There you are. Good horse." Grayson rubbed the horse's nose. He centered the saddle, tightened the girth, and swung his leg over the saddle. The faster they got Destiny, the faster he could continue on his way to Colorado.

Billie had picked up the broken pieces of the chair and stacked them near the fireplace, but something told her burning the chair wouldn't erase the memory of what had happened. Her body tingled with awareness when the Yankee walked into the cabin. She kept her eyes on the wooden bowl in her hand and filled it with stew.

"There's not much in the way of dishes." She offered him a bowl of stew and a chunk of bread, stealing a quick glance at his face. "And only one spoon." She held out an army knife-fork-spoon combination.

"You can use it. I have my own." He pulled one from his pocket before he settled beside her on the floor. She stiffened slightly but relaxed when he didn't touch any part of her body.

They ate in silence. The fire crackled, the stew bubbled, and the faint howl of a coyote wafted through the chinks in the logs.

"That was good." The Yankee sounded surprised. "May I have another bowl?"

The compliment warmed Billie. Not many men praised her cooking, but even Fletcher had liked her rabbit stew.

The Yankee ladled more stew into his bowl. "I don't know how you rode Destiny that night. I was sure Gerret broke some of your ribs."

Without thinking, she touched her rib cage. "He didn't break anything, but I could hardly move. I wouldn't have tried to ride any horse except Destiny."

"Your friend had a good disguise. For all of you."

A little smile of satisfaction curved her mouth. "When did you realize you saw us in Albany?"

"Not until I returned home and learned Jacob had traced you to an apothecary's wagon."

She couldn't help it; her smile broadened into a grin. "I worried when Fletcher insisted we go to Albany. He insisted you wouldn't recognize us. It was harder to disguise Destiny, but we were lucky. That woman caught your attention."

She grabbed the loaf of bread she had bought from the Seguin baker and sawed off a piece of the two-day-old bread. Why did the thought of the woman in the green dress make her angry?

"Ah, the inestimable Fletcher." The Yankee scanned the cabin as if looking for something. "He didn't accompany you to Texas?"

Bristling at the implied criticism of her friend, she stopped hacking the bread. "He has other plans for his life. It was enough he helped me get Destiny."

"And almost killed you in the process. Is Fletcher the one who insisted you leave that night?"

"He had nothing to do with the timing of my departure. I had no choice. Seyler had come after me."

The Yankee stared at her, then grinned. "You were in the chimney staircase."

It was a statement, not a question. She tore off a ragged chunk of bread. Pulling it into two pieces, she handed one to the Yankee. "I was exploring the stairs the day Seyler came."

"Then you heard everything?"

"I heard the bastard say my father sold him Destiny."

"What about his claim to be your guardian?"

"How can he be my guardian? I'll be twenty-five years old tomorrow."

"That's a good question, Angel. Does Mr. Seyler know you're a twenty-five-year-old female?"

"I'm not your angel, and Seyler knows how old I am. He has known me since I was a child." Afraid she would reveal too much, she began sopping up stew with her bread.

"All the more reason to wonder why he didn't recognize you when you pretended to be Shaughnessy's grandson during the war."

Her sopping piece of bread halted in midair on its journey from the bowl to her mouth. She eased it back to the empty bowl. "Shaughnessy talks too much."

"He tried to explain why Seyler hates you. I'm afraid his Irish brogue got in the way."

She sighed, wondering what the groom had told the Yankee. "Seyler didn't come to the farm often. When he did, I hid. He saw me often enough in Gallatin to have no reason to suspect I played any role in the war."

"Now he knows you spied for the Confederacy."

"He knows."

"And plans what? To retaliate by being named your guardian?" Frustration colored his tone.

"Once he figured out I was playing the boy again, he probably decided you wouldn't mind releasing me into a guardian's care. I doubt he would have used the ploy beyond getting custody of me in New York." She wouldn't think about what he planned to do with her once he got her to Tennessee.

"But why? Tell me why Seyler wants you."

"Not just me. He wants anyone who worked for Fletcher."

"Fletcher?" The Yankee's lips tightened with disapproval. "What is so special about Fletcher?"

"He's Major Fletcher Darring. The most sought-after Confederate spy in Tennessee."

"Darring! You worked for Darring!" Grayson made no attempt to hide his shock. Every Federal officer in Tennessee had been warned about Major Darring. A master of disguise, he had slipped in and out of the enemy camps like a ghost. And this man had dragged Billie into his world of subterfuge and deceit.

"It was a privilege to work with Major Darring." Billie's spine was as stiff as her words.

Grayson corralled his horror. The war had ended. The young woman across from him no longer played the part of spy. He had pledged to help her get Destiny back. "None of which explains why Seyler followed you to New York or why Dewey took Destiny."

She stared into the fire. His gaze was lured to her eyes, where the fire's light grabbed the golden flecks hidden in the emerald depths, bringing them to life. She hadn't been able to hide the thick sweep of auburn eyelashes, but he had refused to look beyond the greasy hair and impudent mouth. Kissing that mouth was no longer an option. He had set his course and must abide by it.

She swept her gaze from the fire to meet his. "Perhaps Shaughnessy told you Seyler hasn't been pleased with the D'Angelo family for the past ten years. When he discovered I had tricked him, it added fuel to his anger. He has—how shall I say this?—unpleasant plans for my future."

"But he needs you in Tennessee to implement these plans." He kept his voice matter-of-fact and hid the disgust that raced through his brain at the images caused by her judicious choice of words. "And he sent Dewey after the horse because he knew you'd follow Destiny back to Tennessee."

Wiping her spoon on her trousers, she folded it back into its slot. She grabbed her bowl and rose. "Of course I'll go back to Tennessee. Destiny is all I have left."

He put his bowl into her outstretched hand. "And I'll go with you. Any court in the state will honor our two claims for Destiny's ownership against his one."

He liked the way her eyes widened when she was surprised.

"Are you mad? We can't sashay into Seyler's home and tell him to give us Destiny. That man is worse than any Union soldier."

"He must be evil personified." His witty comment may as well have been spoken to the wall; Billie was too engrossed in her own argument to hear him.

"I'll have to find Destiny and steal him, again. It's the only way. I have plenty of friends in Sumner County who'll be glad to help me."

He was on his feet in one fluid motion. "You expect me to steal my own horse?"

"For the last time, Yankee. Destiny is not your horse. He's mine."

"The animal in question was seized in the name of the Federal government, and I legally purchased said horse from the government." He was tired of explaining the situation to this obstinate female. From the mutinous expression on her face, she tired of hearing his explanation. Which meant she wasn't going to like his next proposition, either.

"You can go back to Tennessee alone and penniless, or you can trust me and let me help you."

"Of course! Why didn't I think of that? Trust the man, a Yankee no less, who stole my horse."

"For the last time, Billie D'Angelo, I commandeered Destiny on behalf of the Union army! I did not steal him." Startled by his own vehemence, he took a deep, steadying breath.

God help him, this woman drove logic right out of a man. He gentled his voice. "Let me help. You won't be alone anymore."

She stepped backward, eyes wide. "I didn't spend half the war shoveling horseshit to keep the Yankees from raping me, to turn around and become a Yankee's whore as soon as the war ended!"

"Ladies do not say 'shit,' and I'm not asking you to be my whore!"

"Who says I'm a lady!" Anger bristled from every inch of her body, flushing her ivory skin and fading the freckles that sprinkled her nose. "And I'm not blind. I've seen the lust in your eyes. Holy Mary, Mother of God, what else would you want from someone like me?"

"I want to marry you."

The wooden bowls hit the dirt floor at her feet with a decided thump. Her mouth gaped open, and she stared at him as if he had become a mound of horse manure.

"What . . . did . . . you . . . say?"

What had he said? Marriage! His heart hammered in his chest as his brain tore apart the five words, looking for some kind of sense. Why had he asked her to marry him? He was supposed to escort her to Tennessee and help her get Destiny. But marriage? What had made him suggest marriage? He grabbed the first reason that popped into his head. "If you marry me, the ownership of the horse will be joint. It will double our chances of getting Destiny."

"Marry you? Are you out of your mind? You're not only a Yankee, you have a fiancée. Or do you plan to marry two women?"

Astonishment whammed into his reeling thoughts. He had forgotten about Sophronia. With a small shake of his head, he collected himself. "Former fiancée. She ended the engagement the day you ran off."

"What difference does it make whether or not she broke your engagement? Can't you see it's impossible? To marry a

Yankee would go against everything I hold dear—my father, Stephen, my home, what we fought a war over, the price we paid." Her list careened to a stop; her shoulders slumped.

Once again she relaxed her guard and exposed her fragility. Once again the need to right her world welled from deep within him. He honestly didn't know why he had proposed such a drastic solution to her problem. All he knew at that moment was that he wanted Billie D'Angelo. He had seen her—God, had he seen her! And he wanted her.

But he admired her too much to take her like the whore Dewey had called her. Only a knave would cause this spunky young woman any more grief than she had already suffered.

Slowly she straightened her spine, her gaze lifting to meet his.

"You have no idea what it's like to lose everything you love, Yankee. To have only hatred to keep you alive. After the war you went home to a safe, comfortable farm and food and love. My home hasn't been safe for years, and there was no food, no comfort. The war ended for you, but not for me."

She took a deep breath. "Courtesy demands I thank you for the honor of your proposal." Her voice rasped into a whisper. "I cannot accept."

Was he doomed to hear how honored women were by his proposal as they threw it back in his face? He reached for her. Curving his fingers around the straight, proud shoulders, he looked into her eyes. Despair and sadness ran bone-deep. For one moment, a tremor of fear winged through his soul. Who was he to think he could make her world right?

"The war wasn't between you and me, Billie. We were caught in a larger event and played our parts. Now the war's over. I can't erase the past, but I can make your future better."

"And wh—why . . ." The quaver in her voice shredded his heart, but he would not unlock the grip he had on her gaze, and waited for her to gather her courage to ask. ". . . would a handsome, rich Yankee want to make the future better for a crippled, destitute Rebel spy?"

Somehow he knew her objections stemmed from this one question. And he didn't have the answer. He didn't know why he wanted this woman. He didn't know why he had asked her to marry him. This was his chance to admit the truth, possibly slip out of a situation impulse had created.

But he didn't want to slip out. For some unfathomable reason, he wanted to convince this woman to marry him. He wanted her to see what he saw when he looked at her. And so, for the first time in his life, he spoke his heart to a woman.

He cupped her jaw with his right hand, feeling the tension in the muscles beneath the warm skin. "I don't see a crippled, destitute Rebel spy when I look at you. I see an intelligent, resourceful, courageous young woman who has survived well without me."

His thumb drew soft circles on her cheek, and he felt her lean into its caressing strength. "I think the time for her to fight life alone has ended. I want to be her champion, to take up her fight and help her win."

"I can't marry you, Yankee."

"Not even for Destiny?"

He felt no twinge of remorse when he played his ace. If she wouldn't have him for himself, then she might marry him in order to get her horse back. Hadn't she said she would follow the horse into hell?

CHAPTER FIFTEEN

"The best way to keep a Rebel spy from talking's to cut out his tongue."

"And we don't want him watching any more troop movements, so we'll jist pop out his eyes."

"What about his ears? He's been using them against us, too."

The knife blade flashed in the sunlight. Billie screamed, but the downward swing of the knife didn't stop.

With a sudden jerk, she snapped her eyes open. Rough-hewn wood festooned with a spider web met her startled gaze. Her heart pounded as if she'd run miles through heavy woods with a pack of wild hogs on her heels. A drop of sweat trickled from her temples into her hairline.

She hadn't dreamed about Stephen in a long time.

Home for a quick visit, he had been captured by a group of Union soldiers who accused him of spying for the Confederacy. Then they tortured him. No one knew for sure what the Federals had done to him, but rumors of the atrocities raced through the community like a lightning-lit wildfire.

The rumors gained substance when the family insisted on a closed casket at the funeral. Billie should have insisted on seeing Stephen. Seeing him would have been easier than dealing with what she'd heard: The soldiers had sliced off his ears, scalped him, gouged out his eyes, and cut out his tongue. Supposely, the Federals had been amazed at what Stephen withstood without confessing.

He hadn't confessed, because he had nothing to confess. He had taken a leave from his unit to come home and visit his family. He was a soldier, not a spy.

Nothing had happened to the Federals. No court of law had sought vengeance for Stephen.

It should have been her. She was the spy.

She stared at the ceiling beams. The web vibrated as a black spider danced across the slender silk strands. She snuggled deeper into her blankets, then winced. The movement woke muscles that ached from hours of trying to set fence posts in the hard Texas soil. Had she set herself an impossible task with this horse-breeding venture? She wondered if Shaughnessy would return with her, but knew he was getting too old to help build a corral on rocks.

She refused to think about the futility of her plan if she failed to rescue Destiny.

Low, rumbling snores sounded from below her. She tried to ignore them, but the Yankee drew her, and she peeked over the side of the bed. He had positioned himself on the floor next to her bed. She had been too tired to test his claim that he would awaken if she tried to sneak out and steal his horse.

He slept in his clothes, his head pillowed on his saddlebags. She studied the Yankee in the gray light of the dawn. He had the most beautiful mouth she had ever seen on a man. It rivaled the mouths sculpted on the statues of Greek gods in the Fairmount garden. His lips certainly belonged on something immortal. Unbidden, the memory of those lips feathering softly across her mouth crept into her mind. An ache that had nothing to do with sore muscles rippled through her lower abdomen.

Sensations from the previous day echoed in her memory. This man had taught her body new feelings she found difficult to forget. With a sigh, she propped her chin on her hand and stared at him. What would it be like to wake up in his arms? To sleep beside him without two feet of dirt and air between them? To feel his well-muscled thighs gripping her as tightly as they did his horse?

As warm as she was, there was no reason to stir up the fire. Her gaze slid from his mouth to his well-shaped nose—one that would look nice on his future children. As would the dark brown eyebrows that bordered his brow. It was a pleasant change for them to be smooth rather than snapping together with disapproval. Ah, yes, she liked the view, and her left hand itched to reach down and run over the sleep-softened contours of his face.

She licked lips anxious to kiss his eyes open. During their acquaintance, she had watched his eyes narrow with displeasure, widen in surprise, and soften with concern. Yesterday she had seen them drunk with passion, and it had taken all her self-control not to drown in their gray depths.

Even as she recalled their potency, his eyes opened.

"Good morning." His sleep-roughened voice caressed her spine with tiny shivers. "I'm glad you didn't steal the horse. It's a long walk back to town."

A liquid heat of desire flickered in her veins. It had to be some kind of spell, this sudden wanting of the Yankee. What it needed was a good dousing in cold water. She pushed aside her blanket and welcomed the rush of cool morning air against her fevered skin. "I'll stir up the fire."

Grayson tightened the cinch on the horse's saddle one last time before leading him out of the small barn. The drumming sound of hoofbeats met him at the doorway, and he could see half a dozen men headed for the ranch.

He dropped the reins, his first thought for Billie. She was pushing aside the deerskin, rifle in hand, when he reached the cabin.

Pushing her back inside, he said, "I'll take care of this." She looked too damn feminine for his peace of mind. "Cover your curls. And for God's sake, put on your coat."

"If they're after the ranch, I've got a deed."

As if a piece of paper would stop men whose accessories ran to guns and knives. As the group of men brought their horses to a noisy halt a few feet from him, Grayson caught the glint of sunlight off metal on the chest of a man whose frame flowed over the smallish horse he rode. A large finger rose to tap the brim of a dusty hat.

"Mornin'."

"Good morning, Sheriff." He wondered what mischief Dewey might have created before leaving Texas.

"Deputy—Deputy Sheriff Weisser's the name."

Grayson kept his tone casual. "Pleased to meet you, Deputy Weisser."

The large man shifted his massive bulk. Grayson was surprised the horse took no notice.

"We're looking for the boy who lives here."

"Oh." Grayson's mind raced with explanations for whatever lie Dewey had told. He decided it was best to admit Billie was there, because it was too easy to search the cabin.

"What's that rapscallion been up to?"

"Bank robbery."

"Why, that's ridiculous! I never robbed a bank in my life."

Billie's angry appearance brought the guns swinging from their holsters. Grayson stepped between her and the men. Now he had her rifle pointed at his back and five hand guns pointed at his chest.

"Billie, my boy." He stressed the word "boy," trusting that

no one had noticed her genteel diction and that she would revert to character before anyone did. "Let's give Deputy Weisser a chance to explain." His tone was mild, meant to soothe her ruffled feathers.

"But I ain't no bank robber."

He heard the familiar whine with relief.

"As if I ain't heard bank robbers say that heaps and cords of times," the deputy retorted. "Sheriff Boggart told us to bring you in. I'm gonna bring you in."

"It seems there's a young man robbing banks in the area. Unfortunately, you fit the description. I think we'd best accept our escort into town, where I'm sure we can straighten this out with the sheriff." Before Billie could protest, he took her rifle and handed it to the deputy.

"Yes, sir. Sheriff Boggart's a right smart man. If the boy ain't the one robbing banks, why, he won't keep him in jail."

"How could I have time to rob banks?" Billie grumbled as she followed Grayson to his horse. "I been digging holes since I got here."

Swinging into the saddle, he pulled her up to sit behind him. This was going to be sweet torture, having her body pressed to his and her warm arms clasped around his waist. And he couldn't steal a kiss, or six grown men would shoot him for being a pervert.

Sheriff Boggart was waiting in his office when the deputy escorted them into the room. Grayson breathed a small sigh when he saw an older man who appeared to be a tad brighter than his large minion.

"Vanderlyn's the name, Sheriff. Grayson Vanderlyn." Hand outstretched, smile on his face, Grayson took the initiative. "I believe there's been a mistake concerning my young friend—"

"Grayson Vanderlyn? *The* Grayson Vanderlyn that writes books?"

Grayson stretched his smile farther. "Yes, sir. I claim that dubious honor."

"The hell you say! If it ain't Grayson Vanderlyn!" The sheriff turned to glare ferociously at his deputy.

"I didn't arrest Mr. Vanderlyn. No sir, I arrested the boy, just like you tole me." With that disclaimer, the deputy shoved Billie into the center of the room. "The boy says he ain't no bank robber, but I tole him you'd be the one to decide."

"Don't be a complete horse's arse, Jerry. This here's Grayson Vanderlyn. My God, he writes books. Fine books, too, Mr. Vanderlyn." The sheriff rubbed his hands together. "This here's an honor."

"Yes. Well, about my friend . . ."

The sheriff waved his hand. "No problem. This boy don't look nothing like the picture on the poster, and he ain't near tall enough. If you say the young 'un ain't a bank robber, Mr. Vanderlyn, then I take your word for it. Truth is, I didn't like the looks of the man who claimed the boy was a bank robber. Shifty sort, don't you know?"

Billie muttered something, but Grayson ignored her.

"Well, thank you, Sheriff. We're happy to have that cleared up." Grayson turned to herd Billie out the door before she said something loud enough for the sheriff and his deputy to hear.

"Anytime, Mr. Vanderlyn. You know, I've been anxious for you to write another book now the war's over. Are you thinking of writing a book about Texas?" He paused, a puzzled look on his face; then his expression lightened. "Oh, I see it now. Captain Dinsmere coming down the Mississippi River with some Indians, maybe as their captive?"

Grayson wasn't sure which delighted him more, the sheriff's fawning attention or the scowl that kept Billie's features from appearing too feminine. When he mentioned they were staying in town for a few days, her scowl grew more ferocious. And when the deputy, eager to please the sheriff, volunteered the information that his mother ran a boardinghouse and had an empty room, Grayson thought Billie snarled.

Room. He liked the singular sound of that word.

Billie didn't.

Nor did she like the idea of being alone with the Yankee in the small room Mrs. Weisser showed them. She waited until their landlady left to throw her blanket roll on the one bed, narrowly missing the Yankee's head. He had stretched himself out on it before Mrs. Weisser closed the door properly.

"What are you doing? Why'd you tell the sheriff we'd be here a few days? And agree to let him show you the town!"

The Yankee laced his hands together behind his head and crossed his long legs at the ankle. When he closed his eyes, she wanted to rip the pillow from under his head and put it over his face.

"If you're referring to the fact the sheriff offered to show me the telegraph office later today, I need to telegraph my brother." The Yankee snuggled deeper into the bed. "Since your friend Dewey stole my money, I have to ask Darrell to send more. We also need money to buy you a horse unless you're planning to ride double to Galveston."

The notion of spending several days pressed intimately to the Yankee's buttocks and clinging to his narrow waist silenced her protests. She couldn't like the laughter she heard dancing in his crisp Yankee tone, either. The man was enjoying himself entirely too much. What she needed to do was rob one of those banks she had been accused of robbing. Then she would have money and wouldn't have *him* interfering in her life and making her feel things she didn't want to feel.

As he lay comfortably stretched out on the bed, those infernal gray eyes that didn't miss a thing drifted open. "Unless you need me for something, I'm going to take a quick nap. From the look on your face, I know I'm going to end up on the floor again tonight."

And from the leer on his face, she knew he'd prefer sleeping with her. "No one's forcing you to traipse around the countryside. It's your foolish notion Destiny belongs to you, not mine."

"And it's my foolish notion that by combining forces, we can rout the enemy." His bantering tone took on a serious edge. "Marriage would protect you from Seyler's claim of guardianship, you know. I'm sure it wouldn't be difficult to find a Catholic priest to perform the ceremony."

And then he would do all those wondrous things to her body every night. Perhaps even in the daylight hours. She marched past his half-closed but too perceptive gray eyes to the door. "I'm going to stable the horse."

"While you're there, would you see if there's one we can buy?"

She paused before she pulled the door open. "I'll sleep on the floor tonight."

Loud, staccato knocks brought Grayson awake with a disoriented start. It took him several thudding heartbeats to gain his bearings. Rolling out of the bed, he opened the door. He had meant to take a short nap because his previous night's sleep had been cradled between a hard dirt floor and lurid images of Billie. From the looks of the sky outside the window, he'd slept away half the afternoon.

"Sorry to disturb you, but Sheriff Boggart said to tell you Dellwood has to take a telgram out to the Diamond D. If you want to send yours, you need to get over there now."

Grayson ran his hand through his hair. "Thanks, Deputy. I guess the time got away with me. Tell the sheriff I'll join him in two minutes."

Pouring some water into the basin, he splashed his face with the cool water and chased away the sluggish feeling he got when he napped at odd hours. He pulled a comb from his pocket, ran it through his hair, and then settled his hat on his head. He cast a quick look around the room. It didn't appear

Billie had returned while he slept. She was probably wrangling with the stable man over a horse.

But she wasn't at the stable when he checked after sending Darrell a telegram. His horse was gone, too. In fact, the hostler hadn't seen anyone fitting Billie's description all day.

When Grayson returned to the boardinghouse, he found Deputy Weisser in a chair on the porch. Feet propped on the railing, he whittled on a piece of wood.

Grayson stopped by the hitching post where the deputy's horse stood. "Have you seen Billie?"

"Yep."

Grayson reined in his impatience. "I'm sorry to sound rude, Deputy, but the boy appears to be missing. Along with my horse."

"I wondered if the boy was stealing your horse when he rode off."

"You saw him?"

The deputy stopped whittling and folded up his knife. "Yep. He rode toward the river right after Ma showed y'all the room. It might take me some persuading to get a posse together even if it is to go after a horse thief. Old Elyard says there's a norther on the way."

Grayson untied the deputy's horse.

"Here, now, whatcha think you're doing?" Weisser said.

"I'm borrowing your horse." He gathered the reins and swung himself into the saddle. "And Billie's no horse thief—if anything, she's a heart thief."

"She?" The front legs of Weisser's chair hit the porch with a loud thud. "The hell you say! That boy's a girl?"

"No." He turned the horse toward the river. "She's a woman, and I plan to marry her," he said over his shoulder. "Can you get me a priest? Telegraph San Antonio for one if you have to, but get a priest here."

"Wait a minute!"

Grayson let the horse dance around to face the deputy, his body tensed for an attack.

"Don't worry," said the deputy, "you can use the horse, but Elyard ain't usually wrong about these things, and he swears there's a norther coming."

Grayson relaxed. "And?"

"You'll freeze your arse off when it hits. The cold comes right quick-like. One minute it's a warm spring day. The next minute you think you're in one of them there icebergs Sheriff Boggart told me about. Give me a few minutes to gather you some ponchos."

When Weisser returned, he tossed a bundle of boldly striped material into Grayson's hand. "Tie that to the saddle with those rawhide thongs. Ma put some biscuits in there, too."

Weisser went to the horse's head while Grayson tied the ponchos to the saddle. "This here horse is a real jewel, Mr. Vanderlyn. She don't look like much, but Dandelion's got heart. And she knows her way home—why, she brung me right to this here porch in a snowfall one night. And if you get off 'er, she'll stay put as long as you leave the reins dangling to the ground. She was a cow pony I got off a stockman what went broke during the war."

"Thank you, Deputy." Grayson leaned forward and extended his right hand. He kept his smile at the horse's name hidden. "I shall return Dandelion to you quickly and in good health."

Billie stopped the horse at the edge of the Guadalupe River. The horse stirred restlessly as if he suspected she wanted him to cross the fast-running water. The Guadalupe didn't look any more frightening than the Cumberland, but she had always been on Destiny when she crossed that river. She had also crossed at well-marked fords, but this afternoon she'd shied away from the usual crossings. If the Yankee was behind her, she had no desire to make it easier for him to find her.

After finding a good spot, she would have to coax the horse into the river. She might as well accustom herself to swimming the horse across rivers, since several others lay between her and Galveston.

"Get up, boy. We won't get across the river by staring at it." She talked to the horse as much to build her own courage as his. Guiding him along the riverbank, she searched the river for a shallow place. With her attention on the river, she never realized the danger until the bank, softened by the overflow of spring flooding, caved under the combined weight of horse and rider.

With a shrill whinny of fear, the horse scrambled on the mud-slicked rocks to avoid sliding into the river. The ground kept crumbling beneath its iron-shod hooves while the panicked animal fought to retain its footing. Billie struggled to free her feet of the stirrups. The horse's body twisted beneath her as it lost the fight to stay upright. Another equine cry of fear tore through the spring afternoon as the horse slid on its side into the river.

She jumped free of the horse at the river's edge, but the rock-strewn soil of Texas, not the tilled soil of Tennessee, awaited her. She hit the ground hard, her head cracking into a large rock. The sounds of the rushing river, the horse's cries, and her own jagged breathing slammed into black silence.

Time meant nothing to her. The blackness dissolved, but she wasn't sprawled on a riverbank. Instead, she seemed to be floating above her body. Below, she could see herself tangled in a young river birch whose slender arms cradled her upper torso and held her head out of the churning water. An ugly gash on her temple oozed blood in a small rivulet down her face.

Then she saw Stephen. Not the Stephen the soldiers had left, but the Stephen she had known. Joy blossomed in her heart.

"Have you come for me? Where do I go now? Am I dead?"

But Stephen didn't answer. He didn't go away, but he didn't communicate with her, either. He hovered beside her and stared at her body as if he were waiting for someone.

She didn't mind that he didn't answer any more than she minded hovering over her old body. A feeling of peace unlike any she had ever experienced flowed through her. Everything was light and beautiful, and she felt no sadness or pain.

As she floated beside Stephen and awaited what was to come, she saw the Yankee. He was riding Deputy Weisser's horse and leading her mud-splattered mount when he found her. She was surprised at the horror and fear she saw etched on his face as he flung himself off the horse and raced for her body.

"Billie!" His crisp Northern accent rang through the anguish in his voice.

She smiled at Stephen. He must have known the Yankee was looking for her. How kind to let her see that the Yankee cared about her. Now that she had seen him, it must be time to go. A wisp of sadness wove through her heart because she had spurned his offer of marriage, but bittersweet pleasure trailed behind it. The Yankee cared about her. Too bad she had learned this truth when she was dead.

But the Yankee didn't think she was dead.

"Billie! Hang on, Billie, I'm coming!" He scrambled down the crumbling riverbank, sliding through the mud to pull her free of the tree limbs. Then he crawled back up the riverbank, half carrying, half pulling her limp body. Rolling her onto the top of the bank, he pushed her beyond the rain-sodden edge.

"You're all right, Billie. Everything's going to be all right."

Pushing aside her shirt, he pressed his fingers against her neck. Unadulterated joy lit his face. "That's my girl. You just keep that heart beating. I'll do the rest."

He moved with incredible speed to bind the wound on her forehead and strip off her sodden clothing. She should have been embarrassed at his actions, exposing her body before Stephen, but she was cocooned by the peace that surrounded her. Then the Yankee stripped off his own clothes.

She suddenly wished she weren't dead. Her Yankee—Fletcher had been right to call him that—possessed an incredibly beautiful male body. She longed to reach out and run her fingers across the wide shoulders and then trail down the well-muscled back to stroke the firm buttocks. His thigh was scarred on the left side. A puckered white line furrowed its way across the thickest part of his leg. Her Yankee had not escaped the war unscathed.

His body wasn't hers to admire for long. Within seconds of stripping off his clothes, he had wrapped them both in blankets.

"Come on, Angel, come back to me. Please."

She longed to be with him, but she longed as strongly for the peace that enveloped her.

"Come back to me. Give me a chance to make you love me as I love you."

He loved her?

She could feel his frantic kisses on her ice-cold eyelids, his warm breath on her face, and his hands rubbing the circulation back into her arms and legs and torso. She could smell the indescribable male scent that belonged only to him and that would have sent her own senses spinning if they hadn't been too cold to spin.

And she felt him pulling her back from the brink.

She also felt rather than heard Stephen telling her it was all right to want to go back.

So she did, slipping as easily back into her body as she had slipped out of it.

Grayson pulled Billie's nude body against his own. God, she was cold, as cold as death itself. But she wasn't dead, because he had found a weak pulse beating in her neck. He refused to let her die—not when he had just found her. But she was blue with cold, and he had seen death often enough on the battlefield to recognize when it hovered nearby.

Its presence made him fight all the harder as he tried to infuse her with his body's warmth. When her teeth first clicked, he almost missed it, but they clicked again, and again until they were chattering with cold. It was the sweetest sound he'd heard in a long time. With a quiet prayer of thanks, he renewed his efforts to warm her.

"Come on, Angel," he said as he snuggled her breasts against his chest and rubbed his hands down her back to curve around her derriere. "You know you haven't finished sassing me yet."

True to Weisser's prediction, an icy-cold wind swept across the sky, pushing any clouds it found back into the Gulf of Mexico. The sun had disappeared, as if displeased by the intrusion of the cold and unwilling to fight over the issue.

He rubbed Billie until he thought she had warmed enough for him to leave her. Slipping quickly from the warm asylum he had created, he grabbed his own damp, chilly clothes. A biting wind chilled him, but he was afraid to take any of the ponchos from Billie.

Dandelion proved to be every inch the well-mannered horse her owner had claimed. She didn't shy away from him when he approached her with Billie and awkwardly swung both of them onto her back. And she carried her heavy burden back to Seguin through the dark countryside.

Mrs. Weisser and a doctor took over the care of his bride-to-be as soon as they reached the boardinghouse. After all, a single young gentleman didn't belong in a single young lady's bedroom, now, did he? And the only way he would get there as far as Mrs. Weisser was concerned was after the young lady recovered her strength and a priest married them. If the poor lamb did recover. The doctor expected pneumonia at the very least after her exposure to the cold and water.

The doctor's expectations were met, but Mrs. Weisser's

were not. Grayson didn't stay out of Billie's room once he had warmed himself with a bath and a change of clothing. Only the actual mouthing of the words stood between him and "in sickness and in health."

Perhaps it was the severity of her illness, or the fear she would leave him again rather than marry him. He never knew what prompted him to do what he did while Billie was ill, but he did know it was the only way it could be accomplished.

And it was for her own good.

CHAPTER SIXTEEN

First she was cold, so cold she ached with it. Then she was hot, burning with a fire that she knew could not be found outside Hades. But she was alive. Stephen had shown her death, and this was not death.

Nor was death something to be feared. It was something to be embraced. She tried to smile at the priest who appeared by her bed, because she wanted him to know she wasn't frightened. Inhaling the familiar scents of the priestly profession that clung to his robes, she welcomed the last rites.

"Tell the priest you will. You can do it, Angel. Concentrate. Say the words."

She knew that voice; it had ordered her back to life. Then it had persisted in interrupting her sleep with various demands such as sitting up and drinking broth. She had done whatever the voice told her to do for a long time. She would again.

"I will." She didn't recognize the faint voice, raspy with disuse. As soon as she said those two words, she fell asleep—the deep, untroubled sleep of the exhausted.

When she awoke again, it was night, because the room was shrouded in darkness. Awareness wove into her sluggish brain. First she was aware of the darkness of the room; then she was aware her body no longer burned with heat or shivered with cold. She felt alive—incredibly weak, but alive.

She shifted on the bed, stretching her stiff muscles with the languor of a sleepy kitten.

Her bare hip bumped into something solid.

Something warm.

Something firmly muscled.

Something naked.

Something in bed with her.

She lifted her hand and trailed it down the body lying beside her. There was a man asleep beside her in the bed.

Fear had no time to register. Her senses, newly awakened, signaled the man's identity: the Yankee.

She also knew this was no accidental napping. It was late night and he was naked. And she was naked, too. She could feel the rough brush of the hair on his leg against her bare leg.

A thousand thoughts raced through her mind. Jumbled images that held little meaning vied for interpretation. She tried to sort them out, but her brain wouldn't cooperate. In fact, her brain and body had no interest in anything except more sleep. . . .

It was daylight when she awoke the second time. She found herself curled beside the Yankee as if they had always slept together. His arm draped her waist, locking her against his chest.

"Good morning, Angel."

Warm breath tickled her right ear. Heat pooled in her stomach. A knob of hard flesh pressed into her spine. She tried to inch away from him. His grasp didn't slacken.

Her brain hadn't worked much since the horse dumped her into the river, and now she was expected to figure out all the implications of finding the Yankee in her bed?

"I'm too weak to protest your presence in my bed." She closed her eyes. Sleep had saved her from facing the issue earlier; perhaps when she awoke again he would be gone.

"That won't work this time."

Her eyes flickered open. She felt the blush start at her toes and work its way up her body to her face. Had he been awake when she found him beside her the first time? Had he expected some protest then? He wasn't being fair; she was too weak to figure it all out and too weak to argue.

Since he wouldn't let her roll away, she rolled into him. The Yankee peered down at her with half-closed eyes that held a hint of drowsiness.

"You needn't worry about the propriety of our sleeping together. It's perfectly legal."

"Legal?" Vaguely she remembered another time when her voice had been rusty with disuse. *"I will. . . . I will. . . . I will."* A sinking sensation trickled through her stomach. "The priest wasn't here to perform the last rites, was he?"

"Oh, he insisted on performing the last rites, too. He didn't believe you were going to survive. I, on the other hand, had all the faith in the world that you were going to live."

"And you had him marry us?"

"It seemed like a good idea at the time."

Her brain was incredibly sluggish. It didn't seem able to comprehend what the Yankee had done. He had married her? She would insist on seeing the paperwork. And the priest.

"It won't work. Once I explain the situation, the priest will annul the marriage."

"He won't. He knows we've slept together."

Her hand fluttered weakly to her stomach. Had the villainous Yankee planted his seed in her while she was too ill to stop him, and worse, too ill to recall the experience?

He nuzzled her neck, spinning her questions into oblivion.

"This is the best way to win." He spoke softly against her throat.

"Win what?"

"Why, Destiny, of course. It'll be difficult for a court of law to deny two legitimate claims."

She couldn't think with his hand curving up her thigh and trailing over her waist as if he had intimate knowledge of her body. Her memory sang with the delicious feelings his hands created when they touched her body, but panic trembled on the edge of pleasure. She didn't know how to deal with the uncharted feelings his touch generated.

To her relief, his hand continued upward to pull the blanket snugly over her shoulders. "There will be no annulment. Now go back to sleep."

Sleep sounded good. She'd argue better after she rested.

Grayson watched Billie fall back asleep before brushing his lips across her forehead. Her sweet scent filled his nostrils, and he wanted to bury his nose in her neck and breathe in her essence.

He had peopled his novels with villains, yet none were as bad as he. None had tricked a woman weak with dying into marriage. A modicum of remorse tickled his conscience, but he suppressed it. Sliding his hands under the blankets, he ran them lightly across her body. She was a soft, curved, unexplored terrain waiting to be surveyed and mapped by him. And oh, so very feminine.

She was also his.

To protect. To cherish. To love.

A strong, unexpected wave of possessiveness swept over him. She needed him as no other human being had ever needed him. He had saved her life and nursed her back to health. Now he would tend her heart. And with time, she would learn to love him.

But he would tread lightly at first. He recognized that some demon dogged her waking hours, but one day she would snuggle as eagerly into his embrace awake as she did now while she slept. One day her mind would follow where her body so readily went.

He was sure of it.

His right hand curled over the hand she had laid on her stomach. He ran his thumb up and down each finger, gently massaging the newly soft skin. In the long vigil beside her bed, he had rubbed lotion into her rough, callused hands. There would be no more shovels full of horse manure or caliche in Mrs. Grayson Vanderlyn's future. There would be maids and grooms.

And children.

He was hard with wanting her, but that could wait. Oh, yes, that could wait.

"Feeling a bit more the thing?"

Billie blinked her eyes, too groggy with sleep to answer the woman standing beside the bed.

The bed. She turned her head to see if the Yankee was beside her.

"If you're looking for your husband, dear soul that he is, he's gone to buy you something to wear besides a nightgown."

Billie remembered her former state of nudity and slid down into the bedclothes. She felt the brush of cotton against her thighs as a nightgown failed to slide with her.

Mrs. Weisser.

Billie recognized the woman who had shown them to their room that first day.

"Why don't you just sit up while I fix those pillows for you?"

Billie obediently sat up.

"You've certainly got yourself a wonderful husband, Mrs. Vanderlyn." Mrs. Weisser seized a pillow and gave it a good thump.

Confused, Billie looked around the room for the Yankee's mother.

"Why, your husband hardly left your side this past week. I had to insist he eat and sleep. I told him it wouldn't do you any good at all to wake up and find him ill, I did." She gave the second pillow a whack before she positioned them both behind Billie's shoulders. "There, now. That should do it."

Husband? Billie leaned back into the pillows. She felt as if she'd awakened into a nightmare even though the morning sun streamed through the window behind Mrs. Weisser, bright enough to make her eyes ache.

"The Yankee can't be my husband—"

"Of course, you don't remember." The older woman patted Billie's shoulder with motherly solicitude. "That dear man didn't want your soul to burn in hell because you two had sinned. Now it's all right and tight between you and your Maker.

"How about a sip of water?" Mrs. Weisser didn't wait for Billie to answer. She filled a glass with water from a pitcher beside the bed. "Your throat sounds awful dry."

Billie took the glass. The scent of minerals wafted to her nose when she drank, but cool water eased the dryness in her throat.

"Mr. Vanderlyn had a priest here and everything," Mrs. Weisser continued. "Why, I was one of the witnesses."

Billie felt a noose closing around her neck. Witnesses? For some reason she hadn't believed the Yankee's claim. What was there to believe when a Yankee spoke? But witnesses?

"It was so romantic. Why, we were sure you were as good as dead, and yet Mr. Vanderlyn insisted on the priest reading the marriage vows over you. The priest wasn't too eager to do it, I can tell you. I think your husband promised him a new roof for his chapel, or was it a new bell tower?" Mrs. Weisser shrugged. "It makes no never mind what he promised. You're married, all legal-like."

Billie wanted to sink back into the oblivion of sleep.

"There won't be many pretty dresses at our dry goods,

but I'm sure Mr. Vanderlyn will see that you get lots of new clothes when you reach Galveston."

"New Orleans, I think, will have the best selection."

The Yankee stood in the doorway, several paper-wrapped parcels in his hands. The smile on his face made Billie's heart beat a little faster. When he walked across the room, she couldn't help wondering if her fevered hands had caressed the hard, muscular planes of his well-formed male body . . . and forgotten.

"But I can't have my wife traveling to New Orleans in her nightgown." He placed his packages on the bed and began untying the string that wrapped the largest one. The dress he shook free of the paper and string was a simple calico.

"What a pretty green. I do believe you've matched Mrs. Vanderlyn's eyes."

"I tried."

Female undergarments joined the dress on the bed, but it was the final package that snagged Billie's attention. It was a pair of ladies' half boots whose left heel was slightly thicker than the right. They were a delightful change from the rough work boots she had worn this past year.

"Why don't I run down to the kitchen and heat you some broth, Mrs. Vanderlyn?"

She barely noticed Mrs. Weisser's departure. Her fingers were stroking the supple leather of a half boot. "You tempt me. Oh, how you tempt me."

"Who would have thought a woman would be tempted by a pair of boots?" mused the Yankee. "Flowers and jewelry are the traditional items of temptation."

She dragged her gaze, but not her fingers, from the new boots. "No matter how you tempt me, I can't stay married to you."

"And why not?"

She couldn't keep the irritation from her voice. "I've told you why. You're a Yankee."

"And I've told you, Angel." The Yankee's voice was gentle but firm. "The war's over. Yank. Reb. We're all Americans."

"The war's not over for Seyler." Fatigue tugged at her body, but she had to convince him they could not remain married, no matter how many pairs of shoes he gave her. "If he finds out we're married, that I have a protector, he'll kill Destiny. I can't lose Destiny. He's my future." He was also her past. Losing Destiny would sever her last link with her father and the horse farm.

The Yankee pried her fingers off the boots. She watched him place them on the bedclothes before he grasped her cold hands. Warmth from his hands spilled onto hers.

"Tell me why Seyler would kill Destiny."

She had trouble thinking with his freshly shaved face so near her own. The faint scent of shaving soap, mingled with the bay rum he seemed to favor, curled its way into her nostrils and muddled her argument. His proximity, scent, and warm gray eyes set off that throbbing sensation in her lower abdomen again. She leaned backward, pushed her head into the pillows, and refused to remember the chair incident. With effort, she quashed her reaction to the Yankee and concentrated on answering his question.

"If Seyler finds out I'm married, he won't be able to fulfill his plans for me. Destiny will no longer be a means to an end."

The Yankee squeezed her hands slightly. "Look at me."

She couldn't. Her gaze locked on their clasped hands. Embarrassment washed over her as she realized how rough and callused her hands were compared to his. How many times had she watched his long, slender fingers wield eating utensils or a sketching pencil while she marveled at their grace? Hands that befitted an artist. Hands that had been shaped with the same loving care nature had bestowed upon his face.

While her hands had become tools of another trade that

required hours of shoveling and raised thick calluses. She tried to tug free of his grasp, but he wouldn't release her hands. Then he loosened his grip and turned her hands over, exposing the palms.

To her astonishment, her hands were soft and smooth. She lifted her right hand from his loose grasp. A close examination revealed traces of the calluses, but the skin was soft, almost as soft as it had been five years ago. Lightly she ran her fingers across first one palm and then the other.

"Aunt Maria would be happy to see my hands this smooth. Each time I stayed with her, she had me soak my hands in special potions and rub lotion into them. She was positive gloves were all that stood between me and social disgrace."

She stared at her smooth hands as she wrestled with how best to answer the Yankee's question. Months of hiding the truth from the enemy made it difficult to suddenly share confidences with him. But the war was over, she told herself. And she was tired of shouldering her problems alone.

"Billie, look at me," the Yankee repeated.

Reluctantly she pulled her gaze from her hands.

"I promise to protect you from this spawn of the devil, but I need to know what threats he has made against you."

She felt the tiny smile dance unbidden onto her mouth when he used Shaughnessy's favorite description of Seyler. Then her smile faded as she wondered if the Yankee wooed her as a path to Destiny. But she found it difficult to believe he had married her to get Destiny. It was a step she could take because she would do anything to keep her horse.

This marriage, if she let it stand, proved she would.

Marriage.

To the Yankee.

Forever.

Her imagination galloped in another direction that made her body flush warmly, but she refused to follow that path.

If she let the marriage stand, and if he traveled with her to

Tennessee, then he needed to know what type of man awaited them. Although mere words could never describe Seyler's depravity, mere words were all she had.

While these thoughts wove their way through her brain, she absently caressed the smooth skin of her hands. The vision of him patiently rubbing lotion into her cracked and callused skin swayed her toward accepting the marriage.

The mere whisper of mental acceptance brought a barrage of implications that led far beyond the present goal of retrieving Destiny. If she allowed the marriage to stand, she would belong to the Yankee. As his wife, she would have to do whatever he commanded and go wherever he took her.

She would no longer be free.

But she would have Destiny.

No, the Yankee would have Destiny. As her husband, he owned all her property.

Her head ached with trying to decide what to do.

"Billie?" His voice stilled her whirling thoughts as his grasp stilled the restless motion of her hands. She slowly brought her gaze up to his.

"I realize this is a difficult situation for you. To come close to death and awaken to find yourself married. But believe me, I acted in your own best interests. In essence I tricked you because I saw no other sensible solution to our problem."

He leaned toward her, and the persistent tug on her hands brought her closer to him. For one panicked yet hopeful moment, she feared he was going to kiss her.

"I have a suggestion to make this situation more palatable to you."

Uneasiness stirred through her veins. "What kind of suggestion?"

In the quiet, suspended moment, intuition told her she wasn't going to like his suggestion.

"After we get Destiny, we can file for divorce."

"Divorce!" She jerked her hands away from him. "That's impossible. You had a priest marry us."

"I thought you'd prefer having a priest do the ceremony."

"Of course I prefer a priest performing a marriage ceremony. But you don't understand. The Church doesn't give out divorces willy-nilly unless you're a king or something, and even then it's almost impossible. I'm sure you've read of Henry the Eighth. When the Church wouldn't agree to his divorce from Catherine of Aragon, he set up his own Church in England. Believe me, an annulment would be easier."

"Well, that's impossible."

She couldn't like the flat finality of his tone.

"No priest," he said, "will grant an annulment to a couple who have spent an entire week in a bedroom together. Mrs. Weisser has been quite vocal about how lovingly I've tended to your every need."

She felt the blood drain from her face. "My *every* need?"

"Your every need. We're married in the eyes of God and man. I've offered to help you rescue Destiny and deal with Seyler. If our marriage is too repulsive for you, we can separate after we find Destiny. I'm on my way to Colorado to do some mapping for a train company. You can bring Destiny back to Texas and continue with your life."

A thousand questions assaulted her exhausted brain: What about his life in New York? His books? And most important, his former fiancée. Would he one day regret this hasty marriage that had cut him off from reconciling with his first love? The uncertainties battered at her, but she was too tired to deal with them.

A knock on the bedroom door kept her from answering him. When the Yankee opened the door, she caught a whiff of chicken soup, but hunger and the murmuring voices couldn't keep her eyes from slipping closed.

* * *

Grayson stared out the rain-wet window onto the muddy street in front of the boardinghouse. He hadn't wanted to suggest a separation after they retrieved the horse, but he hadn't wanted Billie to become overset, either. Her agitation at the news of their marriage had not meshed with the doctor's orders of complete quiet and rest.

Letting the dimity curtain fall gently back into place, he turned to look at Billie. She had been sleeping for several hours, but he expected hunger to awaken her soon. Settling himself into the overstuffed chair Mrs. Weisser had offered for his use at the onset of Billie's illness, he contemplated his bride.

He grinned at the memory of her reaction to his announcement he had cared for her every need. In truth, he could draw her body from memory; she had been his in every way except one, and if he wooed her properly, he hoped to demolish the last barrier before they reached Tennessee.

Even as he watched, the sound of her breathing changed and lost the deep, even pace of sleep. Taking the hand that lay alongside her thigh into his own, he waited for her to awaken. His patience was rewarded when a pair of drowsy green eyes looked at him. The sleepiness fled quickly, to be replaced by silent reproach.

"I kept the broth warm while you slept. Are you ready to eat?"

Her stomach answered for her, growling in response to the aroma of chicken broth that filled the small room. He pulled her limp body forward, feeling her stiffen slightly as he positioned the pillows behind her back.

Easing her gently back down to the pillows, he said, "I've always found it easier to eat while sitting upright, haven't you?"

Although he longed to run his hand down her spine and mold her buttocks with his fingers, he didn't. He kept his hands on the business of making her comfortable while she ate. He knew he had to touch her to calm her fears, but he had to touch her in nonsexual, nonthreatening ways. She had to be seduced without knowing she was being seduced, until she came to him of her own accord. He could only hope he wouldn't go crazy with wanting her before she welcomed him into her body.

He filled a bowl with broth from the pot Mrs. Weisser had nestled near the hot coals in the fireplace. Billie still hadn't said anything, nor did she protest when he offered her a spoonful of soup. Obediently she opened her mouth. He concentrated on the spoon, making himself ignore the way her tongue slipped out to catch the drops of liquid that clung to her lips. He could feel that same tongue licking its way along his . . .

"Seyler won't kill me outright. He has . . . special plans for me."

Her words shattered his fantasies of what he longed for her tongue to do to him. "Special plans?"

She weighed her answer before she spoke. "Seyler's going to rape me. When he's had his fill of me, he plans to put me in a brothel frequented by Union soldiers."

A hot, burning rage surged through him and shook the hand scooping up the next spoonful of soup. He slowed his actions and focused on the ritual of transferring soup from the bowl to her mouth, defusing the anger that consumed him. The slight quiver that trembled across her lips when she opened her mouth to accept the spoon was nearly his undoing. He wanted to kiss away her fears and slay her dragons.

Rather than do that, he withdrew the spoon and announced, "You'll stay here while I return to Tennessee and get Destiny."

Her green eyes flashed with brittle outrage. "And let you take Destiny back to New York? Not on your life. I'm going after Destiny, with you or without you."

To her obvious dismay, the show of defiance used up most of her strength. Her mouth twisted into an angry moue as she sank weakly back into the pillows.

He had been around her long enough to recognize when she was being obstinate. Frankly, whenever it came to that damn horse, she was obstinate. He also knew her well enough to know if he left her behind, she'd follow him unless she was jailed or hog-tied. Although both prospects intrigued him, he knew he wouldn't leave her behind. He needed her with him if his plans to woo her into his bed were to be successful.

"I intend to bring Destiny here." Injured dignity steeped his tone.

She folded her arms over her chest. "You said you'd protect me if I told you what Seyler wanted. I told you what he wants. Now you can protect me."

He bent his head to hide his smile at her belligerent pronouncement of his duty. Oh, he would protect his little rapscallion as surely as he would entice her into his bed. He didn't like taking her into Tennessee if Seyler was as obsessed about destroying her family as Shaughnessy claimed, but their marriage changed Billie's status. Seyler would hardly molest a married woman under the protection of her husband.

Husband. A sly grin touched his lips as he stirred the broth. A grin that he wiped from his face before lifting a filled spoon toward her mouth.

"Of course I'll protect you. As long as you travel to Gallatin as my wife, I see no problem with taking care of you."

He wouldn't have been at all surprised if steam had whistled out of her ears. Her lips pursed into a tight, angry line, and her pupils narrowed into tiny black dots, leaving her eyes a hard, brilliant green.

"If Seyler does anything to Destiny because of this marriage, I will hold you personally responsible."

"If Seyler does anything to Destiny, *I* will hold *him* personally responsible."

By the way she relaxed back into the pillows, she liked his answer.

He hoped she would take the news he owned her childhood home this well. She might even be grateful enough to
accompany him to Colorado. After all, Angel's Valley wouldn't
be fit for habitation for months. She could hire local people
to do the repairs while they went west. He was more than
willing to try his hand at horse breeding, and they could live
in Tennessee after he fulfilled his obligation to the railway
company.

Why not have the best of both worlds? With the new
trains linking the East and West, they could spend part of the
year surveying the West and part of the year raising horses in
Tennessee. He couldn't imagine no longer surveying and
mapping unfamiliar terrain, but all the notes taken in the
field had to be translated into inked lines and symbols. That
portion of his work could be done during a Tennessee winter
as easily as a Colorado winter.

"As for this separation idea of yours . . ."

Her voice shouldered aside his idyllic thoughts.

". . . I think I have a better solution. I'm sure my priest in
Gallatin will be willing to annul our marriage once I explain
the situation to him. After we get Destiny, of course."

CHAPTER SEVENTEEN

Grayson drew Billie into his arms and gently curved her somnolent body against his own. She had not denied him the pleasure of sharing a bed, although sleeping beside her without making love to her was more torture than pleasure.

Once again his angel had thrown him off balance. Although he had planned to bed her by Gallatin, now he couldn't allow her to return home until he had claimed full conjugal rights. He doubted she would ask her priest to annul the marriage if they consummated it. He hoped she would have no reason to want an annulment once she tasted the delights of the marriage bed.

Delights he was eager to teach her.

For now, he had to content himself with feathery forays across her sleeping body, letting his fingertips scout the soft-contoured terrain with gentle thoroughness. He delighted in the way her nipples puckered when he brushed across them and the way her legs parted at his touch, his probing fingers greeted by a warm wetness. Oh, she wanted him when she was sleeping. It was while she was awake that she denied her body's desires.

And the denial began the moment she drifted into consciousness. At the merest hint that she was awakening, he removed his hands and regulated his own breathing. He could do nothing about the stiff shaft pressed against her buttocks.

As soon as she edged into wakefulness, she would untangle herself from his embrace and roll away. Torture. Sleeping with her was sheer torture. But he was a patient man, and one night the door would open into sheer ecstasy.

Billie awoke once again to find herself intimately entwined with the sleeping Yankee. It had become quite a habit over the past few days—one she seemed unable to break no matter how hard she concentrated on keeping as much bed between them as possible before she fell asleep. The Yankee was never holding her, yet she was always nestled against him, her bare buttocks pushed against the hard evidence of his arousal, and her nightgown hiked to her waist.

Usually, she rolled away, but it was becoming more and more difficult to part from him. Every particle of her body yearned to remain in contact with him. Each morning she awoke with a dampness between her legs, and her nipples hard with an unfamiliar longing.

This morning she lay quietly and listened to the rhythmic sound of his breathing. If his hard shaft weren't pressing into her buttocks as usual, she would have wondered if only she awoke this aroused each morning. Perhaps it was usual when two people of the opposite gender slept together. She doubted if she had lain this close to any other human since her mother nursed her.

If she extended her right hand, she could trace the scar that ran down his thigh. When her hand settled on him, the Yankee grunted slightly. She stilled her hand and breath until he quieted.

She had made a point of ignoring him on the first two

nights she was well enough to realize when he was coming
to bed. Although curiosity nagged her, she kept her gaze
averted while he undressed. Lying there, stiff with fear, she
waited while he made himself comfortable beside her. It
took her another hour to relax enough to fall asleep, and she
was tempted to tell the doctor he should banish her husband
from her bed if anyone expected her to recuperate. The idea
of explaining why her husband should be banned not only
made her giggle, it also kept her from saying anything.

It was the third night before she saw him nude. She had
fallen asleep while they played a game of checkers. When
she awoke, slightly disoriented by her nap, it was to find the
board and pieces gone, all but one oil lamp extinguished.

As she tried to orient herself, her sleepy gaze settled on
the Yankee. He was in the process of extinguishing the lamp
next to the bed, and the sight of his nude profile robbed her
of breath. His lean, muscular body seemed strangely familiar, as if she had seen it before, but that was impossible.
Within seconds, the brief spider web of familiarity evaporated. What became embedded in her memory was the scar
that furrowed his thigh. It began its disfiguring run at his hip
and angled down his leg, its full length blocked from her
view by the bed. It seemed almost a blasphemy against the
gods that his otherwise perfect body should have this flaw.

The mattress gave as he slid under the bed linens and
rolled on his side to face her. His harsh voice shattered her
mesmerized silence.

"I apologize if my scar offends you. Few of us left the war
unscathed."

She flinched when his hand closed around hers and, without a word, guided her fingers to the scar. She couldn't stop
the tremor that cascaded through her fingertips.

"There's no need to be frightened." His tone had gentled.

Frightened! As if a healed scar bothered Billie D'Angelo.
It was the warm feel of his puckered skin that made her

tremble. Snatching her hand back, she asked sweetly, "You weren't riding Destiny when you were shot, were you?"

She regretted the words as soon as they left her mouth.

"It was a saber, not a gun, and no, I wasn't riding Destiny." The Yankee rolled onto his back. "He didn't spend much time on active duty. I sent him to New York a few days after I commandeered him."

He had banked the fire for the night, but the glowing coals dimly lit the room. She propped herself on her elbow and stared into the shadowed face of the man lying beside her. "Why?" she asked.

"Why what?"

"Why did you send Destiny to New York?"

She hadn't gotten a clear answer. His eyes closed, and he growled an incomprehensible reply. She had fallen back onto the bed, stunned by the realization Fletcher had been right. The Yankee had saved Destiny's life.

For the first time since that night, she reached out to run her fingertips gently along the scar. His skin quivered beneath her touch. Worried her touch had awakened him, she lifted her fingers. He turned over onto his stomach, almost capturing her hand beneath him as he went.

Warm heat pooled in her abdomen while her heartbeat slammed into a gallop. If she had been one second slower pulling her hand free . . .

She steadied her breathing, then rolled away, leaving him for the cool, lonely part of the bed. A single sunbeam evaded the worn curtains and played across her hip. She watched the dust motes dance in its path and wished she didn't have to spend yet another beautiful spring day indoors. She sighed. At least the doctor had proclaimed her well enough to spend a few hours in the parlor yesterday. Perhaps he would agree to an hour on the front porch. She decided to ask for an hour and settle for ten minutes.

Beside her, the Yankee rubbed his bearded stubble into

the plump pillow. She buried the unexpected, treacherous wish to be his pillow as she turned to look at him. He rolled onto his back, stretching himself awake and giving her a bright but sleepy smile.

"Good morning. Feel like a picnic today?"

She couldn't help smiling back; it was as if he had read her thoughts. "A picnic? Outside?"

"Yes, by the river."

"What a lovely idea!" She pulled herself upright and hugged her knees to her chest. "I feel as if I've spent my entire adult life in this bedroom."

He sat up, his well-muscled torso rising out of the bed-covers with a fluid grace. Her heart fluttered. She stared at his face and told herself not to look at his chest even if she was a little overheated by the way the hair flared across it and then arrowed down his torso to disappear beneath the bedcovers. Her right hand twitched with its desire to follow the line of fine hairs.

She couldn't like the lack of response on his part. Why, he acted as if sitting half naked in a bed with a woman were an everyday occurrence for him.

"Mrs. Weisser offered to pack us a lunch. I thought we'd go down to the river and sit in the sun."

Maybe sitting half naked in a bed with a woman was an everyday occurrence for him. In truth, she barely knew the man.

"No swimming, though. Doctor's orders."

His words and teasing grin brought her skidding into the conversation. "Tell him not to worry. I can't swim."

"Can't swim!" He shook his head in exasperation. "That figures. You can't swim but you try to cross a swollen, unfamiliar river miles from the ford."

"It's not as if I haven't crossed plenty of rivers on horseback."

"If you're going to persist in doing it, I suggest you take a swimming lesson or two before you drown yourself."

She remembered Fletcher's offer to teach her to swim. Perhaps she should have accepted. Then she would be in California, married to Fletcher. The idea didn't please her.

All thoughts of Fletcher scattered when the Yankee leaned over and brushed a light kiss on her cheek.

"Come on, sleepyhead. Much as I prefer to spend the day in bed with my lovely wife, I'm sure you're tired of being here. Not, of course, for the right reasons."

His outrageous words caught her attention, and she was looking at him when he threw off the blankets and bounded out of bed. She reassessed her impressions. The Yankee had a major reaction to sitting nude in a bed with a woman.

Grayson knew Billie liked looking at him. Over the past week, he had created as many opportunities as possible to focus her attention on his body. It was all part of his campaign to reduce her fear. And seduce her.

Although she tried to hide her interest, he saw it. This morning she grabbed the flying bedcovers and pulled them to her nose as if she weren't already covered from neck to toe by a thick cotton nightgown. Then her unshielded eyes stared at him for a few unguarded seconds before she turned aside. From the blush that stained her forehead, she knew he knew she had been studying his flagrantly swollen manhood.

He waited until she wasn't looking to smile. When he had felt her hand lightly exploring his scarred leg, it had almost killed him not to groan aloud from the sheer pleasure of her touch. He had even tried to trap her hand against his body by rolling over, but she had evaded his little ploy.

As he struggled with his drawers, he bit back a few choice words. He had to admit his strategy had its flaws, and putting clothing over a rigid shaft was one of them. The thought of a cooling dip in the Guadalupe River seemed appealing but impractical. Perhaps the soothing repetition of shaving would get his mind off the delicious body lying three feet away.

It didn't. His razor was poised for a downward swing over

his lathered cheek when he realized Billie would need to change from her nightwear to outerwear for the picnic. A small nick on his chin attested to his lack of attention to shaving. The fingers that he wrapped in toweling to dab at the cut trembled with eagerness to undo the ties that held her nightgown together.

Humming quietly to distract himself, he resumed shaving.

Fifteen minutes later, he peeled the blankets away from Billie's lax grip. She had fallen asleep. Ah, that would make the first part of his plan easy. Planting a hand on either side of her body, he bent over and gently blew the tendrils of hair away from her ear. He kept his kiss more of a nibble as he tasted her earlobe and inhaled the sleep-warmed scent of her hair.

Her hand, clumsy with sleep, batted the air near her ear, but his gossamer kisses didn't wake her. Fingers that had touched countless delicate plants without bruising a leaf had no trouble untying the three ties that kept her breasts hidden from his hungry gaze. He slid the neck of the nightgown open and trailed his finger down to stroke the top of a breast. Every time he saw her breasts, he wondered how could he have been so blind. With his eye for details, how had he missed all the clues to her gender? He had to content himself with the realization that his eye was trained to catalog topographical data such as rocks or road conditions or bridges, and not the contours of the human body.

Still, how had he missed the woman beneath the boy?

Carefully he dragged her upright against the pillows and peeled the nightgown over her head. Sleepy green eyes fluttered open, and she slapped at his hand, but her aim was too erratic to ensure contact.

"What're you doin'?" Her tongue failed to wrap itself fully around her words.

Tossing the nightgown aside, he picked up a chemise and waved it under her nose. "Getting you dressed for a picnic."

It was almost comic to watch her struggle against the lassitude of sleep. When she realized she was bare-chested, she tugged at the bedcovers. "I'm perfectly capable of dressing myself."

She had straightened herself on the bed. There were no female hysterics, no bewailing her fate. There was only Billie mantling herself with an innate dignity and facing the situation. He wanted to wake up every morning next to this woman.

When he dropped the chemise over her head, the narrow straps caught in her hair and gave him a chance to run his fingers through her soft curls. He covered his actions with a brisk tone.

"I don't want you wearing yourself out before we get there. It's not as if I haven't been dressing you these past days."

He tugged the chemise into place, resisting the temptation to smooth his hands down its satiny surface and feel the warmth of her body as it penetrated the finely woven fabric. Instead, he pushed back the bedcovers and swung her feet over the side. As usual, he kept his actions nonthreatening because his immediate goal was to accustom her to his touch, not frighten her.

He had the advantage; she was drowsy and recovering from a serious illness. If any whisper of guilt tickled his conscience, he didn't hear it. He was too engrossed in trying to balance his need to touch her against his need to maintain an impersonal, nurselike role.

After buttoning and tying her into a dozen pieces of clothing, he seated her at the scarred dressing table and picked up a brush. Running it slowly through the dark red curls, he was mesmerized by the way they fell in silken abandon around her head. Had she not dyed and greased her hair when she posed as a boy, no one would have accepted her masquerade. With patient care he threaded the green ribbon he had bought to match her new dress through the curls. His fingers lingered over the tying.

Was this how Sophronia felt about John? Did she hunger for John's touch, John's smile, John's laugh? John's best friend would have been a poor substitute if Sophronia harbored the same feelings in her breast that he harbored for Billie.

This hunger for Billie headed toward an obsession.

Like a skittish filly, she shook her head as if to free herself from his touch. He looked down into the scratched mirror and her reflection. Fear skidded through her eyes as she watched him. He knew his hunger for her showed too brilliantly in his eyes. With effort, he banked the fire and tied the ribbon.

Gentling the hunger in his eyes, he molded his hands around her shoulders. Even as he bent to plant a feathery kiss on her cheek, he met her gaze in the mirror.

"You look lovely."

A tentative smile curved her lips. Did he see a hint of trust buried deep in her gaze? Or was he imagining what he wanted to see?

The picnic in Texas differed from the picnic in New York. There was no Destiny or Dinsmere to carry them to the site, although the doctor lent them his buggy to keep his patient from doing too much on her first day out. And this time Billie was dressed as a female, with her hair the right shade of red and her body molded by a dress instead of hidden behind baggy trousers, breast band, and bulky coat.

It had been a long time since she'd run her hand down a crisp new skirt, but when she found herself smoothing damp hands down the front of her dress for the umpteenth time, she knew she was nervous. Why a few hours spent with the Yankee on a picnic should make her feel slightly giddy after she had spent the past ten days in constant companionship with the man, even sleeping with him every night, was beyond her grasp. She laid her feelings on the altar of weakness from her recent bout with death.

When the Yankee spread a quilt on the ground, she was

reminded of the picnic in New York. There had been no so-licitous attention that day. A warm glow of satisfaction should brighten her morning; hadn't she wished for such a scene as this? But sadness, not satisfaction, mantled her shoulders. She had told the Yankee her priest would annul their marriage as soon as they reached Gallatin.

The sooner she mended, the sooner they would be in Gallatin and the sooner their marriage would be ended. She tried to drive away the sadness by reminding herself she would have Destiny.

For the first time in years, it didn't seem enough.

The rich, bubbling song of a meadowlark pierced the air. Spring was heating into summer in this part of the Texas hill country and she could not be sad long when faced with the joy of being outdoors. And it seemed a sin not to enjoy what-ever time she had with her Yankee.

Who was smiling at her.

While she had fretted, he had emptied the contents of the basket on the quilt, laying out thick slices of cured ham and sourdough biscuits for her scrutiny. Several baked potatoes, still warm from the huge oven that dominated Mrs. Weisser's kitchen, nestled beside a jar of blueberry jam. Billie felt her mouth water.

"Are you hungry?"

"Famished for real food. It seems ages since my teeth had anything to chew."

Unsure how her body would respond, she ate sparingly from the plate he fixed her. She couldn't help but close her eyes as her taste buds reveled in the salty flavor of the ham. For the first time in a long time, she was glad to be alive. Life didn't seem as daunting when the sun hung in a cloud-less sky and the chirruping songs of birds and insects ac-companied the river's trickling melody. She opened her eyes to find the Yankee looking at her.

"I feel like Rip Van Winkle," she confided with a smile. "It's as if all my senses have been asleep."

"You didn't quite sleep twenty years, but you knocked at death's door."

They ate in a congenial companionship punctuated by an occasional comment about the river or the lovely day or the brown thrasher who found them and their picnic interesting. After they finished eating, the Yankee pushed aside the food before settling himself comfortably beside her.

"Nap time."

"I don't feel the least bit exhausted," she lied.

He didn't pay attention to her protestation. Instead, he leaned over and untied the ribbons of the white straw hat he had given her that morning. The light brush of his fingers on her chin sent tiny shivers along her spine. Without asking, he plucked the hat from her head. Then he arranged her body on the quilt and put her head in his lap. She was too drowsy with food and pleasure to resist. Nor did she pull away when his fingers brushed the loose tendrils of hair from her forehead.

Eyes closed, she was teetering on the edge of sleep when he whispered, "I have to admit. I prefer you as a female."

She smiled.

"I can't help but shudder when I think what might have happened to you if your masquerade had been discovered."

The patronizing criticism chased away the drowsy contentment. She pushed herself upright and out of his reach. The glare she sent him should have blistered his skin.

"And I shudder every time I think of what could have happened to me in the role of an unprotected female."

Her wrath failed to intimidate the Yankee. "Then why didn't you live in Gallatin with your aunt? Around people who could protect you?"

"How could I look after the farm if I lived in Gallatin?"

"Why didn't your aunt move to the farm? Surely with Shaughnessy and your aunt at the farm, you would have been safer."

"Aunt Maria in the country? She was petrified of Yankees.

She was sure they'd as soon kill a secesh as look at one. To her, living in the country guaranteed they would find you alone and end your life." She gave his muscular frame a quick appraisal. "After they had their way with any woman they found."

The thought of this particular Yankee having his way with her excited rather than frightened her. He didn't see her measuring glance—he had found the last sourdough biscuit too tempting to ignore.

She dragged herself back to the argument.

"My aunt didn't have a strong constitution." Billie felt her lips draw into a tight line as she thought of Lieutenant Adams. "Angel's Valley had the honor of serving as a temporary Federal headquarters. When they deemed it no longer of use to their war effort, they took or destroyed what little they had not already ruined. My aunt couldn't have watched the Yankees burn priceless pieces of furniture as firewood." It wasn't easy to keep the bitterness from her tone, but harping on the past didn't change the future.

The pungent scent of freshly baked sourdough tickled her nostrils when the Yankee waved the biscuit beneath her nose. "I've seen your former home, Angel. Perhaps you should have accepted reality and stayed in town with your aunt."

Former home. Then Seyler had Angel's Valley now. She wouldn't think about that or what the Yankee would have seen had he visited the horse farm five years ago. His words opened another wound.

"If you're implying I failed to protect my family's property by staying on the farm, you're correct." The truth seared her soul. She had failed to protect anything. The horses had been taken, the fences burned to warm soldiers, the house stripped to its shell, even its floors and walls scarred by careless men. The memories were painful, and she hated it when they slammed unexpectedly into her gut.

The home she loved was gone. Her father was gone; Stephen was gone. Reality was a jarring truth she had fought for years. Her earlier indignation evaporated as she shifted her gaze from the Yank's face to her lap. A tear dripped onto her tightly clasped hands, sliding down the back of her left hand until only its slick path was left.

She lifted her head and set her chin at a defiant angle. Defiance often seemed all that she had left.

"They destroyed my home, but I got revenge."

"What? By spying?"

"Yes. By spying. I shoveled muck and bore insults, but I also listened to the Federals make plans. Encrypting those plans for Fletcher gave me a great deal of satisfaction."

"You were a fool." The anger in his voice startled her. "God only knows what would have happened to you if anyone had found out about your game of charades."

Her tight, angry tone matched his. "I have an excellent idea of what could have happened to me."

"Stephen?" The quiet question exploded like a case shot landing amidst a cavalry charge.

"How'd you . . ." The question died aborning. She saw by his expression he was guessing, but the connection was correct. What surprised her even more was the desire to talk about Stephen that blossomed to life in her heart. She had kept her guilt buried a long time, but the incident at the river had somehow freed her. She needed to talk about him.

"Why don't you tell me what happened to Stephen?" Beneath the soft prodding was a touch of steel.

The desire to tell him warred with her ability to talk. Between the jumbled thoughts dashing around her head and the way her mouth trembled every time she tried to use it, coherence seemed impossible.

When she spoke, her voice held a raspy, distressed quality. "Stephen came home to visit me and his family. On his way back to his company, the Yankees captured him."

The cold, clammy lick of horror rippled through her body and clamped itself around her heart. Gone were the soft trickling sounds of the river and its birdsong accompaniment. She was at the funeral breathing in the smell of freshly dug earth and newly hewed oak. Her ears rang with Stephen's favorite hymn, and she could see the closed coffin as the men lowered it into the ground.

Her words came as quickly as Destiny running through a meadow, because if she stopped to think about what she was saying, the pain would split her asunder.

"They claimed he was a spy, and they interrogated him. They cut out his tongue and gouged out his eyes and cut off his ears."

"God, I'm so sorry, Angel." The Yankee's fingers gently wiped the tears off her cheek.

She grabbed his arm, felt her fingers clutch the fabric as if it alone stood between her and drowning. "You don't understand. It should have been me. I was the spy, not Stephen."

"Hush." The Yankee pulled her against his chest while he stroked her hair. When he spoke, his voice rumbled in his chest beneath her damp ear.

"War is a glimpse of hell—the dead, the maimed. It's men who sell worthless guns that jam in battle or explode in a soldier's face. It's rape. It's murder. But there's a glimpse of heaven, too. Courage, heroism. Soldiers who face cannon fire to rescue fallen comrades. Doctors and nurses working days without sleep to ease the pain of the injured.

"It's one person dying while another lives." He pulled back to look down into her face. "I know it's hard to accept. I feel guilty because I survived and my best friend, John, died. My guilt made me propose to his fiancée. I thought I had to live the life he wasn't there to live, I guess."

The Yankee was a blurry, slightly sparkling image. She wiped at her eyes, because she wanted a clearer view of his face when she tried to explain why she could not forget or forgive the past.

He didn't give her a chance to say anything. "I was your enemy. You were mine, but you can't hold me responsible for

Stephen's murder any more than I can hold you responsible for John's death. The war's over. It's time to forgive the past and get on with the future, our future."

Forgive the past? This Yankee asked a lot of her, yet the promise of a future with him nibbled at her resolve.

CHAPTER EIGHTEEN

New Orleans

Billie twirled her parasol, enjoying the way the late afternoon sun glimmered off the stripes of green and yellow silk that matched her dress. Twirling the parasol kept both her hands busy and made it easier to resist the urge to pat once again the tiny new bonnet perched jauntily on her head.

She grinned as she watched the parasol twirl. *Won't Alice Ann Denton be pea green with envy when Billie D'Angelo Vanderlyn waltzes into Gallatin dressed in the latest fashions from New Orleans?* She could see Alice's pinched-up face as clearly as if they were still students together at the Clarksville Female Academy.

A shiver of anticipation ran up Billie's spine at the thought of Alice Ann's first sight of Grayson. Why, the poor girl would probably burst with jealousy. Billie refused to dwell on the fact that Grayson would be a free man within days of their reaching Gallatin.

Beside her the Mississippi River crawled with movement as steamboats, barges, and flatboats lined the shore as far as the eye could see: arriving, departing, loading, unloading. The panorama fascinated her as much as buying new clothes had. Her first instinct upon their arrival in New Orleans had been to balk at the Yankee's suggestion they get completely outfitted before leaving New Orleans.

He had argued his point well. "Men such as Seyler use the trappings of wealth to intimidate." The Yankee had settled himself into the upholstered chair in their hotel sitting room. "It gives them a sense of power, a feeling of control."

He had bought her a new wardrobe, tempting her with a rainbow of dresses, parasols, bonnets, lacy undergarments, and shoes. She had sat on the edge of the bed, lacing up her new half boots.

"If we're going to beard the proverbial lion in his den," the Yankee continued, "then it's important for us to be well dressed, too."

Billie slipped off the bed and lifted her skirts to better view her shoes.

"You are satisfied with your new clothes, aren't you?"

Had there been a note of doubt in his question? She peeked over her shoulder at him. If she hadn't become attuned to his every nuance in the past few weeks, she might not have noticed the tension in his relaxed position.

She pretended to admire her new leather half boot a second longer, turning her right foot this way and that. As she hoped, the movement caught his attention. She edged her skirts up higher, revealing more of her leg. The heat in his gray eyes made her stomach quiver.

With a quick flounce of her skirts, she lowered them. "Of course I like my new clothes. What woman wouldn't enjoy having all this?" She waved her hand at the wardrobe that was stuffed with dresses. "But Seyler knew me when I was wealthy and wore lovely gowns. And he already knows you have money, because he saw your home in New York."

Then he came up behind her and put his arms around her waist, a distracting habit he had picked up in Seguin. "I want

Seyler to understand you're my wife and he can't make threats against you without threatening me."

She liked the feel of his chin resting lightly on the top of her head, his warm breath stirring the curls beside her ear and sending shivers up her back, but she didn't want him to know. Slipping out of his embrace, she crossed to the cheval glass and pretended to admire herself in its full length.

"I'm not sure clothes will sway Seyler from his course," she said as she leaned toward the mirror, "but Fletcher would agree with you about being dressed for the occasion. He always said it takes people a while to see past the clothes a man is wearing." She smiled at the Yankee's reflection in the mirror. "Or a woman. I knew I couldn't stay long in New York, because sooner or later, you and Lina would have seen past the clothes to the person beneath."

She ran her hands down the skirt. She doubted if she would ever tire of running her hands across the rich fabrics he insisted she buy.

"I know I've been appallingly greedy since you dragged me to the first dress shop, but it's been years since I had a new dress. It seems as if I've spent most of my life as a dirty urchin or ragged old lady."

She left one thing unsaid: that he fanned her desire to be a fashionably dressed young woman into an obsession. He was the one who put the sway in her walk, the coquettish tilt to her head, and the becoming blush on her cheeks. As if buying her clothes weren't enough, he had ensured that every outfit had a pair of matching shoes or boots. And each left shoe possessed a slightly higher heel.

Her hip seldom bothered her these days.

The whistle of a steamboat broke into her reverie. She stopped twirling her parasol to gaze down at the river. Not one of these roustabouts running up and down the landing stage would recognize her as the boy who had traveled downriver with Destiny. Her trip up the Mississippi River was going to be quite different from the trip down. This time she wouldn't be sleeping by Destiny's stall, or listening to obscenities, or keeping out of the way of rough and rowdy deckhands.

She repositioned the parasol above her head where it was supposed to be. As if the frothy mix of satin, ribbons, and lace could shade even a ladybug adequately. It might not be practical, but it was feminine. As was she, even if the Yankee persisted in sleeping in the same bed without demanding his conjugal rights. Not that she wanted him to, she reminded herself firmly. Father Fitzpatrick would never annul their marriage if they had . . . mated.

Oh, but sleeping beside the man was driving her to distraction. She couldn't forget the strange sensations his touch sent shimmering through her body. And her dreams possessed a growing erotic quality over which she had no control. More than once she had awakened to find herself wrapped intimately around his thigh and rubbing herself shamelessly against him. It was a wonder the dampness didn't seep through her nightgown and wet his leg. She was getting more frustrated each night and could only hope she wouldn't go on her knees and beg him to quench the fire in her before they reached Gallatin.

She frowned as she watched a mud clerk scurry around the wharf, pencil flying over paper as he tracked the freight being loaded on the main deck. Sometimes she had odd dreams, and the images teased her thoughts during the day. In one dream she was lying on a riverbank and the Yankee was leaning over her.

"Let me show you I can love you."

Was there any truth twined in the image? During those weeks of illness, it had become impossible to winnow fact from fantasy.

Her frown vanished and her heartbeat accelerated when she saw her husband wend his way through the mounds of cargo heaped on the docks. He cut a magnificent figure in his finely tailored trousers and frock coat, with his new hat cocked to one side. She loved to watch him walk, his confident stride betokening power and strength. Ah, yes, her Yankee was easy on the eye. She lifted her hand, ready to flutter the ridiculous scrap of embroidered linen that passed as her handkerchief, to get his attention.

A gaudily dressed woman came out of the crowded dock and touched his arm, arresting his progress. Billie's hand fell limply to her side. It was suddenly hot instead of balmy, and the humid air too thick to breathe.

The Yankee's mouth flashed a sudden smile. Her heart sat in her chest like the shoe of a draft horse. She didn't have to be within hearing distance to know what the woman offered.

Exactly what Billie denied him.

Jealousy was as unpleasant as Shakespeare claimed.

She began breathing again when the Yankee tipped his hat and continued toward her. Mingled with the jealousy was an unexpected feeling of possessiveness that startled her. Not only had she wanted to rip the she-devil's eyes out for looking at the Yankee, but for one blinding moment she had wanted to shout, "He's mine! Leave him alone!"

Grayson's gaze had been on his wife when the prostitute propositioned him. Nor had his attention left Billie while he politely declined the woman's offer. No, he had his own plans for pleasure during the trip to Memphis, and they centered on the beautiful woman whose green eyes flashed with jealousy when he approached her.

"Sorry to keep you waiting, Angel. Our trunks have been loaded, and it's time for us to board."

"Must you insist on calling me Angel?" she snapped as she took the arm he extended.

"Why, yes. I must." He didn't bother to point out she insisted on calling him Yankee. "I hope you like our accommodations. I planned to secure us rooms on the texas, but those were already booked." He swept her full dress with a laughing glance. "What I booked isn't too large. We shall have to be in our undergarments when we're in the room together."

"Or you shall have to wait outside until I'm in bed," she replied tartly.

Her saucy manner faded as they neared the edge of the river and he slowed his stride to match her faltering steps. This time he was prepared for her reluctance to board a boat. In Galveston her fear had caught him by surprise. His Angel had seemed so unremittingly fearless that this chink in the armor was encouraging.

Covering her gloved hand with his own, he smiled his reassurance when she glanced up at him. She responded with a wry grin and a subtle straightening of her body. Head held erect, a tight grip on his arm, she stepped onto the landing stage.

That was his Angel. Taking life head-on, unwilling to admit defeat or fears. Being her protector was decidedly difficult.

Once on board, she glanced back at the dock, unable to prevent the tiny shudder that ran through her body. "I seem to have developed an aversion for rivers."

"An understandable reaction after your recent experience." He contented himself with patting her hand when he wanted to take her in his arms and kiss away her fears.

Still covering her hand with his, he guided her into the saloon, down a long hall, past red velvet draperies, gleaming mirrors, and gilt-trimmed chairs. A waiting attendant opened the door to their stateroom and stood aside.

Grayson, who thought the word *stateroom* larger than the minuscule chamber that awaited them, didn't follow Billie into the room. Her skirts almost brushed the bed and wall simultaneously, but her attention seemed caught by the two narrow berths.

He leaned against the door frame. "Naturally, I'll sleep in the top berth."

"Naturally."

"Unless, of course, you wish to squeeze together on the

bottom one." He couldn't keep the hint of mischief from his voice.

"I doubt we could get much sleep squeezed together on that narrow berth."

"I hadn't thought to get much sleep."

For once she didn't leap into the fray. Instead, she pretended to be engrossed in the porcelain chamber set. He was surprised that a basin, pitcher, and chamber pot with shepherdesses and sheep dancing around the edges could be so fascinating.

"There's barely room for me and my dress in here."

He took pity on her. "It's only for a few days. We've managed to get you dressed and undressed for weeks, and I'm sure we can manage it here. You said you didn't want a maid."

"I think I said that before we reached New Orleans and bought two trunks of dresses with dozens of small buttons up the back."

"Why don't I unbutton you before I take my nightly stroll on the deck? By the time I return, you'll be safely tucked in bed."

And then, he thought, she'd have a fine view of his assets dangling over her head when he climbed into that damn upper berth.

If she was looking.

He wondered if he should sleep in his drawers while they were on board the steamboat. He had offered her plenty of opportunities to become accustomed to his body while they slept together the past five weeks. She knew exactly what he looked like nude, while he had seldom had occasion to study her body. She persisted in keeping herself covered from head to foot whenever he was in the same room with her.

Even though her head was turned away, he could see the furious blush on her cheek. These new-style bonnets were a welcome change from the older ones because these gave a man a clear view of a woman's face. From where he was standing, he had a sneaking suspicion her thoughts had strayed along the same path his had taken. The prospect had obviously shaken her.

Perhaps he would dangle his assets, after all.

CHAPTER NINETEEN

As the steamboat made its way upriver from New Orleans to Memphis, Grayson courted Billie. His siege on her heart was every bit as cunning and lethal as Grant's siege on Vicksburg. He invaded her emotions as relentlessly as the Union army had invaded her homeland. His assiduous wooing made going to bed alone difficult each night, but he had learned patience hunched over a camp table, inking in meticulous maps for his commanders.

They ate, they strolled the deck, they talked, they danced, and they sat in the gallery. He took every opportunity to touch her. Laying an arm across her shoulders as they stood at the railing and watched the sunset, brushing a stray tendril of hair from her forehead, and always there with his arm extended so that she could tuck her hand next to his side.

Steadily he campaigned to win her to his bed.

It wasn't an easy campaign, not with the aftermath of the war littering the riverbanks to remind her of the past. And his role in it. It wasn't so much what she said as what she didn't say when the burned hulk of a plantation house or fields overgrown with weeds and neglect slid past the boat. Then she would look at him, and he would see bewilderment and a tinge of pain in her eyes, and he would wonder if all the love in the world could eradicate the past.

And how he loved her. At first, he told himself she needed him because she needed someone to protect her, but then he realized he had tricked her into marriage because *he* needed *her.* She had entered his life and unwittingly put it back on course. The war had ripped his world apart as it had hers. The death and destruction he had seen had almost extinguished his zest for living. Returning home, he had set about molding a safe haven complete with complaisant wife and staid profession. He had been willing to marry without love and live without challenge.

Until Billie had tumbled into his life and saved him from a boring, monotonous future.

That alone was reason to love her.

And then she gave him the idea for a new book.

They were seated in the gallery one afternoon, and he was watching her nap. Or at least he thought she was asleep until she opened her eyes and said, "Sheriff Boggart was right. You should be writing the next Captain Dinsmere book, not following a horse around the South."

The next Captain Dinsmere book was the furthest thing from his thoughts, which were filled with visions of her body, nude and entwined with his.

"What could be more important than helping my wife retrieve our valued horse?"

"Can't you be serious for one moment? It's easy to understand why you stopped writing during the war, but it's past time you wrote another book."

"You sound like my publisher." He found he could either look into those serious emerald eyes and think about bedding their owner, or he could tear his gaze from them and try to answer her with a degree of intelligence. Since his brain had spent most of its time these past few weeks besotted with the charmer sitting next to him, he wasn't sure if it could answer her intelligently.

Restless, he went to stand beside the rail and watch a keelboat passing them on its way south. To share a truth that had hit him over the head some months ago would be painful, but he sensed Billie would understand. And he wanted to tell her.

"I'd like to write another book, but it seems the war had a strange effect on me. Although I made copious notes in my journals for a novel during the war, those observations fail to ignite my imagination now. I find I can't write about the war in which I participated. Nor do I seem able to write any more inane stories about the intrepid Captain Dinsmere."

To his surprise, he had gripped the rail with both hands. He stared down at white knuckles, forcing himself to release his grip while he waited for her searing ridicule.

"Your stories weren't inane. They were . . . They were quite exciting. I think Captain Dinsmere was an excellent hero."

He turned and leaned his hip against the rail. "Who, unfortunately, doesn't look a thing like me."

She shot him a shrewd look. "Captain Dinsmere may not resemble you physically, but I think he possesses your worst trait."

Laughter danced in the depths of her eyes; he layered his tone with silk. "My worst trait?"

"Oh, yes. I distinctly remember the scene in which Dinsmere waited for three days outside the Indian camp for de Chartres."

"De Chartres had led the Indian attack on the Dinsmere farm. He practically murdered Dinsmere's family himself." He was startled at how vehemently he defended his character's actions.

"Three days in the same spot. I declare, my muscles ached just reading about it." There was a deceptive sugar coating to her tone when she asked, "Exactly how long did you spy on me before sneaking into my cabin in Texas?"

"Patience," he said with exaggerated care, "is a virtue."

She giggled. "Then your cup runneth over with virtue."

Their time in New Orleans had been well spent, he thought. Anxiety no longer shadowed her every expression. He found her occasional giggles delightful. With effort he dragged his thoughts back to their conversation.

"You're annoyed because you didn't expect me to follow you to Texas."

She looked at him oddly, then said, "If you're having trouble writing imaginary stories about a war, why don't you organize your journal notes into a memoir?"

"As if every old soldier won't be doing that for the next thirty years."

"But none of those memoirs would include your detailed maps."

Her suggestion smacked into his brain like a cannon shot. A book about the war, illustrated with the maps he had drawn. What a perfect idea. And it revived a part of him he had come to believe killed by the war—his desire to write. His brain sang with ideas while his fingers itched to wrap themselves around a pen.

"Lina told me those lovely maps stacked against a wall in the library were drawn by you." The questioning note in Billie's voice cut into his whirling thoughts.

"They were, and you're a genius!" He picked her up, twirled her around, put her toes back down on the deck, and kissed her mouth as a soft "Oh!" of astonishment whooshed out. He inhaled the "Oh" along with the sweet scent of her lavender cologne and the wet breeze of the Mississippi. Although he liked kissing her, his excitement drove his lips from hers. He had to talk.

"You have given me the perfect idea." He looked into her startled eyes and suddenly knew he had never expected to be this happy.

"You're welcome." She smiled at him, then reached up to straighten the bonnet he had knocked askew.

Her smile touched the core of his being, inviting him to share the plans her suggestion had triggered.

His hands dropped from her waist, and he paced the gallery, which was thin of company with dinnertime approaching.

"I can see it now. I shall write a military history that describes my surveying experiences and illustrate it with the maps I made during the war. This winter, when I can't survey, I'll have time to match the text with maps. A year at the most and I'll have a book ready for publication."

He whirled to back to face her. "Thank you, Billie. A military history won't appeal to my Dinsmere fans, but I don't have another Dinsmere book in me. Before you fell into my life, I wondered if I had another book in me at all. Now I know I do."

Unknowingly, she had returned something precious to him, and he knew only one way to thank her: to get Destiny.

A melodious bell chimed, signaling dinner. Since he had selected the *Richmond* because the steamboat boasted a French chef and a fine cuisine, he couldn't be too annoyed by the interruption.

With a happy grin, he offered Billie his arm. "May I escort you to the dining room?"

The *Richmond* also boasted an excellent selection of wines, essential to the last stage of his seduction campaign. For one brief, sparkling second Grayson's conscience twinged. This lovely young woman had given him so much; should he seduce her and force her to remain his wife?

But the captain had projected their arrival in Memphis by late the next afternoon. Grayson had one night left to bed Billie and make her his wife.

A waiter appeared at their dining table with the bottle of champagne Grayson had ordered earlier that afternoon.

He smiled at Billie's raised eyebrows. "I had thought to celebrate our last night on board. Now we have even more reason to celebrate, don't you think?"

"I haven't tasted champagne since . . . for a long time." Billie picked up the fluted glass of sparkling wine the waiter had poured for her.

Grayson raised his glass. "To the day I commandeered Destiny."

Her startled gaze met his steady look. A cheeky smile curved her lips as she offered her own salute. "To the day I stole Destiny."

He grinned, then tapped his glass against hers. His plans for tonight didn't include arguing with her. He had instructed the waiter to keep her glass full—a fact that escaped Billie, who emptied her wineglass repeatedly.

A tipsy Billie proved as delightful as a sober Billie. Her cheeks, hidden from the elements for the past few weeks, had gained a creamy glow. Now the wine tinged them rose. Her eyes held a dreamy aspect he found alluring when she tried to focus them while she talked.

"Commandeered, smammandeered." Billie waved a fork-ful of Croquettes of Potatoes in the air. Her middle-Tennessee drawl had grown more slurred, but she articulated her words with slow care.

"Admit it, Yankee. You took Destiny and bought him from a government that didn't own him in the first place. I admire the fact you paid for him—few of your Yankee comrades were as obligin'. Too many of them 'commandeered' everything of value for the use of the Federal army."

The potatoes and fork stabbed the air in front of him.

"I doubt if General Paine and his men paid the gover'-ment for any of the furniture or artwork they sent north during the war."

He watched as the potatoes made it to her mouth, where they were thoughtfully chewed and swallowed.

"What truly amazed me was how fas-tid-ious you looked that day."

It took him a minute to absorb the new direction of her conversation.

"Even dust couldn't hide the cut of your uniform. When I saw you on Destiny, you reminded me of General Morgan on Black Bess. Only Destiny is larger than Bess, and you," her green eyes grew owlishly wide as they studied him. "You're larger than General Morgan, I believe. I mean, I never actually stood next to General Morgan, just saw him once, on Bess."

If possible her eyes grew even dreamier, but they snapped briefly into focus with astonishing speed. "And then I thought, *That damn Yankee's stealing my horse. I don't care who he looks like. He doesn't belong on Destiny.*"

"Will madam have her usual dish of ice cream tonight?"

The glare in her eyes shifted back into a slightly disoriented gaze as she looked up at the waiter. Wrinkling her nose, she examined the man as if he were an unfamiliar breed of horse.

"Do you know I've had a dish of ice cream every night since we arrived in New Orl'ns? It seems a shame to refuse one tonight, but for some reason, the thought of ice cream makes me nauseous."

"I believe the lady will forgo her dessert tonight."

"Perhaps a cup of coffee?" Even the waiter had noticed her enjoyment of that beverage.

Grayson shot one quick look at Billie and again answered for his wife. "Not tonight. Thank you, anyway."

In an unladylike gesture, she plunked her elbow on the table and rested her chin on her hand. The gesture brought his attention to the intricately designed ruby brooch she insisted on wearing each night. The lights of the chandelier twinkled softly on its multifaceted surfaces.

"I believe," she rolled her eyes toward the ceiling. "The lady is . . . how should I say this? Drunk?"

"Not really. I wouldn't let you have that much."

"Ah."

Silver clinked against Spode china. Conversations flowed around them, punctuated by light laughter. The aroma of cooked beef mingled with sweet smells of cologne, all tempered by the ever-present scent of the Mississippi River.

Billie's forehead wrinkled. "You wanted me to feel giddy but not unconscious?" She tilted her head and looked at him. "I wonder why."

He leaned back in his chair as if to distance himself from her accusation. "You can't blame how you feel on me, Angel. I'm not the one who asked the waiter to refill my glass four times."

"Holy Mary, Mother of God. Four times?" She blinked, awed by the number.

"Since we've been sharing our meals for the past few weeks, I admit I was surprised by your sudden gluttony for wine."

"One glass. I drink one small glass of wine with a meal." Her finger wavered in the air.

"Exactly. That's why I signaled the waiter to stop refilling your glass."

"You took it upon yourself to tell the waiter not to give me any more wine?"

He wondered what he'd said wrong. "I'm your husband. I'm allowed to do what's good for you."

She thrust herself to her feet. "You may say you comman . . . comman . . . comman . . . deered Destiny as many times you wish, but he will always be mine."

With exaggerated dignity she turned on her heel and left the table. He watched the provocative sway of her skirts as she maneuvered around the tables. She didn't stop until she faced the row of stateroom doors. Although he had leaped to his feet the moment she stood, he settled back into his seat when she left. As he suspected, she couldn't remember which stateroom was theirs.

Her return was every bit as regal as her departure. He came to his feet more slowly this time.

"Would you please escort me to our stateroom?"

Not even for a gold-plated compass would he grin at the

belligerent woman before him. As he guided her through the saloon, he felt the steady beat of the huge engines below their feet slow while the steamboat's direction shifted slightly. The tendency of Mississippi steamboats to stop at every wharf for freight or passengers had driven him to distraction on his trip downriver. This trip, he welcomed the errant path of the floating palace. The longer it took them to reach Memphis, the more time he had to bed his wife.

He followed her into the tiny stateroom and closed the door behind them. The hem of her gown, shaped by the crinoline beneath it, brushed across his feet as he stepped closer to her. She bent her neck slightly, offering him an unobstructed view of the row of tiny pearl buttons that paraded down her back as well as a whiff of the lavender scent she favored. He could see the small knot she had made in the ribbon after she had woven it through her hair. Two months without a haircut had added another inch of length, and the tendrils curled delicately below the hairline and around the ribbon.

His fingers actually trembled when he tried to undo the first button. Licking dry lips, he concentrated on the task before him. If his hands could be steady enough to print minuscule notations on a map, surely they could remain steady while unbuttoning these tiny buttons. Not that he had faced such delectable distractions while he printed map legends. No bared neck, dark red curls, or lavender scent had teased him when he worked.

Halfway down her back, he stopped unbuttoning buttons and surrendered to the need to feather kisses where the Mechlin lace met her skin. He almost missed the sibilant gasp, but he definitely saw her arch her neck. Encouraged, he continued unbuttoning her gown while his mouth followed the opening his hands created.

When he reached the last button, he eased the bodice of her gown off her shoulders. Pushing aside the straps of her petticoat, he curved his hands around her bared shoulders while trailing kisses up her neck to her right ear.

She moaned softly and melted against his chest. Gown and petticoat crumpled toward her waist, leaving her breasts bare. He could no more ignore the tempting opportunity than he could resist sketching an unusual land formation. Gently he closed his hands around the warm, full weight and ran his thumbs across the puckered peaks.

She arched her back, filling his hands with her breasts. He could hear the increased tempo of her breathing and feel the heat of her from his chest to his knees. His own heart pounded the blood through his body and filled every inch of him with desire.

"Oh, Angel. I want you." He breathed his request in her ear.

A long, shuddering sigh was his answer.

He pressured her. He doubted he could live with this aching hunger much longer.

"Be mine. Tonight."

She stirred in his arms, and he worried he asked too much, that he was a fool not to wait longer. But he wanted more, much more.

Eyes closed, she tilted her head against his shoulder and whispered, "Ah, Yankee, when you touch me I forget all the reasons I should say no. You make me feel things I've never felt before. . . . You make me want to do things I've never done."

Unmitigated joy shot through him.

She was to be his.

Tonight.

He had laid siege to her heart and triumphed.

"What things?" He nuzzled her neck, wondering if she could hear the thundering beat of his heart.

She turned her head to stare up at him with beautiful green eyes, pupils enlarged by passion. "I want to kiss you . . . all over."

An intense wave of pleasure swept him. As if she were

made of the finest Sèvres porcelain, he turned her in his arms until they faced each other. "Kiss me, Angel."

Obediently she slid her hands around his neck and pulled his head down to her own. Her lips pressed against his in a sweet, girlish kiss that clarioned her inexperience. But it was the sweetest kiss he had ever received. With gentle care, he nudged her lips apart, nibbling at her lower lip, licking his tongue over the upper lip and then caressing the inside of her mouth.

Her response was immediate.

And overwhelming.

Lips parting more fully, she welcomed his invasion and then tentatively copied him. To feel her innocent tongue licking its way into his mouth dazzled his senses. Awe warred with need when her tongue gently entered his mouth. She offered him so much, she humbled him.

But he needed her.

He pressed her against his chest, feeling the fullness of her breasts through the layers of fabric separating them. His hands traced the delicate shape of her back, his fingers curving into her waist. Each fingertip sang with the joy of exploration.

His campaign was coming to fruition. She had surrendered, but he would make sure she never regreted her surrender.

Dragging his mouth from hers, he marked the path from her chin to the top of her breasts with hot, tiny kisses. He dipped his head to her breast, kissing his way down the mound until he could suckle gently on a nipple. She responded by pushing herself more fully into his mouth. Then she moaned. A faint, tantalizing moan. The sound sent an ache quivering through his groin.

How he wanted to touch her all over, but he settled for resting his hands on her waist and pulling her hips into his while he kissed his way back to her mouth. Savoring the ambrosial taste of her, he was awed by the tumult of feelings she unleashed in him.

He didn't want to pull away from her, but the awkwardness of the small room told him he must. Their first encounter was too important a moment to be ruined by the antics of two people trying to undress with no room to turn around.

Regretfully he pulled her bodice back into place and smoothed the fabric over her shoulders, the metal of her brooch cool against his fingertips when he brushed against it. Unable to resist one more kiss, he gave her a quick peck on the tip of her nose.

"Ten minutes?"

Huge green eyes, smoky with the passion he had lit, met his gaze. "Ten minutes."

His resolve evaporated at the invitation in her eyes. When he found himself undressing her yet again, he brought the kiss to a halt.

"Ten minutes."

He backed out of the room and closed the door. With a few quick tugs, he straightened his clothes, then strolled toward the huge paddle wheel housed on this side of the deck. A few feet from the wheel, he stopped and let its steady thump and splash soothe his ruffled equilibrium. Behind him stateroom doors opened and closed, soft strains of music wafted through the night air, and the busy life of the floating palace continued. Yet two minutes ago the noise of the engine, the wheels, the people, the music—all had faded into oblivion when he held Billie in his arms. Nothing else had existed for him.

If only he could make her feel as he did.

Beneath him the steamboat picked up speed as it left behind the now invisible landing where it had stopped. The Mississippi River was a dangerous mistress, but he had selected their boat with great care, choosing one that boasted two pilots well known for their experience with steamboats and their knowledge of the treacherous river. Of course, no pilot could foresee every peril, nor did a pilot have control over the explosion of a boiler, but the *Richmond* was relatively new. From his experience, an explosion was less likely on a new steamboat.

Planting his elbows on the rail, he stared at the dark riverbank slipping farther away in the cloud-shrouded night. But he wasn't looking at the scenery or even enjoying the cigarillo he had lit; he was working out the logistics of making love to Billie on one of those narrow stateroom beds.

Two men halted their promenade down the deck while one of them relit his pipe. Once it was going to his satisfaction, he waved it toward the riverbank.

"I'm surprised Captain Hillard bothered to stop at the Dupre place. He must know no one's farming it unless one of them carpetbaggers bought it. Lord knows, the South is crawling with them and their money."

"Take a parcel of money to get that place going again. It was ruined during the war. I heard old man Dupre shot himself when Lee surrendered."

"Can't say as I blame him. How many plantations can a man carve out of the wilderness in one lifetime? And this area has become wilderness again, or the closest thing to it."

Grayson, lost in his own thoughts, let their conversation flow around him as he smoked his cigarillo. A few more draws and an eternity of waiting would be ended.

"I can't think a lady would leave her stateroom dressed like that," one of the men said. "Unless the boat blew up and she was tossed out."

"If he pushes her to walk much faster, she's likely to fall."

"You think she wants to go with him?"

"Well, she ain't protesting too loudly, now, is she?"

By the time this odd conversation penetrated Grayson's reverie, the couple they were discussing had reached the top of the stairs leading down to the main deck. Curious, he turned to see who had caught his fellow passengers' attention.

When the couple passed the open door of a stateroom, the escaping light dappled over Dewey's features before illuminating Billie's frightened face. Then they were once again two shadowy figures, one pulling the other along the boiler deck to the rear stairway.

CHAPTER TWENTY

"Damn!" Grayson tossed his cigarillo overboard. Dewey had Billie.

His hand flew to his side, but his gun wasn't there. He had tucked it and his money belt into a secret compartment in the trunk.

He sprinted down the deck, dodging the few passengers who hadn't chosen to gamble in the saloon. About ten feet from the curving set of twin stairways, he climbed over the railing and dropped onto the cargo piled along the main deck.

He missed a sleeping roustabout by inches.

"What the hell . . . ?"

Ignoring the man, Grayson padded across sacks of rice, whose contents crunched beneath his boots. Dodging yet another sleeping body, he flattened himself on top of the sacks when he saw the two shadowy figures near the bottom of the stairway.

On this deck the steady hiss of steam from the boilers vied with the thump and splash of the paddle wheel. A group of roustabouts, who had chosen to drink and throw dice rather than sleep, were gathered near the engines.

He didn't have a gun, but Dewey didn't know it. He decided to take the risk.

"Unhand my wife or I'll shoot."

Billie skittered to a halt when she heard the Yankee's voice. Relief surged through her. She had no idea how he was going to get her out of this predicament, but anything had to be better than climbing over the side of the steamboat into the small boat Dewey had tied alongside.

"You shoot me and I shoot Miz Billie. It's as simple as that, Yank."

Something hard pressed into her lower back. "No reason to stop moving, Miz Billie. I told you to git in that boat. Now git."

She doubted the Yankee was armed, since there'd been no time for him to return to the stateroom and retrieve his gun. But in case he had a gun, she had to get out of his line of fire.

When Dewey shoved her forward into the narrow trail that wound through the piles of cargo, she stumbled. With a small cry of surprise, she pretended to trip over a trunk, giving the Yankee a clear view of Dewey.

When no shot rang out, she flipped open the catch on the ruby brooch. The pin portion was two solid inches of pointed metal.

"Damn it, woman, get up!"

Dewey reached down to drag her to her feet. She jammed the pin into the tender skin behind his left knee. The pin slid though the homespun fabric of his trousers until it was embedded hilt-deep in flesh. Jerking the pin free, she flattened herself against the trunk.

Dewey bent double, grabbing at his knee. "Damn you to hell! What'd you—"

The Yankee tackled Dewey, slamming his body into a hulking stack of cargo. Over the thudding grunt of one man knocking the air out of another, she thought she heard the sound of a gun skidding across the wooden deck. Whatever it was came to a stop near her.

She repinned the brooch to her dressing gown with fumbling fingers, then patted her way along the deck toward the two shadowy figures struggling a few feet from her. It was a quiet, deadly fight played out against the background of the monotonous thump-splash of a paddle wheel and the rhythmic hiss of steam. The mingled odors of damp wood, sweet molasses, and machine oil warred with the champagne that swirled in her stomach. The combination threatened to send her scrambling for the side, where she could heave out her insides in peace.

There was no time for theatrics. She had to find the gun, not lose her dinner. Panic vied with nausea in her stomach. She refused to dwell on what would happen if Dewey killed the Yankee.

She had to find the gun. She had to shoot Dewey.

It was as simple as that.

Oh, and she mustn't shoot the Yankee by accident.

Crawling forward, she fingered every inch of damp wood slick with God knew what vileness. Then her fingers encountered the cold metal of the gun barrel nestled against a coarse burlap bag. Just as her fingers closed around the barrel, someone grabbed her by the hair and hauled her to her feet.

A sharp steel point pressed against her throat. Onion-tainted breath wheezed in her ear.

"She's goin' with me, Yankee, or I kill her right now."

The Yankee, one knee on the deck, breath rasping in and out of his lungs, stayed where he was.

Dewey dragged her toward the edge of the deck. The gun went with her, hidden in the swirls of her dressing gown. She held it by the barrel, afraid to shift the grip into her hand. She had a sneaking suspicion her throat would be slit before she had time to turn the gun around, find the trigger, cock it, and fire it.

"Yankee, the gun!"

With the gun winging its way to the Yankee, Dewey either had to slit her throat or stop the Yankee. To her relief, he tossed her aside to free his throwing arm. Her relief evaporated when he kicked her as she went down. She grabbed for anything to stop her fall, but her fingers found only air, and she tumbled over the bow, into the river.

As the Mississippi closed over her head, she heard the deafening roar of a gun. She hoped Dewey was dead. Too bad she wouldn't live to find out.

If only she'd had the sense to ask who was at the stateroom door before she had unlocked it. But she had expected the Yankee to be at the door, not Dewey Perkins. When he said Seyler had tired of waiting for her, she had followed him. He had a gun, while she wasn't even dressed to be outside a bedroom.

Or in a river. Not that she knew how one dressed to drown.

And this time death wasn't going to be effortless, with Stephen to ease her way. This time she faced a painful fight to get air, blessed air, into her straining lungs. This time fear ruled.

She knew fear; it had been a frequent companion during the war.

Fear she would be discovered.

Fear of what the Yankees would do with her if they knew she was a spy.

Fear of Seyler.

Oh, yes, she had lived with fear, but not this kind of fear. A fear that devoured all hope of survival and offered death as the only option. Death dressed in the guise of the Mississippi River, whose current pulled her along and pushed her down, laughing at her heroic struggles to keep her nose above the water, while gleefully carrying the *Richmond* beyond her reach.

Until she was alone and exhausted in a dark river that

dragged at her flailing arms and saturated her gown and robe with impossible weight. The invitation was always there: to give up, to cease struggling, to let the water close over her head one last time. Then she heard Fletcher's reassuring voice:

"That's all you have to do. Relax, keep your nose out of the water, and paddle like Cato."

Paddle like Cato. Relax. Keep my nose out of the water. She let her feet sink, fighting the fear her body would drift down, too. Cupping her hands, she paddled like a dog, keeping her nose and mouth a scant inch above the water.

She paddled, gulping in mouthfuls of the dank air that hovered over the river—air as sweet as any breathed from a Tennessee mountain on a fine spring day. Sometimes she gulped in more water than air, which sent her into coughing spasms, but she kept her head afloat.

From her position she couldn't see the riverbank, but she paddled with the current while angling toward what she hoped was the riverbank. Bobbing along, she searched the darkness for a light from a house, another boat, or a break in the clouds. Anything that would orient her toward the riverbank.

She could have kicked herself for not having bedded her Yankee in New Orleans. At least she would go to her watery grave with that experience to cushion her death. Damn, she wished she could remember their coupling when he'd bedded her in Seguin while she had been ill. Why hadn't she allowed him to do it again, when she would remember?

Her arms screamed with fatigue. Where was that damn riverbank? She was so tired. She needed to rest. But when she stopped paddling, her head sank and her body drifted down. Down into the dark depths, where she couldn't tell top from bottom.

Panic grabbed her. She needed air. If she expelled the stale oxygen that kept her alive, liquid death would rush into its place, through her mouth, down her throat and into her lungs.

Where was the surface? My God! She didn't want to

drown. She couldn't let Seyler win! Water thrashed. She turned her head toward the gurgling sounds. She hoped it wasn't an alligator.

Clawing her way toward the noise, her head broke the surface, and river air rushed into her lungs. A pair of strong arms grabbed her. Adrenalin slammed into her exhausted body. Twisting and turning, she fought.

"Damn it, Billie, it's me. Stop fighting or you're going to drown us both!"

She had never been so happy to hear a Yankee accent in her life. Joy vied with relief, mantled with a strange warm, fuzzy feeling in the pit of her stomach. She avoided all her reactions by flinging herself on the Yankee.

He went under. Coming back up in a wash of water, he shook his head, showering them both. "Good God, woman! Are you trying to drown me?"

He peeled her arms from their choke hold around his neck.

"Hold on to my shoulders, not my throat." He shifted them in the water until she was behind him. "I promise I won't let you drown."

God, how she loved the raspy, hoarse sound of her Yankee's voice. She grabbed handfuls of the finely woven cotton shirt. Her legs were wrapped around his torso in an unseemly fashion, but she tightened her grip. Propriety wasn't an issue when one was being saved from drowning. Pressing herself against him, she felt her brooch grind into the soft flesh of her breast, but she didn't mind. The discomfort told her she was alive.

"That's better. Now, hang on and I'll get us to shore."

His instructions were superfluous; she wasn't about to let go, not even when she felt the water falling away from them as they neared the riverbank. She could feel his leg muscles straining against the pull of the mucky river bottom, but still she held him. Nor did she let go when he fell to his hands and knees, gasped for breath, and crawled the last few feet to the riverbank. No, she continued to cling to him like a baby opossum riding its mother for the first time since leaving the pouch.

She didn't like these near-death experiences at all, not one bit. From now on, she was keeping away from rivers.

"You . . . can . . . let . . . go . . . now."

She heard him wheeze out his instructions, but she couldn't obey him.

"Billie! Let go. It's all right. We're safe."

She doubted if she would ever feel safe, but she let him push her hands from his shoulders while she loosened the viselike grip of her legs and crumpled to the ground beside him.

Above them the clouds were shredding apart, blown hither and yon by a high celestial wind they couldn't feel. A bright fingernail moon paraded onto the night stage, its beams rippling across the river at their feet.

"What the hell was sticking into my spine?"

She stared down at the brooch pinned to her chest. "I . . . was . . ." She stopped to clear her throat. It felt like someone had run a currycomb down it. ". . . putting my pin in the jewelry case when Dewey knocked on the door."

The Yankee eased himself onto the ground beside her, falling onto his back. "I'm surprised he didn't steal it."

"He didn't know I had it until . . . I, uh, stuck it in his leg."

"So that's why he screamed."

Her body felt as if a team of Clydesdales had carted two tons of freight across it, but she had to touch her Yankee. When she lifted her arm, droplets of water sprinkled the air. Damp fingers met damp face.

"You saved my life. Again." His jaw was firm and strong, the minute stubble of his day-old beard scratching lightly at her fingertips. "I don't think I thanked you for the first time."

Shadows dappled his face, and she couldn't read his expression. He turned his head into her hand and kissed the fingers caressing his face. Tiny vibrations of warmth flickered from her fingertips to pool in her abdomen.

Memories of the accident in Texas crowded her thoughts. She had to tell the Yankee what she remembered.

"That day at the river in Texas when you found me. Stephen was there. I'm not sure what happened, but he came for me. There was such a feeling of . . . utter peace. Then you found me. I wasn't in my body. . . . I was with Stephen, somewhere near . . . and I watched you strip off our clothes and wrap us in blankets. I heard you say things."

When he would have responded, she put her fingers over his mouth. "Please. Let me finish. I chose to come back to be with you, but I was ill. I wasn't sure if I remembered correctly. If you had really said those things to me."

A taut, expectant silence stretched between them as she searched for the words she needed. She ran her thumb lightly across his lower lip.

"Tonight, in the river, I kept thinking I was going to die and I'd never experience you inside me. Please, Grayson . . ." She paused to savor the feel of his name upon her lips. "I have this . . . hunger for you."

"Ah, sweet Angel, I hunger for you, too."

By all rights she should have been cold, but his mouth on her thumb warmed her from the inside out. Death had shadowed her soul twice, and she could no longer see the past. She could only think of the here and now.

Here and now.

Man and woman.

Mating.

She wanted him to claim her the way Destiny claimed a mare. She wanted him to mount her and ride her. She wanted to feel the power in his thrusting hips.

Hands shaky with eagerness slipped down to unbutton his shirt. How many nights had she pretended to sleep while watching him undress? Her appetite for him had grown as her gaze repeatedly traced its way up a pair of sinewy legs to well-muscled thighs, pausing to study that part of him only a wife should see, and finally coming to rest on the thicket of brown hair that adorned his chest. She had enjoyed the play of lamplight across his flexing muscles as he had pulled off his shirt and then bent to remove his boots. And each night on the steamboat she had missed his warm body lying beside hers.

How she had dreaded dying without having known him.

He had erased her fear of intimacy until she craved his touch and thought of him constantly. She needed him in ways she had yet to examine.

God had given her another chance. And this one would not be thrown away.

Her hands would go where her gaze had been. She would engrave the taste and texture of his skin into her memory with her mouth. Then she would run trained hands up the muscles of his legs, across his chest, out his arms and along his fingers to their tips, until her hands corroborated what her eyes had told her about his conformation.

With a gentle shove, she pushed him onto his back.

"Ah, a woman who knows what she wants. I am yours to seduce, my Angel."

She finished unbuttoning his shirt, then slid her hands into the opening. Slowly she spread the shirtfront apart. When she leaned over his exposed chest, droplets of water slid from her head to splatter softly in the wiry hair.

"I'm dripping water on you." She bent her head down to his chest where the water had dripped.

"I doubt another drop or two . . . of . . . water . . . will . . . matter." His voice was hoarse, but not with river water this time.

She licked the drops of river water from his chest, enjoying the harsh catch of his breath as her tongue touched him. With her hands splayed against hard muscles, she inhaled, separating his personal scent from that of the Mississippi

River. She could feel the acceleration of his heart rate with her fingertips, pleased its tempo matched her own pounding heart.

She slowly kissed her way to his throat. "Mmmmm, I've wanted to do this for quite a while. You know, you are a shameless man, cavorting naked in front of me day and night."

"You are my wife. And I wasn't cavorting. If you want to know the truth, I was seducing you." His hand eased into the wet curls at the back of her head.

"I thought as much." She smiled against his throat, then moved closer to him, molding the soft contours of her body to his hard planes. Her body hummed at every inch of contact. And craved more.

She crawled on top of him, sliding her legs to either side of him. Her wet gown and robe rode high on her hips; her naked inner thighs clutched the raspy cloth of his trousers. She leaned forward, pushing herself against the hardness she knew would be waiting. Her hands played across his shoulders, along his arms, memorizing the configuration of his body.

Her brush with death had magnified her ability to feel, smell, hear, taste, and see. She rejoiced in the simple acts of touching his body, inhaling his scent, listening to the sound of his breathing, tasting his skin, and watching his eyes as she traced his body with her hands.

She craved the feel of his body against hers.

To touch him. To kiss him. To love him.

Ah, how she loved him. Had loved him for quite some time, arguing herself out of her feelings, burying them, but the threat of death had stripped away all the reasons not to love him. She was left with this wondrous feeling.

She should fear it, but right now she couldn't. Right now she wanted him. Needed him in ways she had never needed another human being.

Grayson's control slipped a notch each time Billie touched him with her hands, mouth, or body. Playing the passive partner in a session of lovemaking raised his self-control to new levels.

But he didn't want to frighten her or, God forbid, change her mind.

But she was driving him crazy.

Between the hands smoothing their way over his body and the lips nibbling their way up to his mouth, he was reaching the end of his self-imposed role of passivity.

When she wove her fingers into the damp hair on either side of his face, he placed his hands on her shoulders. The slightest tremor—whether of tension or pleasure, he didn't know—ran through her.

"May I?"

She tensed, then asked, "May you what?"

He rubbed himself against the juncture of her legs. "Have a turn."

Her head lowered a fraction. "What are you going to do?"

"This." He captured her mouth with his. She tasted of champagne and Mississippi River and Billie. And he wanted more.

Without breaking their kiss, he pushed the damp robe off her shoulders and untied the tapes to her nightgown. Then he nibbled his way from her mouth to her throat, down to her bare breasts.

"You are beautiful." He had felt her pebble-hard nipples press into his back during their swim in the river. Now he could taste them and lick off the Mississippi until they tasted of Billie again.

When he came up for air, she mewled a protest.

"Give me a minute," he said. With quick, deft movements, he stripped her gown and robe off, then peeled off his own wet breeches and shirt. There was something to be said for stripping off half your clothes before diving into the river: It didn't leave much to divest for lovemaking.

Once he dispensed with their clothes, he put himself on top to shield her from the cold. Not that they were cold. They should have been. They were soaking wet, lying on a moss-covered bank of the Mississippi River while the river itself lapped at the edge of the bank only inches from their feet.

But their bodies burned.

Now it was his turn to commit her body to memory. To touch, to taste, to smell. He made love with the same methodical thoroughness he drew maps. Surveying, sketching, and then creating a beautiful masterpiece. He drew his fingers over her, seeking to learn the peaks and valleys that constituted his wife. With expert fingers he searched for and found those places that would give her the most pleasure, enjoying her ragged breathing, her spontaneous moans, and her sighs of delight. He didn't stop his explorations until he felt and heard her shuddering climax.

Now his fingers were wet with her readiness for him.

Ever so slowly he mounted her, pushing his rigid shaft against the entrance he had painstakingly prepared. He felt her knees bend slightly as she tilted herself to better accommodate him.

He pushed himself inside her.

She was wet.

Welcoming.

Enveloping.

The thin barrier stretched and broke.

Beneath him, her body tensed. A little mewl of pain escaped her clenched teeth.

His body screamed for relief, but he stopped moving. "Are you all right?" The words rasped out of his mouth on a gush of air. He steadied himself, feeling his hands dig into the damp river soil on either side of her head.

"I don't understand. I thought we already . . . you acted as if we . . . Am I a virgin?"

His brain scrambled for an explanation.

"I am! I was. You lied in Seguin. We never did this. The priest could have annulled the marriage."

Hysteria laced her rising tone. Damn! He'd forgotten all about his ruse to keep her from getting an annulment.

"You lied!"

"I admit I implied we made love. I never said it outright."

"That's the same as lying."

God, it felt good to be inside her. If she wriggled much more, he'd explode.

"I admit I took advantage of your illness to marry you. I didn't take advantage of it to do this. Do you think I'm the type of man who would have forced myself on an ill woman?"

"You're a Yankee."

Sweet Jesus in heaven, if she didn't lie still, he could not be responsible for what happened.

"No. I'm Grayson Vanderlyn. Your husband."

She stilled beneath him. He eased himself a little deeper, hoping it no longer hurt. Leaning down, he brushed her mouth with his.

"Do you want me to stop?" That had to be the most difficult question he had ever asked in his life. And he had no idea whether he could stop if she asked.

"No. It feels too good. Too right."

To his undying relief, she pushed up to meet him. He eased himself deeper, searching for the rhythm that would please her as well as him.

Somehow he held on until he heard her cry of pleasure; then he entered her one last time, pumping his seed into the warm recesses of her body. As he shuddered into satisfaction, a vision of their future flashed into his thoughts. He saw Billie with a child at her breast, and he liked what he saw.

Careful not to rest all his weight on the woman lying beneath him, he eased himself toward the ground. He wanted to sleep, but the night river air crept over them and coolly reminded him of how vulnerable they were if anyone should come looking for them.

And Dewey might not be dead.

Although he believed he had killed Seyler's minion, he had no idea how many others had accompanied Dewey, or if they would continue the mission. It wouldn't be difficult to use the small boat tied to the *Richmond* to return down the river and verify whether the two of them had survived.

Lying naked on the riverbank provided little protection for them if Seyler's men returned.

He brought his senses back to reality. Above the sound of Billie's even breathing, he heard the nightly serenade of cricket frogs searching for mates. Deeper in the forest behind them was the occasional crackle of a twig broken by an unseen denizen who preferred to edge away from the humans rather than confront them.

He wasn't as worried about the forest dwellers as he was about Seyler's men. He and Billie might be hidden from the river by a sheltering group of honey locust trees, but they weren't safe from eyes searching specifically for them.

Billie stirred restlessly in his arms, bringing his attention to his sleeping wife. Already he was hungry for her again. He could feel himself harden at the idea of waking her for another round of lovemaking. It seemed impossible he had thought to find happiness in Sophronia's arms. They had been friends, not lovers. He would have lain with her and never experienced the fulfillment he felt with Billie, who completed him in ways he hadn't known existed.

He loved her. He couldn't dance around the truth any longer. He had insisted the priest marry them because he knew she wouldn't agree if she were conscious. Then, to keep her tied to him, he had insinuated they had made love.

And he wasn't the least bit sorry.

Next to him, Billie shivered in her sleep. They had to find a safe place where they could build a fire and dry their clothes.

There was pleasure in being her first. Not that he would

have loved her less, but he was pleased neither Stephen nor Fletcher had known his wife.

My wife. He liked the feel of those two words on his tongue. He liked the feel of her on his tongue. Leaning over, he nuzzled her ear. It was time to awaken his wife.

"Angel."

The insistent voice interrupted Billie's sleep.

"Wake up. It's time to dress."

Her thoughts had scattered like dandelion spores blown this way and that in a spring breeze. She scurried after them, catching each sensation and rebuilding the exquisite experience.

She stretched, feeling sexually replete. A languor such as she had never known crept into every nook and cranny of her body.

"We have to go before Dewey's men come looking for us."

She opened her eyes. Grayson leaned over her. Oh, dear. Those sensations he had unleashed in the core of her being were not going to stay satisfied. She felt them begin to uncoil one by one. With a smile, she raised her arms and wrapped them around his neck.

"Hmmmmm." She tugged his head down.

"I like the way you reward a man for fishing you out of the river."

His lips hovered a scant inch above her own. "I have a confession to make, Angel. You weren't dreaming that day by the Guadalupe River. I did say I love you."

He paused. His warm breath trickled across her lips. "And don't tell me you love me. I'm not interested in any profession of love from a woman who almost drowned an hour ago. I don't want to wait much longer, but I want you to be sure. For now, I'm content you liked what we did." His teeth flashed in the moonlight in a sudden grin. "You did like it, didn't you?"

"Hmmmm." She was glad he hadn't pressed her for an avowal of love, because she wasn't sure she could get her mouth to say what her heart felt. Not yet. Soon her brain would be in step with her heart. Then she would tell him.

Right now she preferred action to words and rose up to meet his lips. He brushed his mouth across hers in a fleeting kiss. She wanted to protest when he stopped kissing her, but he gave her no time.

He unwrapped her arms and said, "You, sweet wife, are a tease. And I'd love to return to our earlier activities, but first we need to find a safer place. And a warmer one."

She shivered when he lifted his warm body from hers. The damp nightgown and robe he thrust at her were cold and clammy from the river, but she had no choice except to don the wet clothing.

"I guess building a fire is out of the question."

She watched her husband button his trousers. *My husband.* She liked the sound of that phrase in her mind.

"We're too close to the river," he said. "I doubt if Dewey's men will follow us, but I have no idea what Seyler promised them."

"Is Dewey dead?"

"One can only hope. It was dark, but I fired from fairly close range. Frankly, I was too concerned about you to worry about whether or not I hit him."

She ran a bare foot up her calf as she looked at the woods behind them. "I'm afraid those adorable bedroom slippers are at the bottom of the river."

"And I'm sure some hardworking roustabout is enjoying my handmade leather boots."

For the first time, she really looked at Grayson. His feet were bare, and he was minus his frock coat. They made quite a ragtag pair. She grinned at him. "I daresay we'll raise some eyebrows when we stroll into Memphis barefooted."

CHAPTER TWENTY-ONE

"I hope Captain Hillard has the good sense to store our trunks in Memphis." Billie limped behind Grayson, relieved to have the scratchy sand of a rutted road beneath her feet. The twigs scattered along the forest floor had jabbed her foot with each step.

"For the fifteenth time, I'm sure he will."

"I can't help it. You've spoiled me. I despise the thought of losing all those lovely shoes you bought for me."

"Why don't you tell the truth?" Exasperation sharpened Grayson's tone. "You're worried about your boots."

"My boots?" She walked into the dark hulk that was her husband, bouncing back in surprise. He turned to face her, his face a pale oval in the starlight. She framed her next question carefully. "Why would I be more worried about my boots than my other shoes?"

"Because the papers for Destiny were in your left boot."

"Were?" Her hands curled into fists.

"The cobbler in Texas found them when he was repairing your boots."

"And he didn't put them back in the heel?"

"I put your papers in a bank in New Orleans."

"Of all the conniving, low-down, Yankee tricks." She planted her fisted hands on her hips to keep them from beating him on the chest. "You stole from a sick woman! Typical Yankee behavior. Steal the horse's papers from a sick woman just like you stole the horse from a defenseless kid." And fool that she was, she had lain with the deceitful man.

"You were ill when I found the papers. Once we were married, I thought it best to protect our proof of ownership in case Seyler tried to steal it. My papers are with yours."

"Oh."

His explanation deflated her anger. She looked down, digging her big toe in the sand.

"You can apologize if you want." He pulled her against the chest she had not beaten seconds earlier. Her fists uncurled, and she flattened her hands across the muscles beneath the finely woven linen of his shirt.

How quickly she had come to enjoy his touch. Here they were, lost and about as bedraggled as any two people could be, and she lusted after him when she should be concerned about getting safely to Sumner County.

"Just what form would you like the apology to take?" She couldn't believe she was flirting, but the feel of his body did strange things to her mental processes. He made her feel utterly feminine, as if she had never played the dirty urchin. As if there had never been a war that pitted them against each other.

"If you weren't shivering in my arms from cold, I'd show you how to make a proper apology. For now, I'll accept a quick kiss." True to his words, his lips brushed over her as lightly as a damsel fly sipping water from a pond. Then he turned her to face away from him. "Look over there. I think I see a place to spend what remains of the night. After you're warm and dry, we'll continue this discussion."

Grayson wasn't sure if the cabin he spotted when he turned back to argue with Billie was inhabitable, but he had to get her in front of a fire. He didn't like the cool, damp feel of her skin. Grabbing her by the hand, he pulled her toward the cabin.

It wasn't much and would look worse by daylight, but it had four walls, a crude bench, and a fireplace that wasn't clogged by bird nests. His matches had remained dry in the tin container Lina had given him as a going-to-war gift many years ago. Each time he pulled out a match, he could hear her patient voice explaining how a soldier needed dry matches as much as the Colt revolver Darrell had given him. The war had offered him many a cold night on which he had heartily agreed with his sister. Tonight he mentally thanked her again. The deadwood he found near the cabin flared easily into warm life.

They didn't find any food, but he found some discarded feed sacks, which he spread before the fire. It wasn't much of a bed, but it was better than lying naked on the dirt floor while their clothes dried before the fire.

Snuggling up behind Billie, he tried to warm her bare backside while the fire warmed her front. His right hand joined the crusade by cradling a breast. He could feel the results of the regular meals she had eaten these past weeks in the heavy fullness in his hand. Nuzzling his nose into her neck, he searched for some hint of the lavender scent she had splashed on herself before dinner. The river had washed it away.

"I guess we should make some plans," she murmured.

"I don't know." He brushed his thumb across the tip of her breast, enjoying its immediate response. "Being with you has taught me the value of spontaneity."

"What do you mean?" Her voice held an erotic, breathless quality that heated his blood.

"Before I met you, I thought my life was mapped out." He

gently circled the taut peak of her breast with his thumb. "I thought I wanted to go home, get married, and start a family. Until you tumbled into my life."

"Are you blaming me because you didn't marry Sophronia?" She slid onto her back and looked up at him. The firelight darkened her eyes to a rich emerald and flickered shadows across her face.

He didn't move his hand, enjoying the spreading flow of her breast beneath his fingers. "Don't get your hackles up, Angel. I'm glad I didn't marry Sophronia. I should never have asked her to marry me."

"Why did you?"

He had given that question a lot of thought since meeting Billie. The answer came easily. "It seemed the right thing to do at the time. When I returned home and saw Sophronia, John's death hit me again, harder than it had during the war. I guess that's when I realized he would never come home. I decided I should take care of her for him. Thank God she realized the folly of our situation and released me from the betrothal."

Smoothing his hand down to her stomach, he relished the feel of her warming skin and stifled gasp of pleasure. He didn't want to discuss Sophronia any longer.

"Don't you owe me an apology?" he asked.

"Oh, yes, I do." Feather-light, her hand trailed across his chest, down his abdomen to his thigh, and then back to his chest. Then her hand stilled. In the flickering light of the fire, he saw a tinge of confusion.

"What's the matter, Angel?"

Her fingers played in the hair that dusted his chest. "I, uh, suppose it's good for a wife to have these feelings for her husband."

"What feelings?"

She shifted restlessly under him. "You know, hot and strange . . . like I felt in the cabin, in the chair . . . but we weren't married and I don't think I was supposed to feel like that when I wasn't married. But now it's acceptable?"

He liked knowing his touch made her feel hot and strange. He also recognized the dilemma she wrestled to solve. The war had stolen much from her, but she had retained an enchanting air of innocence.

"It's not wrong to feel the way you do when I touch you, Angel. It's good you feel this way. Society tells us we aren't supposed to recognize these feelings before we're married, but that doesn't mean they don't exist. The human body has rules, too. And one of those rules is the attraction between male and female."

"If that's true, why haven't I felt this way before?"

Sincere bafflement colored her tone, and he liked hearing it. "Are you saying you didn't experience these feelings for your fiancé?"

"Stephen and I were good friends." She paused as if struggling to find the right words, then blurted out, "If he hadn't been on his way to war, I wouldn't have consented to marry him."

Beneath the confession, he heard the guilt. Why hadn't she loved Stephen enough? Why had she lived when he died? He heard the guilt because he knew how guilt gnawed at you day and night.

The need to protect and cherish the woman beside him flooded his senses.

"Do you know how you make me feel?"

She shook her head.

"Very hot . . . and strange." He cupped her face with his hands. There was a heat in him that had nothing to do with the fire burning three feet away. "Thank God you came for Destiny," he whispered as he lowered his mouth to cover hers.

Her hand slid between his legs.

He sighed, "Oh, yes," into her mouth.

"Do you like this?" Her hand curled softly around him. Her touch was tentative, unsure, and it drove him wild with longing.

"Oh, God, yes."

Moving upward, her hand stroked and rubbed along his rigid shaft. Her body followed the actions of her hand, rising to press against him while she rubbed herself the length of him. Any plans he had of going slow evaporated.

Coherent thought vanished. With a gentle shove, he toppled her back and covered her body with his own, pressing for an entry she eagerly met. Once sheathed inside her, he placed his hands beneath her hips and tilted her slightly. He was surprised by the unexpected strength of her thighs. They gripped him with muscles carved from a lifetime of horseback riding.

Her hair, no longer river-wet, curled around her face in ringlets damp from their union. Perspiration sheened her body as his hold on her buttocks tightened and he entered the clenching interior. It was almost impossible to leave, but a primeval instinct drove him out of her. And then back in.

Tiny moans of pleasure rippled in the air between them, and he watched her eyes shimmer their surprise as he drove himself into her one last time. The deep, guttural cry of his own pleasure resounded in the small room, startling him by its intensity. With a shuddering release, he once again tried to create life with the woman he loved.

He wondered if Billie had explored all the ramifications of their repeated unions, but he wasn't going to bring up the subject of annulment. If anything, he planned to make sure the subject would lose validity by pregnancy. Satiated and highly pleased with himself, he eased down onto the pillow of her body.

Billie had to admit, being lost with a topographical engineer had its advantages—the man carried a compass in his pocket.

He found Memphis the next afternoon. Or rather, he found

a secluded glade and insisted she remain there while he went for supplies.

"It's bad enough I've got to walk into the city without boots or a coat. I'm not taking you into civilization without a proper dress or shoes."

From his stance, she figured it useless to argue with him. "Take this." She unpinned her brooch. "You'll need money to buy clothes and food.

"Keep your brooch. I'll send a telegram to Darrell for funds."

"How will you pay for it?"

He shifted the pieces of wood he carried, fished into his right pocket, and held up his compass. "I am not without resources."

"And what about Seyler?" Her fingers stilled on the clasp of the brooch.

"I don't plan to send him a telegram, if that's what worries you."

"You might as well send him one if you plan to walk into the telegraph office."

He dropped the wood at her feet. "What's that supposed to mean?"

"Seyler's men are probably watching the telegraph offices."

"Why would they do that? They think we drowned or were washed miles downriver."

"I've known Seyler for years. You met the man once. He won't take their word we drowned. He'll want proof. And while they search the riverbanks for our bodies, he'll act on the assumption we're alive. Alive and possibly without funds. The telegraph offices will be watched. He knows if you need money, you'll go there."

Grayson hunkered down and began building a fire. "I think you overestimate our friend Seyler."

"No," she said as she swatted at a buzzing insect who took exception to their invasion of the glade. "You under-estimate him. Seyler put together a statewide system of informers during the war. Many of those men continue to work for him."

"The war's over. Why look for spies now?"

"Not spies, information. Don't you think the governor finds Seyler's men a useful tool in controlling the state?"

"Hand me those twigs, will you?"

Grabbing a handful of twigs, she squatted down beside him. "Believe me, Seyler will have men watching the telegraph offices." She passed the twigs to him and waited, giving him time to mull over her words.

Beside her, he blew gently on the miniature fire and coaxed it into life. Satisfied with his efforts, he leaned back on his haunches and fed a thicker branch to it.

Then he looked at her and smiled. "All right. You made your point. I'll take the brooch, pawn it for food, clothes, maybe a horse, and stay away from the telegraph offices. We can wire Darrell from Nashville and have money waiting for us in Gallatin."

"It'd be better to telegraph him from, um . . ." She racked her brain for towns between Memphis and Nashville. ". . . oh, Lexington, and have the money delivered to Nashville. And use an alias."

"Why on earth would I need to use an alias?" Surprise sent his eyebrows winging toward his hairline, and, at long last, his complete attention to her.

She took a deep breath and told herself to curb her impatience. He didn't know how to operate in her world of subterfuge; she would have to guide him.

"I'd rather Seyler didn't know when we reached Sumner County. If your brother sends the money in your name, Seyler will know in a matter of hours. Just as he knew about the letter you sent to my father. And Dewey knew to follow you to Texas."

"You've made your point." The fire crackled. He fed it another limb. "You know the man better than I, but I think you're giving Seyler too much credit for knowing our every move."

"I'd rather overestimate what Seyler can do than under-estimate him."

When he didn't react to her sarcastic reference to his earlier comment, she felt a niggle of guilt. Dismissing it, she unpinned the brooch.

"How long has the brooch been in your family?"

"A long time, but I find when one weighs jewels against food, food wins every time."

The intensity of his gaze when he looked up from the fire startled her. He reached out and uncurled her fingers from the brooch. His gaze never left her eyes. "Don't worry, Angel, I'll redeem your brooch. It won't be a permanent loss."

The ruby brooch bought them a dilapidated wagon, a horse who had survived the war because he was already ancient when it began, food, a coffeepot, a skillet, two pots, a pair of boots for each of them, several sets of unfashionable clothes, and ammunition for a gun Grayson found on his way to Memphis. Thus equipped, they began their journey across Tennessee.

Billie spent her time in the glade devising a plan to rescue Destiny, but she didn't spring it on Grayson immediately. Living with her father and Shaughnessy had taught her the rudiments of dealing with men. She knew they responded best to female persuasion when they were well fed and relaxed. It wasn't difficult to create such an atmosphere two days into their trip.

First she positioned herself against the sturdy trunk of a yellow poplar tree while they ate their midday meal. Then she mentioned how tired the aging horse looked. Finally, she suggested Grayson nap while the horse grazed and rested.

Before she could blink, her husband was stretched out on the ground, his head heavy on her thighs. All thoughts of why she had suggested he lay his head in her lap fled as she drew her fingers up the curve of his jaw and into his hair. He turned his head and brushed a tiny kiss on her palm.

When he failed to follow this gesture with a more demanding action, she realized he intended to sleep.

"Uh, Grayson."

"Hmmmm?" He nestled his head deeper into her lap.

"I've been thinking . . . I mean, I have a plan to get us into the county without Seyler's knowledge."

"That's nice, but I have no intention of sneaking into Sumner County." He covered his mouth and yawned.

"Oh, I suppose you intend to ride up to Seyler's door, brandish that aging revolver you found in some ditch, and demand Destiny?" Thoughts of coaxing him into a tryst under the trees vanished in the heat of her anger.

Her outburst failed to annoy him. He didn't even open his eyes.

"The revolver's serviceable. Once we reach Gallatin, I'll make an appointment with Mr. Seyler and we'll discuss the horse." For all his sleepy demeanor, there was an ominous undercurrent of steel in his voice. "I believe I can persuade him to return Destiny."

She didn't believe. Seyler was evil. She doubted her husband understood the blackness of Seyler's soul. But she did. Evil had hovered over her family for years.

If Grayson expected a civilized system of law and order in which his stronger claim on the horse was honored, he would be disappointed. He didn't seem to understand how much law and order had collapsed in her county. The end of the war had not brought about its restoration. No, Seyler's brand of frontier justice reigned. The strong ruled the weak, and there were few legal constraints to protect anyone. She didn't like it, but she'd been forced to live with it and had learned to cope with the system.

Grayson hadn't.

She was certain of one thing: She had to offer a logical

argument and convince him her plan would succeed while his would not.

"Are you mad? We can't sashay into Seyler's home and ask him to return Destiny. That man is worse than a Union soldier." The words were said before she realized whose head lay in her lap. She looked heavenward. What had happened to logic?

"He must be evil personified."

She peeked down; his eyes remained closed, but a tiny smile played at the corners of his mouth. An apology seemed in order.

"I, uh, spent four years despising Yankees. . . ."

He waved away her apology. "Don't worry. I understand."

"Good." Now she was free to argue the real issue. "I was worried you'd taken some fool notion your money would ease the way. That Seyler would give you the horse if you asked politely, because you're from a wealthy New York family."

Snuggling his head deeper into her lap, he reached out and tugged at the frayed edge of her skirt. Was he intentionally trying to distract her?

"I don't think money will pave the way . . ."

The lazy rub of his fingers on her calf made it difficult for her to concentrate on the discussion.

". . . but short of stealing my own horse, how else can I get him back?"

"Our horse," she corrected tartly as she reached over and pushed her skirt between her stocking and his hand. Much as she enjoyed his touch, they had a major problem to solve. "And stealing Destiny is exactly what I had in mind."

"What?" Gray eyes stared up at her, and his fingers ceased their distracting caress. "You want me to steal my own horse?"

"Our horse," she corrected again. "Stealing him is the only way you're going to get Destiny away from Seyler."

"So much for an after-lunch nap." He pushed himself into a sitting position. "Stealing, in case you forgot, is against the

268 *Ginger Hanson*

law. Since we have proof we own the horse, the law is on our side. Not against us."

She drew her legs to her chest and wrapped her arms around them. If she didn't keep her hands tightly clasped, she'd grab him by the outmoded lapels of his frock coat and shake him to better make her point.

"In New York the law is on your side. Not in Tennessee. And you told me your proof was locked in a safe in New Orleans." The even keel of her tone surprised her.

He plucked leaf debris off the arm of his frock coat with as much care as if his coat had been sewn by his New York tailor. "A notary public made copies of the documents."

"Oh, and they survived your swim in the Mississippi."

"The copies are in our trunks, which are on their way to Gallatin." A stray thread caught his attention.

"So much for legal copies," she muttered. Her calm, rational side fought with the side that wanted to bang the coffee-pot over his head until he saw the light. And to make him stop preening and listen to her.

She sweetened her tone instead. "Look, we won't be stealing Destiny in the strictest sense of the word, because he belongs to us. And you know as well as I, Seyler won't give up Destiny simply because you ask. I mean, you didn't give him the horse when he asked."

"Perhaps he didn't ask correctly."

"He didn't ask correctly?" All attempts to remain calm evaporated. She jumped to her feet, unable to rant without also pacing.

"He didn't ask correctly? The person who has men combing the state right now with orders to kill us didn't ask correctly? Do you realize we'll be fortunate to reach Gallatin alive? No, you don't. But ignorance won't stop you, will it?" She stomped back and forth, her mind whirling with how to convince him of Seyler's power.

"You think you can ride into Angel's Valley, ask Seyler

for Destiny—ask Seyler *correctly* for the horse—and he will give him to you. Holy Mary, Mother of God! Seyler will have you killed before you set one foot in Angel's Valley!"

Her stomping tirade came to a halt when a pair of arms encircled her from behind.

"This man really frightens you, doesn't he?" He pulled her against his chest.

She turned in his arms. "He scares the hell out of me." But in Grayson's embrace, she felt safe. If he comprehended the danger they faced, he could help her deal with it. She needed him to understand. "He's taken away everyone I love."

She didn't like the way her voice trembled on the last sentence.

He hooked his finger beneath her chin and tilted her head so he could see her face. "That bodes well for me, then. Unless you've fallen in love with your Yankee?"

Well, maybe somewhere between Seguin and Memphis she had, but she wasn't going to tell him. The feeling was too ethereal to put into words. It was easier to counter with her own question. "Are you ready to hear my plan?"

His searching gray eyes didn't seem ready to let her go. They scanned her face as if he were surveying her features to put them on paper. Whatever he saw brought a gentle smile to his mouth. A smile that warmed her from head to toe.

"Thank you, Angel. I accept your warning that I should be careful. Now tell me your plan."

Rather than unravel his enigmatic words, she took a deep breath. It didn't help much; her voice remained wobbly with a strange welter of feelings she didn't have time to analyze.

"Disguise ourselves, get into Sumner County undetected, find out where Seyler's stabled Destiny, and steal him." Fletcher had often told her simple plans had a better chance of success. Thus, she had kept her plan simple.

"And what disguises do you have in mind for us?"

Well aware of his fingers stroking the skin beneath her chin, she thrust her jaw forward and offered her suggestion. "Two old women would be perfect."

"Two women!" He pushed her off his chest to hold her at arm's length. "You want me to dress as a female?" Shock riddled his question.

"Fletcher dressed as a female during the war." It felt good to be on the firmer territory of disguises. Her voice had lost that wobbly edge. "He said it was the most effective disguise he ever used."

Grayson dropped his hands from her shoulders and ran one through his hair. "And naturally I should follow in the footsteps of the indomitable Fletcher Darring."

She smothered a grin. Was that jealousy she heard? The notion gave her an unexpected warm glow, but there was no time to bask in the thought.

"Why not? He was excellent at his job."

"I suppose he thought up your little masquerade. It didn't seem to bother him your life would have been forfeited had you been discovered."

"But I wasn't discovered," she pointed out. "And playing the part of a crippled boy was my idea. Fletcher wasn't at all pleased, but I persuaded him. To give credit where it's due, he suggested I act slow-witted. Fletcher says people see what they want to see. During the war people wanted to see a crippled half-wit, and that's what they saw. *You* wanted to see an old woman in Albany, and that's what you saw."

"I wasn't looking for you in Albany. I thought you were safe on the farm."

Did she hear a touch of grudging respect beneath the censure? "Fletcher had to choose some type of disguise to get us through New York safely. We thought you would be right behind us."

"It's time we were going."

"Does this mean you won't dress as a woman? I mean, Fletcher did it." She kept her eyes wide and innocent as if

unable to comprehend why he wouldn't do something Fletcher
had done.

Her ploy didn't work.

"I absolutely refuse to dress as a female."

She wondered how he had spit out the words with his
teeth clenched together, but she knew better than to argue.
His refusal was rock-solid. She trailed him as he stalked to
the horse.

"Will you consent to any other disguise?" She started to
tell him the horse would shy away from the anger radiating
from him, but let him find out for himself.

Two feet from the restless horse, he swung around. Unprepared, Billie stumbled to a halt. Their booted toes touched.

"You're right," he said. "Fletcher chose the perfect disguise
for you in New York. Your admiration for the man is valid. I
realize now he had no choice except to support your odd starts
because you're a stubborn, willful female who won't listen to
reason. But I refuse to masquerade as a female—if you feel
we should be disguised, I will consent to a male role."

She was too disconcerted by the fact that he had labeled
her stubborn and willful to enjoy her victory. What happened to "intelligent, resourceful, and courageous?" She had
hugged those words to her heart since he had said them. And
now she was stubborn and willful?

Grayson grabbed the harness off the wagon. If he didn't
control his anger, he'd never get the horse harnessed. Taking
a deep breath, he pushed aside the appalling vision of himself dressed as a woman.

"Easy, old boy. It's a harness. You've worn one hundreds
of times." To his relief, the horse responded to his tone and
let him approach. But he couldn't keep his thoughts on har-
nessing the horse. Rather, he fumed over the fact that Billie
had asked him to masquerade as a woman. Fletcher had done
it; why couldn't he? Well, he didn't care if Fletcher Darring
had portrayed a hundred females. Grayson Andrew Vanderlyn would not pretend to be a woman for one second.

"I guess Fletcher was man enough to play a woman."

"And I'm not?"

The horse flinched at the snarling voice next to his ear.

"Sorry, old boy." Grayson softened his voice.

"Oh, that was unkind of me. I never meant . . ."

"What!" He shoved the bit between a set of large worn and yellowed teeth. "To insinuate I'm not the man Fletcher Darring is? That I'm a low-down, stinking Bluebelly? What did you *not* mean, Billie?"

"Well . . ."

"Be happy I'm all those things you think I am. Because if I'd been in Fletcher Darring's place, I never would have allowed you to play the part of spy."

To his disgust, her defense of Fletcher was immediate and staunch.

"Fletcher let me spy because he's a friend. He knew how important it was for me to help. And he was one of our best intelligence officers. Why, he hoodwinked all the Federal forces in Tennessee for four years."

"Friend?" He gave the check strap a final tug. "Does a friend send a woman alone to Texas?"

"He's the best of friends. He got me through the war."

He looked at her over the horse's head but said nothing. His skeptical stare brought him more than he expected.

"He asked me to marry him."

Her defiant words ignited an unexpected fireball of jealousy in the pit of his stomach. The horse lowered his head and snuffled Grayson's hand. The velvety lips nibbled at the sleeve to his frock coat.

"Why didn't you marry this paragon of the Confederacy?" He didn't mean to ask, but his mouth ran off before his brain could stop it. He hated the idea he would have to deal with Fletcher Darring's specter for the rest of their lives.

She looked away. "California called to him. Texas called to me."

A tiny flare of hope flickered in his heart. She had refused to marry the paragon of the Confederacy. He wondered if she would ever tell him why. For now, it was enough she hadn't married Fletcher.

"All right, we'll wear a disguise to keep our arrival in Gallatin a secret. We'll adopt the elderly-couple idea you and Fletcher used. You'll have to carry any conversation, I don't want my accent to give us away."

"Thank you."

"I'm not convinced Seyler has the power you think he has, but you've lived in Sumner County and I haven't. I bow to your experience." He tugged on the lead rein and headed for the wagon. "Oh, and next time you want me to do something, just ask. You don't have to soften me up with food and a nap."

Although he didn't share Billie's fear of Seyler, he respected her instincts. She had relied on her wits to survive in a dangerous situation. He would accept her assessment of the situation until he had time to gather data and reach his own conclusions.

Meanwhile, he treated their trip as he had any clandestine movement of troops during the war. Two or three times a day he left her to drive the wagon while he scouted the area for less-traveled roads to carry them across Tennessee. He made her keep the revolver tucked into her skirts. The old Le Mat might not be as good a weapon as his Colt, but it was a weapon. Foraging ahead of the wagon on foot, he made better time than the horse, who was slowed by bones that creaked as loud as the decrepit wagon he pulled.

In this almost idyllic fashion, they made their way across Tennessee. As the aging horse ambled along dirt roads, Grayson and Billie ambled through a variety of conversational topics. He discovered his bride was an artful mix of common sense and imagination. Her unusual education had been an odd combination of the feminine arts and horse breeding with a smattering of the classics thrown in for good measure. Her knowledge of nature was limited, but she loved geography and had read all his novels several times.

He could not think of a better recommendation for a wife.

Sitting beside her, their thighs rubbing in intimate rhythm as the wagon rolled down a dirt road, he saw this trip as a prelude to their time in Colorado. It was easy to picture them mapping unfamiliar terrain by day and making love by night.

Because their lovemaking made the trip memorable. Just as he sought the best ways to get them across Tennessee undetected, he also sought the best ways to please her. From the cries and moans his hands elicited, she must have liked his penchant for thoroughness. And her body was his to explore each night and sometimes during the day.

All too soon they were camped outside Nashville.

CHAPTER TWENTY-TWO

Billie leaned on her cane and peered nearsightedly through her spectacles at the clerk.

"May I help you, ma'am?"

"Yes." She threaded a higher, softer tone into her deepened Southern accent. "I'm expecting a telegram from my brother, Mr. Darrell."

"Why, yes, ma'am. I believe I received that message two or three days ago."

The clerk bustled off to get her telegram; Billie heard the door open behind her. The fine hairs along her neck rose. She didn't need to turn around to know Norval Perkins had entered the small telegraph office. He had been seated on the bench outside the office.

She hadn't seen Dewey's cousin in years, but the Perkins trademark ears made him easy to recall. She doubted he had recognized her beneath her elderly-widow disguise, but she knew better than to let her guard down.

Folding her gloved hands over the top of her cane, she waited for the clerk. Fletcher had always told her this was the difficult part: convincing her intended audience that her disguise wasn't a disguise. Everything she did had to convince others she was an elderly widow.

She looked like an elderly widow. Black bombazine swathed her from head to toe, leaving little of her for anyone to see. As she had in Albany, she looked out at a world tinged black by the veiled bonnet perched on her head. It and her dress were fashioned in the style popular before the war, signaling to the world she had failed to retain the wealth commensurate with her social position. The back of the bonnet curved upward to reveal silvered hair wound into a chignon and delicately covered with black lace.

"Here you are, Mrs. Gray." The clerk counted out some bills.

Billie tried to concentrate on the money, but every cell in her body focused on Norval. He stood behind her, and she prayed Grayson hadn't allowed any of her own hair to show when he helped her put on the silver wig. She swallowed, alarmed at the pace her heart was hammering in her chest. She drew in a breath, easing it out slowly, calming herself.

"If you will sign here . . ."

Taking the pen the clerk offered, she let her hand shake slightly as she slowly wrote her name. Then she took her time about unfastening the clasp on her large reticule, placing the money in a large black change purse and, finally, pulling the strings of her reticule tight.

"Thank you," she said. Turning, she jabbed her cane down on Norval's mud-encrusted boot.

"Gawd damn! You broke my toe, old woman!" Norval grabbed his foot and hopped backward.

"Heavens, where on earth did you come from, young man?"

"Sir! There's a lady present."

"That old witch done broke my toe!"

Billie toddled out the door, letting it close on the rising altercation. The hotel was down the block and across the street. She tapped her way there slowly when she wanted to pick up her skirts and run.

Time inched past at an agonizing snail's pace.

Then she entered the hotel, crossed the lobby, went through the hall and out the rear entrance to find Grayson snoozing on the seat of the wagon.

She wanted to bop him on the head with her cane. Instead, she tossed the cane into the wagon bed and scrambled into the seat. Snatching the reins out of his slack grip, she clucked at the horse and slapped the reins on his back.

"Let's go, Molasses." She had named the horse Molasses because she always named her horses, and this horse moved too slow for any other name.

The wagon lurched, waking Grayson, who grabbed at the seat to keep from being thrown off. "Damn, Billie! You trying to kill me? What's your hurry?"

"Norval Perkins."

Grayson unlatched one hand from its death grip on the wagon seat and rubbed at his eyes. "What's a Norval Perkins?"

"Dewey's cousin."

A short silence met that announcement. She was too busy guiding Molasses through the wagons and carriages that littered the streets of Nashville to worry about Grayson's reaction.

"Did he recognize you?"

She curbed her impatience at the horse's slow pace. "Norval saw what he wanted to see."

"Which means you had no problem getting the money."

"It's in my reticule."

When a drummer's wagon veered into their path, Molasses halted.

"Mind if I take the reins?"

"Am I doing something wrong?"

"You handle the reins better than most men."

Implicit in the praise was the fact he wanted to drive. She stood up, felt him slide across the seat behind her, gave him the reins, and then scooted to where he had been sitting. She peered anxiously behind them.

"We can't wait here all day. Norval might be looking for us."

"I thought you fooled him."

"Temporarily. Norvel's mind works a little slow, but he might realize the frail old widow jabbed his foot a little too hard for an old woman. When he doesn't find a Mrs. Gray at the hotel, he might decide to send a message to Seyler."

"You jabbed his foot?"

The drummer's wagon blocking the road was as gaily painted as Fletcher's apothecary wagon.

"Did your brother send enough money to purchase that wagon?"

He followed the direction of her pointing finger.

He looked back at her. "Are you thinking what I think you're thinking?"

"Why not?"

"Why not? Let's see. Oh, I thought you wanted to enter Sumner County inconspicuously. That wagon's not inconspicuous. It's gaudy."

She grinned at him. "It is, isn't it? Which makes it perfect. Seyler will never suspect we're in it, because it's too obvious."

Within fifteen minutes Grayson convinced the drummer to sell his wagon. The money Darrell sent them sealed the transaction. Thirty minutes after spotting the wagon, they had moved their meager belongings into it. Once they were outside Nashville, Billie climbed into the back of the wagon to change. When she rejoined Grayson, she no longer sported a widow's dress, although the gray wig still adorned her head and she peered at the world over metal spectacles.

Their new wagon moved as slowly as their old one because the drummer had refused to sell his horse. She was pleased they were too rushed to find another horse, because she hadn't wanted to abandon Molasses. It was, she told herself, because he lent an air of authenticity to their disguise. She wasn't willing to admit she had come to like the old horse.

She settled onto the seat next to Grayson. Disguising him had proved to be more of a problem than she'd anticipated. She surveyed her handiwork with a frown.

"I should've paid more attention to Fletcher's tricks. I doubt anyone will think you old."

Grayson slid his finger under the rim of the overly large hat she had found for him and scratched at his scalp. Billie had tacked some gray yarn to the hat, and the stuff itched.

"Then I guess you'll have to play the part of my mother."

He laughed when her frown deepened. "And I'll be deaf and dumb."

As he hoped, a smile replaced the frown. "That idea has merit."

Her smiles and conversation had lessened the closer they got to Gallatin, and he could feel the past sliding between them. When she talked, she would talk of everything except Angel's Valley.

And their future.

For the past few days, her infrequent conversations centered on Texas and horse breeding. He wondered if it helped her deal with what she saw.

Their trip through Tennessee brought them face-to-face with the aftermath of the war: burned buildings, sagging fences, fields gone to weed. The countryside was mute testimony to the prize middle Tennessee had once been. A devasted land, it would need a long time to recuperate.

Later that afternoon they passed a particularly fine-looking plantation house. It wore the air of desolation with dignity.

"I can't stand the thought of Archibald Seyler living in my mother's house."

Her soft statement, tossed into a long silence, caught him off guard. He had been studying the classical lines of the dingy Corinthian columns that paraded across the front of the house. Her comment broke his concentration. Here was his chance to tell her he had bought Angel's Valley; Seyler would never live in her lovely house.

As he mentally framed his announcement, a half-dozen men poured out of the woods on either side of them.

"Morning, strangers."

Confronted with six horses, Molasses halted. Grayson squelched the urge to reach under Billie's skirts and whip out the Le Mat. From the armory their visitors sported, he doubted one gun would even the odds.

Beside him, Billie leaned forward, tugged her spectacles down a notch, and peered intently at the leader.

"Why, Jonas Reece, have you broken parole?" She pulled off the bonnet and wig with one hand while running the fingers of her other hand through the flattened curls.

"Miss Billie D'Angelo! I thought you went out west somewhere." A grin softened the harsh planes of the older man's face. "Are you up to your old tricks again? Is Fletcher under that slouchy ole hat?"

Six pairs of eyes fastened on Grayson, their dawning warmth extinguished by Billie's next words.

"No, it's not Fletcher. He's on his way to California."

Grayson noticed Billie didn't bother to identify him.

"Why are you wearing enough guns to be a Texan? I thought you signed a parole."

Reece scowled. "Me and the boys here are just getting rid of a few varmints. Seems the Federal garrison can't keep straight who should be in jail and who shouldn't." Shrewd blue eyes swept over Grayson, but his question was directed to Billie. "Why're you dressed like an old woman?"

Grayson wondered if an ex-Union soldier fell in the category of varmint. He'd heard tales of intimidation, pistol-whippings, and outright murder when they stopped in Lexington to send Darrell the telegram. Reece and his band appeared dressed to commit any atrocity.

Billie rested her hand on his arm, either to reassure him

or warn him to keep quiet. Or both. He remained silent because they were on her home ground, not his.

"I was in Texas," she said. "Seyler found out where I was and sent Dewey to steal Destiny."

"And you're here to get him back." Reece shook his head. "Lordy, Miss Billie, how many times are you gonna have to steal that horse?"

"As many times as it takes until people stop stealing him from me."

Grayson caught the quick scowl she sent his way in his peripheral vision. Why didn't she write, *This Yankee stole Destiny,* on a sign and wave it over his head? Not that he had stolen the horse. It had been a wartime comandeering. He hoped the armed-to-the-teeth former Reb understood the difference.

"Sounds like you're on a mission." Reece rested his hands on the pommel.

"Can you help me find Destiny? Have you seen him at Angel's Valley?" Billie scooted toward the edge of the wagon seat.

Grayson glanced down to make sure the gun remained hidden.

"Why would Seyler take Destiny to Angel's Valley instead of the Massengail place?"

The question whipped Grayson's attention back to the Rebel, who shot a quick glance in his direction. Grayson's stomach tensed into a knot. He should have told Billie about the auction weeks ago.

"Didn't Seyler purchase the horse farm when it was up for auction?" Surprise tinged Billie's question.

A few seconds ticked past before Reece said, "No, he didn't."

"No one bought Angel's Valley."

Hope flickered in Billie's voice, ripping a hole in Grayson's heart and locking his tongue to the roof of his mouth.

"Why, Miz Billie, didn't you hear?" One of the men pushed his horse forward, eager to share the news. "Some Yankee from New York bought it. He's got Shaughnessy and half the county making repairs. My brother James is helping with the carpentry. We figured the Yankee went back north to get his wife."

Grayson knew the moment Billie digested this information and jumped to the correct conclusion.

"Holy Mary, Mother of God! *You* own Angel's Valley."

From her tone, one would think he was a poisonous species of insect worthy of immediate squashing.

A number of responses jammed his brain. Noncommittal seemed safest. "In a manner of speaking."

It didn't appear to appease her. She glared at him. Freckles sprinkled her dainty nose; fury snapped in her green eyes.

"Either you own it or you don't, Yankee."

He sighed. She was back to epithets instead of first names. If his crisp accent hadn't alerted the men to his origin, her name-calling did. They straightened in their saddles and eyed him suspiciously.

"Now, Billie. I bought Angel's Valley for you."

His soothing answer mollified her for about two seconds. "Of course. You bought Angel's Valley for a scruffy little boy."

Her logic dented his defense.

"He must be the Yank who stole Destiny during the war," Reece said.

"Shaughnessy said he wrote those Dinsmere books," offered another of the men.

The former Confederates nodded in unison. Grayson ignored them and gave Billie a quelling look. "We can discuss this later."

"Why didn't you tell me? All this time I've been imagining Seyler in my mother's house. . . ."

His plan of surprising her seemed shallow and stupid when confronted by the genuine distress in her eyes. And there was no way to assuage her pain, not in front of these men. He would have to do that later. For now, he needed to salvage a rapidly deteriorating situation. He looked at the men, who had edged closer to the wagon while he and Billie argued.

"Mr. Reece, the name's Grayson Vanderlyn. I've accompanied my wife to Tennessee to retrieve our horse."

His bald announcement of his relationship to Billie shocked everyone into momentary silence. Reece broke it.

"Is that true? Is this here Yank your husband?"

"Unfortunately, yes." Billie scooted sideways, putting several inches between their thighs. "He tricked me into marrying him. He plans to divorce me as soon as we get the horse back."

Her accusation caused a dangerous undercurrent to ripple through the men. More than one hand came to rest on a revolver or rifle.

"Women!" Grayson edged his voice with exasperation. "I'm not the one who wants the divorce."

"I want an annulment."

Her announcement raised six pairs of eyebrows, curled six mouths into a smirk, and turned her face bright red when she realized what she had said.

Grayson rescued her. "She's angry at me because Dewey stole her horse right out from under our noses. When I volunteered to accompany her to Tennessee, she pointed out the impropriety of our traveling alone together. Marriage seemed the best solution. I offered to divorce her after we located the horse, if that was what she wanted. . . ." He gave an eloquent shrug.

In his role of a beleaguered male who sought understanding from other males, he paid no attention to the woman beside him. His assumption of control was subtle but sure.

"Gentlemen, we're here to retrieve Destiny. With your knowledge of the local situation, Mr. Reece, I imagine you could be of assistance. Perhaps we could discuss the matter over a meal? You and your men, of course. You may not know this, but Mrs. Vanderlyn is quite adept at cooking over an open fire."

Reece turned his head and spit a stream of tobacco juice, narrowly missing his own boot. He swiped a stained sleeve over his mouth. "It's a little hard on the soul to see Miss Billie married to anyone except my cousin. Seeing as how she was almost kin and seeing as how she spent the war working with Major Darring, it would be plumb dishonorable to refuse to help her even if she did up and marry a Yank. That said, I reckon we'll accept the dinner invite and we'll answer your questions about Destiny and Seyler as best we can."

"Good," Billie said. "The faster we get Destiny, the faster I can divorce this lying trickster Yankee."

"That's the way I see it, Miss Billie. Then you'll be free to marry a real man."

Grayson started to remind Billie she was a Catholic and couldn't divorce him, but he clamped his mouth shut when the former Confederate winked at him.

Billie slammed the frying pan onto the stump, pretending the pan had made contact with Grayson's head. It wasn't as satisfying as reality, but it came close.

The Yankee had bought her house and never told her. He hadn't bought it for them, because he hadn't known she was a female when he went to the auction. Had he planned to entice Sophronia back into his life with a lovely home in Tennessee? He still could. All he had to do was divorce Billie. After all, he belonged to some heathen church called the Dutch Reformed. They probably divorced each other as easily as Indians.

Holy Mary, Mother of God! She couldn't decide which was worse: Seyler living in her beloved home or Grayson living there with another woman. The first image enraged her while the second shredded her heart. What had possessed her to let her guard down for a low-down, good-for-nothing Yankee? Hadn't her experiences with them during the war showed her their perfidious souls?

Fool! Falling in love with a Yankee. She wanted to scream out her despair. Her heart felt as if it had crushed itself into a knot.

"That were mighty good succotash and corn pone, Miss Billie."

She looked up from the skillet she had scrubbed beyond clean. The man who complimented her food had been beaten by life until there wasn't much reason for him to live. It hadn't always been that way. She remembered the small grocery store Mr. Roberts had owned before the war ruined his business, chased his wife into an early grave, and starved his children into illnesses that led to death. She guessed riding with Jonas Reece gave Mr. Roberts a reason to get up each morning.

Shelving her frustration, she smiled at him. "I'm glad you liked it."

"My Sallie was a fine cook." The older man stared into the past for a few moments, then shook his head as if to dispel his thoughts. "I wanted to tell you not to be too hard on your Yank. He gave Shaughnessy money to hire men and make repairs. I stopped by the other day and saw the changes. Your pa would be pleased."

It took effort, but she kept her smile in place. "I appreciate you telling me this." And she was pleased the Yankee hadn't dismissed Shaughnessy, because in spite of the horse trainer's weakness for whiskey, she loved him. But she refused to be pleased Grayson was restoring her lovely home for another woman. Hiding her pain at the thought tested the limits of her acting skills.

She attacked the heavy iron skillet with renewed energy. Two seconds later, the pan was rescued by a pair of heavily callused hands.

"My, my, this is one clean frying pan."

She looked up into a pair of blue eyes. There was the merest hint of amusement in them. "I wasn't planning to hit you with it, Jonas."

"Well, I figured that, but Stephen always said you had a hot temper. We got some serious talking to do, and you might do it better without a weapon in your hand."

She followed him to the fire, drying her hands on the apron she had scavenged from the wagon. Reece sat her on a log beside Grayson, although she made sure her skirts didn't brush the Yankee's leg as she sat. Nor would she look at his face.

Reece stood by the fire, his fed and drowsy men lounging behind him. "It's like I told you earlier, Mr. Vanderlyn. I cain't afford to ride with a man I don't know, even if you're married to Miss Billie."

Anger flared briefly in Billie's chest. Holy Mary, Mother of God, they'd been discussing Destiny while she was elbow-deep in corn pone. Her patience had been tempered in the fire of war, but it had been a hard lesson that didn't always stick. "Exactly where did my *husband* want to go with you?"

"He asked me to take him to Seyler."

"I asked him because I can't agree to his plan."

She kept her gaze on Reece. "What is your plan?"

"It's simple enough. Y'all stay here while me and the boys get Destiny."

"No!"

"No!"

At least she and Grayson agreed on one point. She hurried to clarify her no first. "I realize Destiny has a reputation as an even-tempered horse, but he's been through quite a number of new experiences. More strangers will probably frighten him. He knows me. I should be there."

"He knows me as well as he does you."

Grayson's patronizing tone grated across her raw nerves. "He hasn't seen Mr. Vanderlyn in weeks."

"He hasn't seen my wife in weeks, either."

Drat the man! Every time he called her his wife, her insides went all mushy. She dragged her thoughts off Grayson.

"He was my horse first. He knows me best. So—"

She snapped her mouth shut when she saw the smile struggling for life on Reece's harsh features.

Grayson must have seen it, too. His next question left the matter of who would accompany Reece unanswered. "What about armed men? Seyler seems to have plenty of people at his disposal."

Reece nodded. "He usually has a small army around him, but he's sent half his men to west Tennessee. From what you've told me, I reckon they're looking for y'all. Then there's a barbecue in the next county. Old Mummy Face is attending, and Seyler's men always guard the governor when he leaves Nashville. If my calculations are right, Seyler's got maybe four or five men left."

"What about the dogs?" She had no desire to have two large dogs nipping at Destiny's heels as they tried to escape.

"Old Mummy Face got them, too. Seyler's dedicated to keeping his man in office. He keeps him well guarded."

"This is the perfect time to get Destiny! You say Seyler bought the Massengail place? Destiny must be there." She surged to her feet in her excitement. She could get Destiny and be on her way back to Texas before the sun set.

"You know a great deal about Seyler's activities, Mr. Reece."

Grayson's casual question snagged Billie's attention.

Reece shot a stream of tobacco into the flattened grass near his worn cavalry boot. "I been studying on him right smart lately. Like I said, me and the boys are cleaning out the varmints in Sumner County."

"I understand why you don't want to ride with a Yankee, Jonas, but you cannot have any doubts about my loyalty. I didn't come all the way from Texas to stand by and let someone else rescue my horse."

"I don't know, Miss Billie." Reece looked at Grayson as if for help.

Billie followed his gaze. Stormy gray eyes glared at her.

She shifted back to Reece. "We'll be in and out of the barn so fast Seyler won't know we're there. And you need me. Destiny will be easy to handle if I'm there."

Reece stared up at the sky and scratched at his beard. The decision made, he dusted his hat against his thigh and gave Grayson an apolgetic shrug. "Miss Billie's right about needing someone to keep the horse calm, Mr. Vanderlyn. Like I said, I'd take you but I cain't afford to ride with no Yankee. I cain't even afford to take your word you won't follow us. Four years drove that inclination out of me. Walton there," Reece jerked his thumb toward one of his men. "He's gonna keep you company."

Flushed with her victory, Billie didn't mind when Grayson drew her into his arms for what she thought would be a farewell kiss. Instead, she was treated to a quick, harsh scolding.

"Don't think to set the tone of our marriage by this afternoon's work, rapscallion."

"Marriage! What marriage? A marriage where you pretend to care for me so you can get my horse? You bought my home."

She turned to the horse Reece had had saddled for her. Gathering the reins in her hand, she put her foot in the stirrup and swung her leg over the saddle, unmindful of the flurry of petticoats and skirt.

"You may have my house, Yankee, but you'll never have my horse."

CHAPTER
TWENTY-THREE

Billie worried about the wisdom of leaving Grayson at the camp. For some reason, freed of his presence, she couldn't think of anything except him. She remembered his promises when he had found her in the Guadalupe River, his care of her while she was ill, his body beside her at night, their conversations on the steamboat, the boots he had bought her, the way his eyes darkened with passion when they made love, the feel of his hand resting on her waist while they slept.

Her anger with him for buying her home cooled into resignation. Whatever his reason, he had saved Angel's Valley from belonging to Seyler. She should be grateful.

And deep down in her soul, she was grateful. Just as, deep down in her soul, she loved him. He should be beside her when they found Destiny.

The closed world of her past had expanded to include a Yankee. He offered her a future. She might not get such a good offer again in this lifetime.

"I don't know what you have in mind for Seyler," Reece said, "but I'll do the killing, not you."

Reece's announcement barged into Billie's reflections. She looked up to find him riding next to her. He had dropped back to where she trailed his men to talk to her.

Kill Seyler? She had planned to steal Destiny and go back to Texas. But her husband owned Angel's Valley. Would Seyler leave her alone now that she was married?

"For Stephen." Reece's voice was firm.

"Seyler killed Stephen?" The sickening truth hit her. Stephen had been her fiancé. Seyler had killed or caused to be killed everyone she loved. Except Destiny. And Grayson.

"It makes my blood run cold to think about it," Reece said. "Ain't no reason for any man to die like that."

"Seyler killed Stephen?" Guilt washed over her. If she hadn't accepted Stephen's proposal, he might be alive today. Or if dead, his death would have been on the field of battle.

"Oh, he didn't do the killing, but Seyler had it done. Truesdail's soldiers were arrested for it. Arrested and released." Reece's clenched fist smacked against his saddle. "Swore they were interrogating a spy who refused to talk."

"But he wasn't a spy."

"You know it and I know it, but those damn Yankees arrested anybody they wanted. They preferred someone with a cotton crop, so's old Seyler could sell the crop, once the man was jailed for spying and his farm commandeered by the Federals. But Stephen was different. He didn't have no cotton and they didn't take him to jail. They tortured him to death."

"How do you know Seyler was involved?"

"Oh, I got my ways. And every one of those soldiers swore they was doing what Seyler told 'em to do."

She didn't want to know how Reece got those men to confess.

"Can you imagine?" Reece continued. "One of those bastards thought to settle in Tennessee after the war."

She wasn't thinking about the Federals. All she could think about were Stephen, her brother, her mother, and her aunt.

One way or another, Seyler had taken them from her. An im-
placable truth settled in her heart: The man would torment
her until she was dead, too. "Seyler has to die."

Reece nodded his agreement. "You'll get your wish. I
plan to kill Seyler."

His comment startled her because she hadn't meant to
speak aloud. She reached for his arm while slowing her horse.
He stopped his own mount and turned in his saddle to face
her.

His men continued down the trail, rounding a bend in the
narrow dirt road.

"You misunderstand, Jonas. That monster killed my family. I will kill Seyler." With those four words, she banished
any possibility of her future. All she had left of her world
were Destiny and Angel's Valley. Grayson would take care of
them both.

"Now, that's no way for a nice young lady like yourself to
talk. I know you can't help you're hitched to a Yankee, but
you're a married woman now. You cain't go around killing
people. 'Sides, I want Seyler to die a slow, horrible death,
and a lady ought not to see what I'm gonna do to Archibald
Seyler. Like I said, I'll do the killing of Seyler."

"I have a bigger score to settle with him that you do."

"You're being stubborn," Reece said. "I've already killed
plenty of men. Killing Seyler ain't gonna change my reputation. If you kill Seyler and are caught, what would happen to
that horse of yours? Your father's horse-breeding plans?"

She slumped slightly. He had a good point. If she were
jailed, who would keep the D'Angelo name alive in horse-
breeding circles?

"That weren't nice of you to stab my foot with yer cane,
Miz Billie. Not nice at all."

Billie jerked around to see Norval Perkins coming through
the woods to their left. He pointed a gun at her chest.

Damnation! She looked around, realizing Reece's men
had traveled ahead unaware that she and Jonas had fallen be-

hind to argue. Three men melted out of the woods to join Norval.

"I'll have yer guns, Reece."

Reece reached for his revolvers.

"Slow-like! Mr. Seyler wants ya in one piece, but I'll shoot ya if I hafta."

Reece gingerly pulled guns from his holsters and rifle scabbard. "I'm sorry, Miss Billie. I thought all Seyler's scum was with the governor."

"Them words are gonna cost you later, Reece." Norval edged his horse near Billie while another man took Reece's gun. "First I gotta take care of the little lady." He held out a hand that hadn't seen soap or water for most of its lifetime. "Mr. Seyler said to give ya this."

Suddenly, she wished Grayson were with her and not Reece.

The paper she unfolded was smudged with dirt, but Seyler's bold copperplate writing sprawled across its interior:

I have Destiny and now I have your friend. Would you like to talk? A.D. Seyler

Her horse stirred beneath her, disliking the strange horses that crowded him. She slid one hand down the horse's neck to reassure him while she stared at the cryptic message in her other hand. Friend? What friend? She racked her brain for a meaning.

Holy Mary, Mother of God! Seyler had Grayson! Friend? Because he didn't know they were married?

"Well, I ain't got all day. Are ya comin' peaceable-like?" Norval's question ricocheted through Billie's thoughts. What choice did she have?

Reece's horse edged closer. In a low and urgent voice, he said, "You know, my men will be back any moment."

"I've run from Seyler enough."

Norval's horse broke between them. He grabbed Billie's bridle.

"Come on, Miz Billie. Mr. Seyler gets real mean when he has to wait." Norval called over his shoulder, "Y'all know where to take Reece. Mr. Seyler'll tend to him after he takes care of the little lady."

"Ah, my dear, so kind of you to join me."

Fear crawled across Billie's skin when she saw Archibald Seyler. Somehow she hid it.

"You speak as if I had a choice with Norval's gun pointed at me."

"Texas certainly agreed with you," Seyler said. "I don't believe I've ever seen you looking this pretty."

Afternoon sun dappled the polished wood floor and filtered through sidelights on either side of the front door. Billie stood in the foyer of Seyler's house in Gallatin, breathing in the homey scents of beeswax and wood while a clock ticktocked from an alcove behind her. An aura of wealth and good taste festooned the home that had once belonged to a banker. She buried her hands in the folds of her skirt to hide their trembling.

Seyler took her by the elbow, his thick fingers grinding through skin and muscle, to bone. She would have a bruise when he unhanded her.

After guiding her into the parlor, he pushed her into an upholstered chair. Comfort enfolded her for a moment; then she squirmed forward until she perched stiffly on the edge. Her elbow ached from his rough handling, but she didn't rub at the soreness. The sweet scent of his cologne hung in the air around her, clogging her lungs.

Seyler crossed to a bellpull in the corner of the room. She eyeballed the distance to the doorway, wondering where Norval and his men had taken Reece. Her gaze swept the room, looking for an escape route. Four French doors lined the wall opposite her. Warm sunlight spilled through their unfettered glass panes. Were they locked?

She stifled the urge to run, knotting her fingers together in her lap. Escape wasn't an option until she discovered where Seyler had taken Grayson and Destiny.

"Do you find my trophy room appealing?"

The soft question startled her. Trophy room? She looked at the room, focusing on its interior rather than its exits.

A dozen waist-high marble pedestals paraded around the parlor. Carved in the classical style, they held an array of mostly tin objects. Displayed as regally as a collection of cherished antique Greek busts was everything from an army mess pail to a saltshaker. Drawn from her chair by the oddity of the collection, Billie examined a knife-fork-spoon combination similar to the one in her own skirt pocket.

"Trophy room?"

"I hear a note of disbelief in your voice, but use your imagination. These are some of the items my company manufactured during the war." He paused to let his chubby fingers caress a lard **can**. "Isn't it interesting what will turn a profit during war? Why, one of my acquaintances made a fortune from selling soap to the Army."

The liveried black man, who had answered the front door when Norval knocked, returned with a tray.

"Ah, Midas is here with the champagne. You will join me in my celebration. It isn't every day that one demolishes a family."

"I'm not here to drink champagne." She turned from a pedestal that held a glass jar rather than something made of tin. An odd chemical smell tainted the air near it. "I'm here to find out what I have to do to get my horse . . . back." She couldn't force Grayson's name out of her mouth. An insane hope flickered in her heart: If she didn't mention him, Seyler wouldn't harm him.

"You are, quite simply, the last of the D'Angelos." Seyler poured two flutes of champagne.

He offered her a glass. When she would have refused it,

he pressed it into her hand. His fat jowls creased in a facsimile of a smile. It didn't reach his eyes.

"Isn't pride ridiculous? It easily gets one killed. Take your brother, for instance. Karl had too much pride, you know. Couple pride with a terrible temper and a tendency to drink . . . Killing him was simply a matter of goading him into a duel at the right time."

The bubbly scent of champagne tickled her nose while bile warred with the back of her throat. Seyler's boast clawed at her chest, reopening an old wound. The pain spilled out anew. For all his faults, she had worshiped her older brother. She put it aside, refusing to let Seyler goad her into saying something that might jeopardize her chance to find Grayson and Destiny.

"Now, your father's death, that was more difficult to accomplish. He was such a popular commander."

His words shattered her fragile hold on her temper. "You lie! You didn't kill my father. He died in a battle."

"So everyone believes. But money opens such interesting doors. And men have such black souls, even the men who wore gray. I hear the coward who shot him in the back didn't survive to enjoy his riches."

Her left hand joined her right to clutch the stem of the champagne glass. Blood pounded in her head; her breath came in short gasps. Seyler lied. General Forrest himself had written her a condolence letter after her father died.

Then she looked into Seyler's cold blue eyes. Triumphant truth stared back at her. Her battered heart staggered beneath this new blow, but she had to focus. She would deal with this information later, after Grayson and Destiny were safe.

"I don't believe you." Her voice whispered her doubts.

"To revenge." Seyler tapped her glass with his.

She stared at the two champagne flutes. Did he expect her to toast her father's death? Or her brother's?

"I don't believe you." She forced a hint of conviction into

her voice, but her hands shook and sloshed champagne against the brim.

Seyler turned away, sipping his champagne as he strolled across the room. "Believe what you wish, my dear."

Glancing down, she wondered if the flute could be cracked against a pedestal to provide her a weapon. She had watched Shaughnessy slit the throat of more than one rabbit. A man's throat could not be much different, given a sharp enough instrument.

"Here's an item of interest to you, my dear. Or has your Yankee lover pushed all memory of Stephen out of your thoughts?" Seyler stood beside the pedestal holding the glass jar. He ran one finger lightly across the lid as if seeking dust.

Dread gathered in the pit of Billie's stomach.

"My men were awed by Stephen's courage. He didn't scream. Not much anyway." He traded his champagne glass for the jar on the pedestal. "Perhaps you'd like this souvenir?"

An errant ray of sun highlighted the grayish object floating in the fluid-filled jar Seyler held out to her. She wanted to take a step backward, away from Seyler, but fear coiled around her feet, locking her in place. She didn't want to know what was in the jar.

He held it higher, inspecting the contents. "The preservative has worked well. His tongue is in excellent condition."

Holy Mary, Mother of God. Seyler had Stephen's tongue. She swayed, trying to keep the room from spinning into oblivion. Something shattered, but the sound barely penetrated the roar in her ears.

"Rosemarie won't be as forgiving of carelessness as me, my dear. If you drop an expensive champagne glass on her floor, it will come out of your pay. If you're not careful, you'll be servicing Yankee soldiers for free."

Somehow she kept the succotash and corn pone in her stomach. The heady scent of champagne wafted from the damp splotches on her skirt, the wood floor, and the carpet, mixing with the chemical odor that mantled the jar Seyler held near her face. She willed the room to stop spinning and hoped she wasn't going to join the champagne glass.

"You're right, my dear. This isn't a proper souvenir for a lady." He returned it to the pedestal.

She wanted to run across the room, fling open a French door, and breathe in gulps of fresh air. And she wanted to kill Seyler.

Bending down, she scooped up the largest piece of glass left from her champagne flute.

Seyler swung back to face her. He eyed the pitiful piece of glass in her hand. "What do you plan to do with that, my dear?"

"Slit your throat." The soft words drained from her in defeat. She stared at the puny piece of glass and wished she had the strength of ten men. Then she could lift one of the pedestals and smash Seyler into oblivion.

But she didn't have the strength of one man. She had only her wits to use against him. And she had to focus or she wouldn't save Grayson or Destiny.

"Tsk, tsk. You'll need a better weapon than that." Seyler turned back to the pedestal and centered the jar, then stepped backward to contemplate his work.

"It's all in the presentation, isn't it? Outward appearance." He retrieved his champagne glass. "Have I told you? Alice Ann has accepted my proposal of marriage. Your Yankee kept me from buying Angel's Valley, but the Massengails had a lovely place. Alice Ann was delighted when I bought it."

"Why?"

"Why marry Alice Ann Denton?" He swung around to face her.

"No." She feathered her eyes closed for the merest second. "Why destroy my family?"

Her question hung in the air between them. He rubbed the delicately etched flower on the champagne flute with his thumb.

"I was ten years old when the county put me with your father. As far as everyone was concerned, a problem had been solved. The county didn't have to worry about me, your father had a boy to help Shaughnessy, and I was to learn how to be a groom. This made me a lucky orphan indeed."

She watched his thumb follow the curl of a leaf pattern, unsure if she wanted to hear about a past her father had created.

"Then your father traded me for a horse."

With her father, it always came back to horses. How she had despised having her life tied to the whims of a man obsessed with horseflesh. Horses, slaves, and her father were interwoven in her mind. And the horses always came first, before her and before the slaves.

She was eight years old before she realized her father wouldn't trade her south for a horse if she misbehaved. By then it was too late for her to change. She needed his approval as desperately as he needed the best horseflesh in the state. He surrounded himself with perfect male specimens, tolerating females only to get the colts he wanted.

She was never sure why he tolerated her.

To please him, she became an excellent horsewoman and learned the science of horse breeding. But deep down she always knew, she wasn't good enough because she wasn't Karl.

And she was crippled.

"The man who took me made me pick cotton alongside the darkies. Me, Archibald Seyler. I was supposed to be a groom. Have a skill. Be somebody people listened to. But no, your father had to have that horse. Two years, two damn long years of picking cotton in hot fields. Then, like a darkie, I ran away north."

The stroking motion stopped. Eyes hardened with past indignities swung up to lock on to her. His soft, fleshy face tightened with anger. "I struggled to make enough money to survive. To make enough money to come back to Gallatin and get revenge."

"But why kill Karl?"

"Your father had to lose something dearer to him than a damn horse. He loved Karl more than he loved horses. More than he loved anyone else."

The words sliced through her like the sharp hooves of a rampaging horse. Her mind cartwheeled with the impact of a truth she had spent her life denying. On one level, she had known her father loved Karl and not her. She had accepted it. But on another level, she had denied it and devoted her life to winning the love Karl received without effort.

She blinked, squinting against the glare of truth, adjusting her eyes to life after spending years in a long, dark tunnel. Her father had died loving Karl and tolerating her. With his death, his feelings were locked in time. What she did in the present and future would never change the past. Her father was dead.

Relief roared into her. She was free to live her life as she wished, without the need to win her father's love.

"I wanted to bring him to his knees, teach him Archibald Seyler has more value that a damn horse. I wanted to crush the D'Angelo family." He saluted her with his champagne flute before emptying it.

Her gaze flitted to the closest French door, but her feet couldn't follow the urge to flee. She had to find Grayson and Destiny. She wanted the chance to live in this new world—with Grayson. She needed to find him and her horse. "Where's Destiny?"

If the harsh challenge in her voice bothered Seyler, he didn't show it. He set his glass on a pedestal, reached into his vest pocket, and pulled out a watch. He clicked open the cover and checked the time. "He should be right out front. I thought we'd take him with us. I know how delighted Alice Ann will be to have you watch while I give him to her." He snapped the watch shut, dropped it back into his pocket. "He's my wedding gift to Alice Ann."

"Alice Ann! I'd rather die than see that heavy-handed jade on my horse."

"By the time Rosemarie is finished with you, death will be a welcome alternative."

Seyler's words slammed the truth into her mind. She was not here as a guest; she was here to find her husband and her horse.

"Don't worry, my dear. I have no intention of harming D'Angelo's Destiny. He's the pinnacle of your father's life, the pride of his stables—as he will be in mine. I promise you he will receive excellent care."

The thought of Seyler owning Destiny fanned her anger into life. "You have me; you have Destiny. There's no reason to involve anyone else."

"Oh, are you worried about our mutual friend?"

She took an involuntary step forward, crunching on shards of champagne glass. "He goes free if I go with you."

"I'd rather not resort to drugging you."

He stated a fact. His tone lacked any hint of emotion and chilled her blood. He set his champagne flute on the sideboard. "Drugging you would ruin my pleasure in this final scene. I wouldn't get to enjoy your reactions."

Held in thrall by the panic climbing up her spine, her feet didn't move when he stalked across the room to her. His ponderous head filled her line of vision as he captured her chin with his plump hand.

"You had to rut with that Yankee, but you won't deprive me of the pleasure of watching Federal soldiers turn you, the last of the D'Angelos, into a whore. Then we'll know who is worth more than a horse—a D'Angelo or Archibald Seyler."

Somewhere she found her shivering pride and pulled it out. "Even a whore D'Angelo is worth more than a lying, thieving killer like you, Archibald Seyler. Your dogs are worth more than a killer like you."

Her words found their mark. She watched his face redden while his mouth tightened into a hard line and the pulse in his temple swelled. She didn't see the slap in time to dodge. The force threw her off balance, staggering her sideways. Glass crunched beneath her boots. Her head reeled from the impact as she grabbed her stinging cheek. Blood leaked onto her tongue from where she had bitten it. Regaining her balance, she tested her jaw.

"I said I'd rather not drug you."

"Take me to see my friend and then I'll go to Rosemarie without a fight."

"Agreed." Seyler shoved her toward the parlor door.

CHAPTER
TWENTY-FOUR

The gig creaked its pleasure when Seyler removed his bulk from the driver's seat at the Massengail place. Billie wanted to leap from the gig and run into the barn to look for Grayson, but she remained seated quietly.

A deserted air hung over the plantation. No one came out to greet them or care for the horses. She watched Seyler tie the gig's horse to a hitching post. Where was everyone?

Then he was beside her. She accepted the offer of his hand to climb off the seat, but when her feet touched ground, she tried to withdraw her hand. He held on to it, pulling her close. Tobacco scented his clothes.

"You will do as I say, or we'll leave now."

She left her hand on his arm.

Behind her, Destiny stamped his foot and shook his head, letting her know he didn't like trailing in the dust behind another horse.

Seyler stopped in front of the large barn doors. "Don't move."

She waited. Gloves encased her clammy hands, but she

could feel the perspiration gathering on her palms. Each uncertain second sent blood pounding into her heart.

Seyler unlatched the large doors and swung them open. The dim light of early evening fell into the barn with the opening of the doors, brightening the gloom as it sliced through the dust motes near the entrance but leaving most of the barn dim. The stale scent of horse, straw, leather, and manure welcomed her. Without thinking, she stepped forward.

"I told you to stay."

The harsh command froze her feet.

"You do exactly as I say, or we turn around now and you'll never see him again."

The word "alive" hovered in the air between them. Her throat squeezed shut. Images of what they had done to Stephen inundated her brain. Had Grayson been killed piece by piece?

"Do you understand?"

No. No. No. She shoved the images back into the darkest recesses of her brain. The war was over. Grayson was a well-known author and war veteran.

"Yes." Somehow she pushed the one raw word from her throat.

"Come on, then. And remember, do as I say."

The gun barrel pressed against her neck was warm from its sojourn in Seyler's waistband. It made his intentions clear should she disobey him again. But his instructions and his gun disintegrated when she saw Grayson's bound, inert form facedown on the stall floor. The dirt and rusty stains on his shirt told her he had not gone down easily. She wiggled out of Seyler's grasp.

"Holy Mary, Mother of God! What have you done to him?"

Seyler grabbed a handful of skirt and petticoats, jerking her back to the sound of ripping cloth as she thumped into his chest. His fleshy arm, surprisingly strong, locked around her waist.

"Let me go, you devil's spawn!" Frantic with worry, she forgot Seyler's gun, forgot her intention not to reveal how much Grayson meant to her, forgot everything except Grayson, who lay injured on the stall floor. Frantically she kicked at Seyler and strained to break free of his grasp.

"Release my wife, Seyler."

At the sound of Grayson's voice, she stopped struggling. Standing not more than ten feet away, apparently uninjured and pointing a gun at them, was her husband. A closer look told her that the bloodied shirt he wore wasn't his. The swell of relief burgeoned into indignation that he would frighten her like that.

"Where the hell's Fletcher?" Seyler's growling question startled her into silence.

"This isn't between you and Fletcher," Grayson said. "It's between you and me. I repeat, release my wife."

"Wife? Why, Billie, you neglected to tell me you married the Yankee." His hold tightened, pushing the air from her lungs.

"And if I don't release your wife? Will you shoot her to kill me?"

"You know I can't let you take my wife." Grayson was advancing across the stall. "Or my horse."

Only the gun digging into her right temple kept her from protesting that Destiny belonged to her.

"It's extremely unfortunate you got involved in this local matter, but I'm afraid I can't let you interfere in justice."

"You call this justice?" Grayson's question dripped sarcasm. "Kidnapping a woman? Killing her in cold blood?"

"Oh, no. No. You have it all wrong," protested Seyler. "I don't plan to kill her. I have something much better in mind for her, don't I, my dear?"

The pressure of the gun barrel didn't lessen as he stroked it down her temple to her jaw. Fear shivered down her spine, but she kept her attention riveted on Grayson. Rage emanated from every pore of his tense body, but it was a controlled rage. She knew he would not do anything foolish. Therefore, neither should she. She kept her body still and

emptied her mind of fear. Together, she and Grayson would
survive Seyler.

"She owes something to those poor Yankee soldiers she
deceived and betrayed during the war."

"The war's over, Seyler."

"Not in Sumner County. It will be a long time before the
war is over here. There are so many scores to settle." Seyler's
voice held an almost dreamy note, but the gun pressing against
her jugular vein was no illusion.

Seyler's tone hardened. "You can have her back in a few
days. A little worse for the wear, but you don't seem to mind
damaged goods."

"Leave Billie. . . . Take me."

Billie peered into the dark recesses of the barn at the
sound of the familiar voice. Fletcher? Here? He sounded as
if he was in great pain.

Seyler didn't seem at all perturbed by the voice or interested in the offer. "There you are, Mr. Darring. I didn't think
you could have gone far in your condition. Broken ribs, if I
remember correctly."

Broken ribs. No wonder Seyler didn't take his gaze from
Grayson.

"As for your generous offer to trade places, I can't release
Miss Billie. Our business will have to wait."

"Have . . . gun."

"Mr. Darring, if you had a gun, you would have already
used it."

Her heart sank. Seyler knew Fletcher well. He also knew
to keep all his attention on her husband, who posed the real
threat. He had a gun.

"Now, Colonel." Seyler purred his triumph. "I'll have
your gun."

Grayson hesitated, his hard gaze searching her face. Then
he stooped to place the gun on the floor.

"Slide it over towards me."

The Le Mat slid to within a few feet of her.

With his gun pressed to her throat, Seyler pulled her down with him. He picked up and pocketed the Le Mat. Then he pulled her toward the barn door. She stumbled over her bedraggled petticoats.

Seyler jerked her closer. "No tricks, or Vanderlyn dies."

Under her boots, the soft dirt of the barn gave way to the firmer ground of the stable yard. Destiny nickered a welcome when Grayson followed them out of the barn. Seyler dragged her past the gig and shoved her against Destiny's shoulder. The horse shied away from them.

"Keep him quiet or I swear I'll put a bullet through his head."

She caressed Destiny's neck. "Easy, big boy. Easy."

Seyler untied Destiny's reins from the gig, then maneuvered the horse between them and Grayson. For a man of bulk, Seyler moved with surprising speed. One moment she stood next to Destiny, the next she had been scooped off her feet and thrown across the horse's back. The saddle bow slammed into her diaphragm, knocking the breath out of her with a loud whoosh.

Destiny danced his displeasure while the ground whirled beneath her dangling head. The familiar black clutch of fear swamped her reflexes. Within bare inches of her head, she watched Destiny's back hooves rise and fall. His tail whipped across her face, stinging her eyes. Unbalanced, she slid toward the ground and his hooves. Her fingers scrambled for purchase while she buried her face in heaving flanks. The familiar smell of horse reassured her. She could do this. One hand locked on to the girth; the other found a flapping stirrup strap.

Hanging on to the agitated horse, she chased her childish fears back into a corner of her mind. She didn't have time to think about the past; she had to stop Seyler.

A plan clicked into her brain. She licked her lips. If Seyler meant to take her and Destiny, he would have a little surprise when he tried to mount. She had worked with Destiny in Texas—he remembered all his old tricks.

Beneath her, Destiny quieted. She felt the reins brush across the thin calico fabric on her back. Tiny stones crushed against the sole of a boot as Seyler heaved himself off the ground and swung a leg over the saddle.

Puckering her lips, she whistled.

Destiny went stock-still as if he couldn't believe her signal. Or perhaps he had not heard the thready, weak sound.

She pursed her lips and whistled again. This time all hell broke loose. She felt Destiny's muscles tense as he gathered himself to follow her command. She tightened her grip and hung on as he went up, up, up on his hind legs. His forelegs pawed the air, and he whinnied his disagreement with her command.

Hanging head down, she had a quick upside-down view of Seyler's thick legs. For a few seconds, he teetered on one foot with the other hung in the stirrup as he hopped after the horse. Then Grayson pulled Seyler free, and the two men tumbled out of sight.

Destiny crashed back to the ground, jarring Billie. Blood pounded in her ears; black dots danced in her vision. Compressed against Destiny's back, her lungs couldn't suck in enough air. She tried to pull herself upright, but Destiny danced sideways to avoid the men rolling in the dirt at his feet. His head swung back and forth; his eyes widened with anxiety. Beneath her cheek, his body trembled. She wanted to soothe him, but she was too scared to release her grip.

Deep in her heart, she knew she'd fall if she did.

The crack of a gun drove Destiny back into the air. His anxiety exploded into terror. With stiff, jackknifing jumps he bucked his way across the stable yard. Billie didn't last over three jumps. Then she was falling . . . falling . . . falling. The hard-packed dirt of the stable yard smacked her into oblivion.

Later, in her dreams, she would hear the killing sounds of Destiny's hooves. It was sheerest good fortune the horse got Seyler and not Grayson or herself.

Good fortune or God's own destiny, as Shaughnessy would say.

Destiny getting shot had never entered Grayson and Fletcher's plans.

As he knelt beside her body, Grayson worried that Billie might shoot him when she regained consciousness. And she would regain consciousness, he told himself, running his hands across her body. This time he met no sassy resistance to his exploration. This time he knew a woman lay on the ground. A woman he loved.

He felt her wrist for a pulse and found a weak but steady beat. His hands curved their way over her chest, feeling for the rise and fall of her lungs. He exhaled his fear when he felt the shallow breath enter and exit.

He continued his search, relieved each time his fingers told him a bone wasn't broken. When she moaned, the knot in his stomach eased.

She was alive.

Kneeling beside her, he waited. Mahogany eyelashes and freckles sprinkled color onto a pale face. Her eyelids fluttered open; dazed green eyes looked up at him. She blinked away the confusion.

"Welcome back, Angel." He pushed a curl off her forehead.

"Destiny?"

The croaked question rammed its way through the emotions of the past few hours and reached what little logic he had left. Fact: He had reunited her with Destiny. Fact: He was doomed to go to Colorado while she secured an annulment from a priest and went to Texas to breed horses.

His heart edged itself into a corner of his logical brain. Had their time together meant nothing to her?

She pushed herself to her elbow.

He shifted his body, blocking Seyler's mangled body from her sight. "Seyler's dead."

She collapsed back into the dirt to digest this bit of information. "I heard a gunshot."

"Seyler's gun went off. He hit Destiny."

He hadn't realized she could grow paler. The sudden well of tears in her green eyes gnawed further at his logic. "He's all right," he reassured her. "The bullet grazed his right rear leg."

As if to lend credence to his words, Destiny lowered his head and blew softly in her hair. She reached up to caress the horse, tickling his chin. A tremulous smile captured her lips. "What a beautiful, brave boy you were."

The horse nuzzled her hand.

"Don't worry, I know I owe you carrots."

Grayson didn't like being jealous of a horse.

Destiny backed away when Billie tried to sit up. She grabbed at her stomach. "I don't recommend riding a horse on your stomach." She waited a moment, then said, "I think I can stand."

Grayson helped her to her feet.

She swept a tangle of curls out of her eyes. "Thank you. Aside from a few bruises, I'm fine." She could see Seyler's body now. He still clutched his gun.

"Holy Mary, Mother of God, Yankee, he could have killed you!"

Yankee.

She had no reason to be mad at him, especially when he was still stinging over the attention she gave the horse. "But he didn't, did he?"

"Billie darling . . ."

"Fletcher! I thought you went to California!"

"Dawdled in . . . St. Louis. Saw . . . Destiny with . . . Perkins. Knew you'd . . . follow that damn horse . . . into. . . . hell." Fletcher tried to grin. It was a lopsided affair, lanced with pain. "Thought I'd . . . help."

"Oh, what did that monster do to you?"

Disgruntled, Grayson watched Billie rush over to her friend, who sat on an aging bale of hay. He shoved his hands in his trouser pockets. Other than her single outburst, she hadn't spared him the same amount of attention she had given Destiny and now Fletcher.

He might as well pack his bags and head for Colorado.

CHAPTER TWENTY-FIVE

"You missed a dandy fight, Billie darling. Your Yankee pulled Seyler off Destiny just as the horse went up, and there they were, rolling on the ground, with Destiny jumping this way and that way, doing his damnedest not to step on them. Then Seyler's gun went off, and the bullet got Destiny in the leg. I reckon that horse went mad with the pain. Next thing I know, Seyler's dead and your Yank's shielding you from Destiny. That poor horse was so confused, he could have easily killed both of you—"

"And we were lucky Grayson got away from Jonas's guard." Billie finished Fletcher's sentence for him.

"Make light of it if you want, Billie darling." Fletcher waggled a slice of toast at her. "I, for one, am pleased your Yankee showed up when he did. I didn't relish surviving the war to have Seyler's men finish me off."

Fletcher and she were in Karl's old bedroom. Billie stared out the window that overlooked the front of the house while Fletcher ate the breakfast she had brought him. It would take months, probably years, for the horse farm to resemble the showplace it had once been.

She wandered around the room and stopped to drag her finger across the polished top of the chiffonier. Its age and hidden location in the attic had saved it from destruction or confiscation. She sighed, inhaling the scent of fresh beeswax.

Fletcher's cup clinked against its saucer.

"Are you going to California after you mend?" She wondered if she could tag along with him until he reached Colorado. Perhaps Grayson would let her stay with him if she showed up on his doorstep unannounced.

"No. It's time to go home to Fairmount."

Startled, she stopped doodling on the chiffonier. "You're going to stay in Tennessee?"

"I couldn't seem to get any farther than St. Louis." Fletcher scooped up a forkful of grits. "And Tennessee will be safer for me with Seyler dead. Reece said he'd give peace another chance if I stayed."

"I'm glad you'll be here." She captured her hands under her arms and leaned on the chiffonier. "He's going to leave me, isn't he?"

Fletcher swallowed his mouthful of grits.

Having voiced her fear, the rest of it tumbled out. "I mean, I have everything I ever wanted. Destiny, the house, the farm. So why aren't I ecstatic?"

"Maybe those aren't the things you really wanted."

His comment hung in the air between them. Words fluttered into her larynx, but her throat squeezed shut, refusing to let them fly free.

She waited, needing Fletcher to help her.

"Maybe what you want has changed."

A mourning dove's coo-ah, coo, coo, coo floated in the open window. The melancholy call wove itself into her heart, accentuating her fears. For years she had clung to the belief she would carry on the D'Angelo tradition. It had shaped her life, given her direction. And then Seyler had freed her from the need to please her father. But freedom was a double-edged ax. Now doubts about what to do with her life swamped her. Doubts about Grayson niggled at her day and night. Coming home to Angel's Valley, she had slid back into the safe world of horse breeding.

Angel's Valley buffered her from the fear Grayson hadn't meant any of the words he had whispered when they made love. If he loved her, why hadn't he told her to forget about asking the priest to annul their marriage? Not that she had asked him. But she wasn't sure if Grayson wanted to be married to her anymore.

"What if he doesn't want me?" She disliked the forlorn, fearful tone of her voice.

"Oh, he wants you, Billie darling."

A tiny ray of hope nudged her heart. Fletcher sounded so positive.

A familiar whinny drove her back to the window. Below her, Grayson was tying a carpetbag to Destiny's saddle.

"It's Grayson. He's taking Destiny." She turned from the window.

Fletcher grabbed her arm before she scooted past him.

"Let go! I've got to stop him."

"One question before I release you, Billie darling. Have you told the man you love him?"

"No." She shook herself free of his grasp. "I haven't."

"For God's sake, woman, tell him!"

Fletcher's command rang in the air behind her as she raced down the stairs. He was right—she had to tell Grayson how she felt. But all thoughts of amorous declarations and images of joyous embraces fled when she opened the front door. He was stealing Destiny.

"Where are you going?" She swept through the front doorway, her full hooped skirt knocking over an empty paint bucket. Without a backward glance, she marched to the edge of the porch. The smell of fresh paint filled her flaring nostrils.

"To redeem a brooch in Memphis. Then to Colorado."

"I mean where are you going with Destiny?"

"Destiny is mine." Grayson tugged the horse's cinch. "I paid hard gold coin to the U.S. government for this horse, and I intend to keep him. Angel's Valley is yours. I've transferred funds to your bank to refurbish it. And you have Molasses."

"But you can't take Destiny." She was sick to her stomach. The past few days had passed in a blur as she cared for Fletcher, discussed renovations with Shaughnessy, and all the while watched Grayson slip between her fingers. Something had happened the day Seyler died, and she didn't know what.

"We both know we only joined forces to get the horse from Seyler. I've got work waiting for me in Colorado. Like I said, I've given you the house and money. And you have your place in Texas. What more do you want?"

He must have thought the question rhetorical, because he didn't wait for her to answer. He swung his leg over Destiny's back. And before she could say "Stop," they were riding toward the entrance.

She wanted to shout, "You! I want you, you ignoramus!" but she was furious because he was taking Destiny. Why, everyone knew she would follow that horse to the ends of the earth.

Everyone knew she would follow the horse. . . . Grayson knew she would follow the horse. Her mouth, tight with panic, softened. Maybe he wanted more than the horse. Maybe his sweet talk on the steamboat had been sincere. Maybe he loved her as she loved him. Maybe he was as unsure of her as she was of him. Maybe he needed her to say something first.

She would never know if she stood here and watched him leave. She puckered her lips and whistled the opening measure of "Fur Elise." Destiny heard the sound and stopped, swinging his head around to look at her. Then he trotted back to his mistress.

When he reached her, she stroked the horse's nose, but

found she lacked the courage to look at Grayson. It was a hot summer day, much like the one on which she had first met her Yankee. This time she wouldn't let him ride out of her life.

"You know, Yankee. I've heard Colorado has wild horses, too." She was lying, because she hadn't heard any such thing, but that didn't mean it wasn't true—and she had to have a reason for going west. "And I find I'm not much in the mood for rebuilding anymore. I seem to have developed a definite interest in travel. What with running up to New York and then to Texas, Angel's Valley seems quite tame now." She shot him a quick glance, her eyes settling on his mouth. Just looking at his mouth made her knees all weak. "Are there any steamboats on the way to Colorado?"

He leaned forward in the saddle, his eyes capturing her gaze. "Do you like steamboats?"

"Hmmmm. I like the small staterooms. They're . . . cozy." Memories of their last time together in a stateroom brought a warm flush to her cheeks, and a wave of shyness swept over her. She could no longer meet his gaze. Running her hand along Destiny's neck, she twined her fingers in his mane and drew courage from the horse's proximity.

She had the horse. She could have the man.

If she had the courage.

All she had to do was tell him she loved him. Admit out loud what her heart had been telling her for weeks. The past be damned. She loved a Yankee.

And she hoped he still loved her.

She wet her lips.

His hand rested on Destiny's shoulder, inches from where her fingers tightened in the horse's mane.

She took a deep breath and said the words that had burned in her heart for so long. "I love you."

Above her, Grayson was silent for so long, she thought her knees would buckle. Then his hand covered hers, stilling the play of her restless fingers. For one heartbeat she watched their interlocked hands, wondering if he was going to fling her hand off Destiny's neck and tell her it was too late, that his love had died.

That she had lost both the man and the horse.

"You wouldn't be heating my blood to get Destiny, would you, rapscallion?"

Her head shot up, but her indignation died a quick death when she saw his grin. Then she knew he had taken Destiny on purpose.

"Well, you are taking my horse. And everyone knows I go where Destiny goes."

His grip on her hand tightened, and he pulled her onto Destiny and into his lap. She slipped her arms around his waist and felt him nuzzle the hair beside her ear.

"I bet my heart on it, Angel."

With one ear cocked backward, Destiny heard Grayson's words, and he nodded his head in complete agreement. The soft jingle of his bridle sounded as pretty as church bells, thought Billie as she offered herself, body and soul, to her Yankee.

About the Author

Ginger Hanson is a former college history teacher who found writing historical romance a natural outlet for her love of history and happy endings. After a vagabond life as an Army wife and Navy brat, Ms. Hanson convinced her husband to retire in Enterprise, Alabama where they now live with their two dogs and cat. Her daughter is a Lieutenant in the U.S. Coast Guard.

She loves to hear from readers and can be contacted at www.gingerhanson.com

DO YOU HAVE THE
HOHL COLLECTION?